Praise for *Live*

"In 1965 I had my own personal *Liverpool Fantasy*. I was a young musician, greatly influenced by the Beatles' music and the whole Liverpool music scene. That December I booked passage to Liverpool on a tramp steamer sailing from New York. In Liverpool I had many adventures including a night at the Cavern and buying the album *Rubber Soul* on the day of its release. It was so exciting to see a whole city so buzzed by the record. The record store listening booths were packed with all kinds of people glued to the speakers and sharing a common experience with 'their boys.'

I was later deported from England for not having a work permit and I made a pretty good splash in the British papers. But that is another story. My fantasy continued in 1970, when after changing careers and becoming a recording engineer, I found myself working with John Lennon on the *Imagine* album. After finding the courage to tell him about my trip to his hometown, he took an interest in me and I was soon hanging out with him after the sessions. We became friends and I worked on projects with both him and Yoko. He also introduced me to George and I worked on *The Concert for Bangladesh* movie soundtrack with him. John and I stayed close over the years, although I became a successful producer (including projects with George Martin), and had no time to engineer for him or Yoko. While producing Alice Cooper in L.A., I was hanging with John during his lost weekend daze, so I know what he's like with a good drunk on.

Six years later the fantasy moves on to new heights when, after not recording for years, John asked me to produce his 'comeback album' which became *Double Fantasy* and the out-takes album *Milk and Honey*. The details of this adventure would fill another book, so they are not needed here. John and

I were working together on 'Walking On Thin Ice,' the two of us working alone, playing guitars in the control room and having a great time, Yoko out in the vocal booth or on the phone doing business. Anyway that night in December, fifteen years from my sailing to Liverpool, I said goodnight to John as he stepped on the elevator, telling him I would meet him at 9 A.M. to master the completed single. Ten minutes later, he was shot dead as he entered his home at the Dakota.

Was Larry Kirwan there with me? Was he by my side in Liverpool when I saw and heard first-hand the love those people had for their Beatles? Feels like he was. Was he a fly on the wall during the *Imagine* sessions? He most have been. Was he hiding somewhere in the studio when George graced me with his spiritual gifts and we mixed for twenty-four hours straight? Or on those drunken nights with John in L.A.? Or with us when at the *Double Fantasy* sessions John would ask me, "are we finished then?" and when I told him we were, he would come into the control room, sit next to me and tell stories about him and the boys that would go on for hours sometimes saying 'you really don't get IT yet Jack.' I do now. Larry gets IT. Larry must have been there with me. How else could he have written a book like this?

His description of the reunion is hair-raising. I had heard John speak of it many times (it was almost at hand) and it is what I imagined it might be. It is a nightmarish book, but when I confront the reality of what happened to John I almost wish for a *Liverpool Fantasy*."

—Jack Douglas, Producer/Composer

"In *Liverpool Fantasy* Larry Kirwan whistles a fine melody between the covers of a novel. If this is a book of a musician, it's a musician with an ear for dialogue, a crack-along pace, a sense of humor, a feel for language and a wonderful awareness of the absurd theatre that we call coincidence, destiny and chance. Who knows what would happen to our lives if not for a glancing blow from the curious angles of fate?"

—Colum McCann, author of *Dancer* and
This Side of Brightness

"Wow, this bloke Kirwan can write! He's got the Liverpudlian patois down to a t-bone. When you read what the four lads have to say and how they say it . . . well, you'll think you're in *A Hard Day's Night*. And the lads—twenty-five years on—I love it. . . . It's a hoot and a half! Good on ya, mate."

—Ray Manzarek, keyboardist for The Doors and
author of *Light My Fire* and *The Poet In Exile*

"Larry Kirwan brings his poet's touch and his musician's understanding to the difficult task of imagining a realistic alternate history for the members of the Beatles. It takes that combination to write a good novel about musicians—especially rock 'n' roll musicians—without falling into a pit of clichés and stereotypes. Kirwan is the real deal—playwright, poet, singer/songwriter, guitarist, bandleader! He knows how to paint the pictures of this particular place and time so you really see them; lets his characters talk and dream so you truly believe them; and writes about music in a way that you can actually hear the heartbeat of rock 'n' roll that burns on every page of this sad, funny, angry, tender novel."

—Vin Scelsa, host of *Idiot's Delight*, WFUV-FM

Liverpool
Fantasy

Liverpool
Fantasy

LARRY KIRWAN

THUNDER'S MOUTH PRESS
NEW YORK

LIVERPOOL FANTASY

Copyright © 2003 by Larry Kirwan

Published by
Thunder's Mouth Press
161 William St., 16th Floor
New York, NY 10038

Library of Congress Cataloging-in-Publication Data:
Kirwan, Larry.
      Liverpool fantasy / by Larry Kirwan
        p.cm.
      ISBN 1-56025-497-1
1. Beatles—Fiction. 2. Rock musicians—Fiction. 3. Liverpool (England)—Fiction. 4. Separation (Psychology)—Fiction. I. Title.

PS3611.I79L58 2003
813'.6--dc21

                          20030402304

9   8   7   6   5   4   3   2

Book design by Paul Paddock
Printed in the United States of America
Distributed by Publishers Group West

Dedicated to

Sir Charles Comer
late of Liverpool and New York City
and
Ita Kirwan
late of Wexford

As I look ahead, I am filled with foreboding.

Like the Roman, I seem to see "the River Tiber foaming with much blood."

That tragic and intractable phenomenon which we watch with horror on the other side of the Atlantic but which there is interwoven with the history and existence of the States itself is coming upon us here by our own volition and our own neglect.

Indeed, it has all but come.

In numerical terms, it will be of American proportions long before the end of the century.

Only resolute and urgent action will avert it even now.

Enoch Powell
Wolverhampton, 1968

PROLOGUE

November 26, 1962
Abbey Road Recording Studios, London

"'Please Please Me' is a number one! You just get Parley-clone to put the bloody thing out and we'll be bigger than Elvis." Lennon took a long drag on his Players, flicked away the butt, then ground it out beneath his boot.

Brian Epstein fingered his tie. That strip of carpet would cost at least forty pounds to replace.

"John." To his horror, his voice modulated to an undignified falsetto. "How many times do I have to tell you? I think it's great, Mr. Martin thinks it's great, but the people upstairs at Parlophone, well . . . " As he gathered himself, his pitch plunged, his accent shed all its northern flavor, and in precise Etonian he brayed: ". . . . to put it quite bluntly, they would prefer to pursue 'Till There Was You.' I'm afraid it's a fait accompli."

Lennon was across the room in milliseconds; he stuck his long nose within inches of his manager's cologned face. "Keep yer froggy talk for yer little nancy boys, Eppy! It don't wash around here. Besides, I never even wanted to record that piece of shit in the first place, and now you have the nerve to tell me it's goin' to be our next single."

Epstein riffled his brain for a witty riposte but, as usual, that sullen Liverpool glare got the better of him, and he keened: "John, I just won't have you talk to me like that."

Lennon sneered and removed a piece of lint from Epstein's

Savile Row suit. "I'll talk to you any bloody way I like, mate. That's what you're here for—to listen to what we want and then put it into action pronto."

He turned abruptly, winked at George Harrison, and tore off the opening bars of "Johnny B. Goode" on his Rickenbacker. George joined in but was left dangling on a suspended E seventh when Lennon choked the chord. Ringo Starr combed back his greasy hair and continued to keep time with a hefty four on the floor; finally, noticing the strained silence, he halted in midbeat and mumbled an unnoticed apology.

"I believe that if you read the terms of our contract," Epstein said, "you'll find that the contrary is quite the case. My duties are, and I quote: 'to advise you in all matters relating to your career.' And the choice of the next single, if I may be so bold, is absolutely crucial to the whole development of this endeavor."

"You can quote and be bold till you're blue in the face, it's all a one to me."

"Listen, you chaps." A megaphonic voice intruded from the control booth. George Martin straightened his silk tie and strode into the studio. In his corduroy pants, cashmere jumper and tan Hush Puppies, he appeared to float across the soundproofed room—a paragon of ease and detachment in this maelstrom of bruised egos, black leather, and sweat-stained guitars.

"Would it be at all possible," he ventured, "to try and approach this from a . . . well, less emotional point of view?"

Lennon unslung his Rick. With a sigh that would have done justice to St. Lawrence roasting on the spit, he grimaced at the lanky Harrison, who raised a nonchalant eyebrow while continuing to glide through his minor scales.

Lennon's look was not lost on Martin. "I have little doubt,

John, that subsequent to the success of 'Till There Was You,' I can persuade my financial people to release 'Please Please Me' as a follow-up. Success breeds success, and—"

"Listen, 'Love Me Do' got to number seventeen without any help from Parleyclone, and you know why?" Lennon jammed his index finger into Martin's cashmered chest. "'Cause everybody and his aunt Fanny bought it up Merseyside. So put that in your pipe and smoke it, Mr. Martin!"

But Mr. Martin was made of sterner stuff than Mr. Epstein and was not inclined to allow some trumped-up Liverpool teddy boy to get the one-up on him. He soaked up Lennon's scowl, then, cool as the other side of the pillow, said, "John, 'Love Me Do' was my product, as well, remember? But I'm afraid the figures were too distinctly regional."

"Listen here, Georgie boy, we're not talkin' about sellin' corn flakes or Morris Minors. This is rock & roll . . . or is that a forbidden term around here?"

"On the contrary, I personally feel that you chaps have a wonderful future in the world of light entertainment; that's why I was thrilled when Paul suggested including 'A Taste of Honey' and 'Till There Was You.'"

Paul McCartney shrugged modestly and smiled. His meticulously tousled brown hair framed a round, boyish face, while his teeth gleamed in the soft glare of the overhead lights.

Lennon creased him with a glare. "It's a wonder we didn't have a go at 'Mary Had a Little Lamb.' Nursery crimes are all the rage nowadays."

McCartney's smile dimmed to a troubled leer. He picked up his Hofner, bounced a couple of harmonics off the G string, and stared strategically off into the distance.

Lennon's guitar began to feedback, and he slapped angrily at the open strings. A burst of raw treble screeched through the studio but expired in midflight when he switched his amp to standby.

The red signal lights from the Vox AC-30's, which had shimmered reassuringly through the session, now seemed to cast a forlorn glow. Ringo sniffled, then cleared his throat in the silence.

Epstein gazed in despair at his pride and joys. Even when they were at each other's throats, they could instantly coalesce and make him feel like the outsider he was. After all, he hadn't even heard of them back in the old days at the Jacaranda; nor had he speeded his brain off on prellies through eight-hour marathons in Hamburg. No, Johnny-Come-Lately Mr. Manager, from toffee-nosed Childwall, had "discovered" them when they were already turning away scrubbers by the score from the Cavern—the hottest thing out of Liverpool since the Mersey Tunnel.

"Look here now, John," he said. "'Till There Was You' is a marvelous song, and Peggy Lee herself has given it her personal seal of approval."

Lennon's guitar had begun sliding off his amp. Without taking his eyes off Epstein, he kicked back and shoved it in place. As he lit another cigarette, his upper lip quivered with rage. "When are you goin' to get it into your thick skull that you're managin' the Beatles, not bloody Acker Bilk! We're a rock & roll group; or, at least, we used to be until you came round and tried to deball us, you—"

"John, please be reasonable." Epstein dabbed at his damp brow with a royal blue handkerchief.

"Reasonable! You know how you spell that word?" He jabbed his Players at Eppy's face. "S-E-L-L-O-U-bloody-T!"

The beleaguered manager retreated until his back was up against the window of the control booth.

"We used to be gear, mate." Lennon spewed forth the bile that had been festering for months. "We used to get up onstage and play our balls off on anything that came into our heads. Then you said: 'You've got to be reasonable, John, you've got to write out a list of all the numbers you propose doing in a night.' As if I know what the hell I'm goin' to do till I get up there and do it."

He shook his head at the thought of such sacrilege; then, sucking in his cheeks, he pirouetted—hand on hip—and lisped, "After that, it was: 'Well, John, we've got to be reasonable, we can't have you goin' onstage like a crowd of teddy boys. So you get us to wear them silly collarless suits, like a pack of King's Road ponces. Well, let me tell you something, mate, this is the way I dress, 'cause this is the way I *feel.* "

He jerked at his black leather jacket and blue jeans. "This is what we've always worn"—he pointed at the other three—"and it did us right well till we had the misfortune to run into a wanker like you."

The sweat was oozing from Epstein. He again reached for his handkerchief, but Lennon snatched it from him and loudly blew his nose in its laundered creases.

"John, this is outrageous! I really must protest."

"Ah, protest my bollocks!" Lennon said. "Once upon a time I could go anywhere Merseyside and hold me head high. Now I have to listen to Marsden, and the rest of 'em, sneerin' behind me back. 'Oh, there goes Little Lord Fauntleroy in his snazzy suit and his shiny boots, all paid for by Queenie Boy Epstein. Next thing you know he'll have 'em wearin' silk knickers and bendin' for him into the bargain."

"Oh, for Christ sake, lay off him and for once in your life be reasonable." Paul pleaded, unaware that the hated adjective was ricocheting around the room—a red rag to a scouse bull.

Lennon flung a half-empty bottle of lager at the carpeted wall. Everyone ducked as beer sprayed the gleaming set of Ludwig drums. "Don't you know any other friggin' word?" he roared, arms outstretched like an Everton Christ.

He grabbed for another half-filled bottle as band, producer, and management ran for cover; but instead, he took a long, thirsty swig. "For Jaysus sake, Paul," he belched, and wiped off his mouth, "if it's got to be one of yours, why don't you do 'Long Tall Sally' or 'Tutti Fruitti.' Somethin' that we can all be proud of. Right, George?"

"Yeah." The guitarist nodded. "My vote's for 'Please Please Me.' It's more us. It just is."

Lennon glowered triumphantly at Epstein and Martin. After some moments of dithering, they retreated to the control booth. But Lennon was relentless. He spun around, gave them the finger, and yelled into an open microphone, "This is a private conversation, if you don't mind!" His voice boomed through their monitors, and the two unmasked eavesdroppers quaked from the shock.

Satisfied, he turned to the others. "They backed down when we wouldn't do 'How Do You Do It.' All we have to do is stick to our guns, and they'll back down again."

Paul counted to a silent three and sighed. "Maybe we should go along with 'Till There Was You' and get them to put it in writin' that they'll release 'Please Please Me' next."

"If we don't hold our ground on this, we'll be just another bunch of puppets and them two spastics in there'll be pullin' the strings. Next thing you know, we'll be dressed in tuxedos and singin' 'Moon bloody River' or the like."

Ringo was in with a rimshot—whistling and brushing along to a dead march version of the Johnny Mathis hit. Paul iced him. "No one's goin' to make us do anything! But Eppy does have a point! 'Till There was You' could do well across the pond."

"Oh, fuck America, and you, too, if that's all you can think of!"

"There's no need for that kind of talk, John, I want to do the right thing as much as the next one. It's just that we've all worked so hard for this break."

"Listen, this time there's no sittin' on the fence, lad. We have to go in there and tell 'em it's 'Please Please Me' or else they can stick their deal where the monkey stuck his nuts."

McCartney's lips hardened, and the baby fat seemed to drain from his face. "I'm not goin' back to Liverpool," he said very quietly.

Lennon took another Players from the pack and tapped it against the heel of his hand. He frowned as he gathered his composure. "That's an odd kind of talk, lad."

"And no way am I goin' back to Hamburg to play all night for chip money."

"Yeah, but at least back there we were our own bosses." Lennon tried to overwhelm him. "Not like on these stupid package tours with a crowd of dossers, wankin' around for twenty minutes a night."

"But that's progress, John! We're takin' home twenty-five quid a week each, and if we get a hit record, God knows . . . "

"Yeah, but if that hit is 'Till There Was Puke,' we'll be playin' the London Palladium to a house full of geriatrics, openin' for Mel Tormé or some other Yank wanker."

Paul paled somewhat at this scenario, and Lennon blazed on. "Listen! What's the worst that can happen? Even if I'm dead wrong, and they give us our papers? We'll make it one way or another, and on our own terms too, right, lads?"

George strummed a diminished seventh and stepped on his vibrato foot-switch. While the chord swirled, he deadpanned:

"I don't know, John, if your aunt Mimi ever hears you turned down a gig with Melly Tormented, you'll be for the high jump."

Paul was unconvinced, but Lennon had a full head of steam. "Bugger the whole lot of them! We'll march out of here with our flags flyin', take the van back to Liverpool, and start all over again. And we don't have to go back to Hamburg neither; we've had a top-twenty hit in this country, and I bet we can get a new record company without Mr. Big Shot Epstein. Where are we goin', Ringo?"

"Home, John?"

"No, you dumb bollocks! Where are we really goin'?"

"Oh yeah, to the top, mate."

"What top, George?"

"To the topper most?"

"What topper most, Paul?"

"To the topper most of the . . . popper most," Paul added reluctantly.

Lennon needled him. "I can't hear you, wack."

"Oh, give over!" Paul pointed at the control room, where George Martin was talking on the phone. Epstein studied him, his chin cocked like a pointer. Once, he glanced out into the studio, his watery eyes darting ferally, but when he caught Lennon staring back, he looked away. They watched, fascinated, as Martin, urbane to the end, smiled, frowned, and silently coaxed.

"Me uncle looks like that when he's talkin' to his bookie," Ringo said, but no one paid him any heed.

The producer put down the phone and, solemn as a curate at a funeral, shook his head. Epstein dropped his forehead onto his palms and ran his fingers through his hair. He rubbed his eyes and nodded an unspoken assent. Then, taking a deep breath, he strode out of the control room.

Outside in the studio, they barely heard the insulated door open. However, to a man, they jumped and then squinted when Martin switched on the full lights that banished shadows and illusions, but not the gloom. John and Paul exchanged glances, each noting the pallor of the other. Epstein came right up to them, his face a study in despair. "It's no use, fellows. They're insisting on 'Till There Was You.'"

Lennon shrugged and switched off his amp. The red light on the Vox faded back into its tiny bulb. He unplugged his Rick and packed it in its case.

"Wait, John, I haven't told you the good part yet."

Lennon pulled his chord from the amp, deliberately wound it, and began to hum "Please Please Me."

"Will you please listen to me," Epstein implored. "Capitol has agreed to release 'Till There Was You' in the States, directly after Christmas. If it does anything, anything at all, we can be over there by Easter. I swear it, even if I have to pay for the whole trip myself."

But Lennon hummed on, and hung a blues interpretation on the bridge, stretching out the "rain" until it flowed like chiseled honey into "my heart."

George noted the stylistic change as he, too, packed his guitar. Ringo didn't care for it, but wiped off his drumsticks and stuck them in his jacket pocket.

"For God's sake, think of what you're throwing away," Epstein persisted.

But Lennon was already on his way to the door, busily deconstructing the last verse.

"John Lennon, don't you walk out on me!"

John Lennon didn't turn around. He threw open the door with a flourish and stalked off down the corridor, roaring the last chorus at the top of his lungs.

The slamming of a street door cut off the song in mid-syllable. For some seconds, a mortuary stillness gripped the studio; then George clicked his guitar case closed and flicked off his amp. Only one red light continued to glow. Epstein grabbed him as he walked past. "George, bring him back . . . please?"

"So long, Eppy. You're not as bad as they say you are."

"You're throwing away a fortune."

The guitarist hesitated a moment, but then, ever conscious of his cool, turned up his jacket collar and countered, "Yeah, but I'm keepin' me integrity."

Ringo battened down his quiff against blustery November and scrupulously removed the ensuing dandruff from his shoulders. "Thanks for everything, Mr. Epstein," he murmured.

Epstein didn't reply. He heard the street door slam behind George and, a moment later, close discreetly behind Ringo. Paul, meanwhile, gave a shrug and reached down for his bass. As he touched the steel strings, a small jolt of static darted up through his fingers. He recoiled, and a wave of rebellion surged through him. "He's just off to the pub. He'll be back soon enough when his money runs out," he snapped, and, firing up the volume, viciously dug into the intro of "Bring It On Home."

Epstein threw one last lingering look down the hallway. Then, with his heart coming apart at the seams, he closed the studio door. The red "recording in progress" light flashed on in the empty corridor.

Chapter One

November 23, 1987
147 Crescent Gardens, Liverpool

THE FRAIL MERSEYSIDE DAWN snuck through a tear in the curtain and threw up all over the ducks on the wall. He yawned and sank comalike back into the lumpy mattress. His tongue dry and callused as old sandpaper, he longed for a cup of tea but shuddered at the prospects of the morning before him. Still and all, a couple of aspirin and a flagon of water might do the trick. He eased out of bed and slipped his stocking feet into the cowboy boots that stood like fatigued sentries on the dusty floor.

Trouserless and trembling, he stumbled to the window, yanked back the curtain, and wiped the condensation from the frigid panes. *Raining again. What a surprise! Isn't it always raining—or threatening to. Well, at least it isn't pissing. Just drizzling, damp and dreary like a wet dream gone wrong. Someday, this whole bloody city is going to rust over, and they'll have to go at it with blowtorches and scour every last one of us the hell out of here; or instead, maybe the whole kit and caboodle will just up on its arse, slide into the Mersey, and lie prostrate like a big barnacled slum for a couple of dozen eons, until some enterprising archaeologist dives down and finds us all corroded, but present and accounted for, up to our necks in Liverpool rust.* Then he caught the idle train of his thought and, in quick succession, yawned, scratched his arse, and grumbled, "What in the name of Jaysus am I goin' on about?"

He turned from the window and had the misfortune to catch a glimpse of his figure shambling by the mirror. The cowboy boots, a size too small, pinched the calves of his long, hairy legs, while his tattered drawers drooped thighward like the diaper old Jesus sported on the cross. He sucked in the folds of his ale gut and twitched his face to straighten the broken nose he'd copped back in seventy . . . ah, back in seventy, whenever.

Oh, Christ! More gray flecks in me sideburns! Like a creepin' cancer suckin' the life's blood out of me manifold illusions. Well, at least I don't murder it with that black-as-the-ace-of-spades shoe polish like Gerry smart-arse Marsden. That chancer should be ashamed of himself, and he dive-bombin' past fifty.

He threw some shapes at the mirror and struck chords on an imaginary Strat. "Pathetic," he muttered. "Even turns me own soddin' stomach."

He fumbled on the floor for his jeans and swept them free of dust balls. Down the stairs, then to the kitchen. *Know every creak and wood groan by heart. 'S like a bloody out-of-tune symphony if you don't follow the freedom trail. And don't lean too hard on that banister either, unless you're insured up to the eyeballs or have designs on meetin' your Maker, sans appointment.*

He switched on the kitchen light and fired up the stove. *At least the bastards aren't rationin' the gas anymore. Easy to tell it hasn't been long since the election—mollycoddlin' still the order of the day—the honeymoon hasn't ended yet. But that and Christmas won't be long in comin'.*

He huddled over the greasy range to catch the heat of the

flame. It was getting harder to remember a time when gas and electricity were taken for granted, just paid the bill and that was that. Since the Front got into the government, you counted on nothing.

He ran the hot tap and held his finger under the flow of icy water. *Ah well, God is good and the devil's no slouch either. Still a profusion of old aqua—be it the Arctic bloody stream. Not like last year, when the waterworks went out on strike and I had to dig a hole down the back garden to shit in. Now, that's what you call makin' do.*

The kettle commenced to sing, and he wet the tea. He rummaged through the dark recesses of his smelly little fridge for the butter. Hard as Blackpool rock, it refused to spread, so he crushed it against the heel of damp bread. He doused the crust in precious sugar and recalled last year's sugar-cane disaster.

Could have sworn it was goin' to work—the summer bein' so balmy. Up them stalks shot like pricks in a whorehouse! Even Lady Maureen Cox-Starkey came to take a gander at me plantation right in the heart of the 'Pool. "Little Barbados," Ringo called it. Turned Marsden green with envy, it did, the flabby little bugger. How quick they all were to jump on the bandwagon: "No reason why cane shouldn't grow in Lancashire. Good a place as any for it. . . ."

But when old Jack Frost came early, the bastards changed their tune. Then it was a chorus of: "Looney's gone and done it again. When'll he ever learn?" Nearly broke me heart, it did. Me gorgeous big stalks of cane wiltin' and dyin', and each one takin' a bit of me with them! The bastards! The bollocksin', beady-eyed shower of begrudgin' bastards! Well, let 'em stew in their own grease. Their one chance to have sugar, regular as rain, on their tables, and they blew it. If they'd been more supportive, who knows what would have happened; maybe Jack Frost would have stuck a Bunsen burner up his frigid October arsehole. If . . . ah, what am I goin' on about? Life is one big four-lettered, free-wheeling if.

He opened the hall door and sniffed at the raw morning. A jungle of weeds, thistles, piss-the-beds, and nettles glistened in his front garden. Rain forest be damned! Come to Liverpool and preserve this fortieth of an acre of brambled and briared virgin wilderness.

Shuddering in the dank air, he threw on his old leather jacket and slammed the door behind him: 147 Crescent Gardens shook to its foundations. *Sod that wanker, son of mine, in his lazyitis! 'Bout time he shook the lead out of his arse, went out, and made some shillings for the good of all concerned. If the ship of state is goin' down, then all hands better jump to the fo'c'sle, and man the oars. The whole pyjamarama shouldn't depend on my command performance down the Exchange.*

He didn't bother with the front gate—the rusted latch had been beyond him for years. Instead, he vaulted over the garden wall, stuck his cloth cap firmly on his head, blew some heat on his knuckles, and headed off to tackle the trials of the new day dawning.

Perched atop BBC aerials, a squadron of great black jackdaws watched him stroll by rows of dreary, semidetached council houses whose manicured micro-lawns had recently metamorphosed into blooming vegetable plots. All it took was the excise tax on imported foodstuffs and Bob's yer uncle, every square foot of unused ground had been dug, fertilized, sown, reaped, and harvested by a legion of manic market-gardeners who would kill, maim, and die any old day of the week for their square inches, perches, roods, and furlongs of consecrated Britannic soil.

He ignored the achievements of his fellow burghers. He hadn't come into this world to be turned into a fat-arsed farmer by the dictates of a shower of xenophobic screwheads. And that was putting it mildly.

At a busy junction, he merged into a surging gray throng of pedestrians who had chosen to hoof it rather than pay the steep fares imposed by the new order. As the slogan on the buses so elegantly put it: "Oil is our heritage—don't give it away."

"More like—walk yourselves into an early grave," he grumbled as he gunned along at a mile a blazing minute. With his hands dug deep in his holey pockets and his head bent low against the soft rain, he looked neither left nor right.

Nor did he spare a glance for the punters as they streamed around him like ducks in a millpond. If they happened to stand in his path, he barged straight at them, and they either jumped aside or collided with a myopic, preoccupied steamroller. Some cursed loudly after him, but he ignored them; others muttered insults while the faint-of-heart just sighed. The man was mad. No question about that. Oh yeah, old Looney Lennon was a legendary nutcase down the length and breadth of the city of Liverpool.

Chapter Two

Britain will always be my homeland
I'm free, I'm no slave
God bless me I'm an Englishman
Purity in my heart
Strength in my hand
God bless me, I'm no slave
I'm an Englishman . . .

HE BIT HIS LIP in disgust. He'd been humming along with them without even knowing it—the words slithering around unconscionably inside his head. And why wouldn't he? Their anthem was the hit of the year and hard to miss: triumphant and claustrophobic, the birth of the blahs, the ultimate victory of the pig.

He spat on the ground, half expecting blood; but time enough for that. It wasn't as if he hadn't warned everyone. He'd shouted it from every pub, pulpit, and piss house that these bastards meant business. And no one was laughing now. The Front weren't a bad joke anymore. They might have got less than ten percent of the vote but, after three months of prevaricating, the Tories still needed their seats for an overall majority. Now they were in the government. The boot was on the other foot and the noose was already tightening.

Lennon could feel it. He knew them and they'd long had his number. He'd hated them from the get-go. Back when they were just another know-nothing pack of racists going nowhere in a hurry. Back well before their Rule Britannica Messiah, the Leader, had graced them with his presence, and become a lightning rod for every pale-faced, unemployed, brains-up-the-arse, disaffected moron. Still, you had to give the little bastard his due—he had a vision, no matter how barmy—the others were stuck in a time warp. He had a dream—the rest put you to sleep.

Lennon latched on to the end of the dole queue and shuddered with suppressed annoyance. He could hear their hullabaloo droning in the distance, then crystallizing until the first banner snaked around the corner. Held proudly aloft by a young blond giant, an iron fist—leaping from a background of red, white, and blue—shimmered in the mist. On either side, but a couple of steps back, the Aryan standard bearer was flanked by two lesser behemoths, holding matching banners emblazoned with the imperial visage of the Leader. All three wore the brown officer's uniform of the Front, immaculately pressed, chests bedecked with ribbons and medals.

A couple of the dole patrons looked up with real respect in their eyes. Most faked it admirably—no point in provoking these head-bangers. Others, of Lennon's persuasion, dug their hands into their pockets and studied the wet pavement, or buried their heads in newspapers and wispy clouds of cigarette smoke. No one spoke. It just wasn't worth the risk.

A brass band of somewhat doubtful musical pedigree was now huffing and puffing by, striving to keep both pace and pitch. Following these intrepid Sousaites, several score of the Chosen marched in strict formation. Blond-haired like their hero, although peroxided in most cases, few wore complete outfits but all featured some pieces of brown, military attire—replete with iron-fist insignia and Union Jack armband. They sang their anthem lustily, at times overpowering the atonal efforts of the band. These were the Chosen of the Leader, and Lennon hated them above all. Some hundred lay supporters marched in their wake, bearing handmade posters that proclaimed the likes of "Britain for the British" and "Coalition Now—Control Later," while the rear was brought up by a couple of short-pantsed boys on tricycles and a Cadbury's assortment of stray mongrel dogs.

Lennon blew his nose in a pothole and looked away. They were everything moronic in the Britain he had come to hate, and he recognized their parades for what they really were—a warning—*we have survived, now we have arrived!* Faces stiff as pokers, the Fronters marched past the hushed dole queue, daring them, tempting them to comment or somehow step out of line, all the while chanting their long-winded mantra as if trapped in some demented tape loop.

A flat-backed lorry stood up the street, draped in Union Jacks and banners sporting the Iron Fist. The open back bristled with an inadequate PA system. Like a well-oiled machine, the Chosen split into three divisions and surrounded the platform in a pyramidic phalanx.

Lennon could take no more. "Put a sock in it, you shower of robotic arseholes!" he yelled, only to be shushed by a chorus of nervousness around him. One of the Chosen stepped out of line and stared back at the dole queue. All heads ducked except Lennon's. They stared at each other, then the Fronter nodded and grimly smiled his recognition before rejoining his comrades.

"Are you friggin' crazy, mate? Get us all in the shithouse, won't you?" Someone shouted down the line. Lennon gave him the middle finger. Then his spirits lifted. The queue in front began to disintegrate when the more politically correct, or perhaps the more politcally discreet, drifted over to the meeting. Lennon worked his way forward and was entering the hallowed halls of the Labour Exchange, when the Chosen erupted into their double-fisted chant of POWER . . . POWER . . . POWER. The word seemed to contract, and the chant transposed into a sickening thud that echoed around the square: POW . . . POW . . . POW.

The remains of the queue shuffled inside, and the chant was drowned out by the murmuring movement of Liverpool's permanently unemployed. They milled aimlessly around the building or meandered down winding lines—gray figures in dun clothes, their cloth caps pulled low over their eyes, not in shame, for they were well used to that, but in search of anonymity—a wasted generation raised on the promise of life-long work in the mills and factories of the industrial North. That and other broken dreams had driven them into the welcoming arms of the Tories and the Front.

But out of the frying pan into the fire, and it was fast dawning on many of them that it would be a cold day in hell before the deflationary policies of the new order would reopen their cobwebbed factories.

Lennon made a beeline for the Final Extension section. Settling in among the crowd of political malcontents and general ne'er-do-wells, he closed his eyes and tried to nap, but it was no use. The line would freeze for long periods, then lurch forward and jolt him awake. Yet somehow it was more than that—a faint prickling in the nape of his neck.

Jesus Christ on a bike! Someone's staring at me. No, not someone! It's him, the geezer gawking out from behind his Echo. Even worse, the bastard's on the Special Extension Line, which means he's a Fronter, a Paki-basher, or God only knows what other form of antediluvial idiot.

Lennon stared steadfastly ahead, all systems wired to red alert. The last thing he needed on this particular morning was to tangle with a Fascist or even some lesser order of gobshite. But from the corner of his eye he could tell the Fronter was squinting at him over the racing page of the local rag. Wasn't wearing any of their doggie medals, but that meant sweet shag all. Your aunt Fanny might be one of them nowadays. *Oh Jaysus, why me, Lord, and on such a miserable Monday too?*

Still, his curiosity got the better of him. He whirled on impulse, spraying the hall with a dirty look. To his amazement, the Special Extensioner winked broadly back at him and flashed a comradely thumbs-up. Shaken by this turn of events, Lennon swiveled back and shuffled forward a few steps, unwilling to acknowledge the unsolicited intimacy.

Maybe he's a bleedin' fairy! I mean, what's the world comin' to if a man's got to keep a tight arse at the Labour Exchange? Is nothin' sacred? Didn't look like one though. Black leather jacket and jeans. Must be some kind of a rocker.

The queue staggered forward again, depositing Lennon at the frosted glass door of one "Beatrice Rogers—Counselor." Relief, for what it was worth, was near at hand; Lennon stole another glance behind him. His admirer was now talking to another patron of the Special Extension Line and, horror of horrors, waving at him.

"Move on, mate, ain't got all day to be fartin' around here," said a voice from the queue.

"In a hurry to meet your stockbroker, then, are you?" Lennon replied, and strolled into the teeth of the storm.

Miss Beatrice Rogers, hatchet-faced and impassive, perched

on a tall stool behind an old clerk's counting desk—Dickens revisited. A couple of cobwebs and a quill pen would have set her off nicely, he thought. She didn't deign to look up, frowning at a bulging manila file open on the desk in front of her. Lennon shifted awkwardly from foot to foot, willing, for another moment or two, to let sleeping dogs lie. At last she closed the file, harrumphed, and peered up at him.

"John Winston Lennon," she said.

He just couldn't resist it. He goose-stepped forward, clicked his heels, and bowed smartly. "Your servant, ma'am."

She cleared her throat once more and wearily examined him. "Mr. Lennon." She paused and adjusted her pince-nez; then, as if on a day trip to Damascus and struck by a fork of her Creator's lightning, she sat bolt upright. "Mr. Lennon, have you ever considered emigration?"

He had not, indeed, nor anything remotely like it; and so he stood stock still and pondered his options. *Easy now, Johnny! This could be a front—pardon the pun. The Labour Exchange in the mornin', Belsen-on-Mersey for afternoon tea and cucumber sandwiches! Better tread carefully here or the old bonyarsed virago'll have me out skinnin' dingos in Darwin or freezin' me balls off up in Baffin Bay.*

"What did you have in mind, Miss Rogers?" he inquired meekly. "I do have family, y'know."

Miss Rogers removed her pince-nez and daintily applied a powder puff to the end of her beak. "Excuse me," she purred. "Ah yes, your esteemed son, Julian."

Julian had apparently made a considerable impression on her; still, she frowned, and her already well-furrowed brow rippled under the strain. "You see, Mr. Lennon, I cannot under any circumstances approve another extension, but—" She halted for emphasis, all the while scratching her ear with the gnarled butt of a pencil. "I am not entirely without sympathy for your plight. I understand you are a musician by calling?"

She smiled sadly, and he could have sworn that her eyes began to mist.

"My late father was a great admirer of Gilbert and Sullivan, you see, and played the pianoforte with some degree of expertise; hence, my continuing interest in your ah . . . sorry state of affairs."

For Christ's sake! The next thing you know she'll have me singin' castrato in the choir.

"You laugh, Mr. Lennon, but if I had not awakened the morning of your prior appointment to the fondly remembered strains of—" And she broke into a surprisingly clear mezzo-soprano—"'Give me some men, who are stout-hearted men . . .'" Her voice trailed off, and, for an instant, she smiled almost bashfully. But only for an instant. "If not for that, you would not have received your last extension."

Miss Rogers paused, allowing this rebuke adequate time to sink into his unworthy head. Lennon let the daggers in his eyes do the talking for him. *Yeah, you old flint-arsed bitch, and if I hadn't awoken to the fondly remembered strains of "Johnny B. Goode," I wouldn't have crawled in here on me knees to apply for it.*

"Mr. Lennon," she resumed, mistaking his silence for some spark of patriotism lying fallow in his deviate breast. "The National Government of Reconciliation is trying to rebuild a new and more vibrant Britain. We are endeavoring to instill in all Britons a fresh pride in their country. We seek to inculcate nothing less than a noble purpose in every citizen in this once fair land."

She halted for an asthmatic breath. Lennon watched in awe as she half rose, half levitated from her desk and solemnly inquired, "What purpose can we inspire in you, John Winston

Lennon?" She lingered lovingly on the middle name and smiled as if at some shared secret.

Lennon rocked backward on his heels and regarded her warily. *Any minute now, this old bitch is going to jump out of her drawers, wave her metal-stayed bra to the high heavens, and sing "God Save the King."*

He considered telling her to go fuck a duck, but hesitated.

"Mr. Lennon," she said fervently. "Do you like sheep?"

Lennon was incredulous.

"Come now, sir, do you or do you not have an affection for yew, ram, or baby lamb?" Miss Rogers had the look of an old greyhound: knock-kneed, half blind, and hard of hearing, but still dangerous when scenting the kill.

"Oh, a lamb chop or a nice piece of mutton does very nicely every now and then."

"Capital, Mr. Lennon! You would get plenty of lamb, and mutton, too, for that matter—no doubt in the world, no doubt in the wide earthly world." She spread her veiny hands to delineate the breadth of her vision. "But tell me, sir, have you ever been in the presence of thousands of these docile beasts as they bah and bleat their woolly way across green windswept pastures?"

The closest scenario he could envision was the Leader's last rally at the Empire; but that had been indoors, and he scarcely felt Miss Rogers would appreciate the analogy.

She seemed to mistake his speechlessness for some small if unexpressed enthusiasm. "An engrossing vision, is it not, John Winston Lennon?"

"Sounds . . . er, healthy?"

"Healthy is one word for it, and many others spring to the sound mind, but consider this, sir. What would you say to uprooting yourself from your ancestral homeland and relocating to the verdant shores of the Falkland Islands?"

She proceeded, in glowing superlatives, to describe this craggy paradise. Lennon reeled under the weight of statistics and the dual promise of a new life and a noble purpose. Then, as the oxygen returned to his alcohol-famished brain, he cried out, "Miss Rogers!" and slammed his fist onto her desk, scattering his file to the four walls.

She woke as if from a trance and gaped at him, her jaw slack and mouth wide open to reveal a cavern full of false teeth and decaying molars.

"I'm a rocker," he roared. "I play rock & roll music. That's all I've ever done, and it's all I ever will do. And bein' a rocker doesn't include goin' to the arse end of the universe to sit on some godforsaken rock so's I can bugger sheep for the rest of me life!"

It was her turn to be speechless. She stared up at him, her teeth—both true and false—chattering away like castanets.

"So chew on that, you old fascist bitch!" He turned and left the office, slamming the door behind him, and plunged angrily into the crowd outside.

Most of them parted before him like the Red Sea before Moses. Those too dispirited or slow to move were sent sprawling. His admirer picked himself up, brushed down his black leather jacket, and swore to his comrade: "That bloody Looney! 'E'll get 'is before this day is over. You mark my words!"

Chapter Three

HE'D WAITED EONS, and now he finally had Herbie Wise exactly where he wanted him—by the short hairs—ten inches shy of the cup on the eighteenth hole. Just one last lousy putt to the dawn of a new era! He dropped to one knee and ran his eye from atop the ball along the manicured green to its sainted destination. Not a bump, a crevice, or an offending blade of grass to stop it. Just hunky-dory, full steam ahead, the way life should always be.

He stood up and flashed the fabled enigmatic smile at his manager, sidekick, bosom buddy, fixer, whatever. They'd been through thick and thin: shared women, booze, uppers, downers, divorces, decrees, subpoenas, and suspicions, you name it—but always this one nagging matter between them—Herbie's dominance on the golf course.

Little bastard has an unfair advantage. Playin' since he hopped bare-arsed and bony out of the cradle. And me? Never even saw a nine iron in all me born days until that rumble in Knotty Ash Town Hall when some Ted cleared the floor with one. Far from golf clubs I was reared.

But I paid my dues—just like with everything else—clawed my way up from bein' the runnin' joke of every clown and his mother to a respectable ninety on some of the toughest courses in this country. Courses that wouldn't even let me caddy for them when I first hit town now treat this guy with respect. I've gone mano a mano with three presidents, and I ain't talkin' banks or insurance— I mean the guys that floss their teeth on Pennsylvania Avenue every night.

Get a load of the little schmuck now—worried as all hell—as well he should be: Ten inches away from finally gettin' what's comin' to him. Ten bloody inches! Guys back home got dicks bigger than that.

Herbie's phone rang.

"We made a deal," Montana howled.

"I gotta take it, man, this is real important."

"You're tryin' to mess with my head, Herbie, and you know why."

"I ain't messin' with no one! This is important, man, I'm tellin' you."

"You're tryin' to distract me, and all because I'm doin' a number on you."

"Yeah, yeah, yeah, yeah, yeah, everyone's doin' a number on me. Listen, it's Morty Schimelman, and I gotta take it, but I'll be quiet, I promise." Herbie put the phone to his ear and whispered something while turning away from Montana.

Let the little runt do whatever he likes. Joshua could blow down the walls of bloody Jericho right now, and it wouldn't stop me from creamin' the little putz. What the hell's he so worried about? Bobbin' his head up and down like a rabbi on speed. Whatever—his problem!

Montana examined the selection of putters in his bag. *Oh yeah, baby, I'll nail him with the custom one he gave me when we signed the last Sands deal. Which scumbag critic said I got no sense of irony? It's cool as all hell lookin' too: shiny and gold with the platinum embossed Montana glintin' like streak lightning.*

He tried a few practice strokes. *Could damn near push it in from here. Just a little tap with the proper gravitas, and I'm in the groovy gravy.*

The sun glared down. Not even a suggestion of a cloud in the blue Vegas sky. Not a sound either, save for the distant hissing of a phantom sprinkler. He could feel his pulse quicken, the way it always did when he had his audience's total attention, and was ready to finish them off with one of his special numbers. But that almost came as second nature now—a piece of cake. This was different. Like the old days—a new thrill, and about time too.

He grounded his feet squarely, a hint of extra weight on the right—just the way Arnie had shown him; then he flexed his fingers, honed in on the purpose, brought the putter back, and, with a song in his heart, let gravity swing it forward again.

"Fucking asshole!" Herbie screeched, flinging the phone down onto the green.

Montana lifted from the ground, and the sudden torrent of adrenaline twisted his delicate putt into a querulous swing, lashing the ball off the green.

"Fucking moron!" he roared as he regained terra firma.

"Yeah, fucking moron is right."

"You're the fucking moron!"

"I'm the fucking moron?"

"You did that on purpose! I was kickin' your ass, and you just couldn't handle it."

"Listen, will you, don't be talkin' to me about golf. I didn't even want to play today in the first place!"

"That ball was in the hole. It was a done deal."

"Don't talk to me about no done deals. Oh, man, I don't believe this shit!"

"Well, I ain't payin'—the bet's off."

"Damn right you ain't! Morty Schimelman just canceled the series."

The blood drained from Montana's face. He clutched at his heart, but this was no hint of angina; the pain went much deeper—all the way down—a poisoned switchblade twisting and probing around the pit of his stomach. He tried to articulate his outrage, but no words came. His voice finally cracked into a hoarse whisper. "He did what?"

Herbie shrugged. It was time for the truth. But how to put it? He swiveled his head this way and that, searching for the right spin, some way to ease the hurt, but all he could unearth was "He said you're too old, man."

The blade plunged even farther—poised within an ace of his testicles. Montana gasped and sucked in a lungful of God's good air.

"He says you ain't cuttin' it no more. The network wants new blood."

"New blood? That scumbag was out at the ranch just last week, feedin' his fat face on caviar and Pérignon. What else did he say?"

Herbie sighed and shrugged again, as if contemplating the unknowable were neither wise nor profitable. "You know Morty."

"Yeah, I know Morty. He stood for one of my kids."

"Don't be takin' it so personal, will you?"

"What way do you want me to take it? Like it happened to me great-aunt Marjorie? That series is my bread and butter. It's my main line of communication with my fans—the American people. I don't got that—I don't got nothin'!"

"Listen, all I'm sayin' is, Morty'd fuck his own mother for another half a rating point. Anyway, there's good news too."

"Like what? He just blew his brains out?"

"Like he's givin' us a summer special—the fifteenth of August."

"Who the hell watches TV in August?"

"I do."

"Yeah, just the demographics I'm lookin' for." Montana raised his arms to the universe. *Should have seen it comin'. All my life, I try to do the right thing, and this is what I get. They wait till you're vulnerable, then grab you by the goolies and squeeze till the eyes pop out of your head. Same old story: the dwarves takin' down the giants.*

A black hole of bitterness sucked him in, and he choked back the rage. *So, this is what it's come to. All the years of fightin' and clawin' my way to the top, only to be dragged back down into the slime by that fuck-faced little midget Morty Schimelman!*

He swallowed hard and wrestled with the fear. But a solitary tear welled up in his eye as he looked to his manager and whispered, "What am I gonna do, Herbie? What the hell am I gonna do?"

REASONABLE . . . R-E-A-S-O-N-A-B-L-E . . . R-E-A-S-O-N-A-B-L-E. The word repeats, caught in some fathomless echo chamber, each nasal syllable at first distinct, but then overlapping and feeding back in on itself until it gathers into one blurred, pounding colossus. In slow motion, John picks up the bottle of lager and hurls it at the studio wall. Through the gathering blob of pandemonium, the bottle flies, sure as a shot, smashing into smithereens.

And one of those alcoholic icicles has my name on it. Even in the distance, I see it tomahawking toward me. I try to duck, but I'm paralyzed. Oh Christ, it's slitting my neck, slicing it in two, heading right through my tonsils, straight for my vocal cords and . . .

"Aaaahhh!" He rose from the bed screaming, clutching for the pain in his throat, the blinking lights of Vegas melding with the strobes darting from behind his eyes.

"Waaahhh!" The current love of his life screamed as she, too, erupted—a vision in violent pink—framed by the gentle glow from his recently acquired crystal planet lamp.

"He stabbed me. I can't breathe."

"Waaahhh!" Luanne Luano screeched in banshee harmony, now up on her knees and wrestling with her sleep mask.

A pounding on the door was accompanied by the booming voice of Big Bill Whalen, Montana's bodyguard. "You okay, boss?"

"Sonofabitch stabbed me in the throat!"

"He's over there behind the curtain. Look at him!" Luanne pointed to a swaying bulge in the velvet drapes.

"Get in here!"

"You gotta open the door, boss."

"Get your ass in here!" Montana roared, then gasped for breath as the realization sank in. "Oh, man, I'll never sing again!"

The door bulged as Big Bill threw his full two hundred forty pounds of somewhat flabby, ex-linebacker physique forward. Montana heard a ghastly groan from the other side, though whether it came from the wooden door or Big Bill, he wasn't sure. But the hinges held firm.

Meanwhile, Luanne dug her long nails through his silk robe. "Look, he's moving."

"Aaaahhh!" bellowed Montana from the real pain in his thigh. Outside, Big Bill listened in horror. He backed up some paces, then, roaring out a bar of the Notre Dame fight song, he charged.

The door splintered, flying off its hinges. Big Bill arrived right behind it. He lurched through the darkened room, upending chairs, a mobile bar, and finally, with a fearsome crash, Luanne's makeup table.

"Over there! Over there! Get up, you idiot!" she urged as he lay groaning on the floor, his shoulder now totally out of whack.

Big Bill stirred and rose slowly from amid shattered jars of Sisley and Clinique. He appeared to be about to speak but froze at an ear-piercing shriek from Luanne.

"Oh, my God, he's coming! Look out, Paulie!" She tried to push her paramour forward. Montana, however, was having none of it.

"Let me go, for Christ's sake!"

Big Bill's huge head swung back and forth, searching the room. "Where the hell is he?"

"Behind the curtain! Behind that curtain!" Luanne pointed at the drapes next to the French door.

Big Bill raised himself to full height, then dropped into an attack crouch. He stalked the billowing curtain with all the deliberation of an ancient master; suddenly, he lunged forward and launched a tremendous karate-chop. With a dull, fearsome thud, his hand crashed through the velvet and into the brick wall behind it.

"Motherfucker! Goddamned motherfucker!" He dropped to his knees and wailed, rubbing his forehead on the carpeted floor.

"Did you get him?" Luanne peered out from behind Montana.

At first, there was no reply. Then a long, low moan of agony. Big Bill crawled along the floor, dragging his damaged fist behind him. The moan sharpened a tone or two as his bad knee—mangled in an epic slugfest with Boston College—ground a jar of cold cream into the carpet.

"What the hell are you doin' to my makeup, you big idiot?" Luanne demanded.

With a titanic effort, Big Bill raised himself to his feet and stumbled to the wall, where, after a moment of fumbling, he found the light switch. In the cool halogen glare, the couple stood etched against the opulence of the master bedroom: Montana, in black silk samurai robe, and Luanne, in a nightie that left little to the imagination, clutched each other atop a majestic heart-shaped bed.

"Where is he?" Luanne glared at Big Bill. "Where is the sonofabitch?"

His face the color of Sierra snow, his breathing like the workings of a bellows, Big Bill leaned his head back against the wall, unwilling or unable to answer.

Hurtling from bad dream to worse reality, Montana looked around in confusion. He took in the wreckage of his bedroom and exhaled mightily. "What sonofabitch?"

"The asshole who stabbed you! Who the hell do you think?" his love replied.

Montana disengaged himself and plopped down on the side of the bed. He failed to notice Big Bill slide down the wall onto the floor.

"My hand is broken," the bodyguard remarked matter-of-factly.

"It was all a dream," Montana said. He put his head in his hands. "If only I could make it go away.

"Dream, my ass! I saw the sonofabitch."

From his sitting position, Big Bill attempted to flex the fingers of his damaged hand. "Lady, you saw the fan blowin' the curtain."

"Don't you dare contradict me. Who's paying your wages?"

"It ain't you, that's for sure," Big Bill murmured.

"Paulie, are you gonna let him talk to me like that?"

"It keeps coming back," Montana said, head still buried in his hands. "The dream won't leave me in peace."

"You gotta be kidding me. That was just a dream?" Luanne was somewhat skeptical.

Montana lifted his head. "How do I make it go away?"

"You go to a shrink like any sane person. What do you think you do?"

"Listen, babe," he snarled. "I've seen more shrinks than you've had hot dinners—for all the good they've done me."

Big Bill stumbled once more to his feet. He shuffled toward the door, his hand held limply aloft before him.

"Where the hell do you think you're going?" Luanne asked.

"I gotta see a doctor."

"No way, José!" She jumped out of bed and placed her impressive body full square in front of him. "You break in here like Schwarzenegger, wreck the joint, and then crawl out like some skinny-assed wimp. Who's gonna clean up this mess? Who's gonna fix the door?"

"I'll send up maintenance."

"You will like hell! You think I"m gonna have every tourist in Vegas staring in at me in my delicates? You'll fix everything this instant."

"Listen, lady, I gotta take care of my hand. These are my bread and butter, see?" He thrust forward his formidable fists.

"They're obviously not your brains!"

Scowling, Big Bill looked to his employer for support— nothing had been right since he'd picked up this piece of trailer trash; but Montana had other things on his mind.

"You know what I need?" he asked, and delivered the answer before either of them could say a word. "I need quiet."

Luanne shook a manicured finger at the bodyguard. "You hear that? The man needs quiet. He doesn't need you barging in here, frightening the life out of us."

"Listen, lady, you were howlin' like the whole front line of Ohio State was on top of you," Big Bill began.

"How dare you! I never in my life got it on with a ballplayer," she protested a tad too vociferously, and added for the bodyguard's information, "especially an animal from Notre Dame."

"Shut up," Montana declared icily. "The both of you."

"Not until he fixes this door."

"Not until she stops runnin' down my school."

"Can't you people understand? I've got to confront this right now, before it slips away. Twenty-five years ago, a guy smashes a bottle off a wall, and I'm still sufferin' for it. Don't that mean nothin' to either one of you?" A moment of silence ensued before he sighed, "What am I botherin' my arse for?"

Montana hopped over the smashed jars and mashed tubes and entered his wardrobe. He dressed quickly, cursing the both of them in particular and the world in general. Then, turning a deaf ear to their protestations, he stormed out of the penthouse and into his private elevator.

In the lobby, the usual collection of rubes and gawkers ogled him, but he was in no mood for signing autographs. Still, his ever-nagging conscience tweaked: *This is your public.*

"My public can roast in hell!" he growled back, frightening a blue-haired matron hot off the bus from Branson, who was clutching his first album.

Got to be careful. One rotten weed can choke a field full of flowers. Five years down the pike, some gossip monger in Buttfuck, Texas, could get a scoop on "Montana's blue-cursing streak in Vegas" and look out! It only takes one. At least, that big idiot Whalen had the smarts to call ahead for the Porsche.

Still gleaming in its custom-made costliness, his cruise mobile was purring in the driveway of the casino—the valet's mouth agape with wonder, his hand opened even further in expectation.

Montana fished for a ten spot. His assistant usually put a roll of twenty Alexes in his pocket every morning, the bare minimum for any self-respecting star on his daily rounds. Anything less and Marianne Mealymouth would rip you to shreds in her column or, horror of horrors, on her syndicated radio show.

"Shit!" Montana hissed. The valet almost leaped out of his obsequious skin. *Where's my money clip? Jesus Christ! What a beginning to a beautiful day.* "Listen, kid, I'll catch you tomorrow. Okay?"

The hand might have retreated slowly, but the wonder instantly transposed into a wounded smugness.

"What the hell's the long face about, I forgot my wallet, all right? Everyone knows Montana ain't no cheapskate. You listen to music? Here's one of my singles! I'll even autograph it for you."

He fumbled in the dashboard pocket. *What's she done with the singles? Bitch gives 'em away at the drop of a hat. Throws 'em out the window at scumbags who can't even name one—not even one—of my hits. She's goin' to pay for this, big time. Nothin' left but a bunch of cassettes.*

He tossed the offending tapes aside. "Listen! Why don't you go tell whoever the hell you like that Montana is the cheapest prick this side of Bootle. And you heard it right from the horse's mouth, you hear me?"

The boy leaped back from the curb as Montana peeled off into the night in a screech of burning rubber. Looking in his rearview mirror, Montana saw that he was the beneficiary of an elaborate obscene gesture. He snorted in disdain and roared down the strip, away from the fancy new gambling dens full of glass and chrome, past the relics of Uncle Howard's crumbling empire. He tried to stare right through the huge billboard advertising his TV show—his own smooth-as-silk, air-brushed face beaming down, mocking him from above with his clarion call: *One and only and forever.*

Yeah, forever and about twenty-four hours, until Morty Schimelman has Wayne Newton's pimply, putrid face painted all over it. What's the matter with this red light anyway? To hell with it!

He tore across the junction, bracing for the whine of a police siren. But the remains of his luck held; soon he was beyond the dazzle and, moments later, all on his own in the starlit desert. The temperature dropped by the second as he barreled down the highway into the moonlike terrain.

Jesus, what a break! Sometimes, that city just chokes the life out of you. It's like your heart is racin' but you can't even feel it, 'cause everyone else's is keepin' time with you. Talk about the Rat Pack! Rat race is more like it.

He sucked in mouthfuls of the bracing air and rejoiced in the silence. But the voices in his head weren't long about needing company, and he fumbled for the radio. Then he heard her, like a chisel scraping off steel, grating on each and every one of his raw nerves. He lurched forward to switch it off, but too late. Marianne Mealymouth was already in her stride:

". . . so that's it, four new dates added to Ol' Blue Eyes' tour. But how about our boy, Montana?"

His stomach did a backflip, but he hung on her every word, poleaxed by paranoia.

"You remember that one and only and forever kind of guy? One and only maybe, but forever? Fuggedaboutit! And you heard it here first. I bet our Paulie ain't sleeping too well tonight after the abrupt cancellation of his ABC series. Oh well, cheer up, Paulie-pie. At least, they didn't totally leave you out in the cold. How about that dog-day-summer special? Now all you gotta do is set up some TVs on the beach."

"Bitch!" But his howl of outrage choked to a dull rattle on her next words.

"Guess the financial pinch is in already, right, Mister One-and-Only-if-Not-Necessarily-Forever? A reliable source reports that Montana, that light-of-touch limey, brazenly stiffed a casino valet who depends on tips to support his mother, six brothers, five sisters, and over forty aunts, uncles, and cousins in sunny Mehico. Montana was seen peeling off down the Strip in his custom built one-hundred-grand Porsche, obviously out of sorts and employing language better left unsaid on these airwaves. Bet you don't use that kind of talk in the White House at one of your family values get-togethers with El Presidente. *Hasta la vista*, Paulie-pie, see you around—the Bowery."

He switched off the radio and wheeled the car abruptly off the highway. He slowed but didn't stop, climbing the dirt and gravel track that led to his spot. Her spot? Which her? *Who cares! All the hers, and their shyster lawyers.*

In a hail of gravel and dust he floored the Porsche, for once not caring what scratches or scrapes tarnished its magnificence. He shot out onto the ridge. Turning off the engine, he let the car coast up to the edge of the cliff—his spot. *Not hers. Not any of the bitches. None of them'd be caught dead here anymore. Too busy spendin' their alimony checks—keepin' their boy toys in rubbers. Later, for all of them!*

And there it was. Vegas, like a jeweled madonna, laid out before him: the lights of Emerald City blowing away the stars that twinkled in the ice-clear moonlight. The tension drained out of him in one long, heartfelt sigh. All the occasions he'd come here through the good, the bad, and, he shuddered, the downright ugly.

Nancy had taken him here first, back in his rookie days, when he was new to the country. New to a lot of things. Trying to break away from Eppy's whining shackles. It had been their spot. He'd asked her to marry him here. She'd told him she was expecting their first here. They'd even broken up here. Seemed like a great idea at the time—like so many others.

Needed my space, didn't I? Couldn't breathe with her and the kids around. Jesus, what a dope! A couple of weeks after the divorce, I was missin' them like hell. But she wouldn't take me back, would she? Took half of everything else though. Not to mention that her old man put a contract out on me.

What's a man without his kids anyway? Had to beg her for every five minutes alone with them. Bitch poisoned their little minds on me. Any bad review, any little piece of gossip, she'd nail to their bedroom walls. Wouldn't even let me bring them home to Liverpool. Said she'd have me up for kidnapping if I took them east of the Mississippi. Never got to meet their granddad. Wouldn't even let them see Eppy. You can imagine what that did to him, and he only hangin' on over here by the skin of his teeth. I'll never forgive her for that. Couldn't leave the country myself after she laid that deadbeat-dad rap on me. Never got to say good-bye to me dad.

And now the kids are all grown up and leadin' their own lives, without the faintest idea of where I came from or what makes me tick. No wonder they look at me funny. Don't even have the time of day for me. Whenever they ring me now, they reverse the charges. I'm an embarrassment to them. Don't want me to be around their fancy friends. But I've poured out buckets of sweat for them on a million stages around the world so that they have the bucks to buy their stuck-up back-slappers. And what have I asked for in return?

Sweet damn all. Shit! I'd sweat double the buckets all over again if, only once, one of them would just call me Daddy, like they used to when they were little.

They'll never know what it's like to go to a foreign country and start all over: Every dimwit fallin' around at your accent. Bottom rung on the ladder, fightin' and gougin' your way up! No time to look back for fear you'll fall down, just on and on until you make it to the next step, then the one after, a whole new set of back-stabbin' bastards to deal with.

Then, when you finally get somewhere, no time to stand still, 'cause the new kid in town is already breathin' down your neck. But I did it. I came through everything, never once looked back, and I've got a boxed-set full of greatest hits to prove it.

He rummaged around in the cassette chest. *Nothin's where it should be. Why can't she keep her greedy paws off my shit? Bitch is outa here tomorrow. Lots more where she came from, and not as many miles on 'em either.*

Then his fingers touched the familiar gold lettering and his heart gave a jump: *One and Only and Forever.* No one could take that away from him. Or could they? He shouldn't have thought about that. Shouldn't have thought about anything. Thinking's the problem. Always has been. Everything else is fine. Just get on with it. But lately, the stress had been out of contol—everything getting hairier by the day. And now, one simple question and his whole world shuddered, just like the time he'd been messing around with Joe Frazier and taken the left hook to the gut. *One and only and forever!* What a joke. They were taking it away from him right in front of his very eyes. Who? They! Who else? He knew this town and how it was run. When you were down, you were really down. Oh yeah, Ol' Blue Eyes had made it back, but only by the skin of his teeth, and he was the Man—almost untouchable. Made no difference, once they gave you the boot down the greasy pole, it was nearly impossible to work your way back up.

But he wasn't going without a fight. He'd been through worse than this. A lot worse! And he'd achieved. Damn right, he had. *One and Only and Forever!* Scream it out loud, sonsofbitches! But the words gave no consolation. Rather, they ripped through him, mocking him, shellacking him, tearing apart twenty-five years of grizzled defenses like they were shredding paper towels. He gripped onto the steering wheel and awaited the arrival of his steely pragmatism. But there was no sign of it. He was suddenly terribly afraid—and alone. To hell with alone! He'd been alone for over half a lifetime. He'd get through this just like he'd got through everything else—head held high and on his own two feet. But then he was crying, tears that he'd been holding back since Liverpool.

Oddly enough, they brought a strange relief. He loosened his grip on the steering wheel and looked out at the Emerald City. His sobbing was only fitful now, but hard as he tried, he could not bring the twinkling lights into focus. Then he felt that he was moving, picking up speed and rewinding through color into black and white, accelerating injudiciously past triumphs and disasters alike, until he was deposited back in a low-ceilinged, shadowy tunnel full of young men and women. They were moving to a silent primal rhythm, their arms raised, their faces flushed and excited. He could smell them, their body odor mixing with deodorants, aftershaves, cheap perfume, greasy food, overflown toilets, and disinfectant. Some were screaming his name. He couldn't hear them, but he could tell by the movement of their lips and the intent in their frantic eyes. The girls wore beehive hairdos, cardigans, and dresses just above the knee, and they toppled this way and that in their high heels; the boys sported white shirts, skinny ties, dark five-buttoned suits, and slathered great globs of Bryl-creem into their well-kempt, unwashed hair.

He looked around the sweat-stained walls and saw that he was on a stage. Behind him, the drummer's head was swaying behind a ride cymbal. He could feel his own fingers digging into the thick strings of a bass, but no sound emerged. He leaned backward and stared at the drummer's right foot, saw the pedal hit the bass drum, and madly willed himself to hear it—then, suddenly, it was there, punching, thumping like the thud of a hammer, giving bottom and balls to the silent song. His fingers were moving in double time to the drummer's foot, and when his bass amp roared on, he could feel his rounded notes gripped in a vise with the kick. Though the singer was screaming silently into the microphone, the instruments and the shouts of the crowd were now popping in and out of his mix. Familiar lead guitar lines were screeching across the high frets and wrapping themselves around the rhythm section like barbed wire around a sheep's back; but when he heard that driving Rickenbacker rhythm surge through its amp, he knew without a doubt that he was back where he started—in the Cavern. Only one thing was missing: Lennon's voice. And now it blasted into, and then soared above, the mix, spewing out a torrent of nasal rock & roll; and for the first time in years, he knew exactly where he was bound. Nothing would stop him this time. There was a gig coming up in London; he'd take the time and the risk, like he'd never done in the past; head on up to Liverpool, check out the guys, see how they were doing; and if they were up for it, he'd fly the three of them back out here, and they'd knock off a set for his TV special—even if it was the fifteenth of August—and anyone who didn't look at it would be a certified dickhead, because he and his three mates were going to blow the tubes out of every television set in America.

His heart began to slow down, the Cavern faded into the past, and the Emerald City came dancing back in all its ice-cold clarity; he felt more at peace with himself than he had in twenty-five years—he knew exactly what he had to do. The kid was going home.

Chapter Four

LENNON BARGED OUT onto the street, almost taking the doors of the Exchange off their rusty hinges. His humor was hardly improved by the sight of the Fronters parading off around the corner. He jabbed a stiff middle finger to the heavens and roared at their wake: "Fascist bastards! Back to the zoo, where you belong, you crowd of bloody Neanderthals!"

"Hey, mate, keep it down," a voice suggested from deep behind an *Echo.*

"Keep it down yourself, you silly git!"

"C'mon, mate, don't want no trouble on this queue, then."

"Oh, bollocks!" Lennon pulled down the newspaper and was confronted by a dwarf of a man crowned by an oversize cloth cap, the butt of an unlit cigarette dangling from his cankerous lip.

"'Ere now!" Cloth Cap stared back through a pair of bloodshot eyes.

Lennon appraised this stunted mediocrity with disgust. He could hear Cynthia advising him to "leave it be, John, he's done you no harm"; but he was far beyond advice, especially hers.

He mimicked Cloth Cap's phlegmy voice of reason: "Don't want no trouble, then. That's what the Jews said before they turned 'em all into lampshades. It's about time someone spoke out against them shower of rag-arses."

Cloth Cap lowered his newspaper and dribbled the butt over a cold sore to the opposite corner of his mouth. This mission accomplished, he advised Lennon in avuncular tones: "You want to watch your tongue, Looney. Them bastards are in the government now, y'know."

"I know they're in the government, then, don't I? Haven't been down in the Algarve workin' on me tan, then, have I? Jesus, the Fronters and the Tories together. It's like the blind leadin' the bloody bland."

Cloth Cap glanced over his shoulder. "Well, you better watch out, mate. That's all I'm sayin'." He leaned forward and whispered, "Things ain't what they used to be!"

Lennon almost choked on the aroma of stale sweat and nicotine. He stepped back and inquired from a sanitary distance, "Who the hell are you, then, Max bloody Bygraves?"

"Laugh all you want, mate. But it's just like Tony Benn said 'fore they threw him in the clapper: 'Even the walls have ears.'"

"Tony big bloody Benn. That chancer couldn't organize a piss-up in a brewery."

"I dunno, mate. He always stood by the workingman, did old Tony," replied Cloth Cap, his voice tinged with nostalgia for this aristocratic champion of the proletariat.

"I'm a lot more interested in the nonworking man meself." Lennon sneered.

"Suppose you got a point there all right. 'S one thing cuttin' back on jobs, but cuttin' back on the dole just ain't civilized."

"Well, I'll give them one thing, they put a stop to the Pakis and them friggin' Irish comin' in and takin' all the work," interjected a matron of indeterminate age, curlers bedecked by a bright orange scarf, head nodding in spastic collusion with her words. She paused for a moment, seeming to savor the sound of her own shrillness, before declaring: "That bunch had it comin' a long time!"

"Are you serious?" Lennon was aghast. "No self-respectin' Paki or Mick'd be caught dead tryin' to get into this nuthouse. The whole country is like a big bloody puzzle factory with half the pieces missin'."

"Better watch out, mate, here comes one of 'em now." Cloth Cap dived back behind his paper as Lennon's admirer emerged from the Exchange and shouted, "'Ey, are you who I think you are?"

Lennon cast a cool but cautious eye on this new arrival in the light of the day. He was some inches shorter than Lennon, but built like a brick shithouse. Though his gut hung well over his belt, still there was an athletic cut to his swagger to suggest that he might have been a handy center-forward in his day. He was probably quite handsome back then too, but his cheeks had fleshed out and reddened from beer and the elements; one of them was adorned by a red weal that stretched from just below his right eye to the lobe of his ear. He tried to conceal this relic of a youthful slashing by cultivating a long quiff that dangled precariously over his face. A rough-looking customer indeed, Lennon surmised, with a face on him like a farmer's arse on a frosty morning. Still and all, he inquired cheekily, "Are you who I think I'm not?"

"Used to be a Beatle, then, didn't yeh?"

"A what?" Lennon played for time.

"Used to play rhythm with the Beatles back when Wooler run the Cavern, then, didn't yeh? Never forget a kisser, mate. 'Arry 'Olt's the name. Used to be a friend of your drummer's." He thrust forward a large callused hand in greeting. Lennon coolly declined the courtesy.

He did, however, motion 'Arry closer; then, in comradely manner, said, "Listen, why don't you do us both a big favor?"

"Sure, mate, anything you want."

"Take a long walk off a short pier."

"Come on, then, no call for that kind of talk. I even saw yez out in Knotty Ash when yez used to be Long John and the Silver Beatles."

Knotty Ash Town Hall. Oh, my God, perish the memory. Dance floor chock full of combustible teds and rockers, axle grease in their hair, bicycle chains welded to their wrists, all hepped up and bullin' for some Saturday night aggro. Look sideways at them or, God forbid, at one of their teased-up dolly birds and they'd beat the livin' shit out of you, eat you up, spit you out, and beat you up one more time, just for the practice. Only one way to survive: play loud, hard, fast, and for Christ's sake keep them jivin'—Jerry Lee, Little Richard, or Chuckie B—and for an occasional smooch, a little Fats or pre-idiot Elvis. Used to call them "blister gigs," your fingers'd be so sore from rippin' through nonstop versions of "Sally," "Molly," "Lizzy," and the like.

He surfaced reluctantly from his memories. "Bit of a historian, aren't you?"

'Arry 'Olt was touched by this belated recognition of his authenticity. "Yeah, I go way back, mate." He thrust out his hand once more in friendship. "I seen 'em all. There was Rory Storm, Kingsize Taylor, Gerry Marsden, the Remo Four. . . ."

Lennon hesitated, then limply took the outstretched hand and listened impassively while the names of friend and foe alike were invoked, judged, and summarily banished back to mothballs. His admirer's next words, however, could have knocked him over with a feather. "Give us yer autograph, then."

"Get on with yeh."

"Yez used to be me favorite group, y'know. I even voted for

yez in that big Mersey Beat Contest years back. Bought up ten copies and sent 'em all in under different names, I did."

"So what? You want a bloody medal?"

"So bloody what?"

"Yeah! So bloody what?"

"Saw yez at least a hundred times down the Cavern. Yez used to be gear."

"Yeah, reverse."

"C'mon, mate, 'ave a 'eart. Give us yer monicker, then."

"Piss off, dickhead!" Lennon stormed off. But a determined hand on his forearm stopped him dead in his tracks.

"All right, mate, you got me number," 'Arry 'Olt confessed. "The truth is, it's not for me. It's for Elsie, me missus. It's 'er birthday, and I ain't got a shillin' for the meter."

"Who d'y'a think I am, Sister bloody Teresa?" But when he tried to break away, the claw grip tightened.

"Won't cost you nothin'."

Lennon glared down at the offending hand.

"Sorry, mate, but it'll mean a lot to old Elsie."

A weariness swept over him, and he longed for home, a smoke, a quick wank, and a long afternoon's read in bed. "Got no paper, then, have I?"

'Arry 'Olt pulled a crumpled newspaper from his arse pocket. "'Ere, you can sign me *Echo*, right over the racin'." He frantically flipped the pages and yanked a pencil stub from behind his ear.

Lennon licked the lead tip, squinted, and signed above the picture of a dappled gelding. 'Arry 'Olt held the paper up to the light and solemnly examined the signature. "John bloody Lennon! I never thought you'd end up 'ere with the rest of us." He shook his head sadly at this baleful state of affairs. "But I suppose that's the way the ball breaks, ain't it?"

"Listen, you got your autograph. You can keep your bloody sermon for the cathedral."

"Good on you, mate, Elsie'll be chuffed. She never saw yez herself, but she's bonkers about that Montana bloke used to play bass with yez. What was his name back then? McCarthy or somethin'?"

"You lyin' bastard! Give it back, then, come on."

He tried snatching the paper away, but 'Arry quick-stepped nimbly out of reach. "No bloody way, mate!"

"Give it back, you hear!"

'Arry danced away from him, skipping over the rain puddles, brandishing his trophy. Though the steam was fast running out of him, he still remained a pace or two in front of Lennon, shouting back: "'Ey! 'Old on, mate. What's the matter with you, then? This'll make old Elsie's day."

"Elsie, my arse!"

"C'mon, mate, 'ave a 'eart."

"I'll give you a bypass, you bloody leech!" Lennon roared.

A crowd had gathered to watch this sport. They drew closer, creating a semicircle around the steps of the Exchange. Tabloids were carefully folded and stored under oxters, and a packet of Players was passed around while Liverpool's unemployed enjoyed the escalating argument.

Lennon finally brought his tormentor to ground against the wall of the Exchange and seized the paper. 'Arry struggled wildly at first, but then let go, afraid of tearing the precious signature.

"'Ey, cut it out! Bloody 'ell, 's only a piece of paper."

"Yeah, but it's mine." Lennon ripped out the racing page. He crumpled the remainder and threw it into the crowd.

'Arry 'Olt was outraged by this sacrilege. "'Ey, Micko, Charlie. This bloody sicko's got what's mine, 'e 'as."

Two large anonymities dislodged themselves from the crowd and swaggered over, à la Bogie and Cagney, ready to affirm the rights and avenge the wrongs of their bosom buddy in dole-hood. Charlie, the larger one, frowned at Lennon and inquired in a surprisingly high-pitched voice, "What's he got, then?"

"'E's got what's mine. That's what 'e's got!" replied 'Arry, frothing at the mouth with indignation.

Charlie lumbered toward Lennon, his hand outstretched. Quick as a whippet, Lennon feinted and dodged past him. He saw an opening in the crowd and made for the wide open spaces of Leece Street. However, he stopped in midstride to avoid Micko and was collared around the throat by the lunging Charlie. Feeling the grip tighten, Lennon grabbed his assailant by the balls, squeezed mightily, and hung on for dear life.

With a bellow of deranged agony that would do a bull calf proud, Charlie lifted his potential castrator from the ground, threw him headfirst into a large puddle, and soundly kicked him in the arse. Spent from pain, he fell to his knees; his eyes rolled upward, seeming to settle somewhere around the roots of his hair.

"Bloody queer! Give it over, then," demanded 'Arry 'Olt, enraged by Lennon's lack of sportsmanship.

Coughing and spitting, Lennon crawled out of the oil-stained water to find his escape blocked. He rolled into the fetal position, stowed his national health glasses in his shirt pocket, and shouted, "Fascist swine!" Then with considerable stoicism, he awaited the pain.

It wasn't long in coming. 'Arry 'Olt landed a place kick in his ribs. Lennon rolled over, stuffed the precious paper in his jacket pocket, and shielded his head with his fists.

Micko, of somewhat softer heart, grabbed his amigo and pleaded: "Give over, mate, you don't want to kill the bastard."

'Arry tried unsuccessfully to break loose, but Micko clung to him like a limpet.

"Get up, you soddin' degenerate, and fight like a man," 'Arry commanded. "Look at 'im! Won't even fight back, 'e won't." He made another valiant effort to kick Lennon from a ten-foot distance and added: "Bloody Communist!"

Charlie, still nursing his bruised and shrunken cojones, crawled over to Lennon and groaned, "You little pervert, if my bollocks ain't in full workin' order, I'll cut yours off and make you eat it."

Since he seemed in little shape to carry out this threat, Lennon ignored him and maintained his fetal station.

"Bastard's gone and fixed poor Charlie," Micko wailed. "What are we goin' to tell his wife?"

"Let me go, mate, I'll just get his address so we can press charges if Charlie's knackered," 'Arry said, but once free of Micko, he circled Lennon like a wounded tiger. "Long way from the Cavern you are now, Mr. 'Igh and Mighty."

Although lying mere feet from Lennon, Charlie now turned to matters of a more spiritual nature. In a quiet but hideous moan, he began to supplicate a selection of the greater and lesser confidants of his Redeemer. "O, Holy Mother of the Infant Jesus and Blessed Martin De Porres, spare me," he beseeched the heavenly hierarchy but, receiving neither balm nor response, returned again to more temporal concerns. "Me wife'll kill me if I come home with me bollocks out of whack."

'Arry 'Olt had little time to devote to his friend's distress. He had Lennon where he wanted him. With legs apart, thumbs jerked into his belt, he towered over the fallen rocker. "Look at 'im! John bloody Lennon, the snivelin' sicko. You know, Lennon, you're not even worth wastin' shoe leather on, but I'm a generous sort of a bloke, so 'eres lookin' at you, kid. Let's 'ear you twist and shout to this!"

He again dug the toe of his boot into Lennon's ribs. "You're not worth the trouble, then. Besides, my Elsie don't even know who you were, let alone who you are." Having delivered his coup de grâce, he bent down, spat on the boot recently defiled by Lennon's Marxist molecules, and polished it with his sleeve. "Not that you were ever up to much anyway, you and the other two wankers."

Lennon didn't choose to address this diatribe, much less get to his feet. Although appreciably the worse for wear, he was, when all was said and done, thankful to be in one piece.

"I'll get you yet, you short-arsed bastard," he murmured ever so discreetly. "One night you'll be walkin' down a dark alley and I'll give you 'Twist and fuckin' Shout.' Throw in a little 'Roll Over Beethoven' for good measure. You'll be pickin' my boot polish out of your fascist hole till the balls fall off the Christmas tree."

He didn't dare rise. Besides, the dirty, wet pavement felt cool and comforting against his throbbing head.

Straight down Leece Street, the sun was working overtime, trying to squeeze through the clouds. The drizzle had stopped for a moment, and a rainbow foraged for roots up under Lime Street Station, but then thought the better of it, and beat a hasty retreat back into the gloom.

"Ah Jaysus!" Lennon groaned.

Chapter Five

HIS GAUNT FINGERS CLUTCHED the receiver long after she had hung up. Her voice still beat tattoos on his eardrum: "See you . . . nice to see you . . . be so nice to see you again."

He put down the receiver. The altar boy was waiting for him to disrobe. Shrugging out of his alb, he kissed the sacred stole while the boy fumbled with the knotted cord.

The frankincense continued to ooze in gray wisps from the thurible. *Damned boy would let it smolder till the whole sacristy smelled like St. Peter's. Ah, let it smell to high heaven.*

Odd that Cynthia hadn't called. Not that he didn't care for Maureen. But Cynthia used to do the inviting even back when his skin crawled at the very thought of seeing anyone.

Ah, Cynthia, how could you have known what was going on in my head, you who always saw the good side of everyone? Dear sweet Cynthia with your long blond hair flowing down over your tight black jumper, your kind eyes and gentle voice—Brigitte Bardot from over the water. That's what John wanted and that's what John got. But then, John always got what he wanted. But did he always want what he got? And even more to the point, was he ever satisfied when he finally got it?

Even so, he was right to walk out of that bloody studio, and so were me and Ringo to go with him. But is right really right when it ends up all wrong? Now, there's a question for the College of Cardinals, or the Synod of Bishops, or the Big Cheese in the tiara himself, or whoever in Rome calls the shots these days. That damned boy is staring again. What the hell does he want now?

Their eyes met and the priest lost his way in the freckled face.

Not much younger than meself when I first met old Paulie back at Liverpool Institute. Always sure of himself, even back then, was our lad. Knew just what he wanted and usually got it too. Different from John though: If Paul couldn't get his way straight off, he'd let the matter rest and pretend he'd forgotten all about it; then later on he'd slip it in again, just like an afterthought. Of course, by then everyone else'd be bored to tears with the original problem and he'd win by default. Smarter than Lennon that way! Old Johnny'd go at it like a bull in a barn full of heifers, and if he couldn't get what he wanted, then he'd make sure everyone else got sloppy seconds, if they were so inclined.

I'll have to go; doesn't seem to be any other way out. Made a promise to Ringo, didn't I? And I wouldn't let him down for the world. Dear old Rings, stood by John and me back in London when he didn't have to. Was with us only a matter of months, wasn't he? Could have snaked off to the States with Eppy and Paulie, but he didn't. And that's why I'll show up, even if I have to strap meself inside a straitjacket and have the dustmen drop me off at the front door.

But enough of that! I'm goin' and that's the long and the short of it. Probably be a relief anyway. Put the whole thing behind me once and for all. Been hangin' over me head like the sword of Damocles, whoever the hell he is when he's at home diggin' into his bangers and mash.

How long since I've seen John now? Has to be ten years. And Paul? Not since the night of the long knives back in Abbey Road. When was that? Twenty-five years. O dear divine Christ, longer than old Stu's entire life.

Sweet Jesus, I've been staring at the little bugger all this time. More grist for the mill in the vestry! Another crazy Father George story—poor old dear is not quite the full shilling when push comes to shove, then, is he?

"Pleasant enough man," he had overheard one of his parishioners pontificate, "a little odd, but I'll say one thing for him, never keeps you too long in the confessional."

Actually, the old barmyness helps in a way: They've stopped inviting me out to their interminable tea-poisonings for chitchat, the like of which could drive Attila the Hun to take up tiddledywinks.

When George dismissed him, the boy's relief was tangible; he scurried off through the vestry door without stopping to empty the thurible.

Ah, let it smoke and smolder till the whole joint burns down. On second thought, maybe that's not the best idea. God only knows where they'd pack me off to on my endless recuperation—Land's End, John o' Groat's, or some other Siberia of the soul.

He opened the side door and dumped the silver censer onto some weeds. The charcoal flamed for an instant in the Cheshire breeze until he stomped it out with the heel of his boot. He leaned back against the wet slate of the annex and pursed his lips. But the images were starting to come again. He flinched as they besieged him, flash frames of the past in dizzying sequences, and always that awful empty feeling that things could have been different.

Nowadays, they seemed to hit him when he least expected it, after a couple of clear weeks when things seemed like they were finally on the up-and-up. He braced himself, clenched his fists, and dug his nails into his palms.

O, sweet Jesus, if I could only stamp out me mind as easy as that charcoal. Make life a hell of a lot simpler, that's for sure certain!

When he reopened his eyes, the rain had stopped and the sky was clearing. Great gray clouds were scudding away from the anemic sun. He gazed across the graveyard, past the neighboring Methodist chapel, and then on down into the once-merry olde English town that was slowly being asphyxiated by corridors of ugly semidetacheds.

Still, there was hope. One end of a rainbow crowned the weather-vaned spire of the Town Hall; the other was hidden from view, but he knew it had cast roots, somewhere across the river, in Liverpool. He couldn't see the city and yet it was ever present, forever pulling him over that aerialed hill down the valley and over the dirty Mersey—home.

He scraped his boots on the foot grille, stepped back into the vestry, and closed the door behind him. A stray ray of sunshine pierced the stained glass window and scattered shifting slivers of color across the gleaming tiled floor. He fastened his Roman collar and took stock of himself in the mirror. An intense ascetic face returned his interest.

A little too thin for some of the parishioners, but then, you couldn't please everyone. A streak of gray here, a line there, but not too bad considering the circumstances. At least, not bad on the outside; but inside, well, that's a whole different kettle of fish, waiting to be opened up and spilled all over this holy sacristy floor, if only I had the guts to do it. But that's not on the cards, is it? Not after what happened back in the cathedral all them years ago.

He grasped the edge of the polished counter and watched the blood drain away, until his knuckles turned white as gleaming fish bones. Again, the familiar, insistent roaring began to swell just this side of his eardrums. He held on, waiting for it to pass. In the mirror, a tiny bead of perspiration gathered itself on his forehead while he struggled to recall that old humiliation. Wasn't that what the shrink had advised: "If you don't want to tell us, take it out and air it every now and again. It'll only go to seed inside."

All very well for him, but he hadn't messed up his life in front of the whole of Liverpool, had he? No, and he didn't spend two years goin' up the walls of a nuthouse with nothin' but a crowd of alky reverends for company.

The roaring began to pulse, and he held on for dear life. *Just got to keep me head screwed on. This too will pass. All things pass if you give 'em time. Jesus, what else have I been doin' but dousin' the past with bucketfuls of precious dwindling days and months and years?*

I've got to go tonight. Got to face up to it. In fact, I've got to get the bloody hell out of here, mucho pronto, before I go down on me hands and knees and do the hokey-pokey all over their holy floor. No! Got to hold on, clear me head first. Can't let them see me go to pickled pieces out in the transept.

Do something concrete, pull meself together! What mass am I sayin' tomorrow? Any births, deaths, weddings, annulments, teas, dinners, garden fetes in the works? Are Everton still in with a chance of the double? Is Elvis still alive or just dead in the head in Grace-land? Who won the Grand National? How is the pound holdin' up? The problem is, I don't give a continental hoot. But please, for the love of Christ, don't let me be givin' a sermon tomorrow. I just can't handle that level of aggravation.

So, put me down for first mass, let me commune with me Creator on me own or, at the very worst, with a congregation of daft old biddies who wouldn't notice Christ resurrected if he hopped down off the cross and took a large bite out of their sanctimonious arses.

His stomach in a knot, his hands clammy and full of thumbs, he staggered over to the weekly duty schedule. *Oh, for Christ sake! How could they do this to me? Eleven o'bloody clock! The headliner, top of the bill, wouldn't you know it! What the hell am I supposed to gab on about this time? Faith, hope, charity, the seven cardinal sins, the nine first Fridays, the Ten Commandments, the twelve apostles, John the 23rd, Paul the 69th? As if any of it made sweet shag all difference; almost put meself asleep, listening to me own dear boring, droning, drab, and dreary noncommittal voice. Can't blame the poor bastards, hawking and spitting, coughing and sneezing, scratching their arses and itching to go home, read their Sunday papers, and watch their creepin' Jesus snooker or darts on the telly.*

As he steadied himself, the sleeve of his cassock caught the altar tray. A small beaker of consecrated wine fell and shattered on the tiles. He rested his hand on the duty schedule and stared at the floor, unable to concentrate, while red rivulets meandered among the shards of glass. Finally, when he could take it no longer, he dropped to his knees and grasped desperately at the jagged end of the beaker; a small gash opened on his index finger. Fascinated, he watched his earthly blood mix with the surrogate essence of his Redeemer.

And then it passed. Just like that! No bells ringing, no celestial choirs, no great insights, much less a parting of the heavens, only a vague, queasy emptiness and a knocking at the knees. A gentle glide back down to earth and sanity, reality, or whatever they called it nowadays.

He donned his black gabardine and, valise in hand, shuffled down the dimly lit transept. At the "Jesus Crucified" Station of the Cross he stepped over old Mary Rosary, on her knees per usual, claiming her billionth plenary indulgence, guaranteed to mainline her straight into the bosom of her dear departed Savior. The old woman gaped up beatifically and, at the touch of his hand on her widow's scarf, she whispered vehemently: "God bless you, Father George."

"If only he would, Mary, if only he bloody well would," he

murmured under his breath. She beamed up at him, assuming his blessing, and he passed on.

Oblivious to this daily drama, the freckle-faced altar boy burst through the upper vestry door, hotly pursued by two angelic companions. At the holy-water font, Freckle-Face turned and, with a sweep of his arm, drenched his pursuers. George stepped into the shadows of a confessional, unwilling to censure these adolescent heathens. The old woman followed him in on the penitent's side. Trapped again.

Reluctantly, he slid open the partition and listened to her drone on, drone on. He forgave and forgave, until she and her spiritual Alzheimer's departed. It was cool and silent in the shadows of the holy box; he lingered on and savored the musty smell of velvet cushions and redemption.

How many times have I sat here on my sainted Catholic backside forgiving human weakness and administering the Great Bearded One's impartial justice? What a sick and sad little litany it's all become. Little lusts, little fears, little people. And back always, a day, a week, a month, a year later with the same little pains. Nothing ever changes. Nothing makes any difference. The world comes, it sins, is forgiven, then it sins one more time and, in the bitter end, the confessional's become just another car wash of the soul.

And who can I confess to? Who'll shoulder the weight of my black despair? How can I tell another of God's dry cleaners that I don't believe a word I'm saying, and that I'm going to go clear out of my skull if I have to put up with another minute of it.

The nerve in his cheek began to twitch, and he was grateful for the darkness. It was safe in the shadows. No one could touch him in here. After all, what was he but a mirror reflecting the world's calamity and confusion? And he'd forgive them anything—big, small, mortal, venial—it didn't make a whit of difference, he'd give them absolution till the cows came home and sweet bugger all penance into the bargain.

At the bus stop he was on remote control, effortlessly trading meteorological observations with a gaggle of squawking housewives. Eventually, they left him to his preoccupations, but he knew his "oddishness" would soon supplant the weather as their main topic of wonder and speculation.

He began to shake again and prayed with all his might that the bus would arrive before his thoughts boiled over and ran down his face to reveal themselves, in all their squalor, to this hung jury of judgmental biddies. Turning abruptly from them, he pulled his felt hat firmly down around his ears; then, squinting into the damp breeze, he hung on until the red double-decker trundled down the hill.

By force of habit, he climbed to the upper floor, sat in the front seat, and stretched out his long legs skew-ways to dissuade any gossipy trespasser from joining him. The bus crawled across Cheshire, and he could smell the Mersey getting closer: a familiar fusion of sea, tar, and sewage. The gulls now fought with rooks and crows for space on the forest of television aerials sprouting from the chimneys of the little red terraced houses.

The bus lumbered up one final hill; then, on the crest, it rounded a bend, and the river lay sprawling beneath them. Close to shore it ran brown and sluggish, but out in the center the foam-flecked waves jigged merrily on the soft swell. He spotted the ferry approaching; he could even distinguish its peevish whistle as it swerved among the motley armada of small craft that plied the river since the introduction of petrol rationing. Across the Mersey, the Pier Head cocked its snout in disdain at Ireland, and Liverpool lay sprawling like an old whore—decayed, toothless, and long past worrying what people thought of her.

"Comin' back tonight, Father?" He hadn't noticed that the conductor, Charlie Something-or-Other, was a parishioner. When the priest fished in his pocket for his newly minted transport pass, Charlie waved him on with a wink.

"No, I'm packin' the whole thing in, Charlie. I'm goin' to get shitfaced and pull meself a big woman."

"You're an awful man for the jokes, Father George."

"That's what the girls used to say."

"Ah, we were all young once. But you'll be back all right now, won't you?"

Although Charlie wasn't expecting an answer, the priest considered this for a moment and then murmured, "I don't know, Charlie, to tell you the God's honest truth, I really don't know."

But Charlie was preoccupied with more immediate calamities. "Well, look out for yerself over there." He flung his arm out ominously across the river as if motioning to Sodom and Gomorrah-on-Mersey. "That bowsy, the Leader, is plannin' a big speech in Anfield tonight. Make sure you get back before dark now. There's a lot of rumors about trouble brewin', and you don't want to get stuck over there."

He pointed at the walls of the terminal: THE LEADER RULES OK! The unveiled threat leaped out at the commuters, with red paint so fresh it still trickled from the letters like tears of blood.

"Them shower of bastards passed through here earlier this morning, and I'm telling you they had something on their minds. All cocky and smirking like. Each one of 'em carrying a big bag—and they weren't full of Christmas presents, I can tell you that."

He waited for the priest to comment. When he didn't, Charlie turned back to the sign. "They did that right in front of me face. Told me to stick it! Ring whoever I liked, the police, the army, the king himself if I'd a notion to. What's the country comin' to at all, Father?"

The priest stared at the slogan and shook his head. How could you give a sermon on charity and not condemn these Fascists? How could you speak of "love thy neighbor" and not rail against their racism? How could you speak of hope and not denounce false prophets—like that blond-headed Antichrist? But, more than anything, how could you speak about faith when the little belief that was left in you was smothering under a sea of doubt?

But that's how he and all the other foot soldiers in Christ had been ordered to preach—in half-truths and innuendoes— never naming names, never going out on a limb, always keeping your holy arse perched squarely on the fence. The archbishop's Paschal Letter had spelled it out in spades: "In this troubled political climate, we deem it imperative that no mention be made of any political party or personage thereof." And that was most definitely that! Orders from the top, prob- ably cleared in Rome with the head sky pilot himself: Don't rock the boat until we see what pier it's going to dock at.

The ferry whistle sliced his thoughts. As the dockers unwound the ropes from the bollards, he took one last look back at the neatly terraced houses of Cheshire, his home within a prison these past how many years? Then he smiled to himself: *Strange, how easy it is to take the big step. You spend years thinkin' about it, frettin' over it, knowin' you won't have the courage. Then one day, out of the blue, you just put your best foot forward and, wham bang thank you ma'am, discover it was no big deal at all.*

Father George Harrison, S.J., cleared his throat, stepped up the gangplank, and spat into the brown river: "Fuck the arch- bishop and the horse he rode in on," he muttered.

Chapter Six

THE RAIN WAS PELTING down outside the Labour Exchange, but it made little difference to Lennon lying arse over elbow in the gutter.

"Hey, what's goin' on here, then?"

"Oh no." Lennon groaned when he heard the familiar voice..

"Well, if it ain't the little drummer boy hisself," said 'Arry 'Olt. "C'mon, Nosey, you want to join your mate down there? 'S where you belong."

"Leave him alone, you big bollocks!" Ringo strutted over and tried to turn Lennon onto his back. Lennon prudently feigned unconsciousness.

"Big bollocks, 'ow are you." 'Arry 'Olt was obviously less than enamored by this description. He noticed a smirk on Micko's pockmarked face and snarled: "Shut it, you!"

"Did the dirt on Pete Best, then, didn't you?" He returned to Ringo. "Best drummer ever come out of Liverpool, till a little ferret-faced bastard like you stabbed 'im in the back. C'mon, Shorty, let's see what you got, then."

"I'm right here, mate," replied Ringo, whose retreat, however, was blocked by Lennon's body.

'Arry moved to within inches of Ringo's ample nose. "You couldn't fight your way out of a paper bag."

"I could do you in me sleep, lah," Ringo muttered not altogether convincingly. Tucking his chin, he leaned backward at a 110-degree angle, a trickle of sweat meandering down the ravines of his brow as he twisted his neck in an effort to loosen his collar.

'Arry turned to his two partners and sniggered. Micko joined in rather half-heartedly, but Charlie, alas, was beyond mirth: fit only now for clutching his testicles and murmuring heartfelt supplications to a lesser litany of saints.

An old crone in the crowd cackled along. 'Arry 'Olt raised his hand for silence, but the lady refused to be stage-managed.

Ringo seized the moment and hopped to the other side of Lennon. He backpedaled some steps and froze into an exaggerated karate position.

In true gladiator fashion, 'Arry placed his foot atop Lennon's shoulder, but warily took stock of Ringo's martial stance. *Little bastard don't look like much, but you never know, could 'ave been spendin' 'is summer 'olidays in Japan.*

Lennon had no such reservations; he hazarded a stealthy glance and awaited the imminent slaughter.

Strategically located behind a Valentine's Brook of a pothole, Ringo crouched in a kung fu burlesque. Resplendent in maroon three-quarter-length jacket with black velvet lapels, blue shirt, matching silk tie, drainpipe trousers, and two-inch-high canary-yellow plimsolls, the drummer appeared all nose and large Labrador eyes. His dark but graying hair was plastered back, with the exception of an offending kiss-curl that dangled somewhere to the left of his right eyebrow. His many rings glistened dully in the soft morning light.

Ringo caught Lennon's eye and winked; then, through clenched teeth, he snarled something unintelligible in pidgin Japanese. Hoisting an imaginary Union Jack, 'Arry 'Olt stepped up to the mark to do battle with this Technicolored samurai.

Lennon braced himself; but lying there with his ear to the ground, he caught the first distant rumble of stamping feet. He arched his right ear to the wind, heard nothing, but noticed Micko tensed and peering up Leece Street, like some Old Testament prophet awaiting Jehovah's latest spin. Miraculously, Charlie's pain had subsided and though still on his knees, he too seemed poised for flight. Suddenly, Micko broke tableau and shouted, "C'mon, mate, it's the bloody Chosen!"

"Christ." 'Arry 'Olt hesitated. "'S all I need, get in trouble over a couple of 'as-beens."

Seizing the moment, Ringo roared, *Sayonara Sushio!* and kicked high into the Liverpool sky, his yellow heels flashing. He landed feet first and ferocious, mere centimeters from a startled 'Arry, who, choosing discretion over getting his arse kicked, fled before this unexpected onslaught.

When he had gained relative safety on the far side of the street, 'Arry picked up a stone, feebly flung it back, and snarled. "That's for Elsie's birthday, Lennon." Turning to flee, he added for Ringo's benefit, "I'll settle with you later, Schnozzleface!"

"I could sort you out with one hand tied behind me back, you dozy bugger!" Ringo retorted. Emboldened by this rout, he kicked high again, this time crash-landing in a puddle and splashing his beloved maroon jacket. "For Christ's sake!" he howled, up to his ankles in muck. Tiring of battle, he hop-stepped to dry land and removed his shoes. "Come back and fight, yez crowd of nancy boys!" he shouted somewhat distractedly and without a great deal of enthusiasm. Then he turned his attention to his stained attire. "Look like the bloody muckman, then, don't I?" he lamented.

But the Front anthem was growing ominously louder, and he swaggered over to Lennon as best he could under the circumstances. "C'mon, mate, you can loosen up now. I run the bastards off."

Lennon peered up cautiously.

"Jesus, John, what have they done to you?" Ringo skipped from foot to foot, shoeless, his orange socks caked with mud.

"Good old Ringo, be late for your own funeral, you will." Lennon, perceiving no immediate threat, groaned and stretched out. "But no panic on the *Titanic*, I can hear the cavalry gallopin' to the rescue." He launched into an improvised parody of the Front anthem:

Britain will always be my Falklands,

I do bugger sheep

But I never touch lamb chops . . .

"For the love of Christ, John, will you c'mon, these are serious jokers to be slaggin'!" Ringo half dragged, half carried Lennon down a side alley and hid him behind a pile of overflowing dustbins. "What did that lot want, mate?" he whispered, despairing now of removing the muck from his shoes.

Lennon's bruised ribs were throbbing like a jackhammer; he bit his thumb for relief, then said: "They wanted a very precious piece of me, that's what they wanted."

"Well, they got a very precious piece of your face, and that's no lie." Ringo crouched under the largest bin and sniffed at some rotten fruit. Turning away in disgust, he spat on the palm of his hand and wiped some congealed blood off his friend's cheek. "What else did they want?"

"Wanted me name, then, didn't they!" Lennon grimaced but Ringo continued to wipe away the blood and grime.

"Yer name, John? Come off it."

"Yeah, me bloody name. Didn't get it though, did they?"

Lennon waved the crumpled paper aloft exultantly. "The only thing I got left in the world, and the bastards wanted it."

"Get down, John, will you!" Ringo hissed. "The Fronters'll think you're talkin' about them."

"And they'd be right." Then he roared out, "Shower of arseholes!"

Ringo ducked down even farther, hastily slipped into his shoes, and discreetly moved to the shelter of the farthest bin. "You keep up that kind of talk and you're on your own. Stay down, for the love of Christ, will you!"

The first red, white, and blue banner streamed past them. Lennon knelt and aimed a gob of bloody spit at the leaders. Luckily for him, the Chosen's attentions were focused on the crush of unemployed outside the Exchange.

"I'll get down as soon as I've finished countin' me molars."

"Well, that shouldn't take too long," Ringo hissed, and risked a glance at the marchers—all fish-eyed glares and self-importance—mowing down the first line of unemployed. The remainder fled in panic before the onslaught, or raced into the sanctuary of the Exchange.

Lennon appeared to have lost interest in matters of politics. After some cautious exploration, he removed a bloody finger from his mouth. "I don't believe it! Me last wisdom tooth is loose."

Ringo sighed. "You lost that one a long time ago, old son."

The parade had passed. The old crone lay stretched out in the mud, still cackling to high heaven. Some others picked themselves up, dusted themselves off, and dragged her into the Exchange. The chant began to recede, and soon the only sound was the rain cascading off the dustbins.

Lennon stood up and gingerly fingered his ribs. This pain was going nowhere in a hurry. A darkness settled in on him.

"Ringo, if you were as good a drummer as a comedian, I wouldn't still be stuck here in some back alley in Liverpool, would I?"

Ringo was hurt. He rose from his hunkers as best his dignity would allow and brushed down his clothes. Taking care to isolate the insistent kiss-curl, he plunged a steel comb through his oily hair.

Lennon watched the drummer's offended ritual and shrugged. "What brings you down here anyway? We get another gig at the Empire or somethin'?"

Ringo took the bait, hook, line, and sinker. "You have to be jokin', mate! Gerry's still pissed at you over that Walrus affair. You'll be lucky if he lets you play the Horse and friggin' Saddle tomorrow night."

He stopped abruptly and considered his next words, while Lennon leaned against a lamppost and waited. "Come down for you I did." He paused, playing for time, and asked none too optimistically: "How'd it go anyway?"

Lennon examined his glasses. He straightened the frame, then spat on the lenses and wiped them in the tail of his shirt.

"Bloody disaster!" He tried on the specs for size, then adjusted the frame one more time. "Do you know what old Bonyarse wanted me to do?"

Ringo was all ears.

"Pack me bags for the Falkland Islands."

"She what, John?"

"Yeah, so I could bugger sheep for the rest of me days."

"That's goin' a bit far, ain't it?"

"Yeah! And then for a little light nostalgia, one of me old fans kicks the shit out of me."

Lennon stuck his head around the corner and glanced up and down the street. Finding the coast clear, he sallied forth.

Ringo, still pondering the deflowering of sheep in the southern hemisphere, followed.

With the departure of the Fronters, the streets began to fill up again; the gray queues of unemployed resumed their vigil, while vendors materialized as if out of thin air, wheeling their carts and shouting their wares. Pedestrians and cyclists flowed between the steady stream of sanctioned official cars, while buses, filled to the brim, lumbered past, the passengers staring straight ahead, sensing that some altercation had taken place and unwilling to take the least chance of getting mixed up in its consequences. After a brief convalescence, the sun began to perk up and shine again, and Liverpool got on with its day.

"You shouldn't argue with the likes of them, John. You'll have no teeth left soon."

"No teeth or no dignity. Take yer pick."

"That's all very well, mate, but you can't eat with your dignity."

"But it saves on me dentist's bills, doesn't it? Anyway, you didn't come all the way down here to discuss my masticatin' habits. How come your Maureen let you off the leash?"

"Got some news, John."

"Yeah, you and the *Echo* both."

"He's comin'."

"Who's comin'? Santy Claus?"

Ringo's muttered reply was so tentative, it got lost in the roar of the traffic. Then, nervous as a cat on hot tiles, he shouted, "Paul's comin', mate."

Lennon stopped as if slapped in the face.

Afraid he might lose courage, Ringo blurted out, "He's comin' to your house tonight."

Lennon stared back at him. All the years he'd been waiting for this news, wishing for it, yet dreading it, and now what came to mind—sweet bugger all. He took his time before answering, afraid his voice might betray him. But in the end, the question appeared almost casual. "How did this come about, then?"

"Some Yank called the salon today."

Lennon's bottom lip had dropped slightly, and the cut under his eye had reopened. Ringo wasn't sure if he was listening, and raised his voice. "Don't you hear what I'm sayin', John? The kid's comin' up to see us. After all these years . . . the kid's comin' home."

The kid's comin' home.' Twenty-five years of waitin', and this is how it ends. "The kid's comin' home." Twenty-five years of what-might-have-beens, and this is all there is? Might-have-beens, my arse! Should-have-beens. Twenty-five years of him rulin' the roost and havin' to swallow his muzackal puke left, right, and center. Twenty-five years of patronizin', pityin', and wholesale whisperin' behind me back: "Oh, Looney's the one what got left behind. Wasn't good enough, y'know. Didn't have what it takes, when it come right down to it. Got all the breaks but couldn't handle the aggro. Gave him the boot, Mr. Epstein did. Him and the other two wankers. Was his fault though. Couldn't move with the times—give the public what they wanted. That's what makes Montana tick, ain't it? Knowin' what the man in the street wants to hear. Not stuck in the past like the other dickhead."

"The kid's comin' home." Not—"The kid's got the electric chair for vomitin' all that shite out over the radio." Not—"The kid's sold his soul, and is now crawlin' back to beg forgiveness from his old mate for leavin' him to rot in this kiphole." No. Nothin' even remotely of that name or nature. Just plain old simple brown bread, hard as rocks, "the kid's comin' home." My sainted arsehole!

The floodgates of defiance reopened; Lennon's lower lip shot back up into place, and the life surged out from his eyes. He grabbed a mental hold of himself. Quietly, and with as much indifference as he could muster, he asked: "He's comin' for definite?"

"Well, it's not dead certain, but near as makes no difference. If the weather clears up they play Wembley, if it stays shit. . . ." Ringo digressed into detailed explanation, but Lennon was already off and walking. He raged down Lime Street—a blitzkrieg in the making—the drummer still explaining, but trailing in his wake.

Lime Street and no Maggie May, Allerton, and no McCartney. I mean, what's the bloody difference? It's all a nightmare now, and who the hell cares if we never made it anyway?

I care! I fucking care! I care more than anything in this shithole of a world! And twenty-five years ago, every punter this side of the Mersey cared; but that was then, and this is now. Eventually, they all slipped back into their lifetime fellowship of the livin' dead. Oh yeah, for a couple of years, scrubbers still looked at me like I was somethin'; then, one day, it all flushed away down the toilet, and the Beatles ended up on your granny's mantelpiece: another sepia-toned memory.

And to make it worse, some days, I, me, meself wake up and wonder if it wasn't all a dream and it could never have been like I know it was. On days like that, I'm nearly ready to believe Maureen's senile sermonizin': "It was all very nice, luv, but you were just a bunch of young lads having a good time; now you've grown up and have families of your own. . . ."

I always make sure I give it to her, right back in the kisser. "Let me define 'grown-up' for you, Maureen Cox. It means B-O-R-I-N-bloody-G. That's what it means. Boring and bland, like you and all the other half-dead wankers in this petrified wasteland of a country."

Twenty-five years now since I've laid eyes on the bastard. Of course, I've seen his ugly mug plastered all over the Echo and, as for the telly, it's Montana this or Montana that or Montana the other thing, till the eyes are nearly poppin' out of me skull from starin' at the cut of him. And each and every time I see the bloody ponce or hear his name, it's like gettin' a large-size belated boot in the family jewels.

Of course, he's the one with the talent, isn't he? And I'm "the sod what got left behind." Well, fuck 'em all and their pukin' pity! I'm as good as him any day of the week. I was as good as him back then, and I'm a far sight better now. I've thrown out classier used arse paper than some of the tripe he's written. And he actually puts his name to that shite too. That's one thing none of them understand. Your name's important. It's all you have, and that's why I wouldn't let that bollocks keep my autograph, even if he'd mashed my balls into gravy. It's my name and it means something to me. McCartney's, obviously, means sweet shag all to him. Paul Montana, my aunt Fanny's false eyelashes! Ah, for Christ's sake, what the hell am I goin' on about?

He stopped dead in his tracks, and Ringo collided into him. "I care," he roared, jabbing his finger into the winded drummer's chest. "And I'll keep on carin', because the minute I don't, I'm as dead as the rest of yez, and I don't ever want to end up like that. Dear dilapidated Jesus—" he sank to his knees on the wet pavement and raised his hands skyward— "if you're up there at all, do what thou wilt with me, drop thine big hairy leg down from the clouds and kick my thick head off; castrate me and hang out my well-wanked mickey for the jackdaws to feast and frolic on; but don't, dear J. C., I beseech thee, don't let me become one of the walkin', talkin' ossified."

Ringo grabbed Lennon's hands and roughly pulled him to his feet. "For Jaysus sake, John, have you totally gone off the deep end? I tell you he's comin' if the weather stays shit."

"Twenty-five years later and he's still waitin' to see which way the wind blows." He ran into the middle of the street, horse-drawn carts, buses, and cyclists alike skidding to avoid him.

Ringo sprinted to the rescue, but the madman held still as Lot's wife, and refused to budge. Like twin islands, they held their ground, the traffic swerving around them, till Lennon revived, and roared through the bedlam, "You're right, lad, he won't come. He'll manipulate somethin'"—he burst into uproarious laughter—"even the bloody weather."

Wild-eyed and worried, Ringo took one last look at the approaching horsepower and bolted for the safety of the curb. "He's comin' all right, mate," he shouted back, on the gallop.

"What?" Lennon yelled. "What the hell did you say?"

Ringo mouthed a reply and waved back madly.

"The little scruff," Lennon grumbled, "can't never hear him when he's got somethin' worth sayin'." He dashed past a foaming-at-the-mouth roan mare and grabbed the drummer by the shoulders. "What did you say?"

"I said, he's comin' all right, John. I can feel it in me bones."

"Your bloody bones? Well, I can feel it in me friggin' spare ribs, and I can tell you one thing for cocksure and certain—that poser'll never set foot Merseyside again."

He stamped on the sidewalk for emphasis, and then shook his mate by the lapels before casting him aside. Without turning to see whether Ringo stood or fell, he took off down the street, roaring at the top of his lungs:

Oh Dirty Maggie Mae
They have taken her away
And she'll never walk down Lime Street anymore . . .

The wary pedestrians made way for this maniac; a lone terrier snapped at his heels but made no impression. He blazed on, leather jacket flapping in the noonday breeze. Ringo smoothed out his velvet lapels and followed.

By the time he caught up, Lennon had lapsed into a moody silence. They matched stride for dogged stride, until the drummer dropped a laconic bombshell. "George is comin' too."

"George?"

The drummer noted the returning intensity and, fearful for the preservation of his wardrobe, sidestepped a cautious pace. "Yeah, Maur rang him up in Cheshire. He's okay again."

"He actually spoke to her?"

"Yeah. Spoke to me too."

"What'd he sound like?"

"Sounded like . . ." Ringo pondered this complexity. "Sounded like George."

Poor old Georgie flipped his lid good and proper. Locked him up with a bunch of his brothers in Christ, the Holy Society of Penguined Pissheads. Wouldn't let me see the lad—and me the only one who really knew what he was going through.

"Be just like old times, John. Just the four of us, right, mate?"

Good old Ringo, a rock of sanity in a sea of madness. But what does he know? He was with us only a couple of months.

Lennon put his arm around the smaller man and hugged him. "Good on you, mate." He laid a big fat slobbery kiss on the other's squirming face and whispered, "Yeah, George'll come all right; might even bring Jesus with him. But Paul won't show. Hasn't got the nerve to face us, then, has he?"

"Sure you got the nerve yourself, John?"

The pain in his ribs was riveting now, and Lennon began walking for relief. He lurched along, arms akimbo, doing the Lime Street wobbly. "Listen, mate," he gasped, finally grabbing on to Ringo's shoulder, "I got every nerve in me body workin' double shift. If there's goin' to be a do, I'll be there. But he won't. I can guarantee you that."

"Whatever you say yourself, John." The drummer shrugged and picked his nose.

"I say me and me spare ribs need an anesthetic. You carryin'?"

Ringo dug deep into his drainpipes and frowned. "Must have forgot me wallet, mate."

Lennon spat at a postbox, then wiped a gob of blood from his lip. "You'd forget your arse if it weren't riveted on."

They stood haplessly on a corner, bonded by misery, until Ringo piped up, "Tell you what. Let's go over to the Dublin Club. Johnny Irish'll be good for a few when he hears the kid's comin' home."

"Twenty-five years later and we're still bummin' drinks on the strength of him."

"He owes us, mate. A couple of drinks is the least we're due."

The drizzle had steadied into a slow pour. Ringo shivered and turned up his collar. Lennon didn't bother to take off his specs, just glared out at the deluge through lenses far from rose-colored. The pain was spreading all over now, drilling through him, curling his lip up to ease his aching cheek. He studied a throbbing vein on the back of his hand, and a fierce loneliness assailed him. He clenched his fist against the hurt. "It costs me, Ringo," he whispered, "it costs me, mate."

Ringo threw his arm around his friend's shoulder and spoke gently. "C'mon, John. It'll be all right now."

Lennon hunched down to fit under the warm oxter.

"You know somethin', sunshine," the drummer observed, "you're just one big, long streak of misery. A couple of pints, and you'll be as happy as a dog with two dicks."

They stumbled down Paradise Street not looking left, right, or center.

"There's somethin' I was thinkin' about, John."

"What's that?"

"This bloke gave me tip for the two o'clock at Chepstow called the Monkey's Nuts. What do you think?"

"Jaysus, Ringo, will you never catch on?"

"But he was serious, John, I'm sure he was. . . ."

Chapter Seven

HE'D BEEN WATCHING the priest for nigh on fifteen minutes. Nothing he could quite put his finger on, but there was something fishy about this particular penguin: the very way he lurked around Mathew Street like he was Sam Spadein' somethin' or other, God knows what? At one point, he was sure the bastard was goin' to rip down one of the Front's pro-clos. *But he didn't have the nerve, did he? Just yanked the end of it, and when it wouldn't come loose, he chucked it in. Read it though, every last red, white, and blue letter. Hope he got the message.*

The young member of the Chosen knew it by heart himself. After all, he'd helped write it and, later, when the Leader spoke at Anfield, with a bit of British luck and some pull from his Citizen's Defense Committee, he'd be up there on the platform with the great man himself: Britain's last hope.

Through hooded eyes, he watched the priest slouch off into the gathering afternoon gloom. The wind had picked up and turned the drizzle into a damp, clammy sheet that democratically soaked mackintoshed monk and bovver-booted Fronter alike. Then the priest stopped dead outside a warehouse and stepped back a pace to examine it.

Julian pulled the hood of his army jacket over his bleached head and moved lithely across the cobbles to within spitting distance of him. The priest turned at the sound of his footfall, but the Fronter had already ducked out of sight behind a piece of galvanized shedding.

The priest removed his felt hat and drained some water from the brim. Wiping his face, he descended the steps to the cellar door. Julian leaned into the rain and squinted. He could see the hat bobbing while the priest wrestled with the sealed door; he dived back, just in time, and watched the disappointed gray face reappear above the steps.

He was about to pack him off about his business, when he noticed that the priest's upturned gaze was now riveted on some letters over the door. And then it struck him like a ton of bricks: Mathew Street—the Cavern.

It wasn't as if he hadn't heard the name a thousand times. No such luck. It had been drummed into him on endless beer-soaked evenings by Ringo and the Old Grouch, while they sat around the kitchen table, pissed out of their gourds, regaling each other with tales of birds, booze, and that bloody band.

The priest was oblivious to the Fronter's musings. The cold sweat had leaked out onto his forehead, mixing uneasily with the rain. He shuddered as a syncopated bass drum kicked him full in the groin, and he jerked back his head when the steel strings of a Fender caught him head-on, and the youth and the songs and the hope and the glory and the teenage lust dripping off the smelly walls all burst out the door and drenched him in memories of a past he had locked up in a compartment labeled 1962.

He tried to escape, but it was too late; the lid had blown off this particular can of worms and there was no putting it back. He stood there drenched in the Mathew Street drizzle, holding back waves of guilt and despair, until he almost dropped to his knees and beat his head against the filthy cobblestones.

Julian had little pity for the quaking figure. And now that he was reminded of him, he had even less for his father. *Bastard had it too bloody easy. Never had to fight for anything; it was all laid out on a silver plate. He could have had any amount of jobs. But old Long John Winston didn't want a job, did he? Sooner sit on his fat arse and feel sorry for himself.*

I'd take a job if I could get one. That's the big difference between me and old Johnny boy. I'm proud to be British! That's why I wear a Union Jack. This country means something to me. That's what's wrong with him and Ringo and all the other alcoholics. Look out for number one! Never think of the generation they're passin' things on to, do they? That's why this country is in the state it's in.

The priest shuddered and dropped his valise. As he bent to pick it up, he almost slipped on the wet cobblestones and Julian made his move.

"Lost your way, Padre?" The voice wavered eerily from behind the shedding.

The priest paid little heed. The voice settled effortlessly into an auditory panorama of feedback, four on the floor and the slashing Fendered chords of "What'd I Say."

Still without emerging, but with more of an edge, Julian persisted, "I said, you lost your way . . . Padre?"

Disoriented, the priest turned. "No, I was . . . I thought I saw . . . " he stammered, vainly scrutinizing the shadows.

"You'd be better off doin' your thinkin' indoors, Padre." The voice lingered sarcastically on the "paw" and "drey" before settling into a disembodied lecture. "These streets aren't very safe for a man of the cloth. Trots and atheists everywhere nowadays! A man of your callin' can never be too careful."

With each movement behind the shedding, Julian's voice shifted erratically. The priest followed the sound with haunted eyes; he even hazarded a few faltering steps, but the voice always seemed to come from another direction.

"You're not from around here, Padre?"

"I used to be."

"The good old days, right?" The voice dissolved into a taunting cackle. Stung by this derision, the priest advanced on one end of the shedding. Wraithlike, Julian slipped out from the other side, darted across the lane, and vaulted down the cellar steps.

"What's your name, then, Padre?" The Fronter cupped his hands and effected a megaphone.

"Who's asking?" the priest challenged without turning.

The authoritative note was not lost on the Fronter, and he barked back, "Citizen's Defense! Your name and destination . . ." His voice dropped to a sneering murmur. "Padre?"

"Harrison, George! One four seven Crescent Gardens!" The priest snapped to attention, clicked his heels, threw an outstretched clenched fist in the air, and sneered back. "Reich-Führer!"

Julian shot up from the cellar steps. "George Harrison? The George Harrison? The One and Only and Forever George Harrison?" he chanted.

The priest coldly watched these antics. "Father Harrison, S.J., to you, Fascist," he spat back.

The insult bounced around the rainy walls. Julian circled him and, for a few menacing moments, it appeared as if he would strike. Still defiant though he was, the priest backed up. Out of the blue, the Fronter's mood swung once again; he snatched at the valise. The priest tried to hang on, but he was dragged around like some disheveled marionette, while the Fronter parodied some lines of "Hippy Hippy Shakes."

"Let go of me!" the priest cried, and finally threw him off, only to lose his bag in the bargain. Julian circled again. The priest followed his every move. The Fronter chuckled at some secret joke; he offered his hand, but the priest refused to acknowledge it.

Julian shrugged and then, in a suddenly cheerful voice, said, "Well, let's go, Father George. I'm sure they're all waiting for you at Crescent Gardens, and we wouldn't want to spoil such a happy reunion, now, would we?" A hint of a sneer returned, and without waiting for an answer, he drawled: "You know, you're not going to believe this, but by a very, very strange coincidence I happen to be going that very, very same way myself, so why don't I carry your bag?"

He strolled off down Mathew Street. The priest hesitated a moment, then followed.

Chapter Eight

"IT'S THE DREAMS that get you. The daytime shit's no big deal. You're always run so ragged, where would you get the time anyway? Always one crisis or another: lighting a fire under someone's ass, dowsing one somewhere else. Nah, it's the dreams. They're so right there in your face, you have to ask yourself: 'Was that what really went down, or is it all in my head?' And you know the worst thing? I just don't know anymore. And if I don't, then who the hell does?

"Like that last one I had. Holy shit, it was so vivid, I woke up screamin' blue bloody murder. I was so out of it, Big Bill kicked down the bedroom door—thought I was being strangled. Luanne nearly had a fit; then the next day, on and on, screamin' at me: 'What is he, your boyfriend or your bodyguard?' Forget about it."

"That dream nearly done me in. It was so real, exactly like I remember it: the last night in Abbey Road, same faces, same arguments, me the peacemaker; then Eppy sayin' Parlophone were insistin' on 'Till There Was You.' Oh man, I can still hear the same dead silence that went on forever, and then John picked up that beer bottle and threw it against the wall, and it smashed into a million little pieces, and one of them stabbed me in the throat and kept on goin' till it cut right through my tonsils, and I knew I'd never be able to sing again and that's when I woke up screamin'.

"It's the dreams that get you, I'm tellin' you, man, dreams are the worst. I can take anything else."

He snapped off the tape recorder just before Luanne groaned, "Honey, you really should see a shrink."

He didn't reply, but cast a withering gaze around the Royal Suite of the Savoy Hotel, as if to suggest that such surroundings called for a more dignified comment. Then he chilled her with the Montana raised eyebrow—the rarely seen B side of his enigmatic smile.

"If I told you once, I told you a thousand times, I do not want to hear any comments about my dream association project," he explained. "I'm confronting a whole lot of painful emotions right now, and I don't want any negative transference from you or anyone else. You should respect the fact that this is highly personal and very important to me."

Anticipating her reply, he turned his back, thereby knocking over the recorder. It bounced on the deep piled carpet and came to rest under the chaise longue.

"So it's not personal or important to me when you describe intimate events from our private life?" She displayed no hint of annoyance, continuing to tinker with her eyelashes. In twenty-nine sultry years, Luanne Luano had conducted myriad dealings with men; she was only too aware of the diversionary value of a well-doctored face.

Montana slyly examined her in the mirror. The current love of his life was draped across the king-size bed, sleek as a jaguar in a black lace slip. With her lovely long right leg raised at a tantalizing angle, she methodically twirled her ankle, occasionally stopping to reference a well-thumbed Bible.

"What do you mean, our private life?" he challenged.

At the suggestion of an edge in his voice, her leg dropped as if the life had fled from it. She closed the Bible with a snap that would have done justice to St. Paul with a hangover. Reclining on his customized mauve satin sheets, she willed the color to drain from her cheeks, and glared at the chandelier. After a strategic pause, she raised herself onto her elbows and pointed her exquisite breasts at him. "I mean, you put the most intimate details of our private life on that tape recorder. Supposing someone from the *National Enquirer* got hold of it? Where would we be then? I'll tell you—up shit creek on an elephant's ass."

He winced at the analogy. It had sounded cute back in Vegas but somehow seemed incongruous in the heart of royal London. He was about to point this out, but the words evaporated as he appraised the lacy outline of her nipples.

With an actress's killer instinct, Luanne took all the time in the world sliding the soles of her feet backward, raising her knees, and arching her back into an extreme bow position before she pouted from somewhere behind her blond tresses, "You know, you wouldn't believe some of the things men think about."

"You can sing that, babe," he whispered a tad huskily while wrenching himself away from the sight of her tanned thighs merging with the elastic of her violet panties. He fought back a Neanderthal urge to fuck her from every point on and off the compass. Instead, he swallowed and stammered: "Anyway, the *Enquirer* couldn't care less about my dreams. There's no story. . . ."

"Listen, sweetcakes, if the *Enquirer* can do a front page on Jesus, alive, well, and runnin' a cat house in Tucson . . . "

"No one believes that garbage! You know, you better get some clothes on, we're runnin' about an hour behind. And where's Herbie and that big idiot Whalen? They're supposed to have the limos downstairs." Leaning into the mirror, he matched a turquoise silk shirt against his eyes.

"Don't try changing the subject." She struggled to keep her composure. "Lotsa people believe that garbage. You said, and I quote, 'I was being strangled and my fiancée, Luanne Luano, was having a fit.'"

"I did not."

"You did too!" She experienced a momentary surge of satisfaction when he didn't dispute the reference to their secret engagement; nonetheless, she propelled her voice to diva heights and lambasted him. "For all they know, I had you hogtied to the bedpost and was perpetrating all kinds of weird sexual acts on your personage. I mean, what else are they supposed to think—that I'm epileptic?"

"Jesus Christ, I don't know how we get into these arguments."

"This is not an argument. It's a healthy, out in the open, honest discussion. You only think it's an argument because of all the childhood repression you were subjected to. That's the reason you have so much hostility bottled up inside. . . ."

"Listen, I don't care if this is an argument, a discussion, or a fucking Knotty Ash free-for-all, but we are going to be late." He stormed over to the wall closet and rummaged through a legion of cellophaned suits.

"Don't you dare use that word around me, mister." She brandished her Bible. "My father was a Methodist minister, and one thing he would never stand for—"

"Oh, Christ on a bloody swing-swong!" His voice had a muffled ring from inside the depths of the closet. "You forgot to pack my tux. How could you do this to me?"

He emerged red-faced, sweating, and demanding answers.

With all the dignity of an imperial grand duchess, Luanne

gestured to the bathroom door, whereon hung his silver-lapeled evening suit.

His sigh of relief was heartfelt. "I can't talk about these dream association pieces right now. In time, I will. In fact, in time"—he stared off into the heroic near future—"I hope to use them in my stage show as introductions to some of my more meaningful songs."

But she hadn't entirely forgiven him. "You think people in Vegas are even remotely interested in the fact that some hood down in Liverpool tried to cut out your tonsils with a beer bottle?"

"How do you know? They've never been exposed to anything like that before." He discarded the turquoise silk shirt and opted for a more formal white.

"Exposed is the word." She affected a particularly lewd burlesque. "You'll be singin' to the busboys while your fans'll all be down the Strip throwing their panties at Wayne Newton."

She might as well have slapped him in the face. He flinched at the prospect of this betrayal.

"Honey," she said, softening a bit at his puppy-dog look, "People go to Vegas to feel good about themselves. If they want nightmares, they go to New York City."

Montana's brow was a mass of wrinkles by the time he finished wrestling with this correlation. He was having even greater problems with his dickey-bow and flung it from him, choosing instead his trademark black leather tie. She watched him deliberate on the style of knot—broad Windsor or slim Kennedy—and melted. "Oh, baby, come over here. Why don't you tell your sweetie what's on your mind? You don't have to go talkin' to that old tape recorder. What's the matter, honey, you can tell your Luanneeeybanneey," she cooed.

He ambled over to the bed and collapsed alongside her.

"Ah, jeez, I don't know." Then, digging his face into the bed-cover, he groaned. "I just can't seem to come to grips with my feelings. Goin' back to Liverpool is pretty traumatic."

"So we won't go."

Her logic had a finality that never failed to annoy him. "No! That's not the problem: I want to go."

"Okay, so we'll go. Listen, it's all settled. Herbie made the call this morning." She anticipated his objection by mounting his back and commencing to dispense a blistering Rolfing massage.

"I know. I know." She forced his face deeper into the satin fabric, smothering his protests. "Your honeydove understands everything. We're gonna take the chopper down to Liverpool tonight. But first of all, we're gonna buy them some presents—perfume for the gals, bourbon for the guys. We'll all kiss and cuddle and reminisce around a roaring log fire, and you and me will be back in London before the Queen puts out the cat."

For a moment, she relaxed her grip.

"For Christ sakes, go easy with that shit!" He gasped for air, considering her rosy scenario with some skepticism. "You just don't know John Lennon."

"Babe," she confided throatily, "I've known more johns than you've known Christmases, but that's a secret between you, me, and our publicists."

She threw his head down again and furiously resumed the pummeling. An odd buzzing sound bounced off the walls of Montana's ears, and tiny pulsing lasers shimmered before his eyes. He had the distinct feeling that he was passing out.

"You might not believe this," Luanne confided to his limp form, "but I was a nervous wreck before I attended my tenth high school reunion. I was positively anorexic from the anxiety. Just the thought of seeing all those girls I hated nearly sent me to Betty Ford. I could just imagine the pity in their eyes as they introduced me to their over-sexed, dynamic husbands and their amazing, adorable, super-IQ children, while I tagged along with some loser from the casino. And then you know what? . . ." She stopped kneading his shoulder blades, the air re-entered his throat with a rattle, and he regained consciousness. "I went and had the time of my life. Everyone, but everyone, was divorced and on pills and having affairs, and their kids were all in reform school, and we all got blasted out of our skulls and ended up watching *Dynasty* in our underwear."

He came to in a wave of nausea and groaned, "I think I'm goin' to throw up."

"That's exactly how I felt."

"This is different, goddamm it!" He gulped in some of London's most expensive air.

"What's so different about it? They don't have *Dynasty* over here?"

He wasn't sure if she was joking; but then, his jury had often been hung on this issue. She regained his attention by almost wrapping his right shoulder around his left earlobe.

"Listen, honey"—she disregarded his cry of anguish—"one set of sticks is the same as another. The only difference between Liverpool and Nob Noster, Missouri, is the price of canaries."

With that revelation, she dismounted, reached for her emery board, and directed total attention to her nails.

Glad to be alive, Montana rolled over and turned away from her. Although still a shade dizzy, he seized the bull by the horns. "You know somethin', honey? Maybe . . . just maybe now, you should stay here in London, take the platinum plastic, and go out and buy yourself a new outfit."

"Not on your life." Luanne studied the travel clock and did

a laborious mental calculation. "We've been engaged for exactly twenty-nine days and seventeen hours, and you want to leave me behind and go off and flirt with God only knows how many old girlfriends. That's an airtight recipe for losing your man, if I ever heard one."

He winced at the door-slamming finality of "engaged" and, not for the first time, wondered what he'd been drinking twenty-nine days and seventeen hours previously. "Nah, goin' up there has sweet shag all to do with old girlfriends. You got no competition, Luanne, I swear. It's just that—well, you wouldn't like Liverpool."

"Honey, you don't know the half of what I like yet." She segued effortlessly into a sexy purr, and stroked the inside of his thigh. "I'm very adaptable."

"I'm tellin' you, they do things different up there."

"Oh, yeah? Like what?"

"Well, like . . . sex, for instance."

"Are you trying to tell me that some bunch of hicks down in the asshole of England got some moves that I don't know about? Hey, babe, I left home on my sixteenth birthday, and I've seen things that'd make Caligula run for the hills."

"That's my point exactly. They don't talk about it up there. They just do it. Wham, bam, thank you, ma'am, and back to the pub before last call."

"Oh, yeah? Well, as far as I'm concerned, that caveman bull-shit went out with Noah and his leaky ark. Us blue-blooded American gals like to take our time about things." She again ran her fingers up his thigh, this time creasing his pants with her sculpted nails.

"Oh, Jesus!" Montana shuddered. He could just imagine Lennon digging into that observation.

"C'mon, honey, relax," Luanne murmured huskily. "You're

all bottled up and tense. You need . . . Oh baby, you know what you need."

She kissed his nipples and moved down his chest toward his solar plexus. When she undid his pants, he half closed his eyes and waited. As he watched the chandelier refract a million shards of electric light, for an instant he was back in Hamburg on a disheveled bunk bed with another blond head bent over him. Then the soft, silky warmth of her mouth enveloped him and the door to the room burst open.

In rushed Herbie Wise, squealing in his ex-croupier's voice: "Champ! Champ! Champ!"

The chandelier imploded, and the warm reassurance of Luanne's mouth was suddenly transformed into a vicious pool of snapping piranha. Luanne arose from her ministrations with indecent haste. Heedless of her paramour's discomfort, she bounded backward off the bed—a vision in tanned thighs and violet panties—and scurried for the solace of the bathroom.

Montana arose too, his pain immediate and searing. "Jesus H. Christ! Didn't you never learn to knock?" He howled at Howie and a bandaged Big Bill Whalen, both of whom stood transfixed in the doorway.

"Well?" he demanded. "Were you born in a bloody barn?"

"No, in a cowshed with swinging doors." Herbie strode over to the phone and dialed a number, his composure apparently regained.

An elderly county couple, up in town for a hunt ball and heading downstairs for early cocktails, wheeled in horror as Montana roared at Big Bill, "Don't just stand there, you big bollocks, shut the effin' thing! You want the whole of London talkin' about me?"

"Sorry, boss." Big Bill stepped into the room and closed the door behind him.

Montana sank back on the bed and gave his wounded loins the once-over, all the while muttering dire recriminations.

Sighing with disgust, Herbie slammed down the phone and cursorily examined Montana's injured member. Perceiving no permanent damage, he growled, "One of the limos has broken down and the other one's out of gas, just like everything else in this crappy country!"

But his mood suddenly brightened. "Champ! Champ! Champ!" he barked in eager succession. "Have I got news for you! I personally, and I reiterate personally, have plucked victory from the jaws of defeat. Rain may stop cricket in Limeyland, but it's gotta be up early in the mornin' to get one over on old Herbie Wise!"

"What are you talking about?" Montana looked at him. "And what the hell have you got on?"

"Not too shabby, eh, old chap?" Herbie sashayed like a Milanese model to display mustard-colored tweeds and a loudly checkered shirt fastened at the neck by a red velvet dickey-bow. His knickerbocker trouser legs had been stuffed into a thick pair of magenta woolen socks. For good measure, he was shod in an outsize pair of twin-toned golf shoes. "Just the ticket for a trip down the country, what?"

Montana burrowed back onto the pillows. "You want to know something? We're off to the back streets of Liverpool, not Balmoral for cucumber sandwiches with the Queen."

Herbie bristled. "Hey, I paid top dollar for this shit down Savile Row. Man said these the only threads for a day in the sticks."

"No. Man saw you comin' and said, 'Whoopee, another dumb Yank lookin' to be fleeced.' And one more thing, I don't know where you people are gettin' all these crazy ideas, but Liverpool is not *Brideshead Re*-ruddy-*visited*, okay? They got guys up there who'd eat Big Bill for breakfast."

At the sound of his name, the bodyguard snapped out of his stupor. "They got hot dogs there, boss? I been askin' all over London, and no one knows what I'm talkin' about."

"The only hot dogs they got are German shepherds to keep the gangs under control."

"Oh, man," Big Bill lamented, "I'd give up my free dental for a coupla two, three Hebrew Nationals smothered in mustard and sauerkraut."

Montana sighed and bent back over his privates for a detailed examination. Howie seized the moment to renew his battle with the British phone system.

Shrugging off another of life's disappointment, Big Bill ran a security check. Without removing his size thirteens, he leaped atop a delicate couch and tapped the frame of a Turner landscape, listening intently for the sound of a hidden microphone. His bulging muscles strained through tight designer jeans, while the gold embossed letters of *Montana World Tour 1987* leaped from his black satin jacket.

"Listen, sweetheart, I ain't gonna tell you one more time who I am," Herbie snarled into the phone. "This is the Montana suite, and you are talking to his personal representative here on Earth. Yeah, yeah, yeah, just like the pope hisself. You know you're a real gas, sweetcakes, but when I say I need two stretch limos yesterday, I'm talkin' right now on the curb outside this flophouse you call a hotel. And if this dump don't deliver, then we're outa here to the nearest Holiday Inn. Okay? Now, snap to it, dollface, or you'll be gettin' your pink slip courtesy of the American ambassador, capisce?"

He slammed down the phone, then glanced apprehensively toward the closed door of the bathroom, from behind which the warbled trills of Miss Luano mixed sourly with the roar of her running bath. Up, down, hither, and thither, her voice slipped and slithered around some dubious microtonal scale in a manner not unlike that of a sucking calf soliciting its mother.

"She's gonna turn into a frog if she don't stop washin' herself," Herbie said, shaking his head and turning his attention back to Montana. "Champ! Champ! Champ! Listen . . ." he began, only to be silenced by a preemptive wave of Montana's hand.

"How many times do I have to tell you that I am not, and never will be, a prizefighter? I'm a songsmith and an entertainer. And if Montana, or Paul, or good old simple Boss don't do the trick . . ."

"Okay! Okay! Okay!" Herbie blasted forth like a souped-up Uzi. "But listen up, have I got the deal of the century for you. Dig this! Me and my own sweet self was doin' the schmooze last night down at this dump's bar, and who do I run into but a point man for a pol. Regular kinda dude, ex-Saatchi and Saatchi, a bit wet behind the ears, but no matter—talked the talk even if he knew shit little about the walk. After a couple of snorts, him and me got to shootin' the shit, and he tells me he's the mouth for the new guy in politics around here. . . ."

Montana waited for him to run out of breath; then, in the millisecond it took Herbie to suck in air, he fired into the breach: "What's this new guy's name?"

Herbie frowned. ""He's called the Boss or the Chief or somethin'.""

"That's me, stupid!"

"Yeah, but it ain't you. This guy's the hottest thing round here since the raincoat, you dig? The new Winston Whatever-His-Name. So I threw my man a coupla two, three hundred for his favorite charity." He sucked in some more air. "Never hurts to grease a few palms when you hit a new burg, right? Bucks in the bank when it comes to keepin' keisters out of jail."

Montana nodded in grim appreciation of how greased palms had, on more than one occasion, kept posteriors out of pinstripes.

"Anyway, whad'ya think happened this mornin'?" Herbie's questions rarely demanded or awaited answers. "The dude called and said that his guy'd be pleased as punch to have my guy onstage with him tonight—his very words—'pleased as punch.' I gotta write that one down."

"We're going to Liverpool tonight." Montana's interruption was caustic to the extreme.

"Yeah, yeah, yeah, yeah, yeah! But guess what? His dude is doin' an early gig down there too, and he'd be even pleaseder than punch if you was to do a walk-on with him. "

"This guy better not be Enoch bloody Powell. They don't go for Tories in Liverpool."

"No way! Powell's just another old fogey goin' nowhere in a hurry. This cat is young and hip and so cool he's got icicles sproutin' from his eyebrows. Ain't you been readin' the papers?"

"What do you think?" Montana gestured to the bathroom, where Luanne had just come a cropper on a high C.

"I told you we should have left her at home," Herbie whispered as if Luanne had the hearing of Superman.

"Yeah, but then I kind of miss her. There's somethin' about her that the others didn't have—somethin' innocent, I don't know."

"Innocent? You gotta be kiddin' me."

"What would you know about it?" Montana shrugged. "It's like she likes me for myself I don't know."

"You know, I've heard this kind of talk before."

"Listen, I get these bloody dreams and I don't like sleepin' on me own anymore. You got a problem with that?"

"So we get you a night nurse. Comes out a lot cheaper."

"You just don't get it, do you?"

"I don't have to get it. I'm not Eppy. Just as long as you're not plannin' number four." But noting a sudden dark cloud descending on Montana, his voice shot back instantly to its normal level: "Anyway, you know me—hit town, hone in! This Leader guy—hey, that's his name. I knew I'd get it. You gotta see this cat: blond hair and a bomber jacket. Marlon Brando with a Union Jack. You gotta tell Spiro about this dude's getup. He could do with a bit of dollin' up, know what I mean?"

"That ain't the big man's style," Montana said, smiling, in spite of himself, at the image of the fortieth president of the United States in black leather. "So what's the book on this Leader guy?"

"Better than the goddamn Torah. This dude's on his way up big time, and it don't hurt to be seen with the movers and shakers. Look at the mileage we got outa Spiro's campaign song."

Montana appeared to slip into the throes of distressed paralysis.

"All right! All right! All right! Who cares what *The New York Times* had to say about it? The fact is, that song put you right back on your feet after the divorce case. Oh shit, I'm sorry! I'm sorry! I'm sorry!"

"Bitch," Montana muttered, recalling the intimacies his most recent ex-wife had shared with the *Star*.

"Yeah, that dame never knew when to shut up," Herbie empathized.

"Whatever." Montana sighed. "Just as long as you don't mess up my visit home. And no bloody Tories, you hear me?"

"This guy has Tories for breakfast. Anyway, what do you think I am? Stupid?"

Montana chose not to answer.

"This is goin' to be good for us, man. I can feel it in my bones, a whole new market openin' up. This could be the start of somethin' big if only . . ."

Herbie's thought would never be completed. The door of the bathroom flew open, and Luanne emerged through a dense cloud of steam—turbaned and toweled to mid-thigh, her face encased in aromatic mud. Clutching the little she'd been wearing in one hand, she dripped her way across the floor to the dresser, mud mask shifting and shaping to violent facial calisthenics.

She appeared to ignore Big Bill's large rump protruding from under her dressing table as he diligently hunted down the suspected bug.

The two men watched her throw slip and panties to the floor, snatch up a jar of lotion from atop the dressing table, turn on her heel, and, without a word, reenter the cloud of steam and disappear back into the bathroom, slamming the door behind her.

Herbie looked as if he was about to make a comment, but, observing the cloud darkening around Montana, he reached for the phone instead.

"Wait a minute." Montana flung himself off the bed and grabbed it first. "What happened when you called Liverpool?"

"Whad'ya mean, 'what happened?'"

"I mean, what happened?"

"Nothin' happened."

"What do you mean, 'nothin' happened'? You were supposed to call them first thing this morning."

"And call I did." Herbie laid his hands on his charge's shoulders and urged him back onto to the bed. "My friend," he said, the essence of sensitivity, when Montana was seated again. "I ask this in all honesty and without any intention of causing a slight, but just how well do you know these people down there?"

"I've known them all my life, that's how well. And once and for all, it's not 'down there.' It's *up there*—in Lancashire. Down there is the friggin' South Pole!"

"Oh, yeah?" Herbie was little concerned with geographic minutiae—if a joint had limo access, he'd be there. "Did you have any idea that these friends of yours are livin' in a ghetto? This Lennon guy's on welfare, for Christ's sake! Dude don't even have a phone. I mean, how poor is that?"

"Lots of people over here don't have phones. I didn't have one till I got to Vegas."

"No phones?" Herbie's expression was beyond horror. "So, how did you ever get anything done?"

"We used carrier pigeons, how do you think?"

But when he saw that his sarcasm had only further clouded the issue, Montana sighed: "Maybe we got nothin' done, and maybe we were happier that way."

He bounded off the bed and glumly kicked at Luanne's discarded panties. By reflex, Big Bill intercepted, threw to Herbie, and then continued reconnoitering under the dressing table.

Still clutching the panties, Herbie pondered Britain's communication problems, but he soon returned to the moment. "All right! All right! All right! You know I wouldn't let you down. I sent a telegram to some broad or other. Said we'd be up there tonight if the weather stays shit."

Montana slammed his fist down on the dresser. "You told my oldest friends in the world that I'd come see them only if the weather stayed shit? Oh man, I can just imagine Lennon runnin' with that one."

"Hey, keep your hair on, dude! You're gonna hurt yourself like you did in Tahoe. Jesus Christ, if they don't got phones over here, what are the hospitals like? Anyway, I told you I didn't send it to *him*! I sent it to some babe in a beauty parlor."

Montana threw a look of pure disgust at Herbie, then marched over to the bathroom and threw open the door. "C'mon, get the hell out of there!" He bellowed into the billowing steam. "Someone might want to take a crap." Coughing and spluttering, he rounded on Herbie. "I can just hear Lennon: 'Twenty-five years later, and that bloody Yank is afraid of a bit of rain.' If the weather stays shit. Jesus!"

"No way did I say 'shit,'" Herbie protested. "I probably said, 'if the weather permits' or 'the inclement weather' or whatever. I got more class than that."

Montana had his doubts on that score, but instead of expressing them, he roared into the bathroom: "Will you turn off those taps and get the hell out of there!"

"Wow," murmured Herbie as Luanne erupted out of the billowing steam like some melting mummy, rivulets of tears and sweat coursing down her caked cheeks. She smashed into Montana, almost upending him, snatched her panties from Herbie, then neatly vaulted over Big Bill's moving rump before throwing herself head downward on the bed and keening: "You son of a bitch, you son of a selfish bitch!"

In the midst of this tirade, the bodyguard materialized from under the chaise longue with more exhilaration than Archimides arising from his bath. In his good fist, he jubilantly held aloft Montana's recorder. "I got it, Boss, I got it! I knew this joint was bugged."

Montana stormed past him. "If Lennon gets on my case for that telegram, you're all fired, the whole bloody lot of you. You hear me?"

Herbie trailed two paces behind. "Champ! Champ! I swear I didn't say 'shit'!"

But the bathroom door slammed in his face, and the lock angrily clicked from within. He stared at the oak paneling for some seconds, despair writ keenly across his sun-lamped cheeks. "You can't fire me, schmuck," he muttered. "I got a contract tighter than the goddamned Ark of the Covenant."

But hedging his bets, he tapped at the door and crooned in his most persuasive barker's voice, "Hey, champ baby, you're getting' yourself all worked up over nothin'. Listen to me now, we gotta be on top of our game today. We got the press at two. The Leader at six."

The door swung open once more. Montana emerged wrathful as Jehovah. He stared wildly around, taking in his entourage and the rewards of a successful life. "The hell with you and your press conferences! And the hell with the Leader too!"

Chapter Nine

LENNON DIDN'T EXACTLY KICK in the door of the Dublin Club, but all eyes turned to behold his entrance. With Ringo in close attendance, he pierced the smoky interior and honed in on a vacant space at the bar. The resident drinkers sniggered knowingly at his rapidly bruising cheek.

Johnny Irish was rinsing out some pint glasses; without the benefit of a glance, he inquired, "Cut yourself shavin' again?"

"Listen, when I want to talk to a booze-jerker, I'll ask the questions. Now, give me a Bushmills and, for once, don't drown the bloody whiskey."

When Irish ignored him, Lennon hopped on the footrest, leaned over the counter, and eyeballed the bartender's blackheads. "Am I talking to the wall or just somethin' that resembles it?"

"Who's payin'?" Irish asked without apparent rancor, all the while examining the chipped rim of a Watney's tumbler.

"Mr. Starkey is doin' the honors," Lennon replied, to Ringo's dismay.

"And what's Mr. Cox . . . beg pardon, I mean Mr. Starkey havin'?"

"The usual, mate, pint of bitter." Ringo's smile masked the bitterness of his thoughts: *Call me what you like, you whore's melt. What's the point in havin' a wife if she won't divvy up for your gargle once in a blue moon?*

Irish plunged the Watney's mug into the sudsy water and came straight to the point: "Mr. Starkey might do well to note that his slate will be forwarded posthaste to Mrs. Cox-Starkey if he should choose to renege on any more of his lawful debts."

He raised the glass once more to the light and ran his finger tenderly around the rim. "Mr. Starkey might also care to note that the aforementioned Mrs. Cox-Starkey has telephoned here twice in the last half hour, inquiring as to his whereabouts in a most—how should one put it—distressful tone of voice. So distressful, in fact,that one was almost tempted to reveal what one knew about certain of her husband's, how shall one phrase it, amorous interludes." He flung the tumbler into a dustbin.

Ringo winced at the sound of breaking glass. He could feel the barman's eyes boring through him, awaiting his submissive response. Ringo, instead, dug deep, maintained both silence and dignity by letting his gaze wander among the various football scarves and rosettes—red for Liverpool, blue for Everton—that adorned the back of the bar.

Irish's smile was not generous when he concluded, "But on the assumption that Mr. Starkey's lawful debts will soon be settled, one for the moment chose to preserve some of life's choicer nebulosities."

Marveling at the wonders of Irish's renowned vocabulary, Ringo, after some scratching of his ear, heaved a heartfelt sigh of relief—what Maureen didn't know wouldn't hurt her. He thrust out an optimistic fist for the pint. "Good on you, Johnny, mate. No bother about the slate either. I got some money comin' on a horse." He shouted down the bar: "Anyone know how the goin' is at Chepstow?"

"Well, if it ain't the gruesome twosome themselves: Ruthless Rufus and the mad drummer." A familiar voice, corrosive with sarcasm, interrupted. Gerry Marsden and his drinking buddy, Billy Kramer of the long defunct Coasters, dislodged themselves from a bunch of other middle-aged, ruddy-complexioned, overweight, off-duty bartenders, bookie's clerks, and seen-better-days musicians. They strode up the bar, their pints held in front of their ale guts, like two gunfighters on busman's holiday from the O.K. Corral.

Lennon tossed back the Bushmills and peered over his National Healths at them. "You know, I've been lookin' all over for you two." In a fraternal manner, he drew them close, draping an arm around each one's shoulder. "I want to thank you both for confirming a long-held theory of mine."

Marsden, who hadn't come down in the last shower, shrugged off the patronizing arm. But Kramer was a more trusting soul. "What's that, John?"

"That misery loves company."

Ringo hooted with glee. "Got the drop on 'em there, mate. Like leadin' two lambs to the bleedin' slaughter."

Marsden smiled primly; it'd be a tropical day in Toxteth before he'd be taken in by Lennon's benevolence, real or imagined. "Out walkin' into walls again?" he inquired.

"More likely he walked into a walrus," Kramer interjected, to the jeers of his cronies, most of whom had witnessed Lennon's fiasco at the recent Mersey Beat Reunion.

"Hey, Looney," a disembodied voice queried from out of the smoky haze. "What's this about you turnin' into a bum boy? Charlie Rossiter says you nearly pulled his mickey out of its socket."

"Always knew there was a bit of an arse bandit in him," Marsden confirmed, placing his pint on the bar and hitching up his trousers over his stomach.

In reply, Lennon feinted a jab at Marsden's testicles, and Gerry leaped back against the bar, thrusting both hands between his thighs as if to prevent his lurching innards from spilling onto the floor. Lennon grinned savagely. "Yeah, and I'm just mad about hernias, right, Ger?"

Marsden's cheeks flushed an even deeper scarlet than usual. Still, he instantly gathered himself and reached back for his pint, taking a long, meditative draft of John Courage; his long-standing rivalry with Lennon demanded that a minimum of emotion be shown.

"Even with your limited knowledge of physiology, Lennon, I'm surprised to find you ignorant of the fact that a hernia has sweet damn all to do with your balls—that's assuming, of course, that you have any in the first place, which is a matter of great speculation in certain quarters round here."

This mouthful was greeted by prolonged cheering and clapping from the denizens of the pub, for Marsden, like Irish, was well known as a keen student of Noah Webster's New Encyclopedic Dictionary. Emboldened by the response, the pot-bellied proletarian etymologist held forth: "I might remind you that Dr. Webster L.L.D. describes a hernia as"—here he paused for emphasis, drawing a wheezy breath—"'a protrusion of all or part of an organ through a tear or other abnormal opening in the wall of the containing cavity.'"

If Lennon was taken aback by this daunting display of memory, his face remained poker stiff. "Oh, contain my aunt Fanny's arsehole! Any daft bastard knows that 'hernia' means your bollocks is out of whack."

"Give the lad a coconut!" Ringo whooped; but his was the solitary supportive voice.

Marsden swaggered over to the jukebox and punched in a set of familiar numbers. He listened in grim admiration to the piano intro of "How Do You Do It," then, painfully bobbing in time to the music, harmonized alarmingly with his much-younger self on the old, unreleased acetate. At times, the scratches and pops threatened to drown out the music, but Marsden knew their each and every position, and he bawled or modulated his harmony as needed.

Lennon could take no more. He pointed at the jukebox and sneered, "We all know you'd have been Liverpool's answer to Chubby Checker if they'd released that piece of shit, but they didn't. So why do I have to suffer through it every time I come into this kip?"

With a majestic wave of his arm, Marsden silenced the hoots from the bar. "It would have been a number one if you and your lot hadn't gone and given every group north of Highbury a bad name. Right, Billy?"

"That's right, John," Kramer said with more than a shade of hostility. "Mr. Epstein never forgave you for makin' a balls of the Beatles! Ruined the rest of us, into the bargain."

The murmuring at the bar ceased. Johnny Irish turned off the tap and swept the room with a warning glare. He would long remember the last time this subject had arisen. Almost cost him his licence, after the fit Lennon had thrown.

Ringo laid a restraining hand on Lennon's elbow. "That was a long time ago, Billy," he said. "We're just havin' a quiet drink."

Lennon shook his arm free and smiled weakly. "Ringo's right, lad, it's all water under the bridge now. It's time we buried the hatchet once and for all."

But Marsden, ever cautious, refused the outstretched hand. Lennon shrugged and walked over to the jukebox; he deposited a coin and studied the lighted menu. After a myopic search, he punched in some numbers.

"How Do You Do It" again blared forth. A murmur of approval, curried with wonder, arose from the bar.

Lennon held up his hand for silence. "What are we fightin' about? It's no secret we all deserved better—Gerry and the Pacemakers, Billy J. and the Coasters, the Searchers, the Merseybeats, Kingsize Taylor, and so on and so forth and so fifth. We gave everything we had—some of us even gave our lives, the Lord have mercy on him."

Here he crossed himself, and all followed suit in silent tribute to their departed peer, Rory Storm. "And all we ever wanted was to make music the way we heard it," he concluded sadly. "Wasn't much to ask, was it?"

A susurrant tide of approval enveloped him, but Lennon, again, held up his hand for silence. "Notwithstanding my many past disagreements with Mr. Marsden and his Pacemakers, I have to admit that this record was one of our generation's finest hours. So let's, one and all, raise a glass to 'How Do You Do It.'"

Like mourners at a wake, the patrons obediently reached for their drinks. Gerry walked across the floor and the decades to Lennon, and hugged him. They stood there, arm in arm, the hatchet well and truly buried. Drinks were called, even an occasional tear was shed before Lennon roared, "And now let's give this piece of shit a proper release party!" He kicked viciously at the jukebox.

With a loud, rending screech, the needle slashed across the face of the disc, propelling it into automatic rejection. Marsden lunged for Lennon, but, anticipating this development, Irish was already vaulting over the bar. He caught Marsden and pinned him to the wall.

"C'mon then, you bloody ponce. I'll fix your hernia for you," Lennon taunted. "Stick your marbles up around your bald spot."

'You'll never work this town again, Lennon," Marsden sputtered from behind Irish's massive frame.

"Who the hell do you think you are, Frankie effin' Sinatra?" Lennon aped an Ol' Blue Eyes shuffle.

"Lennon, you go stand over at that bar or I'll put you right through it!" Irish ordered, hard pressed to hold back Marsden.

Just then, the needle plunked down, and the harmonica intro of "Love Me Do" pealed through the pub.

Ringo cheered lustily and beat out time on the bar. A couple of the patrons smiled, but many more muttered into their drinks as Lennon bowed left, right, and center. Ringo noted the sour mood. "I think we should be goin', John," he murmured.

Lennon looked him full in the face. He caught the drummer's drift, but there was no moving him now. "I'm not lettin' any crowd of dumb dickheads run me out of a pub."

Ringo checked the distance to the door, then sighed, "Jesus, John, isn't gettin' your arse kicked once a day enough for you?"

Lennon kissed him on the forehead and smiled. "You stick with me, mate, I'll see you all right."

Then he strutted past the still-struggling Marsden, blowing him the most discreet of kisses, and shouted, "Barkeep, when you've taken adequate security measures, a double Bush, if you please. And a pint of your best bitter for my friend and faithful companion, Mr. Starkey."

Then he turned to his mate and laughed. "That settled his snot for him, right, Ringo old son?"

No matter how hard he tried to catch up, the Fronter always seemed to be ten yards ahead of the priest. But now the young man had stopped and was peering through a window.

"Well, fancy that," he called back. "I had the oddest feeling."

"Give me back my bag!"

Julian looked at him as if seeing him for the first time. "You know, you'll go a lot further in life," he said, "if you learn to ask nicely."

"The last thing I need in life is advice from the likes of you."

"I suppose you're right." The Fronter smiled almost sympathetically. "Still and all, for what it's worth, I would keep a cool head, Father George. Things are fast comin' to a boil around here."

The valise landed at the priest's feet with a thud, and the Fronter strode off around the corner.

"Little bastard," the priest said under his breath.

The rain was sweeping down the street in sheets, and so he stepped into the doorway of a social club, bent down, and opened the bag to check on his few paltry possessions: a black polo neck, pair of slacks, some socks, and a package of faded clippings. Everything present and accounted for.

The club door opened and two men, pulling on mackintoshes over their suit jackets, sauntered out. They barely looked at him, but there was something familiar about the cut of them. He stared at their broad backs as they hurried into the rain. Then he caught a snatch of the song before the door closed.

"Oh Christ, not again." He couldn't take much more. Still on his haunches, he checked his hand for the shakes. Not even a hippy, hippy one, he noted, raising himself to his feet and picking up the valise.

He zeroed in on the sound and isolated the different frequencies. The door filtered out most of the treble, but the bass pattern was unmistakable. The old familiar feeling washed over him. A lone raindrop coursed down his nose, dangled, and then plunged onto his trembling upper lip. He brushed it off and opened the door. The harmonica engulfed him, and then Paul's innocent voice skidded across the walls.

The smoke and memories brought tears to his eyes, but the stale smell of beer and potato chips felt oddly comforting. The bar, too, looked vaguely familiar. He took in the various red and blue football scarves and he knew well he'd been here before, but the music was overpowering, disorienting, beating tattoos all over his forehead. He leaned up against the wall and steadied himself.

He could feel an odd tension in the room, and was suddenly fearful that it was directed at him. Was this the Fronter's work? Had he been led into some kind of trap? But, as yet, no one had even noticed him. All the attention seemed to be focused on the other end of the bar.

Finally, one of the patrons noticed him and touched his cloth cap. George instinctively acknowledged the salute. Though his eyes were still smarting, he thought he recognized some blurry figures in the distance. He squinted into the haze, and they came into focus—the drummer, head nodding in time to the song, and the guitarist in the familiar, if worn, leather jacket, strumming his imaginary Rick.

He honed in on the tall, slightly stooped figure and noted the scars of time: the creased face—blotched and ruddy from drink—thick neck and sagging beer belly. And then the figure moved down the bar and held out his hand for a glass of whiskey. The priest could see his eyes. They hadn't changed an iota: Proud and arrogant, they hid their myopia behind a cool arrogance; and still they flashed with the old fire. The priest smiled grimly. He knew that age had not mellowed this one: What had to be said would be said without fear of ridicule or even violence. And if the whole world were to go out of whack, at least there would be one voice raised in scathing protest, one outraged madman left to carry on the good fight.

The voice, too, had changed little, a bit coarser perhaps, but there was no weariness in it, no mistaking its distinctiveness; it cut right across the noisy room, boasting to the drummer: "That settled his snot for him, right, Ringo old son!"

The priest blinked, and the younger Lennon metamorphosed: slim, trim, and brimful of energy, just off the stage in Hamburg, the sweat pouring down his electrified face, grabbing for a bottle of lager, the biker jacket, then new, creaking and reeking of fresh leather; tossing his Rick carelessly onto a chair, more where that came from, the world his oyster, nothing goin' to stop him.

"Can I help you, Father?"

George removed his dripping hat and squinted in the direction of the voice. A burly tattooed bartender, his white shirt rolled up at the sleeves, approached.

"There's a snug down the back, you might be more comfortable." Irish stopped abruptly. "The dead arose and appeared to many," he said in wonder. "Hey, lads, it's George. It's Father fucking George!"

"Love Me Do" faded back into 1962, and the patrons turned as one in the ensuing hush. George walked forward, at first hesitantly. Familiar faces held out welcoming hands, but he barely noticed. Even Marsden stood there openmouthed, all his spleen dissipating at the sight of this apparition.

Lennon watched the gaunt figure approach, the glass of Bushmills untouched. They embraced and, for a couple of moments, the many heartbreaks down all the broken years seemed easier to bear.

Lennon's whiskey spilled down the priest's back as he whispered, "What kept you, lad? You knew where I was."

At first George said nothing, just held on. Then he dug his head in Lennon's shoulder and said, "Ah Jaysus, John."

The jukebox needle jumped onto the next record, and a familiar voice shared his hurt:

I waited for you when hope was all gone
Through gray empty mornings long after the dawn
Should have helped me put the run on my fears
Still I waited, I waited for you
Oh, my darlin', my own bitter blue
I waited, I waited for you
My own dear sweet bitter blue . . .

Chapter Ten

EVEN A YEAR LATER, her hand shook at the sight of him. She turned abruptly to the mirror and watched him swagger through the doorway of the Horse and Jockey. He scanned the bar, eyes abrim with bluster, guard up and firmly in place. Even a year later, he couldn't admit that he dropped by most afternoons only because of her.

And Ringo right behind. That's odd. It's usually a busy day at the salon. Why isn't he there helping Maureen? And who's the other one they've got in tow? Pale as a ghost and most definitely not used to pub crawls.

She winced at the swelling on Lennon's face and bit her lip. But it was too late. He'd noticed her concern and now he was his cocky, sarcastic street-self, not her John.

"Walked into a lamppost, then, didn't I?" he answered her mute inquiry. She wrapped a clean dishcloth around some cubes of ice and handed it to him.

"Three pints of Guinness, luv?" Ringo winked.

She pulled the pints solemnly, poured three measured shots of Bushmills, and glanced warily down the bar.

"You're one in a million, China." Ringo acknowledged the free gargle by draining his Bush in a quick gulp. He grimaced fearfully as the whiskey coursed through his veins, burped twice, then winked at her: "That puts a different light on things."

Lennon looked down the near-empty bar and nodded at a couple of pensioners nursing pints and the glowing butts of cigarettes. The old men stared in bleak determination at the flickering images on the silent TV set, passing the long afternoon hours in her company before they'd shuffle home to watch more television. None of them returned his greeting.

Despite the lack of patrons, the bar was shrouded in cigarette smoke. She wore her long hair up and covered it with a soft red scarf. Despite this precaution, she'd still have to spend hours tending to its waist-length silkiness when she got home. The red was her only concession to the black skirt and blouse she wore, except for a small gold cross, one he had given her, which hung from a chain, and nestled just below her pale throat.

"Who's your friend?" she asked Lennon.

"You don't recognize him?"

"Should I?" Their public conversations were always to the point, but unfailingly cryptic to any eavesdroppers.

"The old pictures?" he demanded.

She studied the mufflered George across the pints of settling Guinness. There was a vague familiarity.

George stared back at her, and she looked squarely at him. She didn't often do that to men; it usually invited a come-on. But not this one. Oh no, he was safe as houses beneath his buttoned-up mackintosh. Those bruised, brooding eyes had seen too much of the world and probed too deeply to be preoccupied with a mere piece of skirt. When he loosened his scarf, she saw the white collar and knew who it must be.

"Good evening, Father."

"Hello."

"Would you like me to mind your bag?" Like a lost child

with a teddy bear, he was still gripping the valise. She leaned over the counter, and he surrendered it with a shy smile that suddenly made him seem a mystery worth unraveling. *Oh my, I bet you broke many's the heart with that look.*

Reassured by her friendliness, George unbuttoned his mackintosh and carefully hung it over a barstool.

"Georgie, this is me . . . friend, China. She just bought us a drink."

"Two drinks, John," Ringo interjected gravely, always one to keep the record straight in matters of booze, birds, and the beat.

"Friend." I suppose that's my official title. Not girlfriend. That would be too intimate, wouldn't it, and far too permanent-sounding by a long shot.

A chill wind swept the pub as Johnny Gustafson barged in, a peroxide scrubber on each arm. The pensioners looked up in annoyance at this blustery arrival. China felt three pairs of eyes dance around her slender back when she strolled down the bar and overzealously greeted the jaunty bass player. She leaned over and kissed him on the lips, yet was careful to pull back before he rammed his tongue down her throat. Something for Lennon to think about!

Of course, he would be engrossed in conversation by the time she turned around. She knew all his surface moves by now. It was the deeper details that derailed her.

She bantered with Gustafson and the girls while serving them, and eventually drifted back into Lennon's orbit. He was now furiously reliving old times, but she could sense his lack of conviction. *What's his problem? It would be so much easier if he'd cut all the bull, drag me over the bar, and tell me I was his only reason for being here. That's what he told me that first night in the alley, when he propped me up against the crumbling wall, pulled back my head, and kissed me with his beery mouth.*

"Give us a round for the road, luv."

"You'll get me the sack, Rings."

That's what he'd whispered as he squeezed my breasts and put his hand up under my skirt, while I prayed no one would stumble on us. He'd said a lot more too as he did everything he could to open me up; and hadn't he been the very soul of gratitude when I curled my leg around his hip and showed him how. Oh God, what words he'd whispered as I balanced there like a drunken ballerina holding on for dear life.

"Ta, luv, I'll be round in the mornin' to settle up," Ringo promised, not a doubt in his mind, but a ton of them in hers.

She took her time pouring three more shots. *That's one of the advantages of having Oriental features. They think you're deep and unfathomable. If they had any idea what you're really thinking.*

That was one of Lennon's attractions: He didn't quite fit in either and understood her reserve. Her father was Chinese. Jumped ship off a steamer out of Singapore. No matter that she was as British as the rest of them—same schools, same accent—she'd always be different. Just like him, with the crowd but not of it. She could always sense him blanking out in the middle of pub conversations, retreating to that secret place where she, too, spent most of her time.

It was Lennon who had christened her China. And she went along with it. Better than Lucy Dung—the name she'd suffered all through school. He didn't even notice the surname, nor its connotations. Just couldn't call her Lucy. Said it had already been reserved.

"Oh, no, look what the cat dragged in, Mr. bleedin' Disgustin'!" Lennon pretended he'd just noticed Gustafson. "Your mob playin' here tonight, Johnny?"

"No, that's your Fifty-Six Strat up there, lah." Gustafson pointed to the gear on the small stage. Battered but gleaming, the sunburst Fender leaned against a Vox AC-30 amplifier. Lennon ambled over and knelt down to examine it. He brushed his finger over the strings and listened for its distinctive metallic twang.

"Give it a try, mate?" For once, Lennon was deferential, even bordering on humble.

"Cost you a couple of years dole if you muck it up."

Lennon picked up the guitar with reverence. "Johnny lad, ain't dole enough in the world to replace this sweetheart."

He switched on the Vox and waited for the surge of power. Ringo sidled up and plonked down behind the drum kit. He hit the snare, grimaced at its trebly overtone, and tuned it down.

"Used to be the Beatles!" she heard Gustafson inform the scrubbers.

"The who?"

"No! The ruddy Beatles."

"Never heard of them."

The scrubbers' dismissal angered Gustafson. "A lot you never heard of, sunshine! Chuck Berry, Rory Storm. . . ." He tossed back his scotch, stood up, hitched his trousers up over his gut, and swaggered to the stage. "Or the bloody Big Three for that matter!"

Grumbling to himself, Gustafson switched on the P.A. and turned back to the bar. "That's the problem with the new generation, they don't know nothing about the history of this fucking town, begging your pardon, Father."

"That's okay, Guso. History has a way of repeating itself."

"You what, Father?" he answered distractedly, the booze and the prospect of a threezie calling him from down the bar.

"You always were my favorite bass player."

Gustafson stopped dead in his tracks, turned back, and

peered at the priest. "Holy Christ! I could've swore you were dead, George."

"No. Just missin' in action, that's all."

When the two men embraced, China turned away. She knew it would kill the hard-as-nails Gustafson if she caught the tears in his eyes.

Lennon struck a barred E chord, letting the bottom string ring. He leaned over, flicked the Vox to ten, cranked the treble, and tore through a screaming, sixteenth note intro. Ringo beat time on the kick and during the fourth measure fired off a machine-gun tattoo on the snare, and they were off into a Merseyside anthem.

Shake my heart, shake my world
Shake the sugar right off my girl
Shake my body, shake my soul
Shake me for the sake of rock & roll

The pensioners drained their pints and fled for home, moaning about "a pack of young scuts makin' a racket." But the scrubbers were agog at Lennon's blowtorch vocals. Gustafson smirked at them, then turned back to the priest. China saw him mouth some words, but the priest shook his head in urgent denial. Never a one to be put off by a mere no, Gustafson ushered him up to the stage. He switched on the other Vox and plugged in a gleaming red hollow-bodied Gretsch.

The priest looked at the guitar almost fearfully, but allowed it to be placed over his shoulders. He caressed the neck with his fingers and gingerly picked at the strings. Gustafson handed him a plectrum, then flicked on the standby.

When Lennon heard Harrison's first tentative notes, he smiled: *It's been too long, mate, too bloody long.*

Gustafson jumped off the stage and yelled down the bar to

the scrubbers. "History lesson, ladies, the best band ever to come out of this hellhole!" Then almost in a whisper, "Can't believe me eyes, China, it's the Beatles."

Almost, she thought. Just one piece missing.

As the first solo approached, Lennon could feel the priest tensing behind him. *Not ready yet, Georgie boy?* He swept into the familiar motif, and listened to George's faltering, rusty counterpoint on the bottom strings. *Getting stronger now, you're almost there, mate. Just hold tight. Give it time, it'll all come back. Just like ridin'.*

A surge of joy spiked through Lennon. He leaned to the side of the mike to lose some middle out of his equalization, and spat in the words.

Shake my money, shake my job
Shake me till I know just what you got
To shake my body, shake my soul
Shake me for the sake of rock & roll

He stepped back and studied the priest out of the corner of his eye.

Nice little lick there on the B seventh, lad. Starting to feel the juice flowin' in the pit of your stomach. Easy now. Don't blow your load. Wait for the right moment. It's only been an eternity—you can hang on another few beats. Don't rush it. Hold back till you're skithering round the edge of the pocket. Then nail it to the wall. Jump, for Christ's sake, or it's gone!

Lennon stomped all over the line and the priest blasted a bastardized Scotty Moore across the face of it. China gripped Gustafson and felt the tension in his arm.

"Welcome back, Georgie, you can do it." The bass player whispered through clenched teeth. As the notes, laced with reverb, whistled across the room, his anxiety drained away, and he relaxed against her shoulder.

Lennon stepped back from the mike and eyed the priest. Beads of sweat and concentration flecked his forehead, but he never looked up. Lennon repeated the phrase and the priest stayed with him, digging deep and ripping through the belly of the song. Lennon snorted in defiance and upped the ante as they locked in a duel between the fifth and seventh frets of the E and G strings.

"Go Georgie go!" Ringo shouted from deep in the groove.

"Go on up and join them," China said to Gustafson over the volume.

"Couldn't, luv, that's the Beatles."

"It makes no matter."

"It'd only break the spell."

"They need you."

"You don't know these things, woman. They wouldn't want me."

"Go!" She shushed him onto the stage. Deadly afraid of rejection, he shrugged at them apologetically. Lennon and Harrison had eyes only for each other, but Ringo welcomed him with an ear-splitting grin. His bass boomed in on the bottom; for a moment, it swung indecisively and soured the mix, but then latched like clockwork with the kick drum. Lennon, cocky and expecting nothing less, ignored the precision, but George looked up and smiled. Gustafson winked back. They were caught off balance, however, when Lennon suddenly segued into "Good Golly Miss Molly." He threw them both a scabrous look and left them fumbling for the key.

"Pack of wankers!" he yelled, and proceeded to squeeze every riotous, rebellious note out of the song, the way he'd seen Mr. Penniman do it all those years ago in Hamburg.

China leaned against the bar. *That voice always does it to me— no matter if it's screaming through a microphone, whispering sweet*

*nothings in an alley, or rasping through a cigarette after a good fuck.
That voice that tells all but rarely reveals anything. Except for the one
night. Jesus, what a session! Stayed in bed the whole time, with an
occasional break for a cup of coffee or a swig of cognac.*

It had all come pouring out: the pain, the turmoil and that
dry-eyed, terrifying fear of failure. She'd listened spellbound,
soaking up his stormy history, but eventually overwhelmed by
the flood of ideas, aspirations, ecstasies, obsessions, and
sudden blind rages. Where did she fit in the midst of this torrent? Was there room for her? Or would she eventually just be
swept away, useless to herself or anyone else?

But he trusted her. That was all that counted then. She knew
he'd never told anyone else. And that was a start. He began right
at the cradle—the loss of a father—bad enough, but even
worse: the betrayal of a mother. And that song he'd written
about her. She'd never heard anything like it. She'd stopped
him—the only time—and urged him to sing it down the pub.

He'd ripped her to shreds, as only he could, mercilessly:
"You're as stupid as she was. Do you think any of these
morons would even look up from their pints?"

And he was right. You bared your soul in Liverpool at your
own risk.

On and on he'd pushed, the know-it-all teachers in school.
The first liberating, soul-expanding notes of rock & roll. The
Quarrymen, Silver Beatles, the early years in Hamburg, the first
blazing night back at Litherland Town Hall when the teds and
rockers looked up from their aggro and copped on that this
wasn't just another crowd of wankers out to get drunk, pull
some birds, and then go home and get on with their lives. No,
this shower meant business, they could rip out rock & roll with
Jerry Lee or Prince Vince. They were the real thing—the best in
the world—and everyone Merseyside knew it.

The scrubbers ordered two more gin and tonics. She wondered if they knew Gustafson's code name for the drink: LOs; or when he was being expansive: leg openers. That was Johnny all over, a bit crude, but sound underneath it all, and a solid-as-a-rock bass player.

And right now he was nailing the three Beatles to the floor, bouncing off Ringo's backbeat like a hammer. But he was no McCartney. She could tell the difference. She'd heard the tapes. Old Paulie had put poetry into the beat with his swooping, lyrical lines. No one played bass quite like him. He'd come up with a style, then chucked it before anyone could copy him.

"Put the gin and tonics on Johnny's slate."

"Doesn't have a slate here, luv." Oh well, she'd get it from him down the line.

Those Cavern days, transcendence in a sweaty, smoky cellar. New songs, first demos, rejection all round. The make-or-break session with George Martin, the chart entry of "Love Me Do," and then that last awful night and the split.

He had collapsed back on the pillow and she was sure it was over; he lapsed into silence, sucked on one of her Silk Cuts, and contemplated his descent into nothingness. But no, after a slug of Rémy he was off again. Of course he hadn't given up! He'd pissed away his few pounds of savings in a couple of months. Then came the various bands: some he'd formed with the other two, some without. All of them unorthodox and great, but always measured against his Beatle past. And when the expected record deal didn't materialize, they'd just fall away, or he'd break them up in a drunken explosion at some important gig. More bridges burned, but no losses mourned.

And for good measure, there were the fights with bouncers, promoters, agents, barmen. An out-of-control scouse at war with the world. But who could blame him? Every couple of months, without fail, Montana's latest hit would come lah-de-dahing over the ocean and pouring out of every radio, spawning a new silk thread of bitterness inside him. Would this guy's line of bullshit never cease?

In the end, he threw up his hands and fled to London; no one knew him there. But that was a problem too—starting all over again—he was the hick from the north. Too stuck in his ways—should have gone earlier. London was suave, solipsistic, and sophisticated, didn't want to hear about his royal raw originality, and he, point-blank, would have nothing to do with shit.

Only one way out, go back to rock & roll with a vengeance. Oh, they liked that right enough. But instead of letting him stretch the boundaries, all they wanted was the standards. Hey, he even cracked the far recesses of the charts with a remake of "Be Bop A Lula." But then they wanted to turn him into the new Gene Vincent, call him "Rockin' John and the Spastics." One smart-arse promoter even wanted him to fake a limp and put on a Yank accent. That was the last straw.

On top of everything, he missed his kid. Never mentioned his wife, which gave her a ray of hope. And so he limped back to Liverpool and the dole. And there he stayed, stewing in his own bile, until . . . "I met you."

Her heart had jumped into her mouth. But he swept on as if he were talking about the weather or West Ham's chances in the Cup. Seeds of words tossed into the wind, dropping aimlessly into any kind of soil. Left there to grow or die unless she chose to nurture them. But oh, how desperately she wanted to, if he'd only give her the chance.

They were deconstructing "Hippy Hippy Shakes" when the priest skidded to a halt, ashen-faced, blood dripping from his uncallused fingertips. Gustafson caught on first and signaled

Ringo, lost somewhere in the thick of the beat. The drummer gawked over his crash cymbal. He kept playing for some seconds and then trailed off. Lennon glared back at him.

"What's the matter now? I was just goin' to do me Sam Cooke."

Ringo motioned to George. Lennon stared for a moment, then laid down his guitar. He stood in front of the priest. "Okay, Georgie?" he inquired matter-of-factly.

The priest was trembling. Lennon tried to remove the Gretsch, but he held on fiercely. "Listen, mate," he motioned to the guitar, "this is not a piece of the true cross, and you are not Jesus Christ about to be splayed all over it. Okay?" He removed the guitar from the priest's shoulders and set it next to the amp. "So give us all a break, will you."

George just stared vacantly ahead. They were unsure what to do with him until Ringo looked at his watch. "Jesus, John, d'ye see the time it is? We'll be murdered."

"Can you make it, mate?" Lennon took the priest's hands, and wiped the blood off his trembling fingers with the cuff of his shirt.

"Yeah," George said, but showed no sign of moving.

They led him down the bar to the door. The scrubbers saluted them with their LOs. "You lads are only brilliant," one of them said, a sense of wonder pervading her words.

"D'yez ever do weddin's?" the other one asked.

Lennon froze.

"I'm dead serious," the scrubber persisted, "if yez don't charge too much. Much better than a deejay."

"Yeah, we do divorces too," Ringo said, pushing Lennon toward the door. "And we'll be playin' at me own, if we don't get home quick."

"No need to get so high and mighty." The scrubber drained

her LO and turned back to the bar. "Maybe a deejay is better. At least, you can tell him when to turn down. Give us another, luv, on Johnny.

"Go on ahead," Lennon ordered Ringo. He walked back to China. She lowered her eyes as he approached.

"Thanks," he said quietly.

She nodded and handed him the priest's valise.

"If, eh . . . you're not doin' anything tonight, you might want to come over," he said. "We're havin' a bit of a get-together."

"I might." She turned to measure two gins and hide her smile. She knew he'd be gone when she turned around again, and he was.

Chapter Eleven

"WHAT IN THE NAME of Christ have you done to me?"

"Keep you hair on, will you! This place is crawlin' with press."

"I know it's crawlin' with press. That's why I want to know what, in the name of Jesus, have you done to me?"

"My friend, I have got you exposure that money cannot buy. Maybe you don't realize it, but we are at the hottest happenin' this side of Staten Island with the innest crowd in this fleabag of a country and"—Herbie halted, not for a breath, but for emphasis—"in a couple of minutes, you, Paul Montana, are goin' to be onstage with the Man around here, numero uno himself, the Leader."

Montana took a step back, sized up his manager, and, not for the first time in their relationship, wondered which of the two of them was the furthest out of their respective skulls. "Do you have the least idea what this jerk stands for?"

"Who cares what he stands for? He's got this dump filled with people. Look at them! And am I, or am I not, correct in postulatin' that this is a young, hip, cuttin'-edge crowd? And might I not also be accurate in reiteratin' that young, hip, and cuttin'-edge is the demographic that we could do with a hell of a lot more of?"

From his vantage point backstage, Montana took a moment

to examine the packed terraces of Anfield Road Football Stadium. He shuddered at the sight. Predominantly young it might be, razor-sharp cutting-edge he did not doubt, but not in a month of Sundays could he see any of these denizens of Liverpool's semifascist right wing warming to the mellifluousness of his one and only and forever anthems.

"This guy's even worse than a Tory. He's a Fascist!" He shivered and groaned. "Oh sweet Jesus on high, if John Lennon hears that I'm within an ass's roar of this clown—" He broke off, unable even to entertain such a calamity.

But Herbie was relentless. "Listen, Champ, I want you to reflect on one thing. Just for me, okay? Why is it that you call every up-and-comin' hip young guy a clown? You wanta think about the undeniable Freudian significance of that coincidence and get back to me in a day or two? Huh?" He paused a nanosecond. "This John Lennon dude, who don't own so much as a telephone, he buy any of your records lately?"

Montana didn't have time to address that particular no-brainer for, from out of nowhere, a deafening cheer, spiced with a symphony of wolf whistles, erupted from the terraces. Both men anxiously squinted down the tunnel and into the lights.

"Get her off that stage!" Montana roared as he caught sight of Luanne in tight pink cashmere sweater and matching leather microskirt, waving at the crowd from atop spike heels. She blew a tentative kiss, prompting another thunderous round of caveman testosterone.

"What the hell for? They're diggin' the shit out of her."

"Yeah, like the lions after the Christians. Get her off before I fire the whole useless lot of you!"

But Luanne needed no assistance. She blew one last, lingering kiss at the surging uproar and tottered backstage, swiveling her hips as only she knew how. "Gawd, Paulie, don't those guys have wives and girlfriends? I felt positively naked up there."

"You don't leave a heck of a lot to the imagination," he said. "What were you doin' out there anyway?"

"I was lookin' for the Green Room, but no one knew what I was talkin' about." She gazed at him quizzically. "They never heard about you neither, hon."

"That's 'cause he ain't headlinin'." Herbie said. "We're like the surprise guest star, or whatever they call it over here."

"Well, I never heard of no guest star that no one never heard of."

"Listen, dollface, why don't you give it a break. Can't you see the Boss is under a lot of stress right now?"

The Boss cast a frigid eye on his companions. He took two deep breaths, tried to visualize a blue sky, and struck out miserably. "Does anyone here want to know what I'm thinkin'? Oh, yeah? Good! 'Cause I'm thinkin' you don't have to be Einstein to know that I got two very specific things on my mind right now. Number one, how did I get into this mess, and number two, how do I get the hell out of it—pronto? Now let's go."

"Where?" Herbie played for time.

"Outa here before someone sees me! Where's that big idiot Whalen?"

"He's gone huntin' for woof-woofs."

"He's what?"

"Woof-woofs! You don't know what a woof-woof is?"

"No. For some obscure reason, that particular reference appears to have escaped my attention."

"Hot dogs, my man, hot dogs."

This time Montana didn't bother with the blue sky. "Has no one pointed out to you idiots that this is Liverpool—

not Coney Island? The big lug'll be lucky to get a bag of curried chips."

"Curried what?"

"Curried your mother! Some bodyguard! I could be getting tomahawked for all anyone cares."

"I seen two guys with mohawks on the street, Paulie," Luanne informed him. "My granddaddy always said, 'never trust an injun—honest or otherwise.'"

"It's Native American to you, babe," Herbie whispered, the soul of sensitivity. "Press might hear you, then where'd we be at?"

"Listen, this is Liverpool, not the Black Hills of Dakota. I'm gettin' out of here before someone spots me." Montana spun on his heel and headed for the nearest exit sign.

Herbie trotted after him. "What about Whalen?"

"Let the big dope find his own way home."

"You can't do that, man. This is like Harlem with white people."

"Then you wait for him. I'm history."

He was too late. The main floodlights dimmed and two huge strobes fractured the night sky. The crowd subsided into a deep murmuring anticipation. Off in the distance, a drone began to mutate into the whirling pulse of a helicopter, and row upon row of Fronters broke into the double-fisted salute as the chant of POWER . . . POWER . . . POWER solidified into the dull thud of POW . . . POW . . . POW.

Luanne and Herbie gaped at this alien spectacle, for once speechless.

Montana broke for the exit sign, but his escape was blocked by a company of the Chosen in full-blooded chorus. He tried reasoning with them, to no avail, and when he produced his wallet, they scowled and consulted among themselves. With his tail between his legs, he scurried back to his mesmerized entourage and uneasily watched the helicopter descend onto the pitch in front of the stage.

As the blades twirled to a halt, the crowd lapsed into silence. The seconds ticked into minutes with every eye in the stadium trained on the chopper. When the door was finally thrown back, a small blond figure—brown leather coat draped over his shoulders—stepped onto the field and all hell broke loose. Thousands of voices ricocheted across the terraces in a dozen competing chants. Gradually, the official mantra of the National Front gained the upper hand and gathered into a pounding, disciplined storm: *N-F-U-K . . . N-F-U-K . . . N-F-U-K.*

Turning away in disgust from the spectacle of the Leader making his triumphant way to the stage, Montana spotted Big Bill. The bodyguard was struggling through the exultant Fronters backstage, his bandaged fist held aloft like the Statue of Liberty's torch, while his other hand balanced a cardboard tray stacked with wafer-thin hamburgers and a mound of greasy curried chips.

"Hey, Boss! Some crowd, huh? Reminds me of the way we used to pack 'em in," he said with a grin, pushing his way toward Montana.

"Nice of you to drop by," Montana replied, but his sarcasm was lost on the beaming ex-linebacker.

"That's okay, dude."

"What kind of a bodyguard ain't around to guard the goddamn body?" Montana bellowed. He felt better already. "I'll tell you: an unemployed bodyguard. And that's what you're gonna be if you don't start doin' your job and get me out of here pronto."

"But, Boss, it's taken me forever to get these half-assed burgers, and look at the shit they poured all over my fries."

"I don't care if they dumped the whole Liverpool sewage system on top of them, we're outa here now!"

The bodyguard mournfully surrendered his tray to Herbie, who sniffed suspiciously at the soggy fries. Big Bill meanwhile raised himself up to his full height and shook out his shoulders. Bobbing and weaving, he did a quick feint and shot out a one-two combination that drew the scowling attention of the nearest Fronters.

"Oh, for Christ sake, go eat your chips!" Montana said, realizing with a sinking certainty that he was trapped. One false move could set off an international incident. "Just stand in front of me so I don't end up all over tomorrow's papers."

With the Leader's approach, various local dignitaries and politicians surged eagerly into the tunnel, pinning Montana and his acolytes against the wall. Then, like a vision, the great man went floating by. He was even smaller up close, his face pale and pasty, vacant green eyes watery and unblinking. The brown leather coat draped over his shoulders—ominous, even sexy, from afar—appeared to dwarf his slight frame, and made him seem vaguely ridiculous. However, he exuded an otherworldly, though confident, air, not unlike that of a religious fanatic who had been granted a brief glance behind the heavenly curtain, and was now patronizingly ready to share his vision with mankind.

"Wow," Luanne said.

"What do you mean 'wow'?" Montana hissed.

"I mean 'wow,' like who's his tailor?"

"Are you out of your skull? I've seen bikers with better taste." Montana made one last, halfhearted break for the exit, but a particularly intense young Fronter moved to block his way. He turned away but could still feel the young man's gaze on him.

Just then, the Leader stepped out into the spotlight, center of the stage, and the choreographed faithful abruptly ceased their chanting and segued into their anthem:

Britain will always be my homeland
I'm free, I'm no slave
God bless me, I'm an Englishman
Purity in my heart, strength in my hand
God bless me, I'm no slave
I'm an Englishman . . .

With the crowd pressing tightly in around him, Montana could clearly make out the nasal tones of the young Fronter who'd cut off his escape. The kid stayed locked in the original key, though the anthem rose in intensity and pitch. *Jesus, a singing Fascist! What's next? Maybe a little soft shoe? Get him a gig in the Sands. What the hell am I on about? I've got to get out of here before Lennon hears about this.*

The anthem peaked, the Leader stepped forward, and the terraces lapsed into reverent silence. The man gazed out over the assembled crowd with what seemed like bleak indifference, as if it were all the same to him whether they'd come or not. Then, just as the stillness began to crack, he spoke, at first in the clipped, measured tones of a public schoolboy, but rising by regular increments to a bracing intensity.

"They call us Fascists. They call us racists. Why don't they call us what we really are—patriots? Because the National Front is the only true British party, the party of the people, the real British people.

"This country means something to me, and I'm sick of it being kicked around by a bunch of welfare cheats and foreigners. So first things first, my friends, let's you and I put the great back in Great Britain."

The guy's got chops, I'll grant him that. Knows how to use a mike, holds the silences to breaking point. If he had a decent message, he'd go places. What am I talking about? This asshole is places. Look at this crowd—hanging on every word. Whalen was right. I had them like this once—eating out of my hand. What the hell went wrong?

"But this country can never be great again until we deal with the twin curses of unemployment and immigration. Our jobs have been squandered by the moneylenders down in London, and our national wealth wasted subsidizing the non-British welfare classes.

"Do you think for one minute that our foreign guests are happy living over here? No! With our program, they and their multitudinous families will get a fresh start back in Pakistan or Jamaica or Bullah-Bullah land."

This latter geographical reference tickled his audience no end; never moving a muscle, he waited impassively until long after the laughter had ceased before continuing at the exact calibrated intensity.

"Then you and I, the real British people, can get back to work and make this country great again. That's our foundation plan. Britain for the British! It's not much to ask, is it?"

The faithful had obviously heard this question before. "No!" they roared back in unison.

"Is it?" Their frigid messiah demanded more.

"No!"

"Is it?" The veins pumped in his forehead.

"No!" Their roar swept down from the terraces, and he nonchalantly basked in the adulation. Then, without the slightest acknowledgment of their applause or the brevity of his address, he stepped back from the microphone, and finished, apparently uninterested in any further proceedings.

"Honey, is he a Democrat or a Republican?" Luanne was perplexed.

"Are you kidding me?"

"I don't believe this shit," Herbie exulted. "Does this cat got an agent?"

The mayor, dignitaries, hangers-on, and general kiss-assers surged forward, ablaze with congratulations and an eye for photo ops. Montana used the confusion to retreat, but he was restrained by the young Fronter.

"Let me go, you maniac!"

"But there's so many people out there eager to see you, Mr. Montana," the Fronter said, squeezing his arm ever more tightly. "I know you don't want to disappoint your many fans."

Onstage, the mayor had gained the microphone and was vainly signaling for silence. A chorus of catcalls rippled around Anfield.

Montana struggled uselessly. *This punk is breakin' my arm. Where's that idiot bodyguard of mine, and what the hell is she gawkng at?*

But Big Bill was absorbed in his curried chips, and as for Luanne, her eyes were dreamily glued to the Leader, visualizing his taste in bedroom moves.

The mayor, meanwhile, had soared beyond the normal superlatives to describe this second coming to Liverpool. Yet a slow rumble of disapproval was gathering on the terraces. It seemed to make little impression on the Leader, who continued to stare idly past the proceedings as if gazing into a future that only he could see.

And still, the cry *No politicians* was loud and intensifying. Gasping for air, with the public figure's sure knowledge that he was losing his audience, the mayor looked around desperately for a distraction. His frightened eyes fixed on Montana. Beaming with relief, he turned back to the podium and gripped the microphone almost tenderly. He had been renewed and his voice was strong again.

"Friends," he said. "The world watches Liverpool tonight. Off in faraway America, a president awaits our signal. His emissary is already among us. Brothers and sisters, one of Merseyside's brightest stars has come home to share this moment with the Lion of Britain. Ladies and gentlemen, I give you the pride of Allerton, Mr. Paul Montana!"

A well-directed shove in the back sent Montana reeling forward. As he stumbled onto the stage, the Leader came to life, grabbing Montana's arm firmly while raising his own free hand high in the Front salute. A storm of flashbulbs lit the night, and Montana found himself mesmerized by the narrowed, speculating eyes of a gambler on the streak of a lifetime. Then, before he could say a word to break the spell, he was being hustled off the stage, another pawn swept from the chessboard.

Chapter Twelve

IT'S ALWAYS THE SAME, isn't it? Leave me to pick up the pieces. Bad enough havin' to look after one, but now I have to wipe the other fellow's arse as well. And me already up to me ruddy neck runnin' the salons! Four of them and eyes needed in the back of me head to keep the girls from stealin' every last brass farthin'. Not that I ever get, or expect, a word of thanks from staff, customers, or, the Lord forbid, our Richard. Well, it's not that I wasn't warned. Me poor mam begged me, on her bended knees, not to marry a musician. Oh, God, if I'd only listened.

But what did I know about the world? The sight of him up there behind his drums, all cool and collected, and every young one in the place fawnin' over him, and me, the lucky one he'd chosen. At least, that's what I thought back then in me delirium of innocence. But look at him now! Barely able to get up in the mornin'—the very hangovers cripplin' him!

He'd lie in that bed till the cows'd come home if I let him. But any man that lives with me has to pull his weight. I mean, what money does he bring in from his drummin'? A fistful of paltry pounds from playin' with God's gift to women, Gerry Marsden.

Still, for all his faults, there's a man knows how to look after himself, I will grant Gerry that. Made the best of his breaks, unlike my husband. Husband indeed! The only time he's interested in me is when he comes staggerin' home from the pub, thinkin' he's Rudolph Valentino, and then gets all in a snitch if I don't greet him like Marilyn Monroe, arms outstretched, lingeried to the eyeballs, and longin' to have his old beer belly come floppin' down on top of me. If only he took his time or did it in a kind and considerate manner— instead of hoppin' aboard, "sinkin' a depth charge," as he so crudely chooses to call it, then rollin' over, snorin', and belchin' to high heavens while I'm left there twiddlin' me thumbs, wonderin' what hit me, and a million problems camped out on the edge of me imagination, waitin' to assault me in me sleepless frustration.

She emptied a bucket of filthy water into the sink, then ran the hot tap and wrung out the dishrag one more time— praying for something a tad more tepid than the Arctic stream. Switching on a battered transistor radio, she was assaulted by a barrage of white noise but flipped the dial until she found some saccharine-sweet dance music. She hummed along while scrubbing the kitchen floor, but the soothing melodies were little match for the jagged misgivings bouncing around the walls of her skull.

Of course, I could drop dead of old age if I was waitin' for him to bring home some flowers of an evenin', take me dancin' or out to dinner or a show. Our Richard's idea of entertainment is a night out in the pub, gettin' ossified and leavin' me to converse with a crowd of brassers, sluts, and common dolly-birds, while he's off in a corner with the other fellow, laughin' and boastin' about all the crumpet they pulled in the good old days.

And where are they now? I'll give you one guess, and I bet it's not at a museum or library or some vocational class, betterin' themselves. Oh no, more likely down at Johnny Irish's vomitorium, that's where! And what do I find waitin' for me when I get here? The house black and deserted and me left standin' out in the rain, can't even get in the front gate. No, I have to climb over the wall and cut me way through that wilderness of nettles, weeds, and piss-the-beds John Lennon calls a garden.

But that was nothin' compared to what I found inside. O Sweet Divine Jesus on high! How can anyone live in such filth? I tell you, the first thing I felt like doin' was turnin' on me heel and out the door before I caught diphtheria or even worse.

And I'd have gone too, and not a bother on me, but what would Paul think of us all? Twenty-five years livin' in the lap of luxury in Las Vegas, and he's reduced to comin' home to a slum the likes of which you wouldn't see in blackest Africa. Even Pakistanis, nice people that they are, wouldn't be caught dead in this squalor.

She screamed in abject horror, rose from her knees, and vaulted onto a chair when an emaciated gray mouse skidded across the linoleum, unable to gain its usual traction now that she had removed the top layer of muck and grime. Maureen turned this way and that, following the mouse's panicky peregrinations until it eventually leaped for, and disappeared through, a crack in the window sash.

From her perch, she took in the filthy kitchen: a couple of rickety chairs sprawling around the table, a chipped enamel sink in front of the window, and the cupboards bare except for a few boxes of moldy corn flakes, a half pound of loose tea, and some cracked china mugs. The wall, separating the kitchen from the parlor, had been knocked down, creating one big room that stretched from the back door to a heavily draped bay window that looked out on the front garden. Part of the side parlor wall had also been removed, causing the already large room to stretch out into the hallway; she could see from the middle to the top steps of the stairs, though not the front door, which was still shielded by about six feet of remaining wall.

The parlor itself was sparsely furnished except for a collapsing, stuffingless couch, two armchairs, and a coffee table littered with bottles and cans. In the far right-hand corner, a battered acoustic guitar leaned against the wall. A Beatles poster from the Cavern, dated October 1962, had been tacked to the peeling wallpaper over the fireplace. Four young faces, confident and eager to confront the world, looked out on the general seediness. The poster itself was torn and faded. It faced four carved ducks flying along the stairway wall, obviously yearning for freedom beyond the front door.

With the coast clear, she climbed down stealthily, keeping one eye peeled for further vermin, alive or calcified. *And isn't it lucky I had me salon clothes with me? What would I have done otherwise? Strip down to me undies to clean this pigsty? That would have been the last straw; but I'd have done it. Because I haven't the slightest intention of gettin' me new outfit ruined. Me good dress that cost over a hundred pounds in the Mature Boutique yesterday. Me gorgeous burgundy satin, a modest inch above me knees, to allow the displayin' of the one good part of me that's left: me legs, enveloped in them black seamed stockings that Paul used to go apeman over.*

Oh, I well remember the glint in his eye when he'd notice them. Of course, back then, Richard would sweep me off into another room to get me away from his rival's fiery orbs. How times have changed. King Kong could be ready to hop aboard now and ravage me till me bells'd be ringin', for all the pass that husband of mine would put on him.

Enough of that! Now, where's the fridge? Used to be right in the corner, by the door. In fact, there's its mark on the wall. How in God's name does any Christian live without a fridge?

Then she noticed the small white icebox under the kitchen sink. She threw it open but jumped back in alarm when a frozen, sour smell enveloped her, assaulting and almost overwhelming her senses. Holding her nose, she looked past a bottle of congealed milk, a couple of beer cans, and a head of decomposing cabbage.

A thick green fungus had advanced outward from the cabbage and clawed its way across the frozen glacier that clung to the walls. Appalled but fascinated, she couldn't take her eyes off it.

And it's moving, too, or is that me imagination? Supposin' Paul or, even worse, his fiancée should come lookin' for ice for their martinis? What would they think of us?

She slammed the door shut and hummed into red-light emergency. With her heart pounding like the hammers of hell, she unplugged the icebox; at once, a low gurgle emanated from within. She stepped back, fearing for her sanity; but then, throwing caution to the wind, she opened the back door and, clenching her teeth, threw her arms around the frozen little tomb, staggered out into the yard, and laid it among the weeds.

Oh God, will this day never end? I better dust off the parlor area a bit. If only Cynthia hadn't knocked down the walls with her high-falutin ideas, I could have kept the company locked in there and out of this Black Hole of Calcutta.

Where is our Richard? When I see him, he's in for a large-size piece of my mind. And I'll give it to him in front of everyone—the very way he hates it. I won't stint on the vinegar either.

Duster and brush in her hand, fire and fury in her heart, Maureen Cox-Starkey stalked into what was once the parlor and threw back the curtains.

Oh, Dirty Maggie Mae, they have taken her away
And she'll never walk down Lime Street anymore
Oh, the judge he guilty found her

For robbin' the homeward bounder
That dirty no good robbin' Maggie Mae

Unaware of such dire retribution about to be visited upon him, Ringo unsteadily honed in on his spouse. Arm in arm, he and Lennon rolled down the terraced streets, bawling to the high heavens, sending cock-sparrows, robins, and lesser fowl chirping for the wires, while stoic crows took their measure, and judgmental jackdaws glared down in barely concealed contempt from a rusting forest of BBC and ITV aerials. The priest followed in their quickstream, humming a jittery harmony.

A watery sun had emerged from the drizzle and was setting anxiously over the little gardens, momentarily casting a rosy glow over all and sundry, but a cool wind had picked up speed, and the Union Jacks fluttered along in staunch, shivering empathy. Storm clouds were blowing in from the Irish Sea, and the first hints of a scouting shower darted up the Mersey. Lights were coming on in kitchen windows and housewives set the evening tea. One or two cast indifferent glances out at the drunken louts parading past their semidetached fortresses.

Lennon didn't give a damn. "C'mon, lad, one more time!" he urged Ringo. "'Oh, Dirty Maggie' . . . what the hell are you gawkin' at, you old bag of bones?" He gave the finger to a startled harridan, who dived for cover behind her lace curtains. "May you all die roarin'!" He directed an Elvis the Pelvis swivel at her offended dignity before shouting back over his shoulder, "C'mon now, Georgie boy, this place is crawlin' with bloody Fronters! Might make you eat your collar for dinner— Spaghetti Il Papa."

Father George smiled back. *Might be insulting, but at least he speaks his mind. Makes a change from Cheshire. Everyone tiptoeing around on eggshells in case they send me diving off the deep end, belly flopping back into the funny farm.*

"Home sweet home!" Lennon bawled as they turned the corner on Crescent Gardens. "Come back to me castle, I have! Right, Ringo old son? Only place an Englishman feels safe and sound these days."

"Right you are, John. I see you have the moat up again."

"Up, cocked, heeled, hunted, and ready to repel all raiders!"

Lennon approached the dingiest-looking house. A number of slates had departed the roof, while the lateral drainpipe had collapsed and hung skew-ways, causing a mini-Niagara to cascade to the side of the front door. One of the bedroom windows had cracked and was held together by a large piece of ugly-looking adhesive tape. Still, the forest of wet weeds in the garden gleamed with an odd ragged beauty in the dying sunlight. He tried the rusty gate, without much conviction. When it wouldn't budge, he kicked out at the offending handle.

"Nothing works in this bloody country," he yelled while painfully hopping the Aztec Two Step on his one good foot.

Ringo winked at the priest, then strode up to Lennon and offered his cupped hands. "M'lord, your stirrup awaits."

"Up she flew and the cock floored her!" Lennon leaped for and gained the moss-backed wall but lost balance on its slimy top and tumbled headfirst into the jungle of weeds within.

"Down she came without a feather on her." Ringo muttered. "You all right in there, old son?" he called out, dragging over a dustbin. "Watch me back, Georgie, will you?"

The drummer gave a sprightly leap up onto the bin, but the lid was no match for a daily regime of eight pints of beer and a pound or two of greasy fries. Still, nothing if not game, he sprang up again, cleared the wall, and landed on top of Lennon with a roar: "Jesus Christ on a bike!"

Lennon grunted from the shock, then threw his arms around the drummer and rolled over on top of him. "To hell with women, lad, I want to have all your babies."

"Better use a frenchie, John, what's Father George goin' to think?" Ringo tried to protect his clothes, leaving himself open to his comrade's amorous advances. After a couple of wet kisses, Lennon turned him over and summarily mounted him.

"To hell with the clergy!" he roared, pumping his crotch into the drummer's back.

"For Christ sakes, John, will you watch them nettles." Ringo's voice was muffled.

The wind gathered strength as the shower branched out from the Mersey and raced over Crescent Gardens, drenching them once again. George wiped the rain from his eyes and peered over at his two friends frolicking in the weeds. He opened his long black coat and leaped nimbly up on the wall, valise in hand. Perching there precariously, he stretched out his arms for balance and gazed in at the glistening jungle, searching for an open piece of ground to land on.

"Well, here goes," he whispered. "Back in the belly of the beast."

Chapter Thirteen

MAUREEN HUMMED ALONG with the dance music from the radio and rubbed the dust and condensation off the windowpane. She crinkled her nose—the height of disgust—and examined her damp imprint. A movement in the dusk caught her eye; she leaned forward and peeked into the fading rainy light.

"Dracula!" she screamed as a luminous winged figure floated down from the wall and crouched amid the weeds. She stepped back into the parlor, clutching her heart. First the fungus in the fridge, now Bela Lugosi unleashed on Liverpool.

Her lament resonated outside in the garden. Ringo raised a cauliflower ear. "That sounds like my missus."

"More like the wreck of the bloody Hesperus, if you ask me," Lennon noted.

"Could've sworn I heard her say Dracula."

"You never know with women, old son. Howlin' for your plasma, more than likely."

"Yeah, she'd start a riot in a ruddy nunnery. Though I suppose we're late enough, all right." The drummer picked himself up, shook off the rain, and wiped the grass stains from the knees of his drainpipes. "Better check her out. Hasn't been actin' herself lately." Then he added darkly, "These past twenty years."

He beat a path through the thistles to the front door. Lennon trod carefully in his wake. "C'mon, George," he called back to the priest. "Up off your knees and bear witness to the manifold joys of married life."

"Are you okay, Maur?" Ringo rapped the door knocker and shouted through the letterbox.

"Jesus save me!" a distracted voice implored from within.

"She's alive anyway," Lennon commented somberly. "Can't win 'em all, mate."

"C'mon, Maur, open up. It's only me."

"Maybe someone's assaulted her virtue, lad," Lennon added without much conviction.

"That'll be the day." Ringo blew on his hands. "Come on, Maur, it's gettin' cold out here."

They waited in silence. Eventually, a woman's figure appeared in silhouette through the frosted glass, and the door opened a crack. "Richard?" a plaintive whisper inquired. "Is that you, luv?"

"No, it's Mr. bloody Right. Open up, will you? It's freezin' out here, and you know how my lumbago acts up."

"I don't want to hear one word about your lumbago—carryin' trays up that stairs, twenty-four hours of the day." She tried to slam the door behind him, but Lennon stuck his foot in.

"Ah Jesus, me bloody corns!" he howled. "What are you tryin' to do? Lock me out of me own friggin' house?"

"Shut up, John Lennon! He's out there, I'm tellin' you. I saw him flyin' down off the wall."

"Ah, will you give over, Maur, I told you, you shouldn't have gone off them pills, that was only . . ." Ringo began.

But she stopped him in midbreath, spun him up against the stairway, her back to the front door, the bile of a quarter century dying to spew forth. "None of this would've happened if you'd been here on time. The smell of drink off you! And me slavin' away here, tryin' to put some shape or semblance of order on this shambles, with guests from America on their way here right now."

"As for you, John Lennon"—her wrath deepened and she took a quick gulp of air—"draggin' our Richard feet first into your web of drunkenness and deceit, and tomorrow the tongue'll be hangin' out of him, and he won't be able to drag one foot after the other out of his bed. And I bet neither one of yez cast a thought for poor Father George, and he lost and wanderin' the streets at this very moment. God only knows what trouble that poor misguided man has got himself into, and him teeterin' on a knife edge as it is, one step away from total certifiable lunacy."

She paused for another breath and stepped backward into the arms of the priest, who murmured, "To tell you the truth, Maur, I've actually never felt saner."

She froze at the familiar, but oddly brittle, sound of his voice; at once, all the anger drained away, and she was a girl again, back at the Cavern with her friends, watching the group; John and Paul already too mighty and remote, but slim and lovely George down to earth, and maybe, just maybe, approachable. He'd smiled at her once from the stage, lovely almond eyes framed beneath those sloping lashes, and all she could do was blush back; later that night, she'd been intro-duced to Ringo, and what did she know anyway, a slip of a hairdresser swept off her feet with his rings and his worldli-ness? But she'd never forgotten that smile, the boyish face, the whole all-the-world-ahead-of-me look, and now she turned around and stared up into his lost eyes before reaching out for him and sobbing, "Oh, George, what's become of us all?"

The priest hugged her back and held on for dear life. *You're right too, girl, the problem is, you're the only one with the balls to say it. But, oh Christ, how good it is to hold a woman again. Just the shape, the smell, the feel, the very essence. All those years thinkin' about it, tryin' not to think about it, knowin' what I was missin' but afraid to miss it too much for fear I'd go totally round the bend. Just a big hole, gettin' emptier by the day and nothin' to fill it with, but endless acres of loneliness.*

The afternoon teas with married women, when it would all get too much and I'd want to scream out: "Just hold me, that's all, I don't want sex or even the thought of it'; in fact, I don't want anything but the warmth of two arms around me, squeezing me and comforting me and catching my free fall for just one long, lousy minute. And sometimes, the tea lady could feel my need from halfway across the room, and she'd recoil, thinking it was something else, and on my next visit there'd be a friend, a husband, or some class of a chaperone sizing me up, sorting me out, and, of course, I'd be on to them and back safe behind one of my masks, stiff as a board, safe as a house, and I'd be no sooner out the door but they'd be telling the lady in question that it was all in her head, that a bit of nooky was the last thing on poor old Father George's mind, God help him, sure isn't he a harmless poor soul. Oh, Maur, you have no idea how good it feels just to hold you, and be held so sincerely, with no questions asked, in return.

She stopped crying and looked up shyly. The hot tears had streaked the remains of the morning's makeup, cutting rivulets down through the dust on her cheeks. "Oh, George, I'm always puttin' me big foot in me mouth, aren't I? It's just that I wanted so much for everything to be right, and look at me now, me face in a mess and me work clothes on, and all I wanted was for you to see me in me new dress and stockings, and lookin' nice for you."

He gave her another hard squeeze, then quickly released

her, afraid of the strength of his own emotions. "Right now, Maur, you look better than Marilyn Monroe."

"Oh, get on with you, will you look at the state of me. I'm an absolute mess."

Then, from inside the kitchen, came a roar of outrage. "Where's me fridge? The bastards have took me bloody fridge."

"Oh, Jesus." Maureen gathered herself.

"What's that, John?" Ringo inquired, glad to have done with all this bothersome emotion. Next thing you knew, she'd be on about "intimacy" or "relating" or one of them other words that led to arguments and making your own breakfast.

"I come home like any decent, law-abiding citizen, ready to stick me ale in the fridge, and what do I find? Me aforementioned fridge is bloody gone, out of here, kaput! Disappeared, like Aunt Fanny's drawers, into thin air."

"Maybe you pawned it, wack, like the last one?" Ringo strode from the hallway into the kitchen cum parlor. A uniform shabbiness, as much as the lack of walls, had united both rooms, and there was little now to differentiate between them except for the furniture.

"Remember the commotion when we wheeled that bugger down the street?" Ringo added, his mind really concentrated on the assortment of food his wife had laid out on the table.

"No way did I pawn it. And anyway, why would I? It's a brilliant little fridge, absolutely perfect for chillin' all manner of gargle."

And breedin' freezin' germs, the like of which you wouldn't experience in Antarctica. Oh God, what am I goin' to say now? If I tell him where it is, he'll insist on bringin' it back in and makin' a show of us all in front of George, not to mention Paul. And then to top it all, the whole lot us could get swallowed up by that creepin' fungus, and never be heard of again.

"Maureen Cox!" Lennon demanded, training a beady eye on her guilt. "You wouldn't happen to have seen anyone suspicious lurkin' around here, now, would you?"

She blanched, and his eye turned positively reptilian. "Well, the back door was wide open when I arrived," she said. "I thought that was kind of odd, but then I figured Julian . . ." She knew there was no need to say more.

"That greedy little sod always had his eyes on it. Pawned the bloody thing, he did. Then showered the money on them blasted Fronters." Lennon looked forlornly out the kitchen door.

Oh God, whatever you do, don't let him see it. But the weeds have probably choked the livin' daylights out of it already. "John, we do have a guest," she reminded him.

"Who?"

She motioned furiously at George, who had lost himself in the Beatles at the Cavern poster over the empty fireplace.

"Will you give me a break, woman, it's only George."

"He's still our guest." Then, like some Mayfair hostess, she directed her rounded vowels and plummy consonants at the priest. "Would you like a sherry, Father George?"

"Sherry's for old ladies. Have a bottle of ale, lad. Though it'll be a bit on the warm side," Lennon lamented as he slammed a six-pack of John Courage on the kitchen table.

"Sherry'll be fine, Maur." George had noticed the battered guitar in the far corner of the parlor. He strolled over and brought it back to the kitchen table; almost absentmindedly, he began plucking at the strings.

"It's freezing in here." Maureen heartily rubbed her hands to emphasize her point. Forgetting about the sherry, she rolled some old newspaper and mixed it with pieces of splintered plywood in the grate. Then, meticulously placing a couple of chunks of coal atop the heap, she struck a match. The flame took its time catching and she blew on it, looking up for a moment to whisper fiercely at Lennon: "Please try not to get drunk tonight."

"Why shouldn't I, then? You'd swear the effin' pope himself was comin'."

"Not in front of Father George," she hissed like a rattler.

"Father George, me arse! Right, Georgie boy? Best guitar picker this side of Birkenhead."

"That's not today or yesterday, John, and me fingers were in better shape too." He ripped off a double blues scale up the length of the neck and winced from the effort.

"Yeah, but we're still as good as ever, and don't let no one tell you any different. Right, Ringo?"

"Bloody well right!" Ringo stared clear through the icy darts shooting from his spouse's eyes. *The cheek of her! There was absolutely no call for the kind of bollockin' she gave me in the hall. And in front of George too! I don't give a rat's arse about John; he's like meself now, barely notices her bitchin' and moanin' anymore. But that kind of carry-on is just not acceptable when you haven't seen a body in donkey's years.*

When the fire was burning to her satisfaction, Maureen produced a dainty goblet and a bottle of Madeira from a small traveling case. Lennon slid over to examine the other contents, but she snapped the case closed and poured George a less than generous half-glass. Lennon raised an eyebrow, but she refused to take the bait. Tiring of this rigmarole, he cracked open a bottle of ale, took a swig, then belched loudly before inquiring, "You play at all now, Georgie?"

"Don't get much time, then, do I? What with bingo, bazaars, and the like."

"You runnin' a church or a flea market?"

"Well, it's like me archbishop says, 'You've got to keep the ship afloat. A penny here, a penny there, it all adds up.'"

"Yeah, Jesus saves but Moses invests." Lennon studied the priest. *Still no rise from him. Just like lookin' through a sheet of glass. Comes out every whenever to test the air, but then straight back behind—doors bolted, curtains drawn—at the first sign of a problem.* He took another long swig. Then, as casually as he dared, "Don't it never drive you round the bend?"

"Jesus, John, take it easy." Ringo cast him a warning look. Maureen halted her dusting, her back arched with anxiety. The long silence seemed to blanket the air, until George rose from his crouch and turned around.

At first, his eyes were cloudy, but then he focused on John and swallowed. "I've been there and back a couple of times, mate. It's no big deal." He halted for a moment, then steeled himself. "'Sides, there's something I should tell you all. . . ."

But Maureen wasn't able for the tension. "We're sorry, George." she blurted out. "He didn't mean anything by it."

That bloody bitch! Almost had him, and she goes and opens her big mouth again. Lennon mimicked her cruelly "We're sorry, George. Will you put a sock in it, you stupid cow. He's with his mates now, and if I want to ask him what it was like in cuckoo-land, I'll bloody well ask."

Maureen raised a hand to her mouth as if she'd been struck. Ringo walked over and put his arm around her. He was still pissed at his wife, but this had gone way over the line. "There's no call for that, John."

Lennon ignored him.

"Where's Cynthia?" George tried to change the subject.

Lennon polished off his ale and leaned down for another.

Confronted by his large arse, George turned to Ringo.

The drummer hiccupped with some flair. "Pardon me." He

played for time, but receiving no help: "What's keepin' Paul, then? I'm starvin'."

"She's not sick or anything?" George was worried now.

Lennon opened a bottle, let the cap fall on the floor. "She left me, mate. Ran off with the milkman."

"The coalman wasn't good enough for her?" George enjoyed the joke. "She's visiting her mother or something?"

There was a long, awkward silence. George looked from one to the other around the room.

"Albert is an accountant with the Milk Board," Maureen finally said, resolutely wiping her hands on her apron. "There, it's said and done. I don't know what all the fuss is about." But when she saw the priest was still confused, she added, "She's very happy, George."

"He's still a bloody milkman," Lennon said.

"You're serious?" George was astounded.

"She's gone this six years. Good riddance too."

Maureen furiously dusted the mantelpiece. She hummed an atonal tune of unknown origin, one she often employed in her dealings with John Lennon. As the swish of the duster grew more vicious, she scoured the room and her mind for some-thing to say. As usual, Ringo gave her an opening. "Richard, don't you dare touch them canapees."

Ringo might not have known canapés from a hole in the wall; still, his hand darted back from the forbidden hors d'oeuvres, but a sullenness set in. "I'm bloody starvin'."

"Eat up, lad. That Yank wanker is not comin'."

"Oh, he'll come all right," Maureen said. "Paul was always very considerate and well mannered."

"You didn't know him like the rest of us. Could be a right little prick if he didn't get his own way."

"And you could be a right little . . . eh . . . eh . . . troublemaker yourself, John Lennon. And that's been said by more than one in this room."

"Yeah, but I'm a right little . . . eh . . . eh"—he rolled the offending word round in his mouth before spitting it back at her—"prick to your face. I don't go behind your back, like some in this room."

That was the limit. Maureen flung the duster down on the table. After all the cleaning and mucking around, to be insulted in this fashion. She advanced on him, and drew a deep breath before declaring, "I've always said my piece to your face."

A shopping list of her back-stabbings flashed in front of him, any one of which had cut him to the core, but Lennon's reply was interrupted by the slamming of the garden gate.

"Oooh, they're here!" cried Maureen.

For an instant, Lennon's guard collapsed, and he looked around in a panic. But then, from outside, a voice bawled: "Off my street, you slimy Trot! Get back to London, where you belong!"

Ringo drew back the curtain and peered out.

A key clicked in the lock of the front door. Lennon turned on his heel and stared determinedly out the kitchen window. The door opened and a figure lumbered noisily through the hallway, but stayed out of sight of those in the kitchen. Maureen alone went into the parlor area, but by then all that was left to see was a pair of bovver boots tramping up the creaky stairs.

"Julian," she called, but there was no reply, just the crash of his bedroom door.

Seizing the opportunity, Ringo sauntered over to the table, gave the hors d'oeuvres a quick once-over, and stuffed the largest cocktail sausage into his mouth.

"Julian's one of them?" George was stunned.

"Yeah, the heir to my throne happens to be the local commandant."

"Little Julian?"

"He's not so little anymore."

"I can't believe it. Especially . . ."

"It had sweet damn all to do with me."

George backed off, shrugging bitterly. "I had a run-in with one of them earlier. He was a right little Fascist."

Ringo stuffed another sausage in his mouth. "I had a piece of a couple of them meself this mornin'. Right, John?"

Lennon winked at George. "Yeah, mate, you were a real animal."

"Bloody well right I was!"

"Richard, I warned you not to get in trouble with them."

"Oh, there was no trouble. But they'll be pickin' my boot leather out of their arses for the next twenty years."

"You know well I don't like that kind of talk. Besides, you could have lost your transport card."

"Ah, bugger me transport card! You never let me go anywhere anyway."

For once, Maureen let it pass. Surprised, Ringo upped it a notch: "That'll teach 'em to pick on a mate of mine. Right, John?"

"Yeah, mate, I bet they're still talkin' about it."

"Oh, they may be talkin' all right, but I bet they're not sittin' down." The drummer swaggered around the parlor, a bantam cock tipping his feathers.

"They told me to shut the salons tonight if I knew what was good for me," Maureen said. "They act like they're the total authority."

"What do you expect? I told you years ago, we should've stood up to them, but you all laughed at me—said I was paranoid. But I tell you one thing, if that little bastard up there slams that door again, I'll . . ."

"Please, John," Maureen pleaded with him.

As if in answer, Julian's door did slam, and he began tramping down the stairs.

Maureen anticipated Lennon's movement and placed herself squarely in front of him. It seemed like he was about to brush her aside; then, just as suddenly, his resolve failed him. Though he shook with frustration, Lennon turned away.

Maureen crumpled the tea towel she was holding into a ball and went out into the hall. "Julian, there's a friend of your father's here," she said, betraying only a slight catch in her voice, "please come and meet . . ."

The only answer was a loud *harrumph* and even heavier tramping. Then the front door hit the wall, nearly lifting off its hinges, and Julian was gone, out again into the Liverpool night, an offending dustbin clattering down the street in front of him.

"Jesus Christ," George said.

"He's no better than the rest of them. Give him an inch and he takes a mile." Lennon turned his bitter back and threw open the kitchen window. The filthy lace curtain blew in and fluttered with the first blast of the night air. He cupped a cigarette in his trembling hands and, with some difficulty, lit it. He took a long drag and blew back fiercely into the wind.

Maureen folded out the crumpled tea towel and placed it neatly on the table. She looked up suddenly, about to give Lennon some kind of argument but, instead, bit her lip. Then she reached for her duster and made a few feeble swipes at the mantelpiece

"I don't know what this country is comin' to, I really don't," she said. "I can only imagine what Paul is goin' to think of us."

Chapter Fourteen

SPEEDING THROUGH THE STREETS of Liverpool in a sleek limo, its tinted windows raised, Montana alternated between cold contempt and red-hot rage. Herbie had just trailed off a long soliloquy by pointing out that: "Hey, you wanted a stretch, so the man rustles up a stretch and one of his own guys to drive it. How bad can this Leader dude be?"

Montana was trying, with scant success, to ignore him. *Jeezus, will this guy never shut up? Talk about a bloody stuck needle goin' on and on, cloggin' my brain. When I get back to Vegas, there's goin' to be changes—big-time changes. When I get back? Jesus Christ, if I get back. Look at that shit out there!*

He gazed out at the scarred streets: his streets, his city, the rosy memories of boyhood now festering under a lacquer of grime and graffiti. Off on the skyline, tongues of fire flared through the gloom, and when he lowered the window, the acrid pall of arson seeped into the limo's cushy interior.

What the hell's happened? I mean, no one expects the world to stay the same; things change and time tramps headlong over everything. You go away and you remember it one way, you come back and it's different. But you ought to feel some connection. And what do I feel? Nada. I got more in common with Big Balls Whalen— dumb as he is—than I do with any of those maniacs at Anfield. At

*least, I can relax around him, let my hair down every now and then,
have a couple of laughs, get drunk, pull a piece of tail. I couldn't get
down with that pack of Fascists to save my life.*

*What went wrong? I used to be one of these people. I know these
streets like the back of my hand. Nights I'll be onstage at the Sands
and off I go into a dream, and the left side of my brain'll be singin'
to the fans, but the right, oh, man, that crazy right'll be on a day
trip up and down the lanes and alleys of this city, and the next thing
I know, the song'll be over, and everyone is thinkin' I'm drinkin' in
the applause, 'cept I won't even be hearin' a DB of it, 'cause the
better part of me—the spiritual side—will still be diggin' the dry
tears of scouse rain drippin' down my face.*

"Paul, hon, I think those guys are going to burn that store."
Luanne glanced out the window for a puzzled instant and then
resumed polishing her nails.

"What are you talkin' about now?" Montana grunted.

A gang of Fronters was systematically breaking the windows
of a takeout; up the street, an older Pakistani man was trying
to restrain two younger men, perhaps his sons, from inter-
ceding. While the Fronters goaded them and waved them on,
their leader—his bare tattooed arms glistening in the drizzle—
doused the building with a can of paraffin oil. One of the
young men broke loose and ran full tilt at the delighted mob,
which proceeded to beat him senseless. The stretch moved
past at a crawl, seeming to savor the scene.

"Let him go, you motherfuckers!" The car screeched to a
halt when Montana opened the door and jumped out. The
Fronters looked around in alarm. Seizing their chance, the
other two Pakistanis darted in to pick up the injured man, and
dragged him up the street to safety.

"If I were you, my friend, I'd get back in the car," the
driver called out, and added, not without a trace of gleeful

anticipation, "if you don't want your brains splattered all over the road."

The mob appeared to grow in numbers and, as it approached, Montana froze. Not so, Big Bill: With surprising agility, he sprang from the car and placed himself squarely in front of his boss. "You boys lookin' for trouble?" he drawled in his best John Wayne.

"He's a fuckin' Yank," one of the Fronters noted in some amazement.

"Are you tryin' to get us killed?" Herbie screamed meanwhile, reaching out to drag an unresisting Montana back inside the stretch.

"I said, you boys lookin' for trouble?" Big Bill reached nonchalantly inside his tour jacket.

"Hey, mate, this is Liverpool, not the bloody Alamo." The lead Fronter backed off a step, his muscled arms a mosaic of Union Jacks and National Front slogans.

"One hick town is the same as another to me, pardner." Big Bill cast a chilly but amused eye on the Fronters. The notion of a concealed Colt .45 appeared to be causing a certain trepidation in the ranks. The ex-linebacker tipped his finger to his forehead and drawled, "Y'all take care now." He swaggered into the back of the stretch, slammed the door, and whispered hoarsely to the driver, "Pedal to the metal, boy."

When the first rock hit the limo, the driver, despite his party affiliation, cut the lights and floored the accelerator; the limo shot forward, sending them all sprawling onto its carpeted floor.

"You stupid fool!" Luanne howled, her nail polish spurting into Herbie's face as they spun head over heels, locked together in a frantic embrace.

Herbie screamed in terror "Aah! I'm bleedin' to death!" He

blindly flailed arms and legs in a struggle to free himself from between her thighs.

"You touch me there again, buster, and I'll call the cops."

"I ain't touchin' nothin'! Get your knee outa my face. I'm cut bad, can't you hear me?"

"I can't hear nothing else but your yelling."

The driver zigzagged crazily to avoid a further hail of rocks, sending his passengers flying, once more, to the far corners of the stretch.

"Who's yellin'?" Herbie screamed. "Hey you, shit-for-brains up front, slow down before you kill us all. I'm bleedin' bad."

"Oh, will you shut up! It's just nail polish," Luanne screamed back.

"Nail polish?" Herbie curled his nostrils and sniffed at the magenta mess congealing on his face. "No way. Smells like blood—tastes like goddamn blood."

"That's because it's organic, flown in special from New York City at sixty-five bucks a fluid ounce."

Another sudden swerve of the limo threw them back together again on the crowded floor.

"I'm warning you. You touch my privates again—I got connections on the Strip."

"I ain't touchin' nothin'. Hey, asshole up front, slow down!" Herbie cried out from amid the tangle of limbs.

"Yeah," Big Bill's voice chimed from somewhere in the mix. "I'll kick your English butt if my hand gets hurt again."

But the driver barreled on through the dismal streets. As the three of them fought to regain their seats, they became aware of a low moan emanating from the floor beneath them.

"That you, Boss?" Big Bill ventured, shining a pocket torch in Montana's general direction. His silver lapels glinted in the narrow beam of light. The bodyguard worked his way across the swaying limo floor. Montana was lying on his back, eyes wide open, apparently in some catatonic state.

"What happened?" The moan was barely decipherable.

Big Bill shone the torch into each eye and squinted into Montana's pupils, but there was no movement.

"This big idiot nearly got us killed, that's what happened," Herbie said with disgust. "Doin' his stoopid John Wayne again."

"No," Montana emoted. "This big idiot saved my life." With each slowly formed syllable, his voice strengthened in conviction. "When none of you would lift a finger to help me, this big idiot put his butt on the line. That's the difference between him and the rest of you. And another thing"—he paused for breath—"my bloody herniated disc is out of whack again."

"I warned you to do your mental imaging yesterday. . . ." Luanne began.

"Shower of fucking arseholes!" the driver interjected with gusto. He switched on full lights and roared at them over his shoulder. "Shut up, yez crowd of dumb Yanks!"

"I'll have you know I was born in Allerton," Montana roared back, his eyes once more blazing, catatonia apparently banished.

"Allerton, my arse! Why don't you just shove it, cowboy."

"Excuse me?" Luanne interjected. "Am I missing something, or do I hear the chauffeur giving orders?"

The driver slammed his foot on the brakes, and the car fishtailed to a stop, once more depositing them head over heels onto the floor. "I'm not your chauffeur, you dumb cunt! Drive your own bloody car." With that off his chest, he threw open the door and strode off into the gathering fog.

"I will not have that word spoken in my company," Luanne shrieked. "Get right back here and apologize, you smelly little zit-faced prick of an Englishman."

Montana groaned, then straightened up suddenly. His back cracked as his head hit the velvet ceiling, and he pitched forward in agony. "Jeezus!" he bellowed, collapsing onto the seat. He exhaled loudly, farted, and then observed to the ether: "Always does the trick."

Herbie licked his handkerchief and dabbed at his face. "Well, this is just great. Look at that fog. Now what are we supposed to do?"

"That's what I pay you twenty per for, but as usual you're about as helpful as a nun in a brothel," Montana said.

"I don't deserve that, Paul." Herbie spoke quietly, but deep down he was seething. *Oh yeah, schmuck, we'll see about that the next time the IRS comes callin'. I have personally saved your ass so many times, it's a wonder I don't shit through it.*

Montana ignored him. Perching himself in the lotus position, he summoned unto himself his inner white light. *Gotta calm myself. With all these dimwits around me, it's a wonder I can function at all. No, I gotta remember, they are not dimwits—merely loose pieces of dysfunctional firmament blown this way and that, without the ballast of their developed inner selves to keep them moored to the reality they perceive. And what's more, I absolutely refuse to allow their distorted perceptions to influence mine. All I have to do is center myself and let my own inner flame rekindle the eternal matter of my soul. Then propel it outward in a million expanding circles which, with a bit of luck, will detonate into a billion subliminal tendrils of white light that will reenergize the extremities of my total being.*

The others watched warily as, with eyes closed, Montana solemnly communed with his latent Enochian being.

The Boss is so deep, Big Bill marveled.

I hate when he pulls this shit! Herbie grumbled.

Has he passed out? Luanne wondered.

Montana's eyes reopened slowly and focused on his body-guard. "You drive," he said in a voice of utter inner certainty.

"But, Boss, they drive on the wrong side over here."

"So, you'll be happenin'! You can't get anything else right."

"You heard the Boss. Now, move!" Herbie snarled.

Big Bill clambered out of the limo and got into the front seat. "The wheel is even on the wrong side."

"It's not on the wrong side, it's on the right side," Montana said. "All you have to do is keep to the left side of the street."

"Yoh what?"

"The Boss said keep to the left side of the street even though the wheel is on the wrong side of what you're used to," Herbie interjected. "Don't you understand English, you big dummy?"

Montana turned to his manager. "I said nothing remotely like that, but since you insist on messing up every last detail of my life, you haul your own sorry ass up there with him."

Herbie's razor face mutated through shades of incredulity, despair, and derision, but finally hardened into brazen contempt. "Management do not ride the front of a stretch," he noted with pontifical infallibility.

"Get your skinny butt up front or management be history."

"No need to shout!" Luanne said.

"And you shut your fat trap or you'll be up there sittin' on his knee."

Luanne returned Montana's outraged scowl. But then, noting its ferocity, opted for discretion over spinsterhood. She plunged into the recesses of her pocketbook, retrieved a new sixty-five-buck bottle of the Big Apple's finest magenta, and set to furiously adorning her nails.

"Well, what's it gonna be?" Montana asked.

Mustering his dignity, Herbie stepped from the limo and threw open the front right-hand door. Big Bill looked up in alarm, but then returned to his puzzled inspection of the gear stick.

"Call yourself a manager? You don't even know what side the wheel is on," Montana gloated.

Herbie slammed the door and, with insulted head held high, paraded around the front of the boat-sized car.

"What's this, then?" a spectral voice inquired.

Herbie stopped dead and gaped out into the fog, from whence a group of ghostly figures began to materialize.

"Champ," he stuttered, his voice modulating up a wavering flattened third. "I think I'm gonna shit myself."

"I wouldn't do that, then, not on a public thoroughfare. We 'ave laws against that type of thing in this country," 'Arry 'Olt cautioned.

"What the hell is it now?" Montana's muffled roar emerged from the limo.

'Arry 'Olt's eyes narrowed at this affront to his authority. He smacked down hard on the roof of the limo three times, and loudly proclaimed: "Citizens Defense! On the street, before I drag you out by the bloody 'eels."

"Jeezus! Did none of you jerks ever hear about migraine?" Luanne swung the door open and clacked forth on her stilettos, her tight dress rising above her stocking tops.

'Arry 'Olt gave a short, sharp gasp at this unexpected vision. The other Fronters broke ranks to crane forward for a keener appraisal.

Luanne shifted her dress down over her hips, and 'Arry 'Olt reached out to lend a helping hand. Smiling coyly, she allowed his fingers to linger briefly on her thigh before punching him full in the face. "You keep your paws off me, you pervert! I've been felt up and fucked by the best, and you don't even come close."

"Bloody bitch!" 'Arry exploded. With blood gushing from his nose, he raised his hand to strike back. Big Bill and Montana simultaneously rushed to her defense, tripping over each other and sprawling onto the pavement in their haste to exit the limo.

"I wouldn't do that, brother." A familiar voice leered out of the fog. "This party is under the Leader's personal protection."

"That Yank bitch just broke my bloody nose!"

"Listen, buster," Luanne declaimed from a defensive crouch. "I have a black belt from Fu Chi Hee himself, and if I wanted to break your nose, you wouldn't be talking right now."

Montana's outrage was palpable as he attempted to extricate himself from Big Bill's tangled frame. "I don't want that bastard's protection!"

"You didn't say that when you took his master class," Luanne countered.

"I'm not talking about that Chinese con man!" Montana shouted. "I mean the Leader, or whatever the hell he calls himself!" And then to his bodyguard: "Will you, for the love of Christ, get off my leg!"

"Pleased to be of assistance, Macker." The newcomer jerked Montana to his feet.

"You again." Montana recognized the young Fronter from Anfield.

"In the flesh. I'll take over from here, brother," he ordered 'Arry.

"No way, mate! 'E called the Leader a bastard. Right bloody ponce 'e is too. Look at the clobber 'e's wearin'."

"I said, I'll take over!"

When 'Arry 'Olt continued to stand his ground, the young Fronter beckoned him to one side and threw a comradely arm around his shoulders. "Mr. Montana happens to be a close personal friend of the Leader's. You didn't see them onstage tonight?"

"'Old on now a minute, mate. You mean that old geezer there is Paul Montana?"

"The very one. And another thing, brother, he has a very pressing appointment—Leader's business—very hush-hush-like."

"I don't believe it! Paul Montana 'isself? 'E look's a lot better on the telly, don't 'e?"

With the aid of a filthy handkerchief, 'Arry 'Olt had succeeded in stanching the flow of blood from his nose. He now appraised Montana—up, down, and sideways—like a bullock at a fair. Something, apparently, was not quite up to speed. Then the veil of memory parted and he marveled aloud, "Jesus, it's 'im all right! Just got a lot of miles on 'im, that's all." Never one for subtlety, he prodded Montana in the breadbasket. "Put on a few pounds, ain't you, then?"

"I keep tellin' him that, but he never listens," Luanne agreed, forgetting their earlier enmity. "Honey, you'll be as fat as Wayne Newton soon."

"Listen, if you want to sleep with that no-talent Newton, you go ahead. See if I care." He ripped open the limo door. "Now, if you guys are finished playin' tin soldiers, maybe the rest of us can get on about our business."

"'Old on there now, mate." 'Arry 'Olt grabbed the handle of the door. "I bet you 'ad no idea that my Elsie adores the very ground you walk on."

"That had somehow escaped my attention."

"I'm dead serious, mate." He grabbed Montana's arm and spun him around like a top. "I bet you'll never guess who I was talkin' to today?"

Montana raised his eyes to the good God of all discombobulated superstars. "Let me guess? Now, it wasn't the Queen Mother, was it?"

"'Ardly, mate, we 'ad her over for tea and crumpets last Sunday. No, I 'ad a run-in with that Lennon bloke you used to play with down the Cavern. Proper wanker 'e is too."

The young Fronter stiffened with interest, but Montana refused to be drawn.

"Give us your autograph, then," 'Arry 'Olt said quite reverentially.

"Here, Boss." Big Bill pulled a sheaf of eight-by-tens from his tour jacket and handed Montana a close-up of his beaming, air-brushed face.

Montana hesitated and took it with a sigh. "All right. Anything for a bit of peace. What's her name?"

"Elsie, mate. She's gonna be so chuffed. Plays your records day and night. Mind you, it's not to my taste—bit on the sugary side compared to what you and old dickface used to play, but there's no explainin' taste, now, is there?"

"Yeah, yeah, yeah." Montana thrust the picture into 'Arry's fist and broke for the stretch.

"Good on you, mate! You be a good boy now, no more callin' the Leader names, you 'ear me?"

"Oh, go fu—"

"I'll keep an eye on him, guy," Big Bill interrupted.

'Arry 'Olt seemed less than reassured.

"That's settled, then." The young Fronter smiled and pointed down the street. "Just around the corner to the left—the one with the stuck gate."

An odd, claustrophobic silence descended as the Fronters dissolved back into the fog.

"Thanks," Montana called after their vanishing shapes, "for bloody nothin'."

"Oh, man." Herbie exhaled. "What was that all about?"

For the first time, Montana's voice veered totally from Vegas twang to scouse slang. "That's bloody reality, pal. Somethin' our arses could all use a good dose of."

Howie noted the change and felt a strange foreboding.

"Get in the car," Montana said. "We have a party to get to."

Luanne shook out her hair. "I'm goin' back to Vegas!"

"Off with you, then, luv," Montana declared unromantically. "Just make sure you turn left at Pier Head."

Luanne looked around at the foggy streets and shuddered. "What's happened to you, Paulie?"

"Nothin's happened to me."

"This country is changing you."

"Get in the bloody car."

"No, I'll walk," she said. "It's just around the bend."

"Around the bend?" Why did she have to bring that up?

Montana shuddered from a jolt of paranoia. He reached out and grabbed the limo door to steady himself. Big Bill glanced over, but Montana turned away, suddenly terrified of any eye contact.

I see the way they're lookin' at me. They think I'm losin' it, but that's their problem. This country is not changin' me—just showin' me up for what I am. I mean, how am I goin' to tell Lennon about Anfield? And what, in the name of Christ, is he goin' to think of this posse of lunatics I got with me? No wonder I'm goin' up the walls.

He took a deep breath and tried counting to twenty, but the numbers splintered and rattled like daggers inside his skull. *I've got to pull myself together. What doesn't kill me will only make me stronger. Yeah, yeah, yeah! More bullshit.*

His heart was kicking triplets all over his chest. His posse was looking at him. They'd been through this before. Now they were waiting for his signal that all had returned to normal. But it hadn't. He risked a look in their frightened eyes, and almost succumbed to the panic. Then he straightened up and threw back his shoulders. *I haven't come this far just to fall apart at the seams. When all is said and done, deep down I am still Paul McCartney. I will get through this if it kills me.*

"Get in the bloody car!" he snarled. "Lennon's been waitin' twenty-five years for this. The least we can do is give him a full show."

Chapter Fifteen

MAUREEN HAD SLIPPED into her new dress. From time to time, she observed herself in the mirror, tucking in a fold here—flesh or silk—filling out a line there, sucking in her cheeks, teasing out her hair, adding lipstick, subtracting mascara, compulsively checking the seams of her stockings.

That shade of blush makes me look every bit like an old lady. What in God's name ever made me put it on? The new foundation works like a charm though, covers up those ruddy big lines, that's for sure. Still and all, will you look at the state of me? If I'd only used that spa membership the girls got me for Christmas. But where do you get the time, I ask you? It's not like I'm sitting at home on me arse, preening and pampering meself, like some I could mention. Speaking of me arse. It's not really so bad now, is it? Mr. funny fingers Marsden likes it well enough. Let his Roman hands linger there that night down the pub during the slow dance, when Richard didn't show up until all hours. Out with John Lennon, I suppose. He better have been!

He'd never do anything like that to me, would he? Carry on behind me back like? The girls in the salon would surely tell me, wouldn't they? Unless it was one of them he was actin' up with. He's got far too much class, our Richard does.

Then the awful voice that kept her awake nights dryly inquired: "Our Richard with too much class?"

The toilet flushed and Ringo emerged, running his fingers through his hair, teasing his kiss-curl to a precise angle—apparent only to him. He yawned, scratched his ear, and headed for the table; he also noted that his wife was surveying him suspiciously, but thought the better of inquiring what the hell she was looking at. Even with back turned, he could feel her eyes upon him. He snorted and defiantly cracked a fresh beer. He let the cap fall to the floor and didn't bother to pick it up. Then he swaggered over to the window, pulled back the curtain, and peered out.

Maureen quickly distracted herself. "Do you think he'll have changed much?"

Father George had come across a tattered Beatles scrapbook that Cynthia had once lovingly put together. He flipped through the pages of his glory days, eyes alternately blank, then quizzical. His thin frame swayed to the beat of some song he was humming while he lingered over a picture and examined it from every which way. He suddenly snapped the book closed, and even more color drained from his already pallid face. As if by instinct, he reached out for the acoustic guitar.

"I said, 'Do you think he'll have changed much?' " Maureen repeated, her voice now sharp as a blade.

Ringo made a point of ignoring her. The priest had his ear to the body of the guitar, listening for some sound obvious only to his ears. Lennon, who had stretched out on the couch, looked up bleary-eyed. "The last time I saw him on the telly, he looked like a right old whoremaster, with all them silver chains hangin' out of him. He's probably even got one on his ankle."

"Well, I thought he looked smashing, hardly aged a day. Not like some I could mention with their big Guinness bellies."

Lennon arose from the couch, Mr. Hyde personified, and

advanced on her in a slow, lecherous shuffle. "How about our big Guinness mickeys, then?"

Ringo sniggered; while George doggedly repeated some bars of "Maria Elena" on the acoustic, coming a cropper on a forgotten major seventh chord.

"Sit down, John Lennon! You're so uncouth."

"Don't try your BBC accent on me, Maureen Cox. I remember when you were just another groupie down the Cavern."

"And you were just another group. Anyway, some of us did try to better ourselves."

"By diddlin' little old ladies out of their pension money?"

He had struck a nerve, and he knew it. Maureen looked around the room for support. Her husband avoided her eyes like the plague.

"I think I hear a car," she said. "Richard, will you check the window."

"You ought to be ashamed of yourself," Lennon persisted.

Unaware that her husband was already in motion, Maureen once more barked her command, this time venomously rolling the R's in his name. "Richard, will you please check the window."

Richard pulled up short. "Ah, go do it yourself. I've a pain in me arse lookin' out the bloody thing."

"Robbin' the poor old dears," Lennon mimicked, encouraged by Ringo's insurrection.

"I give them twenty percent off all perms, and free rinses, and that's good value by anyone's standards."

Lennon snapped to attention and saluted smartly. In his best Admiral Halsey voice, he serenaded her.

God save our gracious Maur
She snips 'eads by the score
Come back for more . . .

"I give good service to my community, and if I do well by it, then more's the better," Maureen haughtily defended herself.

"More strength to your elbow." Lennon slapped Ringo on the back. "Another couple of drinks, and I'll sing high mass for Father George."

Ringo sniggered and rewarded himself with another bottle of beer.

"What are you laughin' at? How come you always side with him, Richard Starkey?"

"Who am I sidin' with? Never said a word, then, did I?"

"Yes, but I know well what you're thinkin'! You should learn which side your bread is buttered on. Any extra money I earn goes for our Zachary's future."

"What'd I say?"

"If I left it up to you, he'd end up runnin' wild in the streets like young Julian."

"There's no call for that kind of talk, Maureen." Her husband's tone was quiet but disapproving. Maureen knew she'd overstepped her bounds.

"Ah, she's right," Lennon said. "Little bastard's probably outside right now, plannin' the final solution."

Maureen wrung her hands. "I'm sorry, John, you know I love him like me own. But he should've stayed put out in Cheshire. I mean, there's no sense nor meanin' to the lad."

"I didn't ask him back," Lennon scowled. "Showed up here on me doorstep, didn't he, then, like a bad penny."

Ringo scooped his finger in the dip and licked it absentmindedly; he twisted his face grotesquely at its bitterness, while saying, "Ah now, John, isn't he only a kid. And you were glad enough to have him when he arrived—you told me so yourself, mate."

Lennon didn't dispute this. In fact, his features softened

and he hid his regret behind the arse end of the bottle he was slugging. *When he was little I didn't have the time then, did I? Always runnin' around from one gig to the next. Then when he came back, he was all grown-up and I thought we could be regular like, go down the pub together, put a few quid on the horses, go shout at Everton or Liverpool on a Saturday. Have a bit of a laugh. What did I know—never had a dad of me own? But our young lad was lookin' for somethin' different, wasn't he, and I didn't have the sense to cop on. And now look at the state of him—like a knife in me guts.*

George had been picking away on the acoustic, the melancholic South American melody providing background to Lennon's regrets. When he became aware of the silence, he put down the guitar. He stretched and then yawned. "He's still generous all the same."

"You must be jokin'!" Lennon said. "The little bastard wouldn't give you the steam off his own piss."

"Paul. Not Julian." George laughed. "Sends a donation to the church fund with his Christmas card every year."

"You mean his secretary does: 'Paul Montana wishes you many more number ones on the hit parade of life,'" Lennon sneered.

"That's the same one we get," Ringo said.

"QE bloody D!"

"Well, I think he's done fab for himself," Maureen challenged them.

"What's he ever done?" Lennon demanded.

"He's done a lot more than some I could mention round here."

"That's enough, Maureen," Ringo said.

"Well, at least he doesn't slick back his hair like you two middle-aged teddy boys. You know, Father George, I have to put grease paper over my Richard's pillowcases. He makes such a mess."

But George provided little comfort for her. He was staring off into space again and didn't even notice her appeal. Lennon strode over and snapped his fingers in the priest's face. George blinked, and Lennon winked broadly at him before rounding on Maureen. "Richard! Richard! The lad's name is Ringo."

"Grow up, John Lennon."

Lennon was about to nail her but was distracted by George, who shook his head violently, then gazed around the room in wonder as if seeing them all for the first time. He strode over to the mantelpiece and stared at the poster for the Cavern. The others watched him squint and hone in on some specific detail. Then he turned around slowly and nodded to himself, obviously having just confirmed something to himself.

"I hear he's been married three times," he said very hesitantly, seeming to try out the words for size.

"That's madness," Maureen said.

"I'd imagine it's a bit confusing all right," the priest agreed, and the others waited, unsure if he was serious. He looked from one to the other and blushed violently. Then he shrugged and began tapping the tops of his fingers together, at first slowly and then gathering speed.

"I mean, you'd hardly have time to get to know one another, then, would you?" Maureen blurted out, unable to take her eyes off George's fingers.

"Maybe that's the idea."

"Speak for yourself, John Lennon. Richard and I have a very caring and mature relationship. Isn't that right, dear?"

"You what, luv?"

"I was remarking on the special nature of our relationship."

"Oh yeah, you can sing that." Ringo sighed with relief at the unimportance of the subject. Then he added, laughing a little too loudly, "The longer you keep the cork in the bottle, the bigger the pop." He slapped George on the back, breaking the rhythm of his fingertips. George folded his hands together and Ringo gave Lennon the thumbs-up—a job well done.

"I sincerely hope that there was no double entendre implied in that remark."

"You imply whatever you like," her husband replied, irked that she hadn't noticed his good deed. He strode over to the table and, with a flourish, opened another beer, though he hadn't finished his last one.

The priest studied them; his eyes were now clear, and sharp hands firmly grasped. *And I thought I was nutty. I should have taken that course in marriage counseling. Get plenty of call for it around here. One left high and dry, the other two as happy as a sack full of wet cats.* "What was the name of his first?" he asked, throwing open the window and taking a deep gulp of Liverpool smog as if his life depended on it. "You know, the 'Boots Are Made for Walkin'' one?"

"Them Sinatras are so common," Maureen sniffed, shivering from the blast of damp air—still upset over Ringo's rebuke. "His second was much nicer."

"I'll say one thing about our Paulie. Never had any trouble gettin' his leg over, then, did he?"

"Do you have to smutify everything?"

"Smutify?" Lennon took a swig and rolled both word and ale around in his mouth. "I don't recall that one in me Concise Oxford English."

"Wasn't a bad-lookin' tart he had on the telly last night."

"Don't act so common, Richard! That tart, as you so crudely choose to call her, is his fiancée, Miss Luanne Luano. Those in the know"—she jutted out her chin to suggest ongoing membership in that rarified circle—"say he just can't wait for his divorce from Cher, so he can tie the knot."

"For Jaysus sake, woman," Lennon exploded, beer and sibilance spraying the room, "he's not comin', and neither is his Yank dolly-bird, Loose Ann, or whatever the hell you call her."

His head still out the window, George called back, "I wouldn't speak too soon, John. Either that's Paul's limo outside or me archbishop is slummin'."

"A fiver it's the archbishop." Lennon said, barely masking his panic.

"Oh, my God, I don't believe this woman."

"Oooh, let me see." Maureen only barely beat Ringo to join George.

Lennon cracked another beer. *What the hell's the matter with me? Waited twenty-five years for this and now me hand's tremblin', knees like rubber, gullet dry as an ash can, and I'm sweatin' like a pig. Well, let him come. What do I care? He's the one that should be on hot pins. I'll soon enough put the bum's rush on the wanker. Nothin' short of a total abject apology is even remotely close to acceptable, and I don't have the least intention of listenin' to a word of his smarmy Yank bullshit.*

"John, get over here, will you." Ringo's voice was urgent. "This bird's got legs all the way up to her arse."

"Richard, you mind your tongue. Oooh, will you look at Paul; he's smashin', ain't he."

"Cor! She's a real knee-trembler—talk about stacked. What do you think, Father George?" Ringo elbowed the priest in the ribs.

"Oh, Lord, give me chastity—but no need to rush."

"Oooh, Father George, you're a one, aren't you?" Maureen smacked him playfully, but then almost choked in dismay. "Oh no, the gate's stuck. John Lennon, you promised you'd fix it."

Lennon elbowed his way into the group. "Kick the bugger, Paulie!" he shouted. "It's just another one of them unoiled gates on the hit parade of life."

"No!" Maureen howled. "She's goin' to tear her stockings on them spikes. Go out and help her this moment, John Lennon."

"I will in my arse," Lennon demurred.

"Richard, I warned you to keep away from them sausages. Now, quickly, luv, go out and give Miss Luano a hand."

"I know the hand I'll give her."

"Richard!"

"Well, what do you want me to do? Pick her up and carry her in on me back?"

Herbie hadn't budged from the car, but Montana and Big Bill had already hurdled the gate and were now urging on a plainly disconcerted Luanne.

"Richard, will you look at your tie." In one swift movement, Maureen tightened his knot, brushed the crumbs from his jacket, and swept the oily kiss-curl back off his forehead. "The state of you! How come you never wear that nice pinstripe I got you for Christmas?"

"'Cause people think I'm the bloody insurance man. They run when they see me comin'."

"Might as well be talkin' to the wall. Now, out you go and welcome our guests."

"What do you think I am? The headwaiter?"

"Well, you can't expect Father George to do it."

"It's his house." He pointed at Lennon.

"You go out and open that door," she hissed, "if you've a mind to have your allowance next week."

This suggestion did little for Ringo's humor. But despite some dark mumbling, he plodded out into the even darker hallway, opened the front door, and must have been all but trampled by the arriving throng—for suddenly, Montana was among them. Beaming and blustering, he swept in, causing shock waves of sheer energy that swept the dust off the knick-knacks on the mantelpiece.

"John! George! Where the hell is Ringo? Jesus H. Christ! Will you take a look at you all."

It was as if the world stopped dead on its axis. They were caught in the headlights, staring, glaring back at him, drinking him up, taking him in; wide, welcoming grins plastered across their faces, masking nervous, anxious eyes. They were so like, and yet so unlike, how he imagined they would be. The ghosts of their youth peered out at him from beneath sunken eyes, lined faces, bulging bellies, veined hands, and hopes long gone astray. Gray now flecked their hair—when it hadn't been artificially banished. None of them had dared, or bothered, to battle the years like he had. And yet, their rare shyness and childlike excitement overcame all his preconceptions and melted his misgivings; he wanted to take them in his arms and never let them go again.

The house was shabby beyond belief. He had grown up in rooms even more humble, but his had been spotless: dusted, polished, and scrubbed with carbolic soap until they gleamed. How could John have descended to this? And why hadn't *he* sent gifts of dollars and made the difference? The ten or twenty grand that he pissed away in a night on the town could have turned this dosshouse into a palace. Or would it? Wouldn't John have mounted his high horse and thrown every last penny back in his face? He tried to find the answer in Lennon's eyes. Hurt, anger, and suspicion leaped right out at him, but they were accompanied by curiosity, affection, and even a gnawing desire to put all the pain behind and start over. Which side would gain the upper hand?

The smell of the room filled him with nostalgia. It was a pungent but familiar mix of burning coal, cigarettes, beer, freshly cut sandwiches, damp carpets, mildewed walls, and memory, all infused with an undying camaraderie and the rock-solid English belief that life must go on. It was home, it was familiar, and he'd been the poorer without it in his air-conditioned, exiled unhappiness.

What was George thinking behind his wry smile? All bruised eyes and marble forehead—his face moody and intense, where once it had rippled with self-assurance. What worlds had he come through in his fling at the God game? There was pity in the priest's face too. Paul could tell it was for him—for what he had become. He shuddered to think of the outsize, buffoonish figure he must be cutting in these modest surroundings?

And with that, the moment passed. Frantically, he searched John's eyes. The two competing emotions were lining up; brotherly love was going head to toe against anger and suspicion. As usual, it was no contest.

He knew what he had to do. He couldn't bear to be lacerated in these first moments of his arrival. He needed time to shield himself—to find out how to fit in. And so he pounced on his old friend and plastered him with a gigantic, gob-smacking kiss. As they spun around the room like twin cyclones, Lennon was forced to clutch on for fear they'd tumble over and break their collective arses. Paul dug his face in Lennon's shoulder so that he couldn't see the real hurt that was sheltering just behind the Vegas glitz.

When he had regained his balance, Lennon caustically inquired, "How are they hangin', mate? How are the balls of your Texan toes?"

"Mate! Mate! I ain't been called mate in twenty-five years."

The mask was back in place. "You're breakin' my heart, John. You're breakin' my goddamn heart."

"Wouldn't want to do that, mate."

"There you go again. 'Mate.' What a blast!"

Lennon tried to focus on the blurred pulsating vision before him. He couldn't remember what he had expected: perhaps a bit of humility, some slight acknowledgment of guilt, anything of that nature would have sufficed; but instead, Paul seemed bigger, full of shit and confidence, ripe for pulling down and putting in his place. Lennon, too, needed time, and the accompanying hullabaloo covered up his disorientation. Though Luanne was something to behold, he couldn't tear his eyes off Big Bill, who had already cased the windows and was now down on his knees, burrowing behind the sofa.

"What's he do?" He pointed at the bodyguard's swaying rump.

"What's he do?" Montana jumped at the bait and replied in tones that would suggest that the very stones on the street could provide such an obvious answer.

"Yeah, I mean, he's crawlin' around me bloody floor?"

"He gives his blood for me. That's what he does—twenty-four goddamned seven! Hey, Bill, this is the guy I've been tellin' you about."

"No way!" Big Bill jumped up, but he had obviously been expecting someone of more Olympian stature, for his face dropped a yard. "The psycho dude with the toilet seat?"

Montana nodded and pulled them together.

"Oh, man, I pissed in my pants when he told me that one." Big Bill bear-hugged Lennon, squeezing mightily on his bruised ribs. Lennon screamed from the pain as he was effortlessly uprooted from the floor. The bodyguard then wrestled him to the ground before roaring, "You are the man, Johnny! You are the goddamned man!"

Truly fearful now of any more American affection, Lennon gingerly picked himself up. But Big Bill had already taken off after Montana, who was zeroing in on a vaguely familiar face. Furrowing his brow, Montana inquired disbelievingly, "Maureen?" as if the Blessed Virgin herself had materialized and was demanding the pleasure of a fox-trot. "Maureen Cox! Waaagghhh!" He plunged forward and swung her off her feet.

Maureen squealed in girlish abandon, vainly attempting to keep her dress below her waist. He plopped her back on terra firma with less pomp than circumstance, and she staggered as he spun her madly across the room.

"Oh, Paul, I'm scarlet!" She gasped for air.

"Let me take a look at you!" He pulled her back into his arms and purred Don Juan-like: "I tell you, babe, if Ringo hadn't spotted you first down the Cavern."

"Oh, Paul, you shouldn't try and turn an old married lady's head."

"Old married lady, my ass. You look better than a Jack LaLanne ad." He dispatched her on her puzzled way. "Will you get a load of George—and is that Ringo? Where the hell have you been, man?"

"I tried to say hello, mate, but you slammed the door in me face—nearly put me through the friggin' wall."

"Sorry, Rings, it's all such a goddamned rush. Jesus, you guys look great." He lied. "What's your secret? You both usin' the same embalmer?"

"Yeah, Paul," George drolly replied. "Two can die cheaper than one."

"Did you hear that, honey?"

But "honey," already furious at the lack of attention, glowered from the doorway like a constipated Venus—her vision of sipping bourbon around a roaring log fire having taken a hammering.

"Oh, Jesus, *pardonez-moi*. I know, I know, I promised, but it's the excitement. Hey, everybody, this is the light of my life, Miss Luanne Luano."

"It's about time, Paulie, the poor girl's been standin' there like a spare prick at a weddin'." Lennon's voice was tinged with sarcasm.

At no extra charge, Luanne included him in her withering sights and added in vitriolic treacle, "Soon to be the new Mrs. Paul Montana."

"Oooh," sighed Maureen, "it's all so romantic."

Montana took Luanne in his arms, rammed into her five-hundred-carat body, and whispered wrathfully, "Lighten up, will ya," before ramming his tongue halfway down her tonsils.

Luanne sucked in and speared him mercilessly with her eye-teeth. She held on while his knees buckled, and his eyes turned glassy.

"Oh, Richard, aren't they gorgeous?" Maureen cooed. The three men gawked on in envious speculation.

When Luanne finally let go, Montana stumbled backward. He felt faint and wanted to take a swing at her, but she beamed back at him, everything at least temporarily forgiven. "Hello everyone. I know every eensy, weensy thing about you all." Without wasting a breath, she descended on Ringo, laid a big buss on his cheek, and cried out, "John!"

Ringo wafted in the fragrance of her opiated perfume and, for one luscious instant, imagined himself balls-deep inside her.

"Ringo!" she squealed, and Lennon ducked a continental double kiss while still managing an exhaustive eye-level inspection of her décolletage before she made a beeline for the reverend.

"George," she marveled with a Lauren Bacall growl, to which he drolly replied, "Bingo."

"Hey, where's Cyn?" Montana inquired.

"Oh, she ran off with the milkman." Lennon grinned.

"She ran off with the goddamn milkman! Jesus Christ on a bike, you haven't lost it, Johnny."

"That's not what she said."

"Hey, what happened to your face, man?"

"Oh, I wouldn't give a bloke me autograph, so he kicked the shit out of me."

"Ah, John, John, I have cried at night for that sense of humor." Montana threw his arm around Luanne's shoulder and dragged her within inches of Lennon. She involuntarily inhaled his sweet and sour bouquet of fags, beer, postponement of last Saturday's bath, and a surfeit of late nights and pissed-upon hopes.

"Honey," Montana gravely announced, "this is John Winston Lennon."

"I thought you said you were Ringo?"

"In another lifetime I was, luv. Then I got reincarnated as a cockroach, though some people call me a Beatle."

"Huh?"

"You'd have to read the book, I suppose."

"Well, what do you think of him?" Montana hastily interrupted.

"Honestly?" She sniffed, certain that the milkman must have smelled like roses compared to this whacked-out bum.

Montana threw her the most discreet of karate chops—his invitation to desist with this line of thought unless she wanted her pink slip, and he wasn't talking lingerie.

"What sign are you, hon?" she inquired.

"The sign of the cross, luv." Lennon stretched out his arms and scrunched up his face in anguish.

"Hey, they don't make 'em like John in L.A. Dig this, babe." Montana skidded away, leaving Luanne to confront Christ crucified in a Liverpool sitting room. "Reverend George! Holy shit, I never thought I'd see the day. And a Jesuit too! Ain't that the elite corps? The storm troopers?"

"That's us all right, mate," George said. "The spiked fist of Jesus."

"I tell you, kid, many are called but few are chosen."

"Or as me novice master used to say: Many are thawed but few are frozen," George gravely confided.

"Say what?" Montana didn't even pause to decipher this riddle. He could feel Lennon's eyes on him, sizing him up—finding his measure. He felt like he was being bounced around the room like a beach ball on a windy day in Blackpool, but he was unable to stop himself. "Hey, my main man, Rings! At least, you haven't changed, right?"

It was Ringo's moment. He swaggered toward Montana but, like a bat out of hell, Big Bill rose from his haunches and whisked his boss out of harm's way.

At first, Montana didn't appear to understand the bodyguard's whispered concern, but then he burst out laughing. "That ain't no pimp. Ringo always dresses like that. Luanne, baby," he cooed. But his nearest and dearest was displaying her engagement ring to Maureen.

"Luanne," he repeated, an edge creeping into his voice, "I'm talkin' to you." Luanne, however, was now in the midst of a talmudic dissertation on her nuptial plans.

"Get your goddamned butt over here!" Montana bellowed, and the Liverpool contingent rose from the floor into petrified orbit.

"I'm comin'. I'm comin'. I was just tryin' to be sociable." Luanne came rushing over.

"I want you to meet Richard 'Ringo' Starkey," Montana continued pleasantly.

"Gee, what should I call you?" she inquired breathlessly.

"Call me anything you like, luv, as long as it's not too early in the morning," Ringo replied, relishing the flush on her cheeks while mentally unhooking her bra.

Montana slapped him on the back, causing a loud burp. "You hear that? These guys should be on Carson! Ah, Rings baby, you don't know how many times I wished I had you behind me instead of Krupa or one of them other hotshots."

"Have drum will travel, Paul. I'll give you me number before you go."

"Good old Rings. Four kicks on the floor, a wallop on the snare, and never a roll unless you send out an invoice for one." He thrust him back at arm's length and studied the many and varied ravines on the drummer's face. "What are you doin' these days, bro?"

"Still playin' me skins, Paulie. You know me, a basher to the end."

"Hey, you got a combo of your own now?"

"Nah, it's not worth the hassle, is it, then?"

"You don't know the half of it, pal. Keepin' a good orchestra on the road these days is one large-size pain. Musicians even want health plans now, can you believe it?"

Ringo wasn't at all sure on that issue, but he stated, not without a hint of pride, "I'm playin' with the Pacemakers now."

"Gerry and the Pacemakers?"

"Yeah, and Johnny's been subbin' with us since Gerry got the hernia."

"You gotta watch them hernias, pal. Exercise, calisthenics, that's the name of the game for guys our age." He demonstrated a couple of sharp L.A. gym moves. Ringo stared blankly back—his idea of a workout limited to the bending of his elbow down the pub.

"Jeez, Gerry and the Pacemakers, our big rivals." Montana took to the floor, threw his arms wide, and, with a big band pounding in his head, gave them the full blast of what made him almost the Man in Vegas. "How do you do what you do to me," he crooned. "That was a good toon."

"You didn't think it was so hot when Parlophone tried shovin' it down our throats." Lennon had heard enough. He flicked open a bottle of beer and a can of worms simultaneously.

"Say what?" Montana replied, his eyeballs almost touching his hairline, a study of incomprehension. But he'd gained the time he needed; he was just about ready.

"You know right well what I'm talkin' about."

"That was a long time ago, John, a long, long time ago."

"Not so long, I don't remember!"

Montana held his glare. He'd dealt with the mob, the feds, and every smart-arsed critic in America. When it came to down and dirty, he was there with the best of them. "Listen, mate." His tone was cold and diamond hard, and it blew through the room like a steel breeze. "We got some shit to work through, okay? But just get one thing clear." He moved forward an aggressive step, and all the Vegas glitz dropped off him like confetti. "I didn't come back here to be anyone's whippin' boy."

"What did you come here for, then?" Lennon asked, not backing off an inch.

Montana now took *his* measure. This was the Lennon he remembered, and they were picking up just where they'd left off. He could blow the whole thing through the ceiling, see where the pieces dropped, pick them up, and put them back together again. But he could sense the general embarrassment and see the heartbreak in Maureen's eyes.

He took all the time in the world, and made each word count. "We'll get around to that later, Johnny—much later."

Chapter Sixteen

HERBIE SHIVERED IN THE LIMO. He could see out, but the bastards couldn't see in. Up the block, an overturned car was burning. The flames cast a shadowy, delayed light on a band of drunken Fronters squinting in through the blackened limo windows. A couple of them laughed hideously and shook the car.

Stop that, you motherfuckers! Oh man, if I'd only brought my piece, I'd put holes in all of 'em. See how they feel about that! What are we doin' over here anyway? Move more units in Iowa. Show some respect, you pricks, quit rockin' my stretch!

As if they'd been party to his mental discourse, the Fronters turned as one and took off down the street in the direction of the burning car. A couple of stragglers on their way home from work saw them coming and rushed for the safety of their semidetacheds. There was something afoot—a new threat hung in the air. The shenanigans didn't usually start until later in the night. These streets were no place to be—the Front unconditionally owned them.

What is it with these people, and what's that Leader dude up to anyway? Drivin' 'em all stark ravin' round the bend. I mean, what's his angle? He's got a good thing goin' just bein' what he is. Man, the endorsements I could get for his ass. Lease a Lear, hop over to

D.C., breakfast with Spiro, lay wreaths at the Iranian wall, meet the press, then up to the Apple, lunch with the media, drinks with the Saatchis, dinner with corpos, tape the Sundays, get down with Letterman, and back to London before the milk is delivered. Hit the system hard and fast but keep the man's ass under wraps. Instead, what's his act? Tryin' to take over this fleabag country? I mean, what's that all about? Gettin' a crowd of screwy kids to burn the joint down?

Up the block, the gas tank ignited, and the car went up in a sheet of blue and orange flames, illuminating the seedy council estate. The Fronters scurried to all sides before resuming their drunken dance around the smoldering remains. No police siren, no fire engine—just a damp blanketing silence broken only by the shouts of the Fronters and the crackle of flames.

Burn, baby, burn! I'd pour gasoline all over this shithouse if I could get outa here one minute faster. But it literally pains me to see such a platinum opportunity go up in smoke. 'Cause that Leader guy's got it in spades—charisma, star quality—whatever you wanta call it.

But it's always the same. The ones that got it are assholes, just like Montana, self-destructive, psychotic pains in the butt. I have personally watched that guy go through three separate fortunes, and why? Because he can't keep his dick in his pants! Don't get me wrong, I like a piece of tail as much as the next guy. Who don't? But when your dick starts fuckin' with your bank balance, then it's time you put a muzzle on it. Get it back in its kennel, lock the door, throw away the key.

But it ain't just their dick, is it? No way! They all got some kind of issue eatin' away at 'em. Somethin' that happened way back that they can't get out of their ugly little minds, and it gnaws away at them till it bores a hole right through their little peanut hearts, and then the shit hits the fan and there ain't nothin' no one can do

*about it. If I said it once, I said it a thousand times. Talent is wasted
on assholes. Oh no! Here they come again.*

Montana, aided by a couple of slugs of top-shelf bourbon
from his hip flask, had mellowed somewhat. A warm glow
of nostalgia enveloped him as he looked around the room.
What had previously seemed dingy now was homely. Even
the ducks on the hallway wall had their appointed place in
the grand scheme of things and did not appear as eager to
be gone the hell out the front door. Though no roaring log
fire, the banked glowing coals had taken some of the chill
and dampness from the air.

Maureen was showing some family pictures to a bored-out-
of-her-skull-but-enduring-it-for-the-sake-of-her-man Luanne.
Lennon, too, had backed off somewhat and was reclining
ungraciously across the length of the couch, balancing a pint
of bitter on his chest. George had retreated back into his
thoughts, Ringo into his cups, while Big Bill, after the explosion outside, kept a gimlet eye on the street and the limo.

Montana leaned back against the mantelpiece, warmed his
arse on the fire, and wiped a trickle of booze from his lip. Cynthia's divorce had shaken him a little, but in the light of things,
what could you expect? Vegas, Liverpool, it didn't seem to
matter: love and permanence seemed to be out of sorts with
each other. Still, it could be a lot worse. He tightened the cap
on his flask and sighed contentedly. *This is more like it. The way
it should be. A bunch of old friends knockin' back a few, shootin' the
shit, lettin' our hair down. Sure we got some issues to get through,
who doesn't; but these are my buddies and I want to do the right
thing by them. Now all we've got to do is let the flow grow and when
the iron's nice and hot, I'll get down to business.*

"Hey, Paulie," said Ringo out of the blue. "We're giggin' down the Horse and Jockey tomorrow night. You could sit in, you know."

"That would be fantastic, Rings, just fantastic."

Luanne snapped the family album closed. "But, Paulie-pie, you promised."

"What's that?"

"You know." The pout trembled on her lips, like Mount Vesuvius before an awakening.

"Ah shit! The Queen and her dinner party!"

"Queen Diana?" Maureen snapped to attention like a setter whiffing a pheasant.

"Yeah, we're workin' on a little charity show," Montana wearily conceded.

"Queen Di?" Maureen was overwhelmed.

"She has got all of Paul's records. And we're goin' to ask her to come stay with us in Vegas, aren't we, sweet thing?"

"Yeah, yeah, sure we are, sure we are." Montana downed another slug of bourbon, then sprang to his feet and said: "Ah, Jesus, this place brings back so many memories."

"Like what, Paul?" Maureen was all ears.

"Well, like old Pete Best."

"Not him again," Ringo moaned.

Montana slipped on his shades and hunched across the room. "Remember when he used to do his Jimmy Dean?"

"Jimmy Dean was from Liverpool?" Luanne was stunned.

This time the karate chop was plain for all to see, aided by a hissed aside: "Are you tryin' to make a total idiot out of me?"

But before she could answer, George pushed back his chair and rose to his feet. "That was the best move we ever made," he said.

The others looked around, surprised at the edge in his

voice. He drained the dregs of his sherry and added for good measure: "Gettin' rid of that wanker."

"Oh, I don't know. He was a decent enough guy, old Pete," Montana said.

"You don't have to live around him," Ringo replied. "I was the most popular Beatle," he mimicked before turning to Lennon. "Remember that night I sorted him out?"

"Yeah, he's nothin' but a bollocks! Pity we didn't fire Epstein at the same time."

"Eppy did his best for us," Montana declared icily.

"Did his best for you."

Montana was stung; he eyed Lennon from across the room. Lennon accepted the challenge and stared back unblinkingly. Montana unscrewed the cap of his flask. He realized he was drinking too fast, but had another snort anyway.

"Well, I for one don't want to spend the whole evening talking about the group," said Maureen hastily. She offered the plate of sausages to George, who gazed upon it as if beholding the miracle of the loaves and fishes. "It always ends up the same. Besides"—she jabbed the plate to within inches of Luanne's face—"we don't want to give Ms. Luano the wrong impression, do we?"

Luanne ducked and countered with her own uppercut of sweetness. "Oh, Luanne to you, honey. And even after I become the new Mrs. Paul Montana, I'll still be Luanne to those who knew me when."

"Oooh, thank you, Luanne!" Maureen savored the sound of the strange name. It rolled off her lips in a cascade of consonants, and she gushed on, now in full flight after this sisterly affirmation. "Anyway, I don't know what all the fuss is about. I mean, we were all just children back then, and now we've all grown up and have families of our own to support." She looked around serenely at either blank or hostile faces. "Well, I was a fan too, but life goes on, doesn't it?"

"You said it, Maur." Montana bounced across the room on the balls of his toes, skipping to a beat only he could hear. He pirouetted to the middle of the floor, opened flask still in hand, and let fly with his happiest hit:

Oh, la la, oh la la
Life is fun, oh oh
Oh la la la la la la. Hey!

His arms reached for the stars demanding a crescendo, then he cut the invisible orchestra dead in a grand finale, simultaneously launching his drink across the room and spraying Ringo and George.

"For Christ sake!" Ringo was thoroughly pissed off. It was one thing for the Fronters to muck up his clobber, quite another for some Yank wanker, be he old friend or foe.

George flicked his tongue out at a drop of bourbon on his upper lip and savored the exotic taste.

"Good for you, Paul! I do love that song." Maureen searched for a superlative. "It's so . . . gear."

"Sounds more like automatic to me," said Lennon.

The smile drained from Montana's face when he inquired, "You writin' yourself, bro?"

"Yeah. But I'm so far ahead of meself, me arse is passin' me elbow."

"You don't do nothin' of your own with the Pacemakers?"

"They only want to hear 'Love Me Do,' and you wrote most of that."

Damn right I did, and don't you never forget it. Your one fleeting brush with fame was on the back of my tune. And when I sang it, the birds screamed so loud, it used to turn you puke green with jealousy.

"Hey, I bet you got some nuggets salted away." He smiled, the epitome of graciousness. "C'mon, let's hear one, for the hell of it."

Lennon turned his back—a mixture of panic and contempt.

"That was a good one you were singin' in the toilet yesterday," Ringo said.

"It's not finished."

"You were in there long enough."

Lennon wouldn't budge. But Montana's blood was up. "C'mon, I'm dyin' to hear what you been up to. You don't know how many times I've told Phillie Spector about you."

"Phil Spector?" Lennon could barely conceal the awe.

"Yeah, the whole of goddamn Hollywood knows about you. I never shut up about him, do I, babe?"

Lennon couldn't help it. He dropped his guard and looked to Luanne's blank face for confirmation. She stared dumbly back, and he knew it was all bullshit. He was about to tell the two of them to go fuck a duck all the way back to Las Vegas, when George whispered, "Go on, mate, you show him."

He stared at the priest in surprise. *Jesus, will you look at him— out of his shell and eyes sharp as hacksaws. There's somethin' bangin' around in the old gray matter after all.*

Lennon picked up the guitar and strummed gently, trawling his memory for words. But all that surfaced was an old accordion line he'd once heard seeping out the door of an Irish pub. With a little nudge and a shake, the melody sat right nicely atop his chordal intro. He whistled it a number of times and then dived right in—the hell with the words, the world, and its consequences.

And I walk down the lane with me head in the clouds
Me brains may be scrambled but I don't heed the crowds
With their football and pools, their weddin's and wakes

Their political goals and their kids' birthday cakes
So I shout at the rooftops and I scream at the breeze
Hey, you out there
Can you hear me Liverpool Fantasy

He whistled the intro again but made the mistake of opening his eyes. Luanne's face was scrunched up in a what-the-hell-is-he-on-about grimace, while Montana was blue in the face from delivering long distance karate chops.

Oh, screw 'em all! This is for you, Georgie. Welcome back to the real world, brother. It may be bitter, bleak, and a right old pain in the arse, but it's a damn sight better than the nevermore you've just come out of!

He spat out the next verse.

And I look at the dawn through the Everton rain
The whole city is snorin' just the milk bottles wait
To be taken and washed and filled up and then
I wish they'd take me and remake me again
So I shout at the chimneys and I scream at the priest
Hey, you out there
Can you hear me Liverpool Fantasy

And I'm sick of the dole and I'm sick of me life
I'm sick of your promises and I'm sick of me wife
And I'm sick of your pity and I'm sick of bein' fired
And I'm sick and tired of bein' sick and tired

And I walk down the lane with me head in the clouds
Me brains may be scrambled but I don't heed the crowd
With their football and pools—

Clink! Maureen hit a bottle with her sherry glass. It wasn't very loud, but it broke him into a million pieces.

"Ah, shit!" He was furious with himself and flung the guitar to the ground. It landed with a crash. The strings resounded and carried for a long time, finally disappearing into the hush that enveloped the room.

Montana felt for Lennon. He really did. This was no threat. This was his brother mired in time, not knowing where he's going, what he's up to. He jumped to his feet and slapped him on the back. He wanted to hug him and hold him and tell him it was okay. We all have these days, suffer through these moments. But when Lennon bristled, he backed off, afraid of giving more offense. "Yeah, John, it's eh . . . yeah, I mean you jazz it up a bit—add a few oohs and aahs in the right spots. You know, I got these three chick belters back in Vegas. They could turn it the hell right around. Make it swing, man, black it up a bit, give it some soul. Yeah, it's eh . . ."

His voice trailed off. *I mean, what can you say? It's like a bloody folk song. The guy's gone backwards instead of movin' with the times. The tune itself is pretty enough, but milk bottles and birthday cakes, I ask you? I mean, who the hell's interested in that kind of crap? Was a nice tune though. Maybe I should strip the whole band down, give 'em all a break for fifteen, just get out there with an acoustic and give it my everything straight from the heart. Yeah, I've got to make a note of that. Give it a shot some matinee. Be different—set me apart from Newton or Blue Eyes or any of the rest of them.*

Maureen pursed her lips and swept crumbs—real and imaginary—from the table. It wasn't a bad song, and she hadn't meant to clink her glass. Still, these things happened. "Well, at least it's better than that thing about the walruses you sang at the Revival Show."

"Yeah," Ringo said. "That was the one that gave Gerry the hernia."

"What does Marsden know about music?" Lennon sneered.

"More than he knows about walruses." George smiled at Lennon.

"What the hell do you know? Sittin' on your arse out in Cheshire, recitin' the rosary?"

"At least I know what I don't know, which is more than I can say for you!" George slashed back, his eyes popping with intensity.

Lennon was stunned. Then a grin broke across his bruised face.

The priest scowled back, and without taking his eyes off Lennon he picked up the acoustic from the floor and ripped off the opening eight bars of "Johnny B. Goode."

Lennon nodded. The padre was definitely on *his* way home.

Blissfully unaware of any such odyssey, Luanne smiled into her compact and touched up her lips. "Paulie-pie," she cooed. "It's gettin' late, doll."

"What are you talkin' about? We just got here," Montana said.

"We've still got our meditation to do."

"Ah, will you give me a break! I've had it up to here with sittin' on me arse, starin' at a bloody wall." He dismissed her and winked broadly at the others. "What do you think, Ringo?"

"What's that, mate?"

"Pay someone fifty bucks to go in and stare at their wall for an hour?"

"He does it all day when he's got a hangover. Lyin' there in bed, the tongue hangin' out of him. . . ."

"Yeah, but it's me own wall and I don't pay fifty pounds to look at it."

"Hey, Rings, what was that ferry thing that Gerry was always on about? 'Cross the Mersey' or somethin'? Boy, that was a cute tune."

The spicy sausages were beginning to gnaw at Ringo's stomach. A wave of gloom and indigestion washed over him. There'd be a lot of wall to stare at the next day. He stretched back on the stuffingless couch, awaiting his second wind, and burped: "Would have been a hit if the record company hadn't dumped him."

"You should cover it, Paul." They were again startled by George's exuberance. "Be good for Gerry . . . wouldn't hurt you none either, mate."

"Get the hell outa here! American kids could care less about the Mersey. Now, if old Gerry had the smarts to call it 'Ferry Across the Hudson' or 'Ferry Across the Mississippi' or even the goddamned Staten Island ferry, for Christ sakes."

"It wouldn't fit," Ringo muttered above the rumblings from his stomach.

"What wouldn't fit?"

"Ferry across the Shetland Island."

"It don't rhyme neither," George threw in for good luck.

"Hey, lighten up, will ya? I know you guys think this is the center of the universe, but back in the States, Liverpool don't mean doodley-squat."

"I thought he was sayin' Liverwurst for the longest time," Luanne said.

Montana seared her with a look. "You see." He gathered himself and frowned. "You gotta go beyond the micro and think macro."

"What's that," Lennon sneered. "A bigger kind of oven?"

Montana turned to Maureen and gave her a full blast of his pearly whites. "You know, that was one of the first things Ol' Blue Eyes said to me." He dropped to one knee and gazed into her fawning eyes. "Strangers in the night," he crooned, giving her the full Frankie.

"Oooh, Paul, you're such a one," Maureen gushed.

"Montana," he mimicked his former father-in-law, "you limeys make a good steak and kidney pie, but you don't got nothin' in the pipes department, 'cept maybe for yourself or Tommy Jones on a good night. And it's true, John. What else have we produced? Cliff Richard? Olivia Newton-John? I mean, forget about it!"

"That's 'cause you and Olivia Neutron Bomb and all the others are a crowd of bloody Yankophiles. You're not bein' yourselves, then, are you? But the Beatles, Paul! We took Chuck Berry and turned him on his black arse, then, didn't we? Come up with somethin' real and Liverpudlian-like."

"Nah, the time wasn't right, John. But there's been a change in the climate lately, and that got me thinkin' about the old days, which—" He paused to let his words sink in and prepare them. "Which brings me to the reason I came."

"Oh, Richie," sighed Maureen. "Don't you just love his accent? Speak some more, Paul."

Lennon rounded on her. "Will you hold your kisser. He sounds like John bloody Wayne. You shouldn't be ashamed of who you are, Paul. We're your mates, remember?"

"Yeah, I remember, but America's been good to me and I've done my bit for it and for the free world, which includes you."

Lennon snapped to attention and in his thickest scouse let fly: "'Oh, say can you see by the dawn's early light . . .'"

"That's not funny, pal. I've been to Iran four times to entertain the troops. I've been commended by three presidents, and if I've got an accent, so what?"

And still Lennon persisted in ripping apart the sacred anthem.

"Shut up!" Montana roared. "I've had enough of your shit.

The fact is, I went away and made somethin' of myself. I've been in the arena; man, what the hell have you been doin'—sittin' on your fat arse up here in Liverpool."

"I've been keepin' the faith."

"Whose faith? Your own? That was always your problem. Johnny knows best, and fuck the begrudgers!" He shook his head in abject remorse. "I'm sorry, ladies."

Luanne poured him a glass of water.

"He's so sensitive," Maureen marveled.

"He is so in touch with his feelings since he started primal therapy," Luanne confided.

Montana almost choked on the water. "Jesus, John," he sighed, tearing his dagger eyes away from Luanne's puzzled stare. "No one asked you to sell out—just give and take a bit."

"You mean give and fake a bit, don't you?"

"No, I don't! I've taken the world as I've seen it, and I've done the best I can."

"And I suppose I haven't?" Lennon kicked back his chair and fumbled for another cigarette.

"Look at you! Just look at you! You had so much talent."

"Present tense, mate—have. I didn't waste it on a crowd of dickheads," Lennon spat out, striking a match on the sole of his boot.

"You missed out on so much."

"Like what?"

"You'll never know, will you?"

"I do know!" Lennon yelled as the flame burned down to his fingers. He lit the cigarette and tossed the still-flaring match on the floor.

"Well, why don't you let us all in on the big secret, then?" Montana's lips curled with the trace of a sneer, but he was immediately sorry. "Ah shit, what am I goin' on about? I didn't come here to fight. All I know is, *you* could have been doin' duets with Lionel Richie."

"Listen, head." Lennon ground the match under his heel; then he took a long, comforting drag from his cigarette. "If I was goin' to sing with a spade, it'd be the real thing—a Sam Cooke or an Otis Redding, not some fuzzy-wuzzy puppet on a string."

Montana stood up and very deliberately pushed his chair back under the table. "Just get one thing clear." He etched out his words so that there should be no misunderstanding. "I don't stand for racial slurs in my company. Now, I understand you've got your problems over here, but I treat that race with respect."

"And I don't?" Lennon said very quietly. He pulled his shirt up from his pants and pointed to an ugly discoloration on his back. "I got that from the Front for stickin' up for a black man they were kickin' the shit out of. Is that enough, or do you want to see more?"

Lennon tucked his shirt back in. But he was shaking. When he spoke again, his voice cracked with suppressed anger. "I may not always use the right words, but I have a stupid habit of doin' the right thing. What have you done lately for the real American people, mate?"

"We had Bill Cosby over for dinner last week," Luanne said.

"Would you ever shut up!" Montana hissed.

"Are you by any chance addressing me?" For once, she was all a frozen stillness.

"No, I'm talkin' to the bloody wall."

"You had better be, mister. Because I can scream too, and I know a lot of things you wouldn't want your precious friends to hear."

"You're just like all the rest of them, aren't you, tryin' to manipulate me?"

"No, baby, I'm not. You know how much I care for you. Let's go, this place is not good for you."

"You don't know anything about me."

"I mean, these people are weird."

"Don't you dare insult my friends."

"Well, look at them," she shrieked. "You want to get back to your roots, don't go showin' this bunch of bums on TV. People'll think you come from the Bowery."

"Shut the fuck up!"

She wilted for an instant, the hurt creasing her face, then she came back swinging. "I've had enough of you. You're crazy, and everyone in Vegas knows it. So you stay here with your friends, 'cause no one's gonna miss you."

She stormed from the room and out the front door. Lennon rushed to the window and yelled after her. "That gate doesn't work, luv. That's right. Put your foot on the dustbin and jump."

There was a loud crash. Lennon whistled in awe. "Jesus Christ, Ringo! She's not wearin' any knickers."

Ringo rushed for the window but was halted in midflight by Maureen's scowl. He shifted uneasily from foot to foot, testosterone and marital caution battling for supremacy. The latter prevailed. "What's the Bowery?" he queried meekly.

"Don't mind her! She's always talkin' through her bloody arse." Montana downed a vicious slug of bourbon.

"Shouldn't we go after her?" Maureen said. "I mean, it's not very safe out there."

"Don't waste your time. Her type always lands on its feet."

"She made it." Lennon closed the curtain.

"She'll just crawl into the limo and sulk for a couple of hours with the other guy. The true comforts of home," Montana said bitterly.

For some reason, the room seemed cleansed, the circle smaller. Maureen could feel a barrier going up around the four of them. She wanted to reach out and hold on to Ringo, but instead found herself drifting back to the kitchen wall.

As the silence gathered, George finally articulated what was on everyone's mind. "What are you doin' here, mate?"

Montana sat down at the table and plopped his head between his hands. "Oh, man, I'm drownin'."

"What's the matter with you?" Ringo asked.

"I'm up to my neck in shit."

"I'm right there alongside you, brother." George collapsed on the couch.

"Twenty-five years out there in America, and they still don't know what I'm talkin' about. . . . Sometimes I don't even know meself."

Maureen edged over to him and laid her hand on his shoulder. "It's okay, Paul. You're back among your own now."

He reached up for her hand. "Thanks, Maur." He almost broke down when she hugged him. Her warmth gave him strength. "Listen, lads, you trust me?"

The silence suggested the jury was out, but he was too far gone to turn back. "I want us all to go back to Vegas and do a set of rock & roll that'll blow their socks off—Chuck Berry, Gene Vincent, Buddy Holly. . . ."

"Are you serious?" Lennon asked.

"I want us to show them where I come from. Show them the real me."

"Like you used to be?" Ringo asked.

"Yeah, just like the old days."

"Like back in Hamburg?" George said.

"Yeah, like nothin' ever happened."

"Just the four of us?"

"You got it, Rings. I want to bring us back together. Get you guys the hell out of here. Make you all a few bucks for a change." He jumped to his feet. "Don't you hear what I'm sayin', lads? I want to bring back the Beatles."

Ringo straightened up from his perpetual slouch. He tightened the knot on his tie, and looked his wife in the eye for the first time in years. "Do you hear that, Maur? I won't be bummin' off you no more. We're goin' to play again."

"Oh, Richie," she replied apprehensively.

George clenched his fist, pumped it in the air, and said, "The Beatles!"

Chapter Seventeen

"GODDAMN SON OF A SELFISH BITCH!" Luanne screeched as her bare bottom hit the damp Liverpool pavement. She yanked her dress down and clambered back atop her heels. *I've had it up to here with him and his psychoses. A wedding ring is one thing, living full-time with a lunatic another. I'm young—well, young enough. I've got looks, brains—despite what he thinks—and men come a-calling. I could have my pick of the litter, and what do I do? Waste my life baby-sitting this psychopathic son of a selfish bitch.*

Doubt, however, would not leave her be. Little pincers of apprehension tore away at her defiance. She considered going back inside, but instead she brushed the Liverpool muck off her stockings and surveyed her surroundings.

"A dungeon horrible on all sides round . . ." She recalled the words a Limey john had made her repeat while she laid a whipping on him back in her bad old days. But a whispered order brought her suddenly back to Earth, if not reality: "Get in the stretch if you don't want your ass kicked!"

She spun to find the tip of Herbie's nose protruding through the cracked window.

"Fuck you!" she declined. While she might entertain reservations about Montana's sanity, his manager was a certified weirdo. The working girls on the Strip had left her in no doubt about Herbie's sexual preferences.

"Get in the stretch, you dumb bitch, if you know what's good for you!"

"Good for me? I wouldn't tie you up with my garter belt, wear a Nazi helmet, and sit on your face if you gave me a million bucks!" she heatedly informed him.

The window shot up with wounded alacrity, and she was left alone with her thoughts. *Well, maybe for a million, but not a red cent less.*

She turned on her heel and clickety-clacked down the street past the smoldering car and some grime-streaked children who were doing a Maypole around it. *Get a little fresh air, clean my lungs out good and proper. And replace it with what? Jesus Christ, does this whole country stink? It's almost as bad as New York, everyone and his mother smokes and blows it right in your face, like they never heard of germs or invading your personal space.*

And as for these chimneys, belching out putrid fumes of God knows what. Talk about saving the environment. Jeezus! Ain't no one over here heard about central heating? It was freezing in that goddamn house. I tell you one thing, that's the last time I'm doing a baresy. I don't care how much it turns him on. Those never-know-when-the-urge-will-come-on-me-puppy-dog eyes! Well, he can go and call himself a hooker the next time that particular notion strikes. Bet none of his old English girlfriends obliged him like that. More likely they wore woolen drawers to keep their flabby butts warm.

Luanne glanced back down the street and could almost feel the ugly vibrations emanating from the stretch. She hurried round the corner to shield herself from Howie's psychic onslaught. At once, the silence gripped her. It wasn't even a silence. More like the stillness when you hold your breath and are afraid to exhale for fear of missing that awful something you thought you heard.

But it was definitely there, menacing and lurking behind the gloom of the shadows, and so close she could have reached out and touched it; instead she moved away, down the darkened street. The ghostly blue tube-lights of television sets glowed from the rows of houses, and she was suddenly very afraid.

She stopped dead in her tracks, frozen with indecision. The fog deepened again; but at times, a shallow breeze would whisk it away, allowing corridors of vision to lighted windows. Then it would solidify, swirling around her ankles, turning hedges and pillars into ominous amorphous shapes. Her hearing seemed to have heightened: She could discern the rumble of trucks some miles away or the random shouts of rioters in other parts of the cities; but close by, every sound seemed muted, as if she were surrounded by a giant damp eiderdown. The city seemed to be waiting for the Front's next move, while something, or somebody, awaited hers.

When the first coin landed at her feet, she almost jumped out of her skin. It didn't have the reassuring ping of a dime or a quarter. No, this was something heavier, foreign, and dull.

She wheeled around on her spikes, poised to bolt for the safety of the stretch. But which way had she come? Another coin landed in front of her. That was it! She ran headlong down the street away from the limo, the rainy puddles splashing at her legs, terror of the unknown clutching at her heart. She knew they were keeping pace with her. Above the din from her own heels, she could hear heavy boots cascading on the pebbly concrete, gaining on her step by panicky step.

And then she saw it looming up ahead: a dead-end wall with a blur of graffiti glistening from its craggy surface. She ran toward it anyway, madly searching for a door, a hole, a crack, anything to escape their pounding feet.

"What do you want from me?" she screamed, and turned around to face them.

But only silence now, swathed in the dullness of their labored breathing. She tried to control herself. "What do you want?" she said, surprised at the steadiness in her voice.

She didn't recognize him when he stepped forward. Just another peroxide punk. But then she recalled his cold-eyed glare. It was the same Fronter who'd pushed Paul onto the stage at Anfield and came to their rescue on the way to Lennon's house.

"We want to help you." His voice might have been reassuring but for the suggestion of a nasal sneer.

She tensed, ready to defend herself. And then the explosion went off; though it was distant, the streets trembled, the TV sets went black, and she jumped into his arms, sobbing. He stroked her hair and murmured. "It'll be okay."

"I want to go home," she wailed. "Please let me go home."

His gentleness was reassuring, and she clung to his taut young body. Still, his voice had an odd hardness. "Not yet. There are things that have to be settled."

Lennon didn't want to come. In fact, he fought tooth and nail. Said he'd never heard anything about any get-together. Ringo was sure he'd told him, but then maybe it had slipped his mind. Happened quite often nowadays, Maureen had acidly commented, but she had promised the girls from the salon that she'd introduce them to Mr. Montana and that was that.

She had fretted about Luanne but had been assured by Herbie that the lady had caught a taxi to the airport and was already on the late-night flight to London. This news had sent Paul into a tailspin of depression but, after a couple of slugs from his hip flask, he had bitten his lip and shrugged his indifference. And now, here they were about to alight from the limo, like kings or bookies, onto the hallowed pavement outside the Horse and Jockey.

"C'mon, man, I promised I'd show you a real English pub." Montana was doing his best to be conciliatory, but Herbie wasn't budging.

"They got hot dogs in there, Boss?" Big Bill ventured from up front, still nervous after the hair-raising ride alongside Ringo.

Montana ignored him but gave Herbie one last shot. "Do me a favor, huh?" The martyr complex was getting old and making him look bad into the bargain. He was missing Luanne already and, through the haze of alcohol, couldn't figure out quite why.

"C'mon, wack, be lots of birds," Ringo whispered back when he noticed Maureen was the other side of earshot.

Herbie's eyes brightened a watt or two, but then flared into alarm mode when Ringo gunned the limo into reverse, smashing a rear light against a parking meter.

"I suppose a bit of tail wouldn't go astray," Herbie said, and then muttered under his breath, "Safer than gettin' mashed up in here."

Ringo shoved the gear stick into first and the car lurched forward to within inches of a white van.

"All right, all right," Herbie shouted as he flung open the door and leaped onto the sidewalk. "I'm comin' in."

"That's the ticket, head, you just stick with me." Ringo leaned out the window and winked. He then shouted at the others as they poured out, "Everyone all right, then?"

"Yeah, apart from a couple of minor heart attacks," Montana said. "I thought you said you'd driven a stretch before."

"I told you, you should never let him near the wheel of a car when he's been drinkin'." Maureen hastily ran a comb through her hair and tried to examine herself in the side mirror of the stretch.

"Just tryin' to make up some time, then, wasn't I?" Ringo grumbled. "And yez wouldn't have been very happy if one of them Fronters had thrown a petrol bomb up yer arses, would you?"

"It's closed." Lennon cast a cursory glance at the darkened window of the pub. "Let's go somewhere else." The steady stream of drink had edged him beyond the warm, fuzzy glow, and he was fast approaching the rugged far side of anxiety. He'd had enough of this socializing and just wanted to put his head down somewhere.

What if China's in there? It's not her shift, but they make her work late for parties and the like. Maureen always freezes her, to say nothin' of what she'll think of Mr. Paul Montana. I couldn't stand it if she fawns all over him like everybody else.

But one by one they all made their way up to the door, except Ringo, who was bent over the rear light of the limo, examining the damage.

"It's quieter than the grave in there," Montana said.

"Maybe the Undertakers are playin'," George suggested.

"I tell you, there's no one there! The lights are all out." Lennon turned to go.

"Oh, no!" Ringo shaded his eyes and looked down the street. "Them Fronters I blew the horn at are on the port bow." He pocketed a piece of red rear light glass and bounded across the pavement. He hammered on the door of the pub, but then, noticing that it wasn't locked, threw it open, and they peered in.

Lennon was right—it was all dark and silent. But then the

lights blazed on, momentarily blinding them, and the first raucous notes of "Twist and Shout" blasted from the P.A. The pub was packed and shaking with expectation.

Montana squinted into the melee. Hundreds of gone-to-seed musicians, old punters, their progeny, and general hangers-on: all alive, kicking and pulsing to the beat. Buried beneath the blotches and flabby jowls, faces from his youth beamed at him, flashbulbs of memory stripping away the years. Liverpool's elite of aging rockers stood, applauded, roared their greetings, slapped him on the back, grabbed him by the arse, feinted knees to his balls, and welcomed him home. Billy Kramer, Johnny Gustafson, Gerry Marsden, King-size Taylor, assorted Searchers, Coasters, Undertakers, Mersey Beats, the Big Three, the Remo Four, the Kansas City Five, and every ligger, gigger, and brasser this side of Dingle, thrilled to bits to see him, and eager to bask in his reflected glory.

He felt like he was on some weird drug. Their faces seemed bigger, magnified out of all proportion as they swayed into his orbit, their hands all over him, hugging him, holding him, randomly breaking both his balls and his heart. He wanted to run but didn't dare. And then his vision cleared, and it all came into focus, the panic subsided, and the pride swelled his heart. He was home, among his own: Why had he ever gone away in the first place? No more loneliness, always the outsider trying to make himself understood, and all the while wrestling with that elastic umbilical cord forever tugging at him, dragging him back across the ocean. To hell with Vegas! This was real life, and he'd forsaken it—for what? An overdone illusion? It made no difference. He was back on home ground. Everything was goin' to be all right again.

Then Billy Kramer's arms were around him. "Jesus, Paul, you don't look a day older."

"Still usin' the old boot polish, then?" Gerry Marsden couldn't resist the dig.

"Hey, Lennon," Gustafson shouted, "you should borrow one of the kid's toupees."

But Lennon had eyes for only one person. He shoved past them on his beeline to the bar, not noticing the smug grins and knowing winks. China poured a pint and placed it in front of him.

"You're back quick," she said beneath the roar of conversation.

"I never heard anything about this. I'd have let you know otherwise."

"It's okay. Charlie couldn't do his shift. The flu." She shrugged. "Besides, I could use the money."

"Speakin' of which . . ." He blushed to the roots of his hair. She took care that no one saw her slip him the tenner.

"Thanks." He almost kissed her. "Just want to be able to buy me round."

"It's okay."

"I'll pay you back when I get me dole." It made her tremble to see the gratitude in his eyes. She knew how hard it was for him to ask for anything.

"I said it's okay." She smiled and rang up the register. "It's a big day for you." She turned back and examined him with some concern.

Lennon took a deep draft of his pint, their eyes still latched. He wiped his mouth and leaned on the bar to steady himself. "He wants us to go back to the States with him."

Without me, I suppose. Lots of nice girls over there! Could have yourself a real good time.

"What do you think?" he asked.

It was the wrong question. But Gerry Marsden saved her. He leaned provocatively over the bar, the better to look down her blouse, rolled his eyes theatrically, and called, "A pint of bitter and an LO, luv."

She ignored him and awaited the question Lennon would never ask. Of course she'd say yes. She'd go to the back of beyond with him, anywhere as long as they were together.

"C'mon, Lennon, give the girl a break, then! This is a pub, not a bloody knockin' shop." Marsden then leaned backward and confided to a redheaded brasser whose arse he was furtively fondling: "A man could die waitin' for a drink in this place, with all the goin's-on."

It was useless to wait any longer. He would never ask now. She pulled a pint and poured a gin and tonic.

"'Bout bloody time, then." Marsden elbowed Lennon in the ribs. But Lennon ignored him; he could still feel the warmth of China's hand and wanted to kick himself for his lack of balls.

Montana barely noticed the band finishing their set. It took all his attention just to keep up with the roiling, raucous mill of well-wishers. Big Bill did his best to put some order on their jovial boisterousness, but they paid the ex-linebacker little heed.

Still clutching his pint, Marsden stuck his tongue down the brasser's throat and then, with some difficulty, mounted the stage, tripping over a monitor and banging his head off the microphone.

"Jesus Christ, got me right on the noggin, that one did. One two," he called out, "one two three. Ah bollocks, it's good enough for rock & roll!"

The crowd surged forward. Old Gerry was always good for a bit of a laugh. "Ladies and gentlemen!" He called for and got most of their attention. "And in some cases, I use that term liberally."

A number of hoots and groans. He again demanded silence and glared down at Herbie, who was animatedly describing some lurid scene to a rapt and bug-eyed Ringo. The Yank's voice trailed off when he noticed all eyes upon him, and Marsden resumed his oration.

"He went away twenty-five years ago to seek fame and fortune. Most of us thought he didn't have a snowball's chance in hell. But, by Christ, did the kid prove us wrong. So let's raise our glasses to the toast of our generation, Allerton's own, Mr. Paul Montana McCartney."

This crowd needed little encouragement to cheer, let alone raise glasses. Red faces beamed and rotten teeth gleamed in the warmth of good fellowship.

"It gives me equal pleasure to welcome back his old comrade in arms, now a man of the cloth, no doubt capitalizing on his experience in sins against the Sixth and Ninth Commandments." Marsden sniggered good-humoredly, and the crowd turned to find George corralled against the bar by an old girlfriend and her teenage daughter.

Then Marsden got down to business, a tear blurring his rheumy eye. "Like many of us, he's had his difficulties. But just so you know it, Georgie boy, it's not the number of times you're down that counts but the number you get up. Ladies and gentlemen, I give you the best guitar picker this side of Birkenhead, Father George Harrison, S.J."

George turned beetroot red. He appeared to be about to protest, but Gerry didn't delay: "There are two others here tonight who some of us see more often than we might care to."

This time the boos and murmurs were not so good-natured, but Marsden held up his hand for quiet. "Despite their many and varied faults and flaws, these two veterans have never ceased in their unstinting fight to keep the one true flag of rock & roll flyin' over our fair city. Ladies and gentlemen, do I need to mention the gruesome twosome, John Lennon and Ringo Starkey."

Marsden stepped back magnanimously as the applause swelled. And though it would kill him when hung over on the morrow, he punched his fist in the air in drunken empathy.

"Once upon a time, the four of them were the toast of Merseyside, ladies and gentlemen, united here one more time, I give you the Beatles!"

"Jesus Christ!" Lennon turned to China. "Not now, of all times."

"It's as good a time as any."

"Where's George?"

She pointed down the bar. His tall frame had bent almost double in an attempt to escape the attention.

"Stupid sod!" Lennon muttered at Marsden. He hurried to George's side. "It's okay, lad." But it was far from that: George was coming apart at the rivets, his body shaking, his hands doing a slow dazzle.

Lennon looked around at the fired-up faces of the crowd. Ringo was already behind the kit, methodically smacking the snare and calibrating the tuning key with a concentration that would do justice to a Swiss watchmaker. Montana had Marsden in a bear hug, the tears streaming down both their cheeks at about the same rate that Marsden's pint was dripping onto the floor.

China handed Lennon a glass of Rémy. He took it without thanks and forced it on the priest. "Get that into you, lad."

George stared back, his mouth slightly agape.

"Drink the friggin' thing!" Lennon ordered, his own nerves jagged and raw.

George took the glass and lifted it to his lips for a discreet sip. But Lennon tipped it back into his mouth. Some went in; the rest streamed down his quivering chin onto his shirt. Then he took the dribbling, coughing priest by the hand and led him to the stage. A host of willing admirers gave George the heave-ho and deposited him next to the beaming Montana.

Lennon strapped on the Strat, relieved to have something dependable in his hands. Gustafson studied George warily, then handed him the Gretsch. "Not to worry, mate, it'll be a piece of bloody cake."

Montana was already in Vegas turbocharge, preening and waving to familiar faces in the crowd. The pub was abuzz with excitement, the expectation spiced by a rare, electrified nostalgia. Gustafson tapped the returned hero on the shoulder and handed him a gleaming Hofner, strings upside down as befitted a lefty. "Got it special for you, Paulie."

"No way, Guso, I ain't touched one of them babies in twenty-five years."

"Still only got four strings, mate."

Montana studied the Hofner as if it were some exotic relic excavated from the ruins of Pompeii, but shook his head. "Nah, you play. I'll stick to me pipes. That's what they pay me the big bucks for."

Gustafson cast a doubtful eye at Lennon. "What's he goin' to say?"

"He loves you, babe, it'll be cool." Montana slapped him on the back.

"I don't know, it don't seem right like."

But Montana had already taken the mike from the stand.

Gustafson shrugged and plugged in his own Fender precision. "Always wanted to be a Beatle, then, didn't I?" he joked to Ringo.

"No bloody wankin', then!" Ringo was all grin and lewd gesture.

"So what's it gonna be, chief?" Montana spun the mike cord like a gunfighter, hemorrhaging Vegas confidence all over the stage.

Lennon couldn't believe his eyes. "Your call, Elvis."

"How about a little 'Long Tall Sally'? Remember it?"

"What do you think?"

"You guys ready to rock?" Montana called back to the rhythm section. He tried to catch George's eye, but the guitarist was fiddling with his volume knob. "All right, then!" He high-fived the crowd, slicked back his hair, and counted in a finger-popping four. "Ah one, ah two, ah one two three . . ."

He swung into the classic, slipping and sliding around the syllables and between the grooves, bopping in and out of the meter, big band, brassy Vegas to a T but a universe away from raucous, rockin' Liverpool.

Up front of stage, Herbie bopped to the swing. The crowd did, too, until they copped on that this version had more to do with Fats Waller than Fats Domino. The mood in the pub turned surly, and most of the dancers limped to a halt; a few less doctrinaire souls continued to jive and lindy to the lameness. Still, by the time Montana had massacred the second chorus, Herbie bopped alone.

Lennon was aghast. Not only was he playing second fiddle to some lounge-lizard wanker dead bent on demolishing a twenty-five-year-old legend, but George was paralytic from a panic attack. The song stumbled along while Montana scatted some limpid shoo-be-doos; a few moments later, it staggered to a mortified halt.

Lennon turned his back on the shock and embarrassment, but Montana continued to beam and bluster until someone shouted: "Bloody sellout! You show him, Johnny!"

The Prince of Vegas had experienced many's the bad night, but nothing quite like this. When the first bottle hit the stage, he tossed the mike on the floor and stalked off in a huff.

Lennon watched him leave in a sorrow laced with disgust.

It was going to take more than a quarter century to live down this fiasco. He was livid with the lot of them, and his voice rang clearly through the pub: "What's the matter with you two spastics? One of you can't play—the other won't."

George stared back, his face frozen with fear. But Lennon was having none of it. "What's that you got in your hand?"

George stared down at his shivering fingers. He tried to mouth some words, but they wouldn't come.

"It's a guitar, lad," Lennon said quite kindly, as if explaining to a four-year-old.

George examined the beautiful red Gretsch—the gleam of its polished surface shooting slivers of light off the stage.

"It's quite simple, George. You just put your fingers on a chord and then hit the strings with your other hand."

The priest followed Lennon's lips but made no move. Lennon took his left hand and raised it so that his fingers rested on the strings. By instinct, they formed a tentative chord.

"Now hit the fucker!" Lennon roared, and slapped him on the shoulder. George's head spun around; his arm followed in a short, sharp arc, and an unresolved chord bounced off the walls.

Lennon nodded and spat from between clenched teeth. "That's an E seventh! Remember what you used to tell me about sevenths, Georgie? They're what make rock & roll tick, because they keep you off balance and never let you resolve. That's the story of our lives, mate. Now, just play the bloody thing and quit bollocksin' around!"

He turned on Ringo and Gustafson. "Listen to me, you two! It's not that we were the best. We *are* the best!"

He had their attention now, and they watched him like two hawks ready to swoop. He held their eyes for a tantalizing second, then spoke to the priest. "And for your information,

Father George, I have no intention of lettin' you waste another minute of your life. 'Money' in E!" he yelled, then added with the slightest of grins, "Seventh!"

Ringo raised the sticks over his head and clicked them in time to his barked order, "One, two, three, four!"

He pounded a jungle beat on the floor-tom. Lennon let the tension build over four fours, then stepped forward and snarled the classic.

George curled a lick on the last beat of the bar before the chorus, at first caressing the chords but then slashing at them, his panic undiminished but now using it, abusing it, ripping through the music, everything falling back into its appointed place, making sense all over again. His face lit up as his fingers took control and the memories of all his patented runs and inversions flooded back, overloading his circuits and adding muscle and sinew to the angular rock & roll; he beamed and blasted figures through the crowd, speeding through riffs interred and silent through all his years of isolation. Ahead of the beat, behind the beat, he teetered around sixteenth notes on the high end of the fretboard before skittering back down the bottom strings into double-time boogie-woogie triads.

Ringo oozed sweat behind the drums, locking in with the hardest-hitting Fender bassman in Liverpool history. Gustafson was on fire and in his element. There'd be a lot of birds pulled from the afterglow of this gig, down all the bluesy, boozy nights of ligs, gigs, and LOs ahead.

But right now the years were skidding off the four of them, and the crowd erupted in a frenzy. Women the wrong side of forty and old teds, their sideburns flecked with gray, jived and gyrated on the floor, and it was hot, sweaty, black-and-white 1962 all over again—the years and the tears and the fears banished for thirty puny, precious, platinum resurrected minutes of vanished youth.

Montana looked on, loss fueled by fascination. Nobody paid him the slightest heed: An unnoticed guest at his own funeral, even Herbie was gaping at the stage. He knew full well he should be up there with his mates, redeeming himself, but paranoia had crippled him, and he was afraid to move for fear of screwing up once more. When the song approached the final choruses, the hurt and pain built until he could stand it no more. He rushed back on, but cast a wart eye at Gustafson.

Eyes jammed tight, Guso was in seventh heaven, pumping like a Three-in-one-oiled piston to Ringo's kick drum. He looked around distraught when his notes went dead. Montana had jerked out his cord, plugged in the Hofner and was fumbling for the key. Like a man interrupted in the heat of sex, Gustafson was livid, but after a pissed-off moment, he swaggered off the stage—Fender swinging down his hip, ever cool—he'd done his job, got the thing swingin', and there was always the lig to look forward to.

Lennon was furious at the interruption and yelled back, "What the fuck do you think you're doin'?" But the next verse was upon him and he wasn't going to blow it, no matter who else did. Stung by the rejection, Montana dug into the strings like he hadn't since that last night in the studio. He leaped ahead of the count, and Ringo had to chase him out of the groove, synchronize with his tempo, and then drag him back by the scruff of the neck beat by wrestled beat until the flamming became tolerable and the kick and bass swung at least somewhere in the same orbit.

But Lennon was still a universe apart. Despite Montana's interruption, the guitar seemed small in his hands, as it always did when he was perfectly tuned in. Nor did tuning itself have much to do with it. His A string was slightly flat, but unconsciously he was stretching it a microtone this way and that, either achieving perfect 440 clarity or thickening the chord with a shade of dissonance, depending on what was called for. He knew raucous rhythm to a T—a past master at strummin' up a storm. He listened to the high hat and the snare and came up with his own pocket in between—driving his amp to the point of overload but pulling back a hair before distortion. He could hear and distinguish the elastic bond between the kick and bass, and he grabbed on to it and swung along right over their heads, always taking care that the drone of his bottom E didn't mess up or muddy the netherlands of the bass. But the rhythm section wasn't cutting it to his refined sense of perfection: He could hear Ringo chasing Paul all over the place, and it pissed him off no end. It mattered little that McCartney hadn't played in half a lifetime. Life's tough—wear a helmet! He was souring the mix and turning Ringo's rock-solid beat into his granny's week-old jelly. He rounded on the two of them and roared "Fuckin' wankers!" over the racket of the amps.

And with that, they began to jell the way all great rhythm sections do: Montana slipping and sliding back and forth in Ringo's greasy pocket, sometimes pounding like a headache dead on the four, other times a whisper ahead or behind it. His style returned too, all in an exultant moment, and he recalled his swooping runs and dips, slips and slides, the tiny booming melodies he bounced off the beat and how he'd single-handedly changed the way the Cavern had listened to the bass—no longer the driving eight on four of the revered Detroit and Memphis players, but his very own innovation: the introduction of the melodic left hand of the British music-hall pianists.

Lennon was still screaming the lyrics, his back arched over

the microphone, mad at Montana and the world; but as the familiar bass lines snaked around the groove, like everyone else in the pub, he felt the smack of recognition. At first he resisted, quickening the tempo and then dragging his heels on the bridge in a self-destructive notion of shaking the section, waking them, breaking the spell that they were casting on themselves and the audience. But then he'd lose track of their antics as he soared with George's fiery, fluid solos, and when he came back down to Earth, he'd find that they had him spiked to the floor in that indefinable but particular rhythmic space where all great rock & roll hovers, halfway between the hammer and the anvil.

And then Lennon segued into "Boys," and the ante upped right through the ceiling. Now he was really in his element: hard-core screaming off the cavern walls, raw, pure, and undiluted. On the outro solo, when George leaned back into his amp and let the feedback fuel his fire, in long, piercing sustained streams of strangled, overdriven notes, Lennon smiled grudgingly and tipped his head—*welcome back, arsehole*—in McCartney's direction.

At first, the crowd was typical, skeptical scouse—unwilling to be taken twice—but for how long could they resist the fury and passion of England's greatest ever rock & roll group? Whipped into one seething, bopping, jiving mass, they cleared the floor of tables and stray chairs, dismantling the remains of any fourth wall brick by sonic brick. And as McCartney reached for his trademark high-harmony "Bop dubay, ah bop bop dubay," they sang along, intonation all over the shop but locked together as they hadn't been since the glory days back down the Cavern. Some laughed, some cried, others were beyond emotion, it made no difference: Their dreams had surfaced again, once more overpowering reality and their dread of what was happening on the streets outside. The Beatles were back—redemption was at hand. The Kid had come home.

They rocked on nonstop for a good half hour, continually raising the roof and expectations, the sweat and the hurt and the pain and the lies streaming off them, bloody welts rising on George's and McCartney's fingers. And when they left the stage to screams, yells, kisses, arse-tickling, shoulder-grabbing, and back-slapping, the four of them, as one, belly-upped to China's bar. They were surrounded by a wave of well-wishers but had eyes only for each other, unwilling to let the moment evaporate, reluctant to come to terms with the present, deathly afraid of being reduced to mere normality again. The link was back, all walls were down, all bridges crossed, fire in their bellies, flames in their hearts, iced white light igniting all over their brains—that delicious, exhausted, head-to-toe riveting moment equaled only by the fuck of your life.

Eventually, the punters had whisked George and Ringo away, but the glow refused to fade. Lennon and McCartney stared straight ahead, twin islands alone, but linked as by lava amid the gleaming bottles of booze.

"Thanks, mate," McCartney said. "I needed that kick in the arse."

Lennon barely smiled. No point in speeches. Words only got in the way.

China pulled them two more pints. McCartney sucked on his, routinely appraised her, and for the first time noticed that she was looking straight through him, eyes only for Lennon. He looked away and took another draft, but from the corner of his eye he could tell Lennon was zeroed in on her every move.

When she turned back to the register, he smiled. "Still haven't lost it, mate?"

Lennon began to deny her but realized whom he was

talking to. They'd shared more than they cared to talk about. What was the point?

"About half your age, Johnny?" She turned back from the register and he took in her lineless face. "Maybe even less?"

"Know a thing or two about that yourself."

"More like chalk and bloody cheese." When he measured China's fragile beauty against Luanne's manufactured élan, the swig of beer tasted bitter. "Tell me somethin'." He wiped his mouth with the back of his hand. "What do you talk to her about?"

"Oh, the national debt, the price of turnips, what do you think?"

"Don't you never miss Cyn?" he asked after a moment.

"No!" Lennon drained his pint, still admiring China's feline grace down the other end of the bar. "Well," he said in very measured tones, "maybe sometimes. The young ones do their best, but they weren't there, were they? Can't really know how it was."

"Yeah," McCartney whispered.

They both stared into their glasses, until Lennon spluttered fiercely. "But there's nothing like this one, no matter what age she is."

"Good luck, then."

"There's more to life than luck, mate."

McCartney waited for Lennon to elaborate, but he just stared moodily at the top-shelf bottles.

"It's the lad I worry about," Lennon eventually sighed, then added vehemently: "I can change him, I know I can, given time."

"Yeah, you think you wrote the book about bein' young, and then you have your own and it's never like it should be."

"Just give me six more months with him, and I'll straighten his fascist arse out."

"If I could only get a year's custody of young Lyndon, I'd make a man out of him. Kid's totaled more cars than Mario Andretti."

But Lennon wasn't listening. He pushed forward his glass for a refill. ". . . if it's the last thing I bloody well do."

Chapter Eighteen

THE YOUNG FRONTER moved through Liverpool to a destination, or lack thereof, that he alone was privy to. The power had failed in some streets, leaving them dark, while elsewhere the lights dimmed and shuddered like old Victorian gas lamps. From time to time, a stiff breeze would mount, and disperse the drizzling fog to reveal a crescent moon racing by; but within minutes, dark clouds big as battleships would come scudding over to deny the city even this fragile light.

Police presence was sparse to none. Patrol cars screamed by, sirens on, lights flashing, but always en route to somewhere else. The Front ruled the streets and the young man and his gang moved through them wraithlike, their path increasingly illuminated by the fiery blue glow of paraffin and petrol bombs erupting into flames. Glass smashed in the distance, angry men shouted slogans and racial epithets, and still they pushed on relentlessly.

And everywhere, because of the young Fronter's rank and reputation, they were greeted with respect. At first, his face burned with enthusiasm, but as the night wore on and the level of alcohol consumption among his brethren increased, his features settled into a grim, disapproving mask.

Luanne hurried to keep up with him. At first, she had sulked and fallen back among the gang, but the dull hatred in their eyes frightened her. He knew who she was, where she had come from, and, hopefully, where he was taking her. To her limited ear, the others were mere steps above animals, grunting in some foreign dialect that occasionally resembled English.

And then there was the fight with the worst-looking of them. She'd tried to thank him, but he was dismissive and the height of gruffness. Still, no one had ever stood up for her like that before. She didn't even know the young man's name; the gang just referred to him as "he" or "him," but in a very different manner than Herbie or Big Bill referring to Montana.

She had never met anyone quite like him: principled but prejudiced, centered but opinionated, willing to make, and take responsibility for snap judgments, and always driven, moving forward incessantly, trusting to some inner faith that manifested itself in his burning eyes. She might have been away from her environment, totally out of her depth, but she had a doctorate in men, and after the first hour, she could sense what his response would be to a problem, could almost call the next street or alley they would veer into. She clung to him—if anyone could rescue her from these twisted streets, it was him.

He tried to avoid her, keep his distance, but there was something exotic about her, as if some vivid tropical bird had landed in their midst. Still, he tried not to forget that she was above all else a card to be played, even a trump, if he could find the right hand to deal it in.

It's her nearness that gets me the most. The way she clings to me, not even physically, but in some kind of a mental way, like we mean something to each other, or some such twat. After all, she's just another dumb Yank and even more out to lunch than the idiots on telly.

Still, it's hard to think straight with her hangin' out of me. No matter where I step, she's right there, like me bloody shadow.

Probably 'cause she's so petrified of the others—not that I blame her—crowd of head-bangers. It's the one thing the Reds and Trots get right on the mark: The NFUK does attract its fair share of head-the-balls. But screw them and their arrogance! Everyone has their reason for joining, and their part to play, including me.

She does smell nice though, I'll grant her that. Couldn't stand the pong at first. Almost smothered me. But after a while, it isn't half bad, very feminine like. And what a body. Jesus! Had to kick Dosser Browne right in the balls, I was so sure he was goin' to mount her right there on the street in front of everyone. And her in my custody too! What the hell was I supposed to say back at Central Office: "By the way, brothers, I'm most frightfully sorry, but I was unable to restrain Citizen Browne from throwin' his leg over Miss America and ridin' her all the way out to Aintree Race Course, whereupon he insisted on doin' three laps of the Grand National—bareback, I might add—and before his breakfast too!"

Would have sounded great, wouldn't it? Be the end of my head-long rush up the NFUK ladder. No, I've got to keep my nose clean. There's big things in the offing. If we can take over this dump tonight, it'll take the army itself to make us give it back. But by then, we'll have settled a lot of scores.

And maybe, just maybe, the dickhead politicians down in London won't take the chance on ordering in the army, what with the number of our blokes already planted in the ranks and so many young officers sympathetic to us. Then what, I ask you? It'll be London next, and after that the sky's the limit. Won't have to depend on anyone, least of all old Looney.

She does have an effect though. At times, I feel like just touching her, not feeling her up or anything, just seeing if she's real like. I mean, it's not that I haven't had my fair share of girls 'round here. But "girls" is the word, and that's what they are compared to this humdinger, 110 percent woman, all there in the raw and ready to be *munched, mounted, and accounted for. Jesus, just the very thought of it boggles the mind! No wonder Dosser lost the run of himself.*

A short burst of gunfire clattered in the distance, and some tracers flared across the night.

"Thick bastards!" Julian screamed, and Luanne leaped away from him. "What do they think they're doin'?"

She stared at him blankly.

"They were warned," he lectured her. "A bit of burnin' is one thing, but absolutely no guns. Bring the army down on top of us before we get our business done."

She nodded her understanding, but he could tell she didn't have a clue. He grabbed her elbow and dragged her on, angry at himself for losing his composure.

There she goes again, rubbin' up against me. Give her a bloody inch and she takes a mile. But the thing is, anytime I look at her, I mean really look at her, she doesn't even bat an eyelid. Much as I'd like to pride meself, I actually don't think she's comin' on to me at all. That's just the kind she is. Jesus Christ, if she really put the make on you, you'd probably die howlin' inside her. But what a way to go! I'll say one thing for old Macker. No messin' in the birds' department, knows exactly what he wants and no slouch about gettin' it.

The Old Man's the same, I'll give him his due. I mean, Mam was a looker in her day, and the young one he's ridin' now is a bit of all right too. Not that I'd be much interested meself. There's enough mixin' of the races goin' on. Britain's gettin' darker by the day without me addin' my lily-white langer to the old chromosome stew.

Be the last thing on old Johnny's mind though, wouldn't it? Just thinks of himself and his own gratification and to hell with everything else. His young one's only about my age too. He should be ashamed of himself, the old fart!

What's her problem now? It's just some of our lads breakin' a few Paki windows. I bet she's never had to sit down in one of their dog-for-dinner, taking-over-our-neighborhoods, so-called restaurants. Not very likely when she's living high off the fat of the land, courtesy of Mister Montana.

Not that I agree with our lot torching their bloody buildings though; bit of a waste, if you ask me, regular English blokes could open businesses there as soon as we've repatriated Mohammed and his fifty snotty-nosed brats. But breakin' a few windows is not exactly the end of the world; just sends a message, that's all. I mean, this is not their country. I'm not over in Karachi openin' chippers, then, am I? No bloody way!

"Look out, you idiot!" Julian grabbed the flaming bottle of paraffin from a drunken Fronter and hurled it at a factory wall. "If you're goin' to light it, throw the effin' thing before you send us all up in smoke."

No one drinks in my crew. They're out on their ear if they do! That's one of the things we're tryin' to eradicate—the lack of discipline that's sent this country to the dogs. And I don't have to look far from home for that. Me bloody dad and his best mate, Schnozzlelface, drinkin' themselves to distraction. And I had to grow up around that: him sloshed every night. Pissin' away every penny of me mam's money and then makin' fun of her when he staggered home, three sheets to the wind. And me, lyin' upstairs in bed, clenchin' me little fists at the sound of him layin' aggro on a poor, defenseless woman. Her shushin' him, "For God's sake, John, you'll wake poor Julian."

Well, poor Julian was wide awake through every last disgusting minute of it; yeah, and even worse, through the odd occasion when they'd make up. Turns my stomach now to think of his drunken groans and that general kind of carry-on between them.

Listen, will you give over now! What are the lads goin' to think? Your hand stuck through me arm, linking me like you're me girlfriend. It's not like we're takin' a turn on Blackpool Pier, inhalin' the sea breeze and murdering cones of ice cream, is it? No, this is the Royal City of Liversleaze goin' up in smoke—the night I've been waitin' for all my life.

Outside a police station, a couple of streets ahead, a car loaded with semtex exploded; windows around them shattered and the street shook beneath their feet.

"Get down!" He pushed her into a doorway and threw himself across her body. She was screaming, out of control, and he shushed her gently. Still, when she tried to cling to him, he pushed her aside and called out, "Everyone all right?"

He listened for the answering shouts of his gang and nodded when he'd finished his count. "That's the Trots or the bloody Irish," he shouted at them. "Our side don't bomb cop shops, so be careful."

He looked at her, thinking he might explain the complexities of civil unrest, but when he noted the uncomprehending look on her face, he shrugged his dismissal.

"What do you want with me?" Luanne wailed.

"Just keepin' you safe while we take over this dump," Julian said, wiping the sweat and grime from his forehead. "Not that you appear to have noticed."

"Please take me home." She threw her arms around him. Her perfume was overwhelming. For a split second, he relented and allowed her to melt into him, just to savor the crush of her body. Then he pushed her off to arm's length. But it was too late. He saw what she saw in his eyes: Something had passed between them, and she edged closer to him.

"We could go to a hotel. I've got credit cards."

He steadied himself. "You can't buy your way out of this one."

"I'm not talking about buying."

"I know exactly what you're talkin' about. It's just that, at this moment, you're not dealin' with a decadent old man."

She halted a moment and looked at him. "Am I dealing with a young one?"

He stared her down with all the weight of his purpose. Within moments she was trembling. He took her by the arm and marched her up past the police station. Unlike the others, he didn't cough or splutter from the pall of smoke. He was focused now and barely noticed that she was clinging to him again.

"Everyone has their part to play," he said.

The rumors surged through the city: *The Trots are blowin' up the cop shops, the IRA are snipin' at the army, the Pakis are marchin' on the docks, the mayor has called in the Fronters to restore order.* . . . The truth was, however, that most of the action was confined to the city center, where the immigrants' restaurants and shops abounded, or to the borders of their housing estates, where they had erected "peace walls" to keep the Fronters from entering. Out in the suburbs and in the "English" estates, they watched the "revolution" on TV or shook their heads and went to bed with their hot water bottles, certain that the army would have things straightened out by the morning.

Though the skies glowed in the distance, outside the Horse and Jockey all was quiet except for the beat pounding through the walls; still, the late arrivals checked their backs and counted their blessings before entering. They might have missed the gig of the century, but they were just in time for the gig of a lifetime. The booze was flowing, the good times were being relived furiously, and there was one hell of a chance of pullin' a brasser, if you had even a passing connection to the good old days down the Cavern. To top it all, the Big Three were ripping up the stage. Johnny Gustafson, Brian Griffiths, and Johnny Hutchinson had been the only band to ever hold a candle to the Beatles, and now they were shaking the joint with their primal R&B.

China had been pulling pints and pouring shots for what seemed like an eternity. But as most of the old heads turned to watch Gus, Griff, and Johnny rip through "Walkin' the Dog," she caught a few moments to wash some glasses and survey the scene.

It's nice to see them all happy and enjoying themselves for a change. Not that they don't have good times, for the most part: It's just that there's always something lingering right under the surface, and when they get in their little huddle, it's like time doing a head flip.

Most of the girls my age, or thereabouts, just go along with them because they buy rakes of drink, their stories are a gas, and they're usually a bit of a laugh, unlike the young lads around here, so serious about politics and whatnot. But I suppose if I wasn't doing a line with John, I'd never have copped on either.

But tonight's different. It's all back in electric spades, putting all the madness outside in perspective. They're in their element now, and the glow on their leathery old faces makes me own heart feel proud. Even my John is letting his guard down, not to mention his hair, and it was absolutely brilliant to watch him blow the whole place away. That must have happened all the time back in the old days, but it's a rarity now with him slogging away at the pub, no one listening or, even worse, that night at the Revival when they all fell around laughing at his song about walruses. Well, it was about a lot more than that, but how would they ever know with their nonstop slagging and putting him down. He's the best and they know it, but no one wants to acknowledge him, because if they did, they'd come slamming up against their own failures.

Will you look at him, his arm around Gerry Marsden, of all people, buying drinks for Kingsize Taylor and Billy Kramer. Easy with that tenner, luv, it won't last forever. It must be such a relief for them to drop their silly arguing. Because when all is said and done, they only have each other now. No one else gives a damn about any of them or what they might have been.

And will you look at the go of the priest, chatting up that young one. He might be out of practice, our Father George, but he's working double time getting back in shape. I wonder how's he going to deal with her in confession?

And good old Rings, belly-up as ever and putting the make on big old peroxide Theresa. Terry Tits, she calls herself when the LOs hit the spot. Oh no, lad, whatever you do, don't go giving her your card with the salon number. Supposing Maureen picks up the phone? Speaking of which, here comes that long-suffering streak of misery herself straight off the dance floor, panting like a pony and sweating up a storm.

Either Ringo's sixth sense, or the eyes in the back of his greasy head, kicked in. Just as Theresa was about to take the card, he slipped it back into his comb pocket and moved a degree or two to the starboard of her ample bosom.

With a seasoned glance, Maureen noted the scene, infinitesimally arching her eyebrows.

"Richard," she pealed in the proprietorial manner that a quarter century of putting up with someone's snoring entitles you to, "get me me handbag, will you, luv?"

"Your what?"

"Me handbag, dear. It's in the cloak room."

Theresa sniggered, and Ringo blushed crimson, but Maureen stuck to her guns. "Run along now like a good lad, me feet are killin' me."

But like a dog in the throes of heat, Ringo was reluctant to trot off anywhere. His lip trembled with the makings of a sneer, and he eyeballed his better half while Theresa and

China gawked on in fascination. But his defiance buckled under Maureen's stony glare, and he exited, muttering: "That's all I am around here—a bloody messenger boy."

With husband safely under wraps, Maureen directed her ire at Theresa, who bristled under the scrutiny, breasts jutting forth like twin warheads. But drummers' wives are nothing if not resolute and Maureen's long tenure of slights and humiliations before the bandstand stood her in good stead. "We're not delaying you, are we?" she inquired sweetly.

Theresa had triumphed in many's the cat fight, but she was ill prepared for this particular approach. She lowered her LO in one seasoned swallow and murmured back even more honey-toned: "Oh no, not at all, Mrs. Starkey." The "Mrs.," however, was laced with strychnine.

As Maureen watched her wobble off, she raised her nose and remarked, "She was cheap thirty years ago, and age hasn't worked any miracles." Then, for the first time, she appeared to notice China. "Oh," she said.

China blushed. On the occasions they'd met, Maureen had made little effort to hide her disapproval. Still and all, China turned to a seated customer and said: "Get up, Ronnie. Let the lady sit."

Ronnie grumbled something about his corns, and women buying their round, but arise he did and obediently buggered off.

"Thanks," Maureen said as she slid onto the stool. "Me feet are killin' me. A vodka and white, please."

"Take your shoes off, luv."

"Ta, don't mind if I do."

China measured out the vodka and, on impulse, added another. "There's a double for you. Look like you could use it."

"Put two cubes of ice in that, please. Don't want to be carried home, now, do I?" She splashed some of the white lemonade in, studied the bubbles, and lowered a hefty gulp before sipping in a ladylike manner. "Haven't danced as much in twenty years," she sighed, and then looked up sharply. "Of course, I should hardly be tellin' you, of all people, me age."

"It's okay."

"Oh, for God's sake, girl, it's not okay!"

China swerved on her heel. She'd tried her best to be friendly, for John's sake, but she'd no intention of soaking up this shriveled-up old biddy on a rampage.

"Turnin' your back on me won't do anyone much good."

China knew she was right, but couldn't bear to be sliced, diced, and dissected by those accusing eyes.

"Oh, will you turn around," Maureen said. "I know I have a sharp tongue. I just say what's on me mind, but it always comes out the wrong way."

China clenched the edge of the bar—the whole day was too much. Maureen reached out tentatively and laid her palm on the young woman's slender hands. "Listen, I've known him for over half me life, since I was a slip of a girl like yourself, and I love him like me own, honestly I do, despite all our fightin'. But he's over twice your age, luv, can't you see that?"

"He's also twice the person of anyone else around here."

"Oh, don't I know, darlin', don't I know. There's nothin' like him. He's the best in the world, it's just that . . . this world is not cut out for him."

She squeezed China's hands and drew her closer, as if what she had to say might be misinterpreted by anyone else. "If you'd only seen him when he was young and standin' up there under the lights, smart as a whip, not an ounce of bitterness on him, just full of hope and dreams, the whole world in front of him. But somethin' went wrong and, try as he might, he hasn't been able to put it right."

"I'll always be there for him."

Maureen finished off her drink and placed it down decisively for a refill. "I know you would, and I give you full credit for it. The last thing I want to do is hurt your feelings. You're a gorgeous-looking girl, God bless you, but"—she looked at the young woman, eyes full of compassion—"I've heard that song before."

This time China gave her only one measure. Maureen noted the change. She poured in the rest of the lemonade. "He's bad for women," she added quietly.

China knew she was right. More than anything, she wanted this conversation to end. Across the pub, she noticed Ringo, hidden halfway behind a pillar, again putting the make on Theresa. Maureen followed her eyes and winced. Then she smiled weakly. "We make our own beds, don't we?"

China turned away. One of the recessed bulbs above the bar caught her profile, and Maureen professionally admired her high cheekbones, her clear skin, and the glow in her eyes. "You remind me so much of ourselves," she said. "How we used to be, like."

China poured a measure for herself, clinked glasses, and drank hers neat. "Cheers, luv." She smiled back as best she could. "You haven't turned out all that bad."

Chapter Nineteen

AND THEN THEY WERE LEAVING—kisses, hugs, pokes in the gut, slaps on the back, quicky borderline feels of the other lads' wives, the rattle of bottles in brown paper bags, hail fellow well met, never to be parted again and all that jazz— the whole boozy, middle-aged cacophony amplified by the quiet, insistent drizzle. Maureen, her Beatles, and the two Americans taking the limo, the rest on shank's mare, soon to catch up at the Lennon household for more liquid refreshments and the divine transmogrification of memories. All quiet on the western front, not an explosion to be heard, not a Fronter in sight!

Ringo, bulling to drive again, had downed a quart of Maxwell House, all the better to pass his wife's muster. With eyes on matchsticks, popping out of their sockets, he led them in a merry dance onto the street; yet for all his new-found adrenaline, he failed at first to notice the handsome figure in a black leather jacket, white T-shirt, blue jeans, and slicked-back hair slyly observing the proceedings, while firing up a Rothmans from under the half-shadows of a flickering streetlamp.

"How're you, Paul?" said the figure.

"Hello?" Montana squinted into the gloom. He vaguely

recognized the voice, even the cut of the figure, yet couldn't place the face through the rain on his shades. The bristling body language, however, let him know that trouble was at hand.

"Don't recognize me, then?" the figure inquired in a diffident mix of hurt and sarcasm.

Montana removed his shades. "Pete?" he said, the years once again falling away as if by magic, but this time a darker, more dangerous spell.

"Heard you were comin'."

Montana cut him off. "Oh my God, Pete Best!" He grabbed his ex-drummer by the hand and smothered him in a bear hug. "How are you, man?"

Best freed himself, acknowledging the others with the barest of nods. He took a pull on his cigarette. "Heard you were comin'," he repeated as if he'd prepared the words beforehand and couldn't depart from the script now. "Just figured I'd say hello."

"Hey, you look like a million bucks, man! Not a feather off you." Montana sized up his old bandmate. Best did look genuinely well.

The others shuffled uneasily, passing around packets of fags, hugging passing punters like they were bosom buddies, working overtime at any diversion that might obliterate this unwanted rave from the grave. Best smoldered at the studied put-down but retained his teddy-boy cool.

"Doin' me best. Work out a bit when I get the time. You look just the same, Paul."

"Gotta do your best, babe! A good gym makes all the difference, right?" Under pressure he had slipped back into Montana mode; still, he was acutely aware that Best's arrival had caused a rupture between himself and the others. Then he stumbled: "You still playin', Pete?"

"Nah, chucked it in. Wasn't the same after yez . . ." Though words were left unsaid, everyone heard them loud and clear.

"Nothin' stays the same, does it?"

"No," Best agreed with a subtle bitterness. Then he brightened somewhat. "Did good for yourself. Always knew you had it in you, mate. Feel proud of you, I do."

"It's no big deal." Belatedly, Montana caught the slight against the others. He could feel their eyes on him now, hardening as they waited in vain for his rebuttal. Instead, he went for a soft landing. "Hey, you know everyone here."

"Yeah," Best said. "We've all met once or twice."

The others sulked on—sparing a nod or a wan smile—but not a peep out of any of them. Herbie, however, with a couple of brandies aboard, stepped forward and grasped his hand. "Hey, you gotta be the only guy from Liverpool I never heard of. How come you never mentioned Pete Best, dude?

Montana swung him to one side, hissing, "Shut up!"

Herbie's eyes narrowed. But Ringo laid a restraining hand on his shoulder. Montana was rattled by the interruption. Best watched him closely.

"Listen, Pete. We're havin' a bit of a do back at John's. You wanna tag along?"

Best swept his old mates with a withering glance. "Nah, wouldn't want to spoil the party. 'Sides, I'm working night shifts out at Fords."

"Sounds . . . interesting," George said, sarcasm dripping from every syllable.

Best veered on him, and it was obvious that there had never been any love lost between them. "I tried visiting you out at the rest home, Father George, but they wouldn't let me in, would they?"

"No big deal, mate. They wouldn't let me out."

Best's smile was wintry, but he appeared to let the matter rest. But then all the years of hurt overcame his studied cool, and he blurted out, "You never did care much for me, did you, George?"

"It wasn't you. It was your drummin'."

"I was the best and you know it."

George just shrugged.

"For all the bloody difference it made," Best added bitterly.

"What was right back then is still right," George said.

"I could have made the difference if yez hadn't done the dirt. . . ." Best's words trailed off. For a moment, they confronted each other in silence, Best then turned to Ringo. "Nothin' personal, mate, but I wouldn't have done it to you."

"Yeah," Ringo barely whispered, and Best walked away.

After a couple of steps, he halted and turned around. "You're lookin' good, John."

Lennon stared past him, stonefaced.

"I just wanted you to know—" Best paused, and it was obvious that he was back on his prepared speech. "I was pluggin' for you at the Revival."

He waited in vain for Lennon to react, then took a long drag from his cigarette and let the smoke drift through his nose before adding, "I was probably the only one."

Lennon stiffened, but George laid a restraining hand on his shoulder. "Don't want to punch in late for work, now, do you, Pete?" the priest called.

Best flicked his cigarette into the gutter and strolled on.

She watched them clamber out of the limo one by one, the achingly familiar faces, the blurred contours of their bodies, each one's moves and gestures the same, but grown even more pronounced and calcified with time; if she strained, she could hear their voices, the bantering, acidic as ever, but more measured now, leavened by heartaches and time.

As they waved good-bye to Herbie and Big Bill—dispatched by Montana to make sure that Luanne had indeed reached the airport—they were caught in the limo's headlights before it lurched off around the corner. She was amazed. The years had hardly changed them. Oh, they were older and the wear and tear was obvious, but when the four of them stood together outside the gate that he still hadn't fixed, it was like looking down the wrong end of a telescope: Though everything was diminished in exact proportion, everything remained utterly the same.

Her husband tensed alongside her. He had never belonged in their world, and he made no bones about his disapproval. And now she had no part in it either; walked out one day, locked the door, put the key under the rock, and crossed the moody river to Cheshire.

She squeezed his elbow. He shifted his weight abruptly and took his foot off the brake of his new Volvo. He'd been holding it down all this time, though the car was in gear and the hand brake on. But it was just the same back home: Whenever John's name came up, everything went haywire. It wasn't that she didn't try. God knows, she did her best, but from time to time his name would pop out regardless, and then there it would be, dancing a fandango between them, strangling all the uneventful normality he treasured so much.

Just look at them. They've never grown up. Bolting toward fifty and still larking about like teenagers, piggybacking over that bloody gate. Still, it's great to see them again and smiling too—beaten and bruised though they all must be. Even Paul, for all his fancy clothes, hasn't had it easy. But then, who has? If my own hurts aren't festering on the surface, you only have to peel back a layer or two to see the scars our John left. But that's all behind me now. And I was right to do what I did, wasn't I?

"You still want to go through with this?" Albert asked, seemingly without any emotion, though she knew deep down he was falling apart.

"We've come this far. I might as well," Cynthia sighed, in an effort to display her own nonchalance.

"Oh well, please yourself."

"Pleasing is hardly the issue. You know what I'm here for." They both knew she was lying.

"I'll come with you if you want."

"No, Albert. Remember what happened when I came for my clothes."

"That was six years ago, Cynthia. Even a madman like him gets some sense."

"I wouldn't count on it, dear," she chuckled, before forcing herself to be serious. "Believe me, it's better this way."

She fiddled in her handbag for lipstick and freshened up. "God, I'm such a mess." She ran a comb through her hair. *Wish I'd never cut it now. John always liked it long. Back to my natural color too and those damned gray streaks. Wonder what he'll think about that? Oh, who cares what John thinks!*

She leaned over and kissed her husband on the cheek. He stared stolidly ahead.

"I won't be long." She closed the door and her life with him quietly behind her, and meandered down the familiar street. *It's odd like that with Albert: When I'm with him, for the most part, I feel content . . . but the moment I walk out the front door, he never crosses my mind. A funny kind of love.*

Still the same cracks in the pavement. Nothing's changed much around here. Except for my beautiful garden, overgrown like a jungle. The summer days, all those years ago, when Julian was a baby in the pram, and I planted it like a little Versailles—meticulously, prim and proper, not a petal or leaf out of place, nothing but the best—just like I was going to look after our lives. John was off in London then. Seemed like things were going to happen for him. Just me and the bees and the baby and my beautiful garden.

And when Julian was old enough to crawl, I had to keep my eye on him all the time for fear he'd eat my gorgeous yellow roses. John thought that was the height of hilarity: said eighteen yellow roses was what you gave someone when you were breaking up with them. Back then, I never thought there'd come the day. I should have gone ahead and had another baby even though he didn't want one. That might have kept us together. Oh, what am I blabbing about? I'm a happily married woman with my own rose garden out in Cheshire, not a yellow one among them, and a husband who likes to help me keep it spick-and-span, not like that lazy slob John Lennon.

She turned around, waved at Albert, and, with some apprehension, confronted the gate. Gently depressing the handle, she lifted the top bar and pushed sharply backward.

Voilà! Works like a charm, same as always. John could never figure out how to do it. But that was John all over, wasn't it? Never took the time, couldn't be bothered with the details. But wouldn't let me replace it either. What if people come to visit? He was adamant: Anyone who wants to see us will figure it out or hop over the wall.

But of course he never wanted to see anyone, did he? Sooner lie on the couch and stare at the ceiling any old day of the week. One of his two ways of dealing with life: Either smash it to pieces or ignore it completely.

Look at them, messing around in there, singing to their heart's content, and John with the toilet seat around his neck. He must be really well oiled. His party piece, he used to call it, wearing that and doing his duck walk. God, the nights we had—the good nights, I

*mean—all the laughs and the larking about. Imagine Albert doing
something like that. That'd be one for the books.*

*And what's that song? The one with all the "ahs," one of my real
favorites? Oh, yes, "Twist and Shout"! Always loved those har-
monies. I mean, there was no one like them, was there? They were
the best, and everyone knew it. Must have been great to be the best
at something, anything. Never happened to me. Maybe, for one brief
minute when John first loved me, I suppose I was loved by the best,
and it felt like sheer heaven on Earth; it just didn't last half long
enough. What am I thinking of? We just didn't work out. That's the
long and the short of it. Didn't work out for them either, for all their
brilliance and their frolicking about in there.*

She hummed along while looking under the rock. Her heart
jumped, and she smiled when she found the key—some little
bit of her left—not everything vanished when she walked away
from it all.

She opened the front door and slipped into the hall, but
then backtracked and returned the key to its spot under the
rock. He'd need that tomorrow; she smiled. Memory wasn't his
forte. She made a point of closing the door sharply, but they
kept on singing. She hesitated, shy and self-effacing as ever;
then she thought of Albert and stepped into the front room.

John had his back to her and was strumming the guitar.
The other three were clustered about him, as ever-circling
moons to his blazing sun. Maureen was her usual bustling
self, buzzing around the room, trying to keep things in order.
The house looked much the same: apart from a few, no
doubt, pawned and glaring absences—just older, dirtier,
damper, fading away into a million gray and brown shades of
not-so-genteel shabbiness.

*Nice dress, Maur. Always tried to keep yourself up-to-date. You
don't look too much the worse for wear, dear; don't know about that*

rouge though, makes you look a bit older. Well, we are a bit older, aren't we? Ah, but it's good to see you, luv, still fighting the good fight, trying to remake Ringo into your own image—with all the success of a leaky faucet dripping on a lump of granite.

The scary thing is, that would've been me if I hadn't got out. Always on the go, picking up whatever John threw down. Mess and clutter never bothered him. Never even noticed it, I suppose. His mind on bigger things. I hope to God he bought toilet paper. That's always Americans' biggest complaint, isn't it? As if toilet paper makes the world go around. Then, in a way, I suppose it does.

No girl with Paul? That's strange. Always had an eye for a pretty face. I wonder would he have married Dot if he'd stayed in Liverpool? Probably not; always ready for the next bright young thing. And who could blame him, the way the birds used to throw themselves at them?

Oh God, look at George, so skinny and drawn. What in the name of God have they done to him out there?

She wanted to throw her arms around him, shield him from whatever was tormenting him, but just then Maureen saw her. For a moment, her eyes lit up, then she glanced apprehensively at John. Cyn silently begged her to be quiet. But Ringo, his well-honed antenna raised as usual, noted the alarm on his wife's face and traced it back to its source. George caught the look in Ringo's eye, and then Paul; it was like a chain reaction, but Lennon kept on singing—myopia preserving his euphoria for precious seconds. He urged the other two on, then glanced over his shoulder at the diversion. The song trailed off.

"Cyn," Maureen said, clutching the pearls around her throat.

"Hello, Maureen. Hello, all."

They all greeted her but deferred to Lennon.

"Is it okay if I come in?" she asked him.

He blushed deeply, and then his face simmered with rage.

But when it appeared that she would turn for the door, he shrugged his indifference.

"Thank you," she said.

The initial shock had worn off Maureen, and she quickly took charge. "You look perished, luv. Have a cup of tea."

"No, I can't stay long. Albert's out in the car."

"Come to deliver the milk, then, has he?"

"Please, John."

"Well, why don't we invite him in?" Lennon rushed over to the window, pulled back the curtain, and roared out: "Hey, Albert! Uncle Albert!"

When he turned back, the dusty curtains lay draped over his shoulders like ceremonial banners. "We were havin' a party and then you come buttin' in."

"I'd better go." She moved to the door, but Montana barred her exit.

"Ah, for Christ sakes, Cyn, I haven't seen you in an eternity. C'mon, John, bury the hatchet, will you."

Lennon was about to launch into a well-earned tirade but realized how ridiculous he must look with the toilet seat hanging from his neck. He flung it from him. It careened along the floor and, with a crash, lodged between the couch and the wall. He threw his ex-wife one last angry stare, then busied himself opening a beer.

"Thank you, Paul," Cynthia murmured, trembling from the stress. He held out his arms to her. She took the measure of him for a moment, then allowed herself to be enveloped in the warmth of his reassurance. "God, you look great," she said.

"Hey, a pound here, a line there."

"Get on with you!" She smiled through the tears. "Oh, dear, it's freezing, isn't it?"

"Miss the old central heating out in Cheshire, don't we?" Lennon leered, rubbing his hands ferociously. He picked up one of the empty brown paper bags and threw it into the grate. They all watched as it smoldered and then burst into flames. "That better, Mrs. Jenkins?"

"Here you are, Cyn."

She turned to see George offering her a sherry. Up close, it was even easier to read the hard years scribbled all over his face. But when he smiled, the warmth fortified her against Lennon's cynicism. She wiped the tears away and took the glass. "I tried visiting you out at the home, George, but . . ."

"Must have been one of me bad days."

"I didn't mean that. God, there I go sticking my foot in it again."

"It's no big deal, luv."

"Oh, George, I'm sorry I didn't come more often."

He shrugged that it really made no matter.

"You're better, then?"

"Oh yeah." He grinned bravely, and that hurt her even more. "They tightened all the screws and changed me oil. I'm in top form now—tickin' over great."

"You could've fooled me," Lennon said.

"Hey, at least he can prove he's 99% sane. Wish I could say the same for meself—or you."

Once again, Cynthia was grateful for Paul's intervention. Even in the old days, smoothing out John's rough edges had been one of his roles. She'd never realized how important that was until he was gone.

"Get on with you, Paul." She playfully clipped his ear. "You haven't changed a bit."

"That's what you think. Another face-lift and me ankles will be up around me eyebrows."

"You always saw the bright side of things, didn't you? How are the boys?"

"Well, the young one's in L.A. with his mother, and Lyndon..." His face clouded. "We don't talk much these days."

He reached for his flask, and when he couldn't find it, he shuffled to the table and searched for a beer. All at once, he looked older and vulnerable.

Cynthia sympathized all too well. "You're not married now, are you?"

"No, I put enough lawyers in a higher tax bracket."

"You do things so different over there," Maureen said.

"Yeah, the men leave the women, right, Cyn?" Lennon answered.

"You know full well why I left you."

"Why couldn't you be like Maureen? She's stuck with Ringo even though he gives her a bright young reason to leave every week."

Ringo sputtered out a mouthful of beer. "For Christ sake, John!" He threw a sideways glance at Maureen, who bit her lip and busied herself at the table.

"Speakin' of happy families," George said. "Will we be seein' Julian again tonight?"

"Well, if he gets off early from the concentration camp, he might drop by for cocktails," Lennon answered.

"Julian's very involved in politics, Paul." Maureen kept her eyes lowered, unwilling to deal with Ringo's nervous gaze.

"Oh, yeah? He's running for the local council or something?"

"No, actually they're running from him. That's the one thing me and my son agree on: liquidatin' politicians. Only problem is, our lad doesn't want to stop there."

"He wasn't like that out in Cheshire," Cynthia said. "It wasn't till he came back here and ..."

"And I started readin' him *Mein Kampf* for his bedtime story, is that it?"

"He's a good lad!" Cynthia insisted. "Just sick of the way things are."

"He was sick of livin' out in Cheshire with that spastic you go to bed with."

"Don't you talk about my husband like that."

"Your husband"—he rolled the offending word round in his mouth—"is a bloody moron."

"At least he doesn't sit around the house all day, feeling sorry for himself."

"Six years later, and you're still twistin' the knife."

"Six years later, and you won't face up to the truth."

"What truth? That I'm as dumb and mediocre as the rest of you?"

"Give it a break," said George. "You're not the only one who's had to carry a cross."

Lennon fell to his knees and blessed himself furiously. "So tell us all yer troubles, me son." He aped a broad Irish accent and shuffled toward the priest. "We give very reasonable penances round here. How long since your last confession?"

"You bastard!" George hunched him roughly on the shoulder, and Lennon went sprawling across the floor. He raised himself on his elbows and crawled toward Ringo. "How about you, Brother Starkey? I bet you have somethin' to confess?"

"Yeah, that's right. I bloody well do!" Ringo was still smarting from the "bright young thing" reference. There was a deeper pain, however, one that had been eating away inside him for years, only to resurface after the run-in outside the pub. "What do you think it was like for me to hear all of them birds screamin', 'Pete forever—Ringo never!' The birds loved Pete Best, they did."

Forgetting her own hurts, Maureen reached out to him, but he brushed her aside. "They didn't want a skinny little scruff like me."

George watched her awkward gesture; though Ringo hadn't reciprocated, there was something about their body language that was reassuring. If everyone else was adrift, the drummer had his life's anchor, no matter how barnacled it might be.

"We wanted you," George said quietly. "That's what counted—not a crowd of scrubbers down the Cavern."

"Yeah, but I join and the arse falls out of the whole thing! If yez had stuck with him, things might have been different." He looked around in a daze, shocked at his own disclosure. "I don't know. Maybe it was me looks or somethin'."

"Yeah, now that I think of it, we did consider plastic surgery."

"Shove it, Lennon!"

He had never used the surname before. It hung on the air like the smell of acid through a factory wall. Lennon scowled back at him and walked over to the kitchen sink. He ran the tap and washed his hands. They watched him search for a towel.

"It had nowt to do with your looks," George said. "Best was just a large-size pain in the arse—more go in a traffic light."

"Whatever he was, we should have told him to his face instead of gettin' Epstein to do our dirty work for us." Lennon shook the water from his hands; then, giving up on the towel, he wiped them on the seat of his pants.

"You can't dwell on these things," Montana said. "They'll drive you crazy."

"Little did we know, he was only sharpenin' his knife for the rest of us," Lennon spat back. He saw Ringo lighting a cigarette and gestured for one. Ringo lit it from his own and handed it to Lennon, but made a point of not acknowledging his nod of thanks.

Montana was fuming. It was hardly his fault that the sensitive Epstein hadn't been able to thrive in the rough and tumble of Vegas. Still, all the guilt of those years came rushing back, and he exploded. "You're a great one to be talking about knives. You have no idea what it did to Eppy when you walked out of that studio."

"Let's get one thing straight, pal. The problem wasn't that I walked out, the problem was that you stayed."

Montana strode over to Lennon and planted himself inches away. "Yeah, I did stay, and you want to know why? Because I don't quit at the first sign of a problem. It takes a bit of guts to hang in there and make things work."

Lennon took a deep drag on his cigarette. At first, the smoke drifted out of his nostrils, then he opened his mouth and blew a full draft into Paul's face. "You couldn't wait to get rid of us," he said very quietly.

"What's eatin' you, Lennon?"

"You want to know what's eatin' me?"

"Yeah, I've traveled halfway round the planet to find out. So enlighten me!"

Lennon stepped back a pace. "What's eatin' me is that we could have turned the whole world on its ear."

"Go, Johnny, go!" George was right behind him.

"Then my son, Julian, and his mates wouldn't have turned into a crowd of bloody Fascists."

Montana looked at him, perplexed. "Hey, slow down a minute, pal. Now you tell me, what in the name of Christ playin' guitar has to do with fascism?"

"I know this is way beyond you, but we could have changed the bloody world."

"Get a load of this guy! Come off it, we were the best, okay. But we were just musicians."

"We could have been a lot more than musicians," Lennon said, his voice low but razor sharp, his belief unfaltering. "A hell of a lot more."

"Oh, yeah, so what could we have been?" Montana waited for an answer but could tell it wasn't coming. He laughed bitterly. "You know, you're a great one at makin' wild statements, John, but when it comes to backing them up with facts . . ."

Montana realized he was losing his temper. He took a deep breath and tried to steady himself. "All right, suppose," he reasoned, "just suppose we'd had twenty number-ones in the States. . . ."

"I'm not talkin' about number-ones. You don't have a clue what I'm gettin' at."

"Just suppose, goddamm it, suppose! Now, what would have happened?"

Lennon took a last weary drag on his cigarette and then jammed the still-smoking butt down a half-empty beer bottle. It sizzled into silence. He knew they were worlds apart, and he wasn't thinking clearly anymore. He could feel what they could have been, could see it, touch it, kiss it, scream at it. But he couldn't put it into plain, any-idiot-can-understand-it, brown-bread words. And even if he could, he'd be laughed out of the house. No, better to keep it to himself. That way the dream would stay pure and not be an object of ridicule down all the years to come. He was tired now and didn't want to fight anymore. He wished he was in bed with China, wrapped around her warm, silky body, listening to her sweet, reassuring nothings and the gentle rain drizzling down her skylight roof. Meanwhile, the moment he'd waited half a bitter lifetime for was slipping out of his grasp.

"Sure, we'd have sold out Vegas for a year," Montana continued, astride his high horse, in the grip of an inexorable logic. "Sure, they'd have given us our own network specials. But what were we goin' to do then? Drop platinum records on the White House?"

Lennon shook his head resignedly. "This is all over your head, mate."

"No way! You just don't have a bull's notion about the politics of the thing."

"Politics has sweet shag all to do with it." Lennon's face was throbbing from the beating he'd taken that morning. He just wanted to go back to drinking and a bit of harmless reminiscing. Besides which, there was something more pressing that he needed to talk to Cyn about. His vision was starting to blur and he sank down on the sofa. Montana noticed the pallor of his face, and all his anger evaporated. He threw up his hands and plopped down beside him. He didn't want to cause him any more pain. When all was said and done, there was no one more precious to him. Very gently, he put his arm around his old friend and gave him a comradely squeeze on the shoulder.

"Oh, stop touchin' me! Jesus, don't you never listen to yourself?" Lennon threw off his arm.

Montana tried to stand up, but he was deep in a hole, both literally and figuratively. He leveraged himself up from the couch with much difficulty.

"Didn't you never have any dreams of things bein' different?" Lennon looked up at him.

"That's the difference between you and me, John. You dreamed—I did."

Chapter Twenty

THEY HAD PASSED THROUGH the smashed glass and upheaval of the inner city and were once again trudging through the relative calm of a ring of council estates. The farther they got from the violence, the more the streetlamps beamed, though they still flickered at times, casting shadows on the Union Jacks that flapped softly in the breeze. The homely glow of a television set still illuminated the occasional window, but many had been switched off; tomorrow was, after all, a working day for some, a dole day for others.

None but the brave or the frantic strayed out on these quiet streets—a mother searching for her teenage daughter, a son dragging a father home from the pub—but even they made themselves scarce at the sight of the approaching Fronters. Luanne's spirits had lifted somewhat now that they had moved beyond the chaos of the city into this grimy suburbia. Then it started to drizzle again, the moon fled behind a bank of clouds, the swirling fog enveloped them in its cocoon, and all was silent save for the tramp of their marching feet and uneven breathing.

She was almost used to the vagaries of the weather by now, knowing that, in no time at all, the fog would lift and the moon would give the illusion of chasing clouds across the sky. The young Fronter never seemed to give the elements a second thought. Rain might pour down his face, the fog might swirl around him, it made little difference, he knew where he was going.

She felt a strange exhilaration. This wasn't Vegas, where she was always taken for granted: a second thought, something to adorn a man's arm. She had come through a crisis. She had proved something to herself; she wasn't quite sure what, but it was substantial. There was a whole world going on over here, a world that she would never have imagined, and she could exist in it. She didn't like it; in fact, she wanted no part of it, but she had survived and now her confidence came flooding back.

She watched the young Fronter's back—his body lithe and sinewy through the military jacket. So sure of himself, so determined. For a moment, she imitated his posture, his stride, and she felt even better about herself. She reached out and grabbed on to his sleeve. This time, he didn't push her away, didn't even stiffen. She smiled.

He's cute all right, a little on the baby side, but different: young in the face, but old in the head. And those eyes, sharp as tacks and accusing, bruised and quivering, always slipping under my skin when he thinks I'm not looking, then blowing hard and cold when I open up.

Who does he think he's kiddin'? He's just another man on the make, and God knows I've dealt with a million of them. But he's just a kid, and kids want family. Don't know who his dad is, or used to be, but he just got himself a new one—that Leader guy. And I bet that's why he's dragging me halfway round this dump of a city. Doesn't want anything nasty to happen to my sweet butt, might cause a diplomatic incident. As if that old creep in the White House could care less what happens to me, or anyone else for that matter.

I thought I'd seen it all, but this place is definitely the pits. They don't even have air-conditioning. Not a single one of them showers regularly. Jeezus! When they lift their arms in that goofy fist salute, they got this gal on her knees. Talk about a secret weapon. Bottle that shit, drop a few crates of it on them Iranians, and you settle that mess pronto.

Another thing I don't get is the way these English treat each other. Beating up anyone who ain't white as themselves. Back in the US of A, we got over that kind of garbage years ago. I mean, you got your minorities everywhere, but God made them that way for His own good reasons, and you gotta suffer them to come unto you, like little children.

At least, this kid's got a head on his shoulders: He don't go along with the real rough stuff. But some of the things I've heard comin' out of his mouth about Jews, and all of it baloney. I mean, why would any self-respecting Jew leave New York City anyway and come to this dump? And on and on about Pakis and Banglaydashis, who-ever they are; they all sound English to me, which is another way of saying: I don't know what any one of them is talkin' about. I thought Paulie was bad, but whatever about his psycho shit, I know what he's saying.

Hey, that burnt-out car looks familiar. And there's that stinky little pigsty of a house. Oh, thank you, Jesus! I knew if I had faith, You'd see me through the Valley of Evil. What's this kid want now? And why is his gang takin' off? And will you get a look at those eyes of his, glowing like rubies in a Tiffany box. I do believe he's going to kiss me. Oh, that's sweet. Nice lips too. He's got his hands all over my hips now.

And that's it? I can't believe he's just holding my hand and how did he get that messed-up gate open? I can still feel his nice lean body and the warmth of him glowing across the silk of my dress. But now he's got the front door open too, and I can hear Paul saying,

"You dreamed, I did!" And I love my Paulie so much and I'll always be true to him forever, so help me, Jesus.

He had center floor and he held it like vindicated Cicero in the Senate. But he realized that he was no longer the center of attention. *What the hell is Maureen lookin' at now? Jesus Christ, what's she seen—a bloody ghost?*

Luanne, indeed, resembled a disheveled apparition who had been stranded for a wet weekend in an urban wasteland. Her makeup was streaked by rain and smoke, her stockings were smeared with mud, while her mouth was agape in an unflattering affirmation of love for Montana and renewed faith in her Redeemer.

"I thought you were supposed to be in London by now!"

This none-too-solicitous statement seemed to release her from a spell. Though it made little logic to her, with a wail she propelled herself across the room—a strike missile, capped by a nuclear love head. "Oh, Paulie! Thank God you're still here." She threw herself into his open but ambivalent arms.

"Where've you been?" He pushed her back to examine her. "What happened to you?"

"Hold me, honey. I will never leave you again, I promise."

"We've been worried sick. Howie and Whalen have been scouring the city lookin' for you?"

"I never seen them, Paulie. But you wouldn't believe the things I've been through."

"Oh, man, now we've got to go out and find those two clowns." He halted her in midflight, but not for long.

"First of all, I was kidnapped by a bunch of revolutionaries and dragged all over this crazy city. Then one of them, this amazing young guy, beat the heck out of this monster of a guy, and rescued me and—"

"Young guy?" He raised eyebrows and midlife hackles.

"That's right, Macker, kept the old eye on her for you, I did." The figure, in army fatigues and Union Jack armband, slouched in the doorway.

"What are you doin' here?" Paul spat out, recognizing his nemesis from Anfield.

"What's this, then? Old farts' night?"

"Julian." Cynthia stepped forward to hug him, but he avoided her.

"Julian?" George and Paul mouthed in tandem. He winked at them but moved on.

"Hello, Mam. Have you come home, then—to me and Daddy?"

"I was worried about you. Your stepfather and I were . . ."

"Oh, Uncle Albert! I just had the briefest of encounters with the dear man. In fact, he asked me to give you a message." He scraped some imaginary paint from his bovver boots. "Somethin' about a little bastard doin' a clog dance on his new Volvo. Said he was sick and tired of the whole lot of us. Drove off into the sunset, he did."

"You put him up to that," she accused Lennon.

"Yeah, every night after brandy and cigars, me and the prodigal here roll back the carpets, put on our clogs, and do a couple of old-time waltzes."

"Actually, it's our one true meeting of minds: the love we share for Uncle Albert," Julian said.

"He did his best by you for . . ."

"All the thanks he gets for it." Julian finished the line for her.

"You never gave him a chance."

"But I already had a loving father, right, Dad?"

It was Luanne's turn to be stunned. She pointed at Lennon. "He's your old man?"

"Yeah, old and in the way," Julian sneered.

"I knew there was something about your eyes."

"As long as that's all you recognize, luv. He does have a taste for nubiles, right, Dad?"

Lennon looked away to avoid Cynthia's questioning eyes.

Montana couldn't believe that he hadn't recognized Julian back in Anfield. The kid was so like a young John.

"Been to any good rallies lately, Citizen?" Julian smiled at him.

Go on, tell him, you little bastard! That's what you've been setting me up for the whole day. So, why don't you quit twisting the knife and break both our hearts.

Julian let him hang before winking. "Mum's the word, Paulie—for now. Oh, and since we're on the subject, lost your way, Padre?"

"You don't know the half of it, kid."

"Funny you didn't recognize me. Makes you think, doesn't it?"

"It wasn't exactly how I expected you to turn out."

"Oh no? Lookin' for an unemployed guitar-strummin' alcoholic, were you?"

"Get lost, you little Fascist!" Lennon put a stop to the charade.

A squall of wind blew the kitchen window open, and the dirty curtain fluttered across the sink. Everyone turned in alarm. Not so, Julian; he never took his eyes from his father but, rather, studied him intently. He clucked his tongue. "I'm surprised at you, Dad. After all, Citizen Montana here is a personal friend of the Yank president—and a fervent admirer of our illustrious Leader."

Montana could feel the knife twist. It wouldn't be long now.

"Unlike you, Dad, Citizen Montana always lands on his feet—knows the winning side when he sees it. That right, Macker? Anyway"—he paused to delight in Paul's discomfort—"we should hardly be discussing politics around the ladies." He blew a kiss to Luanne, who blushed furiously.

A distant flash lit up the night sky and, a moment later, the windowpanes trembled. Luanne gripped Montana's hand. He squeezed it, but when Julian smiled knowingly, he stepped away.

"Fancy a stroll in the city, luv, catch a glimpse of merry olde England—on its last legs?" Julian said. "No? Well, I must be off. Oh, by the way, has anyone got a loan of a tenner? I appear to have mislaid my American Express."

"It's in my purse, Julian," Cynthia said.

"Oh, no, Mommy dearest. It must come from a Beatle. After all, they owe us, right?"

"What are you goin' to spend it on?" Lennon asked. "A down payment on a gas chamber?"

"Oh, John, I have cried at night for that sense of humor," Julian replied in a heightened American accent. "As a matter of fact, I have it on the best authority that the Beatles are havin' a reunion at the Horse and Jockey tomorrow night, and I want to make sure my seat is reserved."

"That's all we need." Ringo snorted. "A crowd of bloody Fronters slaggin' us."

"Oh, far from it, Brother Rings. We'll be on our very best behavior. After all, I've been waitin' for this moment all my life. You bringing Uncle Albert, Mom?"

Montana fished a bank note from his wallet. "Here's a twenty, kid, bring a date—if you can get one."

"It's not that easy, then, is it?" Julian's sneer vanished and his face drooped to a clown's hangdog. "All the young girls around here seem to have the hots for old men. Hey, Dad, you bringing Suzie Wong?"

Lennon avoided Cynthia's eyes and snuck a glance at his wrist, but his watch was missing. He tried to remember what China had said about coming over later. But all was a fog.

Julian winked at Luanne before reaching out for the twenty.

"Take that, and I'll wipe the floor with you," Lennon said very quietly.

His son's voice matched Lennon's in breathy intensity. "Easy, Johnny. He owes us, don't he? Runnin' out on you like he did. This is just one back for old Long John and the Silver Beatles."

"You're askin' for it."

No one existed now but the two of them. It had been ever thus as a child, always waiting for him to come home; then the cursory tousling of his hair and the bag of sweets tossed on the kitchen table before the long hours of silence, when he would gaze up into faraway eyes as his father wrestled with some lyric or chord change, the battered guitar a barrier between them.

"You know, for the first time in my life, I'm proud of you, Johnny."

"I bet you are."

"No, I really am. I mean, look at you. Off to make the big time in Las Vegas. Now all your dreams will finally come through, and you'll be just another—golden oldie."

Lennon struck out and smacked him full on the face. Julian didn't flinch except to push the distraught Cynthia away. His eyes swelled with tears, but they never lost track of his father. Lennon stared down at his hand, appalled by what he had done.

"Feel better now, Johnny?" Julian whispered. "Look after

him, Mr. Montana. He's never been the same since you left. Me and Mom were obviously no substitute."

He ripped the twenty from Montana's hand, then shouted, "Sieg heil, fab four! Viva Las Vegas!"

He backed toward the door, then disappeared, singing:

Britain will always be my homeland
I'm free, I'm no slave
God bless me, I'm an Englishman
Purity in my heart, strength in my hand
God bless me, I'm no slave, I'm an Englishman.

They listened to his voice evaporate down the hallway and tensed for the slamming of the door, but it closed quietly. There was a faint echo from the garden, then just the rustle of the wind in the kitchen window curtain.

His exit seemed to leave a void in the room. They skirted each other's eyes.

"Whew!" Montana finally exhaled. "Chip off the old block."

Cynthia clicked her purse closed. "It's not his fault. He's just never been able to get a steady job, that's all."

"That little Nazi could be packing us all into the gas chamber and you'd still be goin' on about a steady job," Lennon said.

Cynthia seethed. She picked up a tea towel and brushed some crumbs from the table, then realized what she was doing and flung the damp cloth back down.

"Old farts' night, my arse!" Ringo said. "He better watch his tongue."

"Richard!"

"Would you ever put a sock in it! All you do is nag me from mornin' to night."

"With good reason."

"Yeah, 'cause you own the bloody salons."

"I did it for us, Richie," she whispered.

"When are you goin' to get it into your thick skull that I'm a drummer, not a friggin' quiff mechanic?"

Cynthia reached out to reassure her, but Maureen was already on her humiliated way to the toilet. They heard her fumble for the broken latch within.

Ringo lit a cigarette and flicked the match toward the kitchen sink. It landed on the draining board. No one moved and it continued to burn. Even when it went out, his hand continued to shake. *Good riddance to her! Thirty years of listenin' to the same shite, day in day out. Do this, do that, don't do this, don't do that! Do the other bloody thing! And puttin' up with it for the sake of a bit of peace. I should've upped and out of here years ago while I still had somethin' goin' for meself. But I stuck it out, didn't I? Damned right, I did! 'Cause, where I come from, once you make a promise, you don't give up on it, no matter how ballsed up the bargain turns out.*

Lennon raised an eyebrow in sympathy, but the drummer looked up fiercely and cut him. *That goes for you too, dickhead! Hangin' in with you has been no piece of cake either. Watchin' your back, onstage and off. Gettin' older by the day with your fat arse stickin' in me face. I should have gone to London. I had lads breakin' down me door to go with them. 'Cause there's not a singer in this land doesn't need a good kick and snare rivetin' his arsehole together. And Paul would have had me out to Las Vegas in a minute if I'd just picked up pen and paper and written to him. But I didn't, and now look at me.* "Gruesome bloody twosome," *my bollocks!*

Montana cracked an ale. "I don't know what's got into these kids." He scratched his face. "Ah, I suppose you're only young once."

"He was never young—him and all the other little bastards with their shaved heads and their Nazi salutes," Lennon said.

"You still don't see why he's doin' it, do you?" Cynthia said.

"What's there to see? That he hates everything I ever stood for?"

"Well, you've only yourself to blame! If you'd spent some more time with the lad instead of locking yourself up in your room with that godforsaken guitar, writing those stupid songs no one ever wants to hear."

"Oh, so it's stupid songs now, is it? Well, they weren't so stupid when you thought I was goin' to make it."

"Make it! Make it! I had half a lifetime of your bloody daydreams." She was right in his face now, and he was taken aback by this newfound ferocity.

"There was a whole lot more than daydreams, if you'd only take the time to remember."

"That lad grew up in a house full of memories and might-have-beens."

"Hey, Paulie, there's a good title for one of your corny songs, and old venial Cyn here won't even charge you royalties." He ripped open his shirt in a bad Montana imitation, whipped out an air microphone, and taunted them both.

Memories and might-have-beens
Broken hearts and old has-beens . . .

"Go on, make a fool of yourself!" Cynthia said, again picking up the tea towel and sweeping more crumbs from the table.

Memories of you and me
And the way it used to be . . .

"You always loved humiliating me in company, didn't you?"

But he had her now, and he had sweet damn all intention of letting go.

Memories and motorcars
Sixties songs and movie stars

She swung toward him, reliving all the nights he'd come staggering home, feeling sorry for himself. "You never wanted our Julian in the first place, and he knew it."

The toilet flushed. Maureen emerged and took in the scene. Lennon had dropped to his knees and was regaling them in a Johnny Ray sob.

You and I will always be
Memories and might-have-beens.

He stretched out the last line, his voice now soulfully quivering a Jackie Wilson plea.

Cynthia flung the damp, crumby tea towel in his face. It hung off him like a veil. She raised her hand to slap him, but Maureen dragged her back.

"You animal! You should be ashamed of yourself." She shouted back at Lennon as she led Cynthia across the room. "C'mon, luv, let's make a cup of tea."

Cynthia broke free and snatched the towel off Lennon's face. "You selfish bastard! What do you think it was like for him with all the other little boys callin' you Looney?"

"Shut up," he said, tensing at the hated name.

"How do you think he felt when you ran naked down the street screamin' about love? He had to live with that, you know."

"Oooh, listen to our Cyn tellin' all the family secrets."

"There's a few more I could tell if I had a mind to."

"Then, out with them!" he shouted. "I'm sure Maureen would love to tell them at all her parties that I'm never invited to."

"Thank God I don't have to put up with this anymore."

"No, not out in Cheshire, goin' to bed with the livin' dead."

"You keep my husband out of your filthy mouth!" She

almost spit at him, defying him to say anything more about Albert. "No wonder they call you Looney. 'Cause that's what you are. Looney Lennon! Looney Lennon!"

He grabbed her by the wrist, bent it backward and yelled at her. "They can call me what they like because I'm right and they're wrong! What do you know about luv? What do any of you know? The wall here knows more about luv."

He dragged her across the kitchen and shoved her into the grimy, sweating wall. He never heard Paul shout, "For Christ sakes, John!" Never felt George pulling at his jacket. He was digging into her wrists, and the tears flowed from her eyes as he roared, "Ain't that right, wall?" He threw her to one side and rained his two fists down on it. "D'ye hear me, wall? All I need is luv! All I need is friggin' luv!"

When the wall didn't reply, he collapsed in front of it. "Answer me, god damn you!"

He leaned his head against its filthy coolness and began to sob. Montana and George, though they were closest to him, exchanged helpless glances. Then Ringo strode over, took his mate under the oxters, and, with surprising strength, dragged him to his feet. "C'mon, sit down here now, John, and have a Guinness."

"Don't want a Guinness! I want what's mine. That's all I've ever wanted." Lennon slammed his face down on the table and covered his head with his arms. But in seconds, he was up again, full of beans, a mad glint in his eye, though his bruised cheek must have been throbbing from the pain. "Hey, Paulie, all I need is luv."

Montana nodded in agreement, eager not to provoke another outburst.

"No, I mean the song. You could cover it. It's in G. Listen!"

Lennon dashed over to the guitar and sang a few incoherent bars. "What do you think?"

"Sure, John, sure. Tomorrow when you're . . ." Montana's words trailed off.

Lennon was suddenly dangerous again. "Tomorrow when I'm what?" His eyes now smoldered with suspicion.

"Tomorrow . . ." Montana searched for the right words. "We can put it on a cassette, and I'll shop it around for you."

"Put it on a cassette." Lennon tried the words on for size. Then he snapped back into reality. "I must have been off me rocker! It doesn't even mention the Statue of Liberty, let alone the Shetland Island ferry. Well, I don't care if it's never number one in Chickenshit, Alabama. It's gonna be top of the pops in Liverpool tonight."

He bolted for the kitchen door, screaming: "All I need is luv!"

Cynthia clutched out at him, but he was gone in a blur. "For God's sake, they'll beat him up again!"

Lennon stood on the doorstep, roaring, "Hey, Eunuch Powell, wake up, you silly bugger! Shaggy Thatcher, shake yer iron corset! *Sieg heil*, you National Fronters, all I need is luv!"

Ringo lunged for him, but he was already out into the roiling, rainy night. No light in his backyard except for the dull red glow of Greater Liverpool in turmoil. The moon was hidden again—not a star in sight through the soupy mix of cloud, fog, and smoke. And still he roared at the heavens, "All I need is luv, everybody, d'yeh hear me?"

"Come back, John, we'll go into a studio and work on it," Montana pleaded, following Ringo in pursuit.

The lights started to come on in the surrounding council houses. Close by, a window screeched open, and a bald head appeared. "Hey, shit-for-brains, put a sock in it, will you! You'll have the Fronters up here after us."

"Fronters need luv too," Lennon roared back.

"Go to bed, Looney! Some of us have to work in the mornin'."

"If you had enough luv, you wouldn't have to work."

Another voice intervened: "You tell my missus that."

Lennon ran toward the latter voice, exhorting this couple to rise above their matrimonial morass. But in the darkness, he ran full flight into a bulky object and was sent sprawling into the wet weeds.

"Jesus Christ! Me shin is splintered." He raised himself painfully back to his feet and was about to kick out at the object, when, to his amazement: "It's a miracle! I've found me bloody fridge."

He dropped to his knees, opened its door, sniffed inside, and was well pleased. With loving care, he picked it up and deposited it in the reluctant arms of Ringo and Montana. "Look after that, lads," he ordered.

With this small, if bruising, triumph under his belt, Lennon was emboldened. He lit out for the front garden, all the while questioning the sexual practices of the Leader's mother. He leaped for the wall and gained a precarious foothold, then, balancing like a spastic acrobat, edged his way up onto the gate pillar.

To the roared tune of "The Stripper," he began to remove his shirt. His friends assembled below him and, like supplicants to some aroused deity, tried to cajole him down. But Lennon was on a mission. Perched on one foot, then the other, he removed shoes and socks. Tiring of the tune, he began to howl at the absent moon, while the lights came on up and down Crescent Gardens. "All I need is luv! All I need is friggin' luv!"

Off in the distance, 'Arry 'Olt cocked his ear and recognized the faint voice. He smiled to himself in anticipation, and hurried toward it, humming a brittle verse of "Twist and Shout."

Chapter Twenty-one

RINGO GAVE UP FIRST and retired to the doorway. He'd seen it all before; besides, there was sweet bugger all that any mortal could do when Lennon went ballistic. Might as well be pissing in the wind. And anyway, he had more pressing matters on his mind. To wit, the body heat blasting off Ms. Luano. Her perfume enveloped him, her curves bewitched him—she was the pig's mickey personified; the mere thought of her set his foot tapping, and when his heart hit a triplet and veered abruptly into five/four time, he knew his blood was well and truly up.

Craning her neck for a view of Lennon's performance, but under no circumstances willing to venture outdoors again, Luanne pressed against Ringo from behind, her right breast firmly implanted in his left shoulder. Ringo held his breath and stayed his kick foot, fearful now that any movement might rupture the spell; but his eyes widened as the pressure increased. Without moving a muscle, his inner radar located Maureen, with her back to him, imploring Lennon to come down off the pillar.

That particular coast clear, he molded his shoulder back against the gorgeous, firm young flesh. His palms sweating, he began to breathe again as his finagling appeared to go unnoticed. When Luanne finally straightened up, he was caught off balance and fell backward, desperately clutching for the wall.

"He's a proper headcase, ain't he?" He threw her a curve from his spread-eagled stance, and doubled up with a man-of-the-world sigh. "Ah, the fresh air'll do him good."

"What the hell is he on?" Luanne demanded, unaware of the havoc she'd been wreaking in the hormone department.

"He should stick to Guinness. At least, that puts him asleep."

"Has he ever considered thorazine?"

"Nah, he was never a great one for the liqueurs."

"Huh?" She examined Ringo for even the smidgin of a put-on, but, discerning none, shook her head. "Jesus, what a way to spend a night off."

"Yeah, it's a nice party all right. Are you enjoyin' yourself?"

"Oh, yeah, I just adore asylums."

"You're dead right, luv. It's the weather, I reckon. It never stops bloody rainin'. Didn't Paul tell you about it?"

"Tell me about it? He never shuts up about it and you guys and . . ."

"Get on with you."

"I kid you not, kid." She gave him another once-over, instinctively straightening her back and easing her breasts forward an inviting centimeter or two or three. Settling on the appropriate thrust, she reached out and patted his hand before confiding throatily, "I bet I know more about you than your wife does."

They both looked out the door and studied Maureen's back. She was busily hectoring Lennon, who appeared about to take flight from atop his perch. Ringo was grateful for this small mercy and, without looking at her, honed in one hundred and ten percent on Luanne. His eyes narrowed as he considered her last statement; it did indeed present possibilities. The question was, could it also be construed as a threat? Best tread carefully.

"Been tellin' tales out of school, then, our Paul?" He tested the waters.

"Tail is the word, kid." She smacked his bony behind. His eyes widened; she even took his hand and swung him around toward her. "Quite a lady-killer in the old days, Ringo?" she said, gazing into his eyes.

"I had me moments, luv," he murmured modestly.

She withdrew her hand and her breasts. "I bet they're few and far between now with that Maureen. Talk about pussy-whipped!"

The arse collapsed on the jaunty five-four time of his heart-beat and settled into a stodgy four on the floor. "Oh, now, I wouldn't go that far," he protested. "I mean, Maureen's a bit of a nag all right, but it's a steady sort of a naggin'—with no sur-prises like. Still"—his sigh was steeped in regret—"it's not a patch on the old days."

"Don't you start up about them old days. No one in Vegas knows what the hell Paulie's talkin' about. It's just like you were his family or somethin'."

Ringo drew himself up to his full, offended five feet what-ever, and solemnly informed her, "We were more than family, luv. We were the Beatles."

"C'mon, babe, you were just another crowd of kids playin' in some glorified garage band."

The insult cut like a spiv's flick-knife. She even pronounced it in the snooty French manner. To which he replied haughtily in proper scouse, "I never played in a garrege in me life! I play weddings, pubs, and the like. But no bloody garreges!"

"Jesus, do you have to spell out everything in this dump? What I mean is, you never played the . . . what's the equivalent of the Copa round here?"

"You what, luv?"

"The Copacabana!" If he was mystified, she was amazed. "You never heard of the Copacabana?"

He gazed at her in mute adoration. Her face had flushed from the mental exertion, and her full lips demanded that the gloss be sucked off them in one almighty snoggle. Was there no end to this woman? She was all points of the compass superior to anything in Marsden's dirty movies. And everyone knew Gerry had powerful taste in brassers.

Just to be on the safe side, he launched another quick wife-scan. With the coast clear, he licked his chops and resumed his suit.

Then the unbelievable! Luanne grabbed him by the wrist and pulled him to her. For a millisecond, he panicked, unable to locate his wife through the musky fumes of Yankee perfume. He rallied heroically; but just as nirvana was at hand, and he was about to die a million times in her paradise of a body, she led him down the hall in a frantic tango. He clung to her—the mating habits of Americans a mystery unto him—and burrowed into her warm lusciousness. She stopped within inches of the closet door and spun him back one more time up the hall. The ducks on the wall gazed down serenely as she lilted sweet nothings concerning this fabled Copacabana in his ear.

Ringo, too, was humming, but not from song. He slid his hand down the curve of her back, grabbed a fistful of the finest American arse, and, when they halted once more at the closet door, pulled her close, and, in a masterly move, latched his lips on hers and shoved his tongue into her mouth.

Montana might have warned him. She bit down hard with ten thousand dollars worth of well-capped teeth, spun him sideways, and smacked him soundly on the puss.

"What kind of a girl do you think I am?" she inquired many decibels too loud for a straying husband's comfort.

Ringo put a finger to his lips and shushed fiercely. His tongue was raw and throbbing, the tears flooded his eyes. "Jesus, luv, I was only jokin'!" he slobbered through the waves of pain, all the while trying to locate Maureen.

Luanne smoothed down her clothes with maidenly virtue. Despite the real agony of rebuff, Ringo couldn't help but follow the movement of her fingers.

"You guys are weird," she howled. "Especially that John! You know he's gonna get Paul's ulcer actin' up again, always goin' on about them Beatles!"

This suit was going nowhere in a hurry. *Better calm the bitch down. Never know what kind of trouble she might get me in, throwin' herself at me like that, then turnin' nasty.*

"That's 'cause the Beatles was his ticket out of here." He tried to make her see sense. "Now, Paul, he was different. He could sing 'Long Tall Sally' and go straight into 'Red Sails in the Sunset' without battin' an eyelid."

Her spirits soared; they had reached common ground. She beamed at him and whispered, "Geminis!"

"You what, luv?"

"Paul is a Gemini. *Comprende?*"

"Nah, you're missin' the point. You're totally missin' the point!"

"I'm missin' the point? You guys are so out to lunch, you wouldn't get the point if it was stickin' up your ass!"

"There's no need to get your knickers in a knot!" He didn't care overmuch for her last analogy. It was crude and unladylike; more what you'd expect from one of them tarted-up Hamburg brassers who used to steal his money. You'd think Paul would have more class, and he with the pick of Yankee women ready to lie down for him. He tried another tack and articulated slowly, as if talking to the permanently brain damaged, "You see, my point is, the two of them were just like fish and chips."

"Excuse me?"

"Just like fish and chips, they were. One of them wasn't right without the other."

"Oh, brother! Beam me up, Scotty." She looked at the cracks in Lennon's ceiling and implored: "Hey, Scotty, yuh-hoo!"

But with the thrill of the hunt behind him, Ringo had lost interest in her. Besides, he had been pondering this puzzle for a large portion of his life. The jigsaw now lacked only one piece: just one last existential detail. "But if they were the fish and chips"—he scratched his head—"what would that make me and George?"

"The mind truly boggles." Luanne hadn't had a cigarette for weeks. To hell with health, teeth, breath, and her mother's emphysema! She stormed into the kitchen and rummaged around the table. *Just like these blasted limeys. They blow smoke into your face all night but are too cheap to leave one stinking butt lying around.*

Ringo followed her, his mind a million miles away from her curves. And then, eyes ablaze with wonder, he shouted: "I've got it!" She moved away from him; she'd witnessed similar epiphanies in gamblers and born-agains.

"We'd be the salt and the vinegar," he intoned, somewhat in awe of his own discovery.

But in the best and worst of marriages, one has little time to celebrate. In a flurry of heels and nattering, Maureen came thundering up the hall. Ringo practically leaped across the room to put modest distance between himself and the American vixen. Maureen rounded the corner at some speed and honed in on her soulmate, failing to notice Luanne. In thick, guttural scouse, she let him have it: "That John Lennon! I'm tellin' you, Richie, the Fronters won't take much more of 'is carry-on. We should be careful about comin' over 'ere."

At first, Ringo was relieved; he was beyond suspicion, and what his beloved didn't know wouldn't hurt her. Still, no need for the old dear to make a proper charlie of herself. "Maureen," he warned, his tongue still throbbing.

But she was up astride her high horse, BBC accent now history. "You just don't 'ave any imagination, that's your problem, and that's why you're in the rut you're in!"

Just like the old wagon! Send for the whipping boy the first minute anything goes wrong. Next thing you know, I'm the one responsible for Lennon doin' a strip up on his pillar, and if it keeps rainin', I'll even get the blame for the bloody weather.

"Maureen!" This time there was more of a cut in his voice.

She didn't like that one bit. "And furthermore, you 'ave absolutely no gumption! That's why you let that John Lennon piss all over you!"

There. She'd said it, and he could bloody well like it or lump it. Who paid 'im 'is allowance every week anyway? And made sure 'e 'ad a roof over his greasy 'ead? And why is 'e takin' it all so calmly? 'E is the most annoyin' man! And what's the silly bugger pointin' at?

She glanced behind her. Her throat constricted, and the breath caught in her gullet. "Oh, Luanne," she gurgled, BBC vowels and consonants once again rattling around in her mouth. "You must think we're awfully uncivilized."

"Oh, honey, why ever would you think that?"

Chapter Twenty-two

THEY WERE PASSING DOWN a leafy street when China began to feel nervous at the prospect of the party ahead of her. Back in the pub it had all seemed like a bit of a lark, but now, as the night grew quieter, the Front patrols became less frequent, and Lennon's house closer, the reality sank in. Where did she fit in his life? Did he really want her to be there? Or was she just something to be enjoyed behind closed doors, with the curtains drawn and the stereo up? And to top it all, she wished she hadn't changed from her sensible Doc Martens into heels. Although the in crowd from the Horse and Jockey was barely huffing and puffing along, her feet were already tired from a double shift. And there was a more immediate problem.

That hand is just too close for comfort. I mean, it's one thing mauling my shoulder like there's no tomorrow, but the man has my bra half off already. Hold on there now, Gerry! What do you expect me to do? Drag you back to the tail end of the crowd and say, "Look, luv, that's a nice, dark lane. Why don't you and me take a gallop up there? I'll drop me knickers, and you can have a quickie—no questions asked. But you'll have to be speedy about it, mind you! Can't be late for the party then, can we?"

Does he, for one instant, think that John Lennon wouldn't notice the change in me? That he wouldn't read the small print of my mind in two seconds flat? I mean, as it is, he can look into my eyes and tell me exactly what I'm thinking; he wouldn't notice that I'd done the dirt on him just a few minutes previously?

But then, to Gerry and his mates, all's fair in love and young ones. Never lay more than a teasing finger on anyone else's wives or longtime girlfriends, though, for fear of gettin' banished bare-arsed out of pub, grub, and family, never to be taken back into the sacred bosom of the gang. A totally different story for the likes of me though, isn't it? Adrift out there in that limbo between a bit of fluff and a steady boiler—a piece of all right, like, but not quite the ticket, if you know what I mean.

Still, I am glad that they waited. Wouldn't hear of me goin' on me own; though I was crazy enough to do it—anything just to spend time with John. "No, no, we'll wait for you, luv, won't we, lads? Can't have our China out on the streets on her own with all this malarkey goin' on. Right? And double scotches all round while we're waitin'. Settle up with you on Monday. Okay, China me girl?"

And a good job they did wait! It's bloody madness out here, with the Fronters throwing their weight around. It's been coming a long time, but tonight the Empire's chickens are really coming home to roost. They colonized us, civilized us, glazed us over with John Bull icing, and everything was prim and proper, right as rain, as long as we knew our place and stayed put in Hong Kong, Pakistan, Guyana, or wherever else their red, white, and blue sun never set upon. But as soon as we showed up on the King's well-scrubbed doorstep with our British aspirations and our not-so-white faces, oh, that was another story, wasn't it?

And now they can't wait to be rid of us. But it's not that simple. We've got roots here, dug bone-deep into the streets of their cities, and we're not going anywhere in a hurry. Old Enoch's going to be wading knee-deep in his rivers of blood before Mrs. Brown's lovely daughter does her pale-faced, knees-up routine around here again.

They heard a low rumble in the distance, and the street-lights went out. Despite Gerry's probing fingers, she was glad to be close to someone. She had mixed feelings when he took away his hand and fumbled in his pocket for a lighter. She even moved closer to him when he flicked on the flame and called out: "Everyone all right, then?"

The gang gathered around him: Kramer, Gustafson, the other rockers, and a gaggle of brassers. Someone passed a pint bottle of whiskey; it was still doing the rounds when the lights slowly regained power.

"Better all keep close, then." Gerry snuggled up in a proprietary manner and draped his arm around her again. When Gustafson lobbed the empty bottle into a dustbin, the others cheered and they moved off toward Lennon's house.

At least my father didn't live to see his nightmare come true. Drove him to an early grave, those Fronter bastards did! And all he ever wanted was to make a decent living for his family. Slaved around the clock at his little takeout, smiling, bowing, and scraping the floor for them, perpetually turning the other cheek when they called him a chink or demanded "contributions" for their "business associations." And who was he supposed to turn to? The police? The priests? The politicians? Fat chance of them doing anything for a "Chinaman."

The hurt in his eyes when they'd try feeling me up on their drunken way home—and why not? I wasn't real British like their girlfriends or their sisters—just a little "slit-eye" to be messed with for a bit of a laugh. And then, the one time he did intervene, they beat him to a pulp, and not one of his regular customers bothered to lift a hand.

I hate them all—the racist pigs with their ragtag uniforms and their stupid red cider faces. That goes for John's son too. I'm sick of the way he looks at me, the way he shades me home at nights, matching step for step. Thinks I don't see him lurking in doorways, sizing me up and down—another piece of yellow trash! He gives me the creeps, he does. That night I lost my keys and John took me back to his house, I could hear him moving about out on the landing, stopping and listening, then sneaking off again—his presence oozing through the walls. Found it hard to do anything in bed that night; then, eventually, when John passed out, I just lay there, knowing he was in the next room, getting off on everything he'd heard. Made my skin crawl—the thought of him so close.

He thinks his father should stick to "grown-up" women—like his saintly mother. I actually feel like I know her from the photos— Brigitte Bardot from over the water, with her long blond hair, creamy English skin, and John's arm draped around her, his eyes everywhere but on her, quite obviously on the lookout for the next piece of crumpet. Her eyes wary, unsure if she's fitting in. Wonder if I look like that when I'm with him?

Hey, hold on a minute, Gerry! That bra cost good money. You'll break the ruddy thing if you stretch it any more.

"Give us a kiss, then?" Marsden breezily demanded.

"You're such a one, aren't you?" There was only one way out. She turned toward him, a hint of suggestion in her eyes. Old Gerry thought his ship had come in. His fingers loosened immediately, all the better to facilitate a surgical strike on her rear end, and she slipped from his grip.

"C'mon, luv, won't cost you nothin', then, will it?"

"Go on with you, Gerry, and you with a girl in every pub."

But he was already reconsidering the options. His beady eye, trained so fervently on her during the walk from the pub, was now zeroing in on old reliable Terry Tits.

You're right too, Ger! Better sure than sorry. Terry might be a bit on the shop-soiled side of things, but any port in a storm and all that. I mean, I might look like a nice bit of fluff, but you couldn't tell then, could you? I might not even put out, for God's sake! Only old John knows for sure, and you know he wouldn't tell you in a month of Sundays. For all you know, the whole thing could be platonic. Might even be spendin' his time spoutin' poetry to me or some other old tripe. And then, you know about those Oriental girls, don't you? Bit on the tight side, like! Wouldn't be able to take a real man like yourself, would they? That's why old John sticks with me, then, isn't it? Never had much going in that department, did he?

She'd heard all of Marsden's whispered speculations from the other side of the bar. *Must think I'm deaf as well as tight! Well, guessin' is the only way you're ever goin' to find out, mate.*

He looked at her long and hard, and she evenly returned the scrutiny. He smiled and nodded, and she caught the mixture of regret and admiration; then he was himself again. "You stick with me, luv, and you'll be all right. C'mon then, let's make sure Terry ain't lonely."

"That's all right, Ger, two's company, three's a crowd."

"Well, you stay close at hand, you hear me? Things are goin' to get worse before they get better round here, and you know they don't like . . ." He didn't know quite how to put it: Chinese, chink, Oriental, slit-eye, or just plain not-as-white-and-all-right-as-we-are. She knew he didn't mean anything by it—that when all was said and done, he'd fuck anything with two legs and half an arse, regardless of creed, color, or the price of cabbage.

He shrugged, lost for the right word. But he was soon off like a beagle with his nose to the ground, one arm grasping his brown paper bag, the other reaching out for Terry's far more accommodating bosom.

The streets had taken a turn for the worse again. Union Jacks hung limply from every window. A burned-out car here, a collection of snot-nosed kids giving them the once-over

there! The air alive with smoke and suspicion. Fronter terri-
tory. Even the drunkest of the rockers could sense it. Move
quickly now, and not quite so much fuss. No point in gettin'
bogged down in stray aggro, when there's a party waitin' up
the road.

She moved into Gustafson's orbit. His eyes tensed and
alert, he grasped her elbow and moved her up into the center
of the crowd. Her feet hurt as the gang picked up speed, eager
to be the far side of this droning silence. They were being
watched—she was sure of it—and not just by kids; but when
she turned around to look, the bass player pushed her on
unceremoniously.

Then they passed from the claustrophobia of the darkened
estate onto an open green littered with cans, broken bottles,
dog shit, and a couple of well-pissed-upon trees. Not much to
look at, for sure, but a safe space where an arse could be parked
and a deep breath taken. A DMZ—for the moment anyway—
but even there they could feel the ground shifting beneath
them. Liverpool was under siege and the city was up for grabs.
The Front was playing for broke—all their cards on the table in
one mad grab for power. Was it too early—another Beer Hall
Putsch—or did they have some support within the establish-
ment, some silent force using them for its own purposes? And
what was the Leader's part in all this? Was he for real, or a
puppet whose strings were being singularly pulled tonight?

Made no matter! It was high time those cheeky sods got
their comeuppance, more bum than brains, Terry Tits suggested. They'd already pissed off the Tories no end, not to
mention the army. And now they'd been given enough rope,
maybe they'd hang themselves, and good riddance. Question
was: Who would they take with them? Better not tarry round
here too long! One of the brassers produced a flask of pink gin

and passed it around. God was good and the devil wasn't so bad either.

China sat on an old milk crate. Though the ground was muddy, she took off her heels. The damp air felt good on her feet. She could feel it soothe the blisters. Not too far to go now, and maybe Maureen might have some plasters. The house should be warm anyway—get out of this foggy dampness. *I wonder what John's up to now? Seemed like him and the Yank were tight as tulips again. God, how I hope it works out, even though it could mean curtains for me. Be like a shot in the arm for him to get away from this mess: the constant slagging and back-biting and him rusting away here Merseyside like some old hulk, with nothing left to look forward to but the scrap yard. What a bit of sunshine and open-mindedness wouldn't do for him? Instead of all his ideas curdling up like month-old milk, souring inside him and turning him more bitter and brokenhearted by the day.*

And anyway, what's to become of him with the Fronters running riot all over the place? That lot is out to settle scores, that's a given. Oh, first it'll be the foreigners and anyone who doesn't look exactly like them, but as soon as that particular clock is cleaned, it'll be on to the Trots and troublemakers and anyone else who ever got up their noses. And you can tell my John is goin' to be right there in the thick of that gravy.

Not that I think these morons have a snowball's chance in hell of taking over the whole shop. Just a crowd of yobs and bully boys out on an endless Saturday-night spree of aggro and drinking. Do they for one instant think that the army and the Tories and every other toffee-nose on this snobby little island are going to put up with the great cider-swilling unwashed running the show? Fat chance! Just using them, that's what they're doing. Get their own nasty way without having to come out in the open and be identified as the racists they are.

Now that the gin had been demolished and the bottle added to the litter on the green, the rockers cut loose, roaring their heads off on old ballads and blues, a beer-fueled gumbo of Chuckie B, Fats D, Jerry Lee, and whatever else came to mind, lustily, bawdily, in tune, out of tune, oblivious to the glow of the red sky around them or the threat of what tomorrow might hold in store.

They moved on through another estate, this one brighter and a shade more well-to-do. An occasional car parked in a tar-macadamed garden, even a small added conservatory or two poking out from front doors, bedecked to the gills with plants, flowers, and assorted knickknacks. More Tory than NFUK, but just like the political wind that could change in an instant, and it did.

A band of Fronters materialized, blocking their way; but the rockers marched steadfastly toward them, buoyed now by a lethal cocktail of whiskey and pink gin, their voices propelled to new heights at the prospect of an imminent dustup. At the last moment, the Fronters backed off, and the gang passed through laughing and jeering. "Blow me bloody nose and they'd fall over!" Marsden sneered.

The Fronters watched them, eyes slit with hatred, bristling with contempt, but that was as far as it went—a dozen blokes and their tough-as-nails tarts looked a bit on the formidable side. Let 'em pass this once, plenty of Pakis and Bullah-Bullahs still to be dealt with. Time enough to sort out these beer-gut granddads another day. 'Sides, they'd have to pass back this way later, wouldn't they?

This bunch of yahoos can't really believe their precious Leader is going to stand by them when push comes to shove? No fear of that! The great New Reality doesn't call for him making any sacrifices. If the whole pack of them isn't interned after tonight's madness, you'll soon enough be hearing the first strains of the great New Accommodation—such as the merging of the NFUK with the Tories; and then, his nibs, the Leader, will be named heir apparent to Powell, and right after that, he'll be spruced up in a monkey suit, dickybowing for high tea with the Queen, touring the inner cities with the King—same old story: out of the cold, into the castle—look out for number one and bugger those behind you. Mark my word. It doesn't take a Harley Street specialist to see what that frigid-eyed little pervert is after.

"Oh, Jesus Christ!" she cried out. Even before they'd turned the corner she'd heard an echo of his voice; but there it was again, clear as a bell and then, in the distance, she saw John himself up on his gate pillar, his shirt, shoes, and socks off, one leg stretched out behind him, and the bawls of him informing the universe: "All I need is luv, yez crowd of dumb bollockses! Sing it with me, yez shower of dickheads, luv, luv, luv is all I need!"

Gathered at his feet, a flock of friends begging him to come down; and surrounding them, a bunch of Fronters pointing at him, guffawing at him, dying to kick the living shit out of him.

China sprinted toward him. Gerry and the others—galvanized for the coming catastrophe—raced behind her. But it was too late. One of the Fronters had grabbed John by the leg and was dragging him off the pillar. He was floating in free fall, time suspended, and she cried out as John came tumbling down into the arms of the leather-jacketed thug, the two of them collapsing on the ground, then John being thrown up against the wall—the priest and the Yank trying to intervene.

Although she was running pell-mell down the street, Marsden, Gustafson, Kramer, and others passed her in a blur, shouting, screaming, and cursing, warning the Fronters that they'd get theirs if one hand was laid on their mate.

And then they were all crashing into one another—blood, flesh, and bone in a crunching thud, muffled by the concrete, the yobs astonished by the ferocity of the rockers' attack. It wasn't supposed to be like this. A family of Pakis or pimply-faced Trots whinging and whining was one thing—quite another a beefed-up bevy of drunks anesthetized by booze, memories, resentment, and revenge, and more than ready to rumble any old day of the week, with a no-good shower of fascist pigs.

Up on the leeward side of a bus shelter, one young Fronter watched the melee with an odd sense of detachment. Oh, his fists itched to be in the midst of the fray, but he had little doubt of the eventual outcome. After all, drinking and boasting was one thing, carrying the matter through to its logical conclusion quite another, and it wouldn't be long till that rag-arsed crowd of rockers ran out of steam.

They think it's all like liftin' pints down the pub, eternally exercisin' their elastic elbows in the sacred task of gettin' plastered. Still, some of them old dickheads got smarts, if not balls. Like that mopey sky pilot— who would have thought? Big Whacker Morgan takin' a swing at him and almost pissin' himself when he sees it's a clergyman.

Whacker must have thought he was at the newfangled mass, acceptin' the priest's handshake and lettin' himself be drawn into an embrace, when lo and behold didn't old Father George lay his anointed forehead on the big gobshite's nose, smashing it into kingdom come. My, my, never thought you had it in you, Georgie boy!

But 'Arry 'Olt has old Johnny's number. Cordoned off by his own heavies, he's playin' with the Old Grouch like a cat with a mouse, a little bit of slappin' around, then some jeerin', like he has all night. Take my advice, 'Arry. No point wearin' yourself out on this one.

Give him a couple of what-fors in the breadbasket. Put him off his ale for a couple of weeks. That's all it'll take.

And get a load of the Yank. Tryin' to break through 'Arry's heavies to rescue his long-lost boozin' brother. Givin' as good as he gets until, oh dear, Dosser Brown gives him a right kick up the arse. What's he mouthin' about now—his "goddamned herniated disc"? Moanin' and groanin' and threatenin' legal action if he misses his telly special! A right daft bastard! Thinks the whole world revolves around him and his shit-in-a-swing-swong music.

And will you look at me girlfriend, Bimbo the Blond Bombshell— come flyin' over the garden wall, layin' into Dosser with a good old boot in the nuts, goin' mental with her karate, savin' her "Paulie," and maulin' any of our lot within spittin' distance. The lads all tryin' to cop a free feel and endin' up flattened like pancakes, won- derin' what hit them.

Still and all, she's single-handedly alterin' the whole complexion of this rumble. Look at Marsden and his mob, even gettin' a second wind. All my life, listenin' to him and the Old Grouch back-stabbin' each other, and now the little fat bollocks is mixin' it up like a Viking—rescuin' his "old Johnny."

Hey now, 'Arry! A couple of licks in the ribs and a few well-placed kicks in the arse is one thing, but there's no point puttin' the old sod in a wheelchair. . . .

'Arry had grabbed Lennon by the scruff of the neck and aimed his head at the spackled garden wall. Just like that, something broke in Julian. Blood and water measured against each other—one found wanting. Nothing premeditated, just a sudden kindling of fury and twisted love, and Julian was off on his own private rampage, all his best-laid plans abandoned in one searing, scalding moment. "You fuckin' prick!" he screamed. "Get your filthy hands off him!"

He cut through the battle—a new force, fresh and

enraged—and burst through the cordoned guard, almost taking 'Arry's head off with a nutter that sent him sprawling in the wake of some clattering dustbins.

Disoriented by this treachery, the Fronters hesitated. Smelling blood and revenge, the rockers followed Julian as he cleared a wide swathe around his father. They didn't stop to reflect on this strange turn of events, nor look a gift horse in the mouth; no, they tore into the hated bully boys and chased them down the street with a torrent of insults and flying stones.

'Arry 'Olt picked himself up as best he could, despite a legion of kicks in the arse and belts in the earhole and, Quasimodo-like, staggered off behind his fleeing brethren. Ducking missiles and threats, he yelled, "We'll be back, you slimy Judas—settle the two of yez once and for all!"

"What are you goin' to do for a face when King Kong wants his arse back?" Ringo's insult rang out above all others. He flung one more rock for good luck, even though 'Arry had limped around the corner. "Come back and fight, yez shower of bumboys!" he added for good measure, looking around at his comrades for approval.

He brushed down his clothes and did a quick line check. Not a thread out of place, everything, including the crease on his drainpipes, all present, in order, and accounted for. And why not? He'd kept a cool head—stayed pretty much out of things—just launched a couple of vengeful drop-kicks up 'Arry's fleeing posterior. No point in playing the hero when the situation appeared to be under control—no profit in risking nose, ears, teeth, or reputation. Looks mightn't be everything nowadays, but no one was even remotely likely to hire a flat-nosed, toothless drummer, no matter how spot-on his chops might be.

He gazed on Luanne with not a little awe. She must have taken out five Fronters in the rumble. Granted, a couple of them thought they were in the backseat of the pictures, putting the hammer on her like she was Marilyn Monroe dropped down out of heaven for a quick knee-trembler, only to find their reproductive organs repositioned up around their eyebrows. He shuddered with just a quark of illicit pleasure: to think something similar might have happened to him in the hallway. Wouldn't have been easy explaining that one back home.

Speaking of which, he sought out his nearest and dearest. "Put the run on them, then, didn't we, luv!" He crowed and swayed his shoulders in a welterweight wobble.

"Oh, Richie, I was so worried about you. Looked all over, I did, until someone said you were in the hallway, protectin' Miss Luano."

He blanched and searched her face for even an iota of irony, but the coast was blankly clear. "Nah, once I made sure she was safe and sound, I came out here and laid into a couple of 'em. Would have done a few more, but I was too busy keepin' tabs on you—never once lost track of you, I didn't!"

"Oh, Richie." She kissed her knight errant and whispered, "they'll be back, you know."

"No way! Haven't got the balls, then, have they?"

"You mark my words!"

But Ringo's psychic alarm bells had gone haywire. He whirled around and located the danger. Over against the wall, Lennon was being propped up by any sporting gentleman's worst nightmare—wife and girlfriend—each of them, for the moment, blissfully unaware of the other.

"C'mon, then," Cynthia ordered after she'd helped him back into his shirt and shoes. "Let's get him in the house."

"Is he going to be all right?" China was distraught.

"For now. But tomorrow won't be one of his better mornings."

Ringo nudged Maureen. They watched the two women assist Lennon, dazed and confused, an arm over each of their shoulders, through the front door.

"What are we going to tell them?" Maureen asked, troubled by the lack of appropriate etiquette.

"Out of the fryin' pan, into the fire!" Ringo was awash with wonder and unease. Still and all, better Lennon in such a lurch than himself.

And then they were all in the house, brown paper bags ripped open, tops of bottles spinning to the floor, foam squirting, war wounds inspected, battle tales reenacted, speedily exaggerated, already approaching mythic proportions; most getting drunker but some already begging leave to go, citing a sick spouse or a nixer to be attended to on the morrow, but everyone aware that this was a mere skirmish, outright war now ahead of them, and it'd be a damn sight more discreet to choose one's own field of battle rather than be caught shit-faced in Looney Lennon's by a reinforced gang of pissed-off Fronters out to right rights and redress wrongs. Besides, the whole bloody city was in a state of chaos, and there was bound to be aggro on the long march home.

The two women lay Lennon down gently on the sofa, but after a few moments he slid down onto the floor, seeking the coolness and consolation of the damp linoleum. There he lay like a wet sack of spuds, one minute snoring, the next his eyes wide open, vacantly surveying the cracks in his ceiling.

Though Cynthia was still unaware of the degree of her significance, China had copped on big time. In the unflattering glare of the naked bulb, she took in John's ex-wife, one part of her screaming out, "Run!"—the other refusing to leave his side. In deference, she stood back as Cynthia rinsed the dirt off his face and dabbed gingerly at his cheekbones. Still, she bristled at the degree of intimacy, the proprietorial quality of her predecessor's touch.

She must have been a looker in her day, not that she's not presentable now, but that hair—makes her look like her granny. She has nice skin though, but that lipstick is a couple of shades too bright, something a fifteen-year-old would daub on for attention.

And listen to me—bitchy as an old fishwife. Whatever her style, she's had a marriage, a kid, and all the things that a woman can expect in life. What's the best that I'll end up with when all this love and drama business is over? A heart shot clean full of holes? But why am I so jealous? She could never be right for my John—not in a million years.

Or is she a lesson to be learned, standing right in front of me? Will I end up like her ten years down the line, used and bitter, clinging to the last shreds of self-respect while I crawl away from the wreckage of it all, before I, too, am discarded for a brand-new younger me, more than ready to glide upon his dreams and delusions?

Maureen fretted around the house as if it were her own: picking up coats, discarding empty bottles, keeping the sink empty, but all the time aware of the task in front of her. Finally, she could take no more. She washed her hands and shook them dry, forsaking the damp tea towel. Then, chewing on her lip, she studied the two women. There was simply nothin' for it. They'd have to be introduced. She steeled herself, but then, to her horror, noticed Luanne making a beeline for the lavatory.

Oh, my God, the one place I never cleaned! Doesn't even have the bare essentials, just a few sheets of the Echo. And, to add insult

*to injury, no toilet seat. That John Lennon was wearing it—makin'
a fool of himself, as usual. Where did he throw it?*

She blushed to the roots of her hennaed hair and made a
mad dash to save the situation. But as she stepped over
Lennon, he rose and grabbed her by the backside. "All fur and
no knickers, Maureen Cox!" he roared as her special-occasion
panties ripped and slipped from his grasp. With the hint of
rarified silk still on his fingers, he collapsed backward and
drifted off to sleep, exhausted from his endeavors.

"You are beyond uncouth, John Lennon!" she bawled back,
grabbing the toilet seat from behind the sofa while furtively
checking her elastic. She gathered herself and primly inquired,
"Were you thinkin' of usin' the loo, luv?"

"The what?" Luanne exhumed a tissue from her purse and,
with some trepidation, accepted the battered seat.

"The lavatory, luv," Maureen cooed, but then, observing
Luanne's continued bafflement: "Oh, I meant . . . the toilette."

"Oh, jeez. And I thought everyone knew my name."

"You what, luv?" Ringo was in like a swami's doormat, cov-
eting any loose spark of enlightenment.

"Loo—Luanne!" she said, her voice hoarse with exaspera-
tion. "The restroom! The potty! Whatever the hell you call it
over here. Oh, never mind, I suppose this will come in handy."
She slammed the door behind her and automatically trilled up
and down her three-octave range—musicians and punters
alike, bemused or alarmed, focusing as one on this choral
cacophony.

Maureen, however, had more serious matters to attend to.
She strode over to the two women, gathered them to her, and
grabbed the bull of etiquette squarely by the horns.

"China, this is Cynthia Jenkins, John's wife, oh dear, I
mean ex." She hesitated for a moment while Cynthia looked

inquiringly at the young woman. "And, Cynthia, this is Miss Dung; that's right, China, isn't it?"

China had gone quite pale, and Maureen felt a deep pang of compassion. Cynthia reached out her hand and Maureen took a breath. "China is . . . John's steady girlfriend."

Cynthia nodded, her hand marooned in space between them. *So this is what it's like. I'd wondered all these years. Rehearsed my various responses: the calm, the diffident, the bitter, the God-knows-what-else that came to mind while washing dishes or making beds out in my germless semidetached in Cheshire. And now all I can do is look at her with my mouth wide open, and drink her in; wonder does she love him as much as I did, does he treat her right, hit her, hurt her, touch her, kiss her, love her, and leave her, like he did with me?*

She's just a slip of a girl really, nice figure and all, and why wouldn't she at her age—not a line on her face, but that'll come with time and John Lennon. She already has the bruised look in her eyes, but that's just a down payment on what's in store. And still, it hurts to look at her, with her gorgeous skin and glowing hair. She's probably good in bed too, or has some notion of what do with herself, unlike me with my genteel nose in the air, but not a clue what a man expects until it was too late and I'd lost him anyway.

"I'm pleased to meet you, Miss? . . ."

"Dung, Lucy."

"I'm sorry, Lucy," Maureen interjected, "I should have known you had a real name instead of—" She hesitated, afraid of giving insult.

"China is what John and his friends call me. But it's quite all right, I don't mind at all, honestly." She blushed, and the other two were silent, both searching for words that would put her at ease.

"Oh, come on, girl," Cynthia finally blurted out. "It's hardly a normal situation, so we might as well make the best of it. Maureen, will you get us a drink, and stop staring like we're goin' to tear each other's hair out!"

China hovered over John, unwilling to leave him, but Cynthia took her by the arm and led her away. "Don't you worry your head about him. It's not the first time he's taken a beating."

"Nor the last either," Maureen murmured as she poured out three dollops of gin.

Chapter Twenty-three

"I AIN'T GOIN' NOWHERE with him behind the wheel again. The big galoot got us lost in the projects—thought we were never gettin' out alive," Howie seethed after bursting into the sitting room.

"But, Boss, there was no lights and I didn't have a map," Big Bill said.

Howie didn't even acknowledge the protest but swept on magisterially: "It's a good thing we're not rentin'. Those maniacs out there put dents all over the good stretch. What are you doin' here?" He paled at the sight of Luanne. Much of his bluster disappeared and he continued unconvincingly. "And we out riskin' life and limb tryin' to find you."

Luanne, in the blink of an eye, simulated taking off her garter belt and hog-tying him. Then, with an angelic smile, she subliminally informed him that from now on he'd better be a good boy or Montana would be informed of his treachery.

Montana didn't decipher the smile but he recognized the origins of the gesture. "Herbie," he asked, "you ever hear of the saying a day late and a dollar short?"

"I guess."

"Well, reflect on it." Montana curtly advised, and then turned to Big Bill. "As for you! Grab yourself a bottle and go guard the limo. Something tells me we're going to be needing wheels before this night's over."

"More like we need the U.S. Marines—get out of here alive," Howie gloomily observed, putting distance between Luanne and himself. "And, oh yeah, there's some dope outside in a Volvo lookin' for a Mrs. Jenkins, like there's a tuppaware party goin' on or somethin'."

Cynthia blushed but shrugged her indifference. There would be time for Albert later—after she got what she came for. In the meantime, she had grown tired of baby-sitting China. Oh, it was okay for a while, and a couple of gins certainly eased the conversation; in other circumstances, she could even like the girl—her sense of quiet austerity and fierce loyalty. But the melodrama of youth soon tried her patience, and really, how many hilarious stories of John's escapades could you tell? How long could you camouflage his thoughtlessness and brooding self-absorption? These flaws, too, along with his creativity, were a major part of the man, and without their ballast he began to seem like some sort of gregarious, flippant clown.

When Herbie materialized by her side, offering to whisk China back to Hollywood and transform her into some kind of a scouse Suzie Wong, Cynthia gracefully eased out of the picture and took a seat on her old springy couch. From there, she watched the party stagger along, riotously and unrelentingly: the lukewarm alcohol greasing the cracks of pain and soothing old wounds; the sunny, larger-than-life memories crowding out and overwhelming old guilt, suspicions, and fears, until one by one, the remaining carousers drifted off. She gazed down at her ex-husband and, not for the first time, tried to make sense of it all. Where had she gone wrong? Or, in the bitter end, had she finally gone right by accident? Or is there even right and wrong after a couple of gins?

"Jesus, is he often like that?" She was startled from her reflections when Montana plonked down alongside her.

"Well"—she paused—"it was bad enough in my day and it doesn't seem to be getting any better."

"He could've got us killed."

"We always seemed to survive." She smiled, waving off a fly that had landed on Lennon's forehead. "It became second nature, I suppose." She sat up and carefully examined her hands, stopping to idly gaze at her wedding ring.

"What happened?" he asked. "I mean, between the two of you?"

"Oh, nothing much." She shrugged and looked up at him. "One day, something changed, and I didn't want to take any more."

"Just like that?"

"It's never 'just like that,' is it? I need hardly tell you of all people."

He didn't reply. She twisted her wedding ring around her finger, as if reassuring herself, before continuing. "I just needed some kindness, a bit of dullness even. I couldn't go on living like this."

He looked around the room and thought of the thousands of other rooms that he'd ligged in since he'd left home—the slaps on the back, the blaring smiles, the drunken promises, the sick, sad, empty mornings.

"There was something missing in me." She seemed to drag out the words. "But, after all the years, I suppose that was understandable. Then Albert happened by—he was kind and thoughtful."

She looked at him almost guiltily, as if awaiting judgment. "My whole world was built around John, and I've no one to blame but myself."

He squeezed her hand, and she acknowledged the empathy with a quick smile; she hurried on, eager to set things straight. "But I could have put up with it, just like I always had. 'Cause there was the great times when he'd finish off some song, and he'd play it to me and it'd be absolutely brilliant, and his eyes would light up, and he'd be so kind to me and Julian . . ."

The glow of those days set her eyes sparkling, and he remembered them too. Who knew them better? The rush when John would bring a verse to him, it would set his mind ablaze; and in an instant he'd knock off the perfect chorus to complement it, or vice versa in all ways and computations, each one sparking the other until it seemed like they could do no wrong, and they'd go on forever.

". . . and then he'd rush off to London or Hamburg or some-where, so full of hope and expectation, and sing it to people and all they wanted was the same old stuff; so he'd come home and come up with something even more brilliant, over and over, and be out of his head with the thrill of it all; and then go away again and have them shrug their shoulders at it, until eventually . . . he stopped going away at all. But he never stopped trying, never gave up, just didn't play the songs for me or anyone else anymore, kept them inside himself." She looked down at John, curled up and sleeping under his leather jacket; somewhat abruptly, she took her hand away.

"Sometimes you just have to cut your losses and get on with your life," she said as if banishing the memories for fear they'd become addictive. "He couldn't and I did. That was about the long and the short of it."

"You leaving must have really put him over the top."

At first, she was puzzled; then she started to laugh. "Oh dear, Paul, you're still such a romantic, aren't you? His pride may have been wounded for a week or two, but he's obviously well over that."

He followed Cynthia's eyes as she clinically examined China, who was gravely absorbing a Howie monologue.

"She wasn't the first—not by a long shot," she said firmly. It was way past their bedtime, and she knew Albert would be fuming outside. "Anyway, Julian is all that matters now."

"There's nothing to worry about there. When the chips were down—he stuck by his old man."

"And you really can't see what's coming next?" She looked at Paul and knew that he was thinking of his own children. She sighed for him but carried on resolutely. "No. John's had his chance with the lad, for all the good it's done either of them."

"These things take time, believe me, young Lyndon tears the heart out of me."

"Our Julian doesn't have time. He has to figure out what he's going to do with his life and not waste it on foolish dreams like we did." She sipped her drink, but the gin tasted bleak beyond its normal dryness.

"There was nothin' wrong with our dreams, Cyn, a bit naive maybe, but that's hardly a crime."

"As long as they don't affect your children." But he was still far away and she lost patience with him. "You know I was so envious of the two of you. Always so sure of yourselves, oblivious to everyone else."

She took a cigarette from a battered pack of Players sticking out of Lennon's hip pocket. "Oh Christ, now he's got me smoking again."

Montana lit it for her and took one himself. He coughed from the first drag and his eyes teared. But he soon got the hang of it again.

Lennon was snoring softly. The pain had dissolved from his

face. Even through his bruises he seemed younger, untroubled. A vague smile limned the corners of his mouth.

"Jesus, he could sleep through anything, couldn't he?" Montana took another drag. Then he looked at the cigarette with disgust and stubbed it out

"Oh Paul, are you so blind? The next time those thugs come back, it won't be just a few bruises. That's why I'm getting Julian out of here."

The leather jacket had slipped off and she tucked it back over Lennon, who recognized its familiar warmth and snuggled underneath it.

"You should go too—the sooner the better—back to your posh London hotel."

"Oh give over, will you! When I go, he's comin' back with me."

"Ten, fifteen years ago maybe," she said wistfully.

A lone gunshot—or was it a car backfiring?—echoed in the distance. Everyone in the room stiffened, and then carried on, a little less forcefully. Cynthia shivered and looked around at the thinning party. Not much help here. She couldn't blame them though. They all had their own troubles ahead.

"You still miss him, don't you?"

This time, she laughed out loud. But when Montana looked up at her, all sheep eyes and innocence, she gave him a reassuring hug and downed the rest of her gin. Finally, it felt better—bitter still, yet hitting its accustomed spot. "Like a pulled tooth. Once it's gone, you're left with the emptiness. But at least the hurtin' is over. Let's get another drink."

"No, wait." He pulled her back down onto the couch. There was a hint of desperation in his voice. "I could never forget, no matter how much I tried. You were all there at the back of me mind. You might fade away for a while, but then I'd hear an old Buddy Holly tune on the radio, or catch a glimpse of a black leather jacket, and there you'd be as real as rain in front of me again."

"I know, Paul, you don't have to tell me."

"I do, Cyn, it's important."

Ringo lurched across the room like a drunken homing pigeon and collapsed next to them on the sofa. Montana groaned at the intrusion but carried on. "If you only knew how many times I picked up the phone."

Though the drummer had just stuffed the mortal remains of a chicken sandwich into his mouth, he still managed to say, "It never rang in my house, mate."

"Don't you start!"

"Ah, I'm gone beyond startin'." Ringo gasped for breath, his eyes popping as some surreptitious cajun sauce assailed his innards. "It's just that one of yez won't remember, and the other one won't forget."

"And which one am I?"

"You take your pick, mate." Ringo looked right through him. He was tired of all the questions and arguments; but most of all he was tired of the three of them taking him for granted.

"Listen, it wasn't easy to come back, but I did, didn't I? What more do you want?"

"I don't want anything. Just play, have a few laughs and a roof over me head." Ringo bent down and roughly pulled Lennon's pants leg down over his shin. "And now your man here is tryin' to wreck the little that's left of me marriage. Then where'll I be? Out on the street with me drums parked beside me."

Montana offered him a swig from his flask. "Happened to me three times. You just pick up the pieces and get on with it."

"It's different over here." The drummer closed one eye and trembled with suppressed delight as the bourbon flooded his bloodstream. He tried to belch, but nothing came. Then from the pit of his stomach a low growl gathered force. He looked downward, marveling at the wonders of his gut. "We don't break that easy," he said. "But, when we do, it's harder to put us back together again."

Montana sat up, straightened his spine, and turned from one to the other, his eyes flashing. "We can do this, I'm tellin' you! A couple of weeks ago, I was sittin' on a ridge outside Vegas, lookin' down at the lights of the city, and I saw the four of us back onstage, young and alive again, and doin' it and not givin' a damn and I made a vow right there and then—"

"You're full of shit, Paul."

People had screamed that same phrase across a room at him, with little or no effect. But coming in a disembodied whisper, mere inches behind his ear, Montana almost hit the ceiling. He turned to see George. "Oh no, just what we all need—the voice of bloody doom."

"You're full of shit, because you come back here with your tail between your legs and want us to put a big plaster over the past without facing up to anything."

"You call hidin' behind a Roman collar facing up to anything? You know, I don't get you, and I never did!"

"Did you ever take the time to ask?"

"I don't recall any of us doin' much askin', least of all you."

"Well, I just finished twenty-five years of it this mornin'." George groaned from the effort as he raised himself off his knees and bounded around in front of them. "And I'm still short a few answers."

In an instant, Montana was on his feet, facing him. "Hey, pal, it was no party for me either."

The conversation around the room came to a halt. The priest and the Yank were goin' for it.

"At least you were playin' music! I was so out of it, I couldn't even draw the dole!"

Lennon started from the priest's roar. He jackknifed up into a sitting position, his eyes wide open but unfocused. Then he eased himself down again, curling into a comfortable position, and pulled his leather jacket around him.

"Well, that's one thing our John never had a problem with." Cynthia smiled.

"I used to sit at home, playin' me licks till the blood'd be drippin' from me fingers, just in case. . . ." George's voice trailed off.

"In case of what?"

"In case you'd come back and do the right thing by us!"

"Listen, mate, I had two families to support. I did the best I could."

"Oh, give me a break with your families. I haven't had a woman this twenty years." George eyeballed the room as if waiting to be contradicted. Then he shrugged. "Well, it's the truth. And I'm sick to the teeth of it."

There was an embarrassed silence and George blushed. Then he looked around wildly and vaulted across the room to pick up the guitar. "There was a tune yez wrote that's been stuck in me head like a prayer gone wrong. Listen!"

He hummed and strummed and stumbled through his own gilded memory. And yet, the melody had an odd freshness—a charming naiveté smothered in a sweet and sour sauce of teenage longings and losses. Lennon's eyes were closed tightly, but he was half smiling, his lips mouthing words to the rhythm.

George soon ran out of steam. He was frustrated and he looked at Paul, pleading, "You have to remember it?"

"I don't think so." Montana lied, and, at once, regretted it.

It had been stuck in his skull too. "Ah, for Christ sakes, George, I don't know what I remember anymore."

"You really don't remember it?"

He knew he should say yes, but he wasn't able to. There was too much else that needed to be dredged up before he could get to it.

"Yez never finished it," George said, resigned now. "But me and Ringo thought it was gear, right, mate?"

"Yeah," Ringo muttered, "if it'd been a hit, I'd own the salons."

Maureen bit her tongue and her eyes began to tear.

"Sure it was gear! We were gear, everything was bloody gear!" Paul said. "But that was then, and this is now, and you've got to keep goin'."

"Goin' where?" George asked bleakly. He picked up a pint of whiskey, examined the green bottle in the harsh light of the ceiling bulb, and poured himself a substantial belt.

"I don't know the hell where! I didn't have your freedom. I couldn't afford to go 'round the bloody bend."

"You sent me there!" George grimaced mightily and slammed his glass down on the table, the years of suppressed rage flying out with the whiskey.

"Don't do this to me," Montana whispered.

"Yeah, you and them bloody voices! Never shuttin' up, goin' at it a mile a minute every hour of the day, tauntin' and hauntin' me about what I could have been, what we should have been, trackin' every wasted second oozin' out of the clock, till I didn't know what the hell was real and what was in me head anymore."

"Nothin' a couple of pints of Guinness wouldn't cure." Lennon had risen on one elbow and was wide awake now.

George shook his head sadly. "I was gone a long way beyond Guinness—a long, long way."

Cynthia reached for the dish cloth and wiped George's spilled drink from the table. "You should have come to us, luv," she said, "we were so worried about you."

Lennon staggered up from the floor. The fire had gone out. He shivered in the dampness and put on his leather jacket. He fingered his glowing bruises and yawned before foraging among the empties for a beer. "Yeah, there was loads of room in my padded cell," he said.

"At least it was your own," George said. "I got shacked up with a crowd of nuts in a monastery."

As Lennon shuffled past, still intent on his search, he patted George on the back. "Not to worry, Monsignor. At the rate you're goin', you'll make the Vatican yet. Pope John Paul George the Sixty-ninth. Got a nice Ringo to it, that."

George shook off Lennon's hand. "You two blew it on me, and I've never forgiven either of you."

Luanne had grown bored with Gerry Marsden's whispered attentions. His running commentary had been amusing at first, but she knew where it was all leading. He had even followed her into the toilet when she was changing into a borrowed pair of Maureen's tights. Now he was lurking around the kitchen sink, where she was attempting damage control on her makeup. She looked over at Herbie—still obsessing over the little Chinese slut—and experienced a catastrophic epiphany: Where were they staying tonight? Had hotel rooms been booked? It was obviously too late for a commercial flight back to London; none of these losers had a spare Lear in their back-yards, and that gleam in Herbie's eye spelled trouble—if he was into Nazis cross-dressing, what wouldn't he do for a good old banzai whipping? It was time to step up to the plate, top of the ninth, the bases loaded, her ace hitter drunk and bamboozled by memory, and everything still to play for.

Leaving Marsden gaping into his own grizzled visage, she abandoned the cracked mirror and strode over to George. "Listen, brother," she declaimed, her finger hopping off the priest's chest, the ghost of her papist-fearing father at her shoulder. "I don't need the Spanish Inquisition makin' judgments on my fiancé!"

"You tell him, Loose Anne, keep the church and the state separate." Lennon clapped his hands in glee.

To her chagrin, George ignored her. "None of you wants to listen, do you? Just like always, think of yourselves and to hell with everyone else." His eyes were pulsing like strobes, and none of them dared answer. "That day, I'm in the cathedral, givin' me sermon, and I look out at all the faces, and then out of nowhere, bang! The crowd's screamin', and I'm playin' me Rickenbacker, and I could feel yez there beside me, urging me on, and I'm goin' for it with the solo of my life, and then"—he paused, a spectral plectrum poised, ready to strike his air guitar—"they're leadin' me away...."

His voice trailed off at this confession—the awful truth his many shrinks had demanded be sculpted into words; he waited, but nothing happened, no thunderbolts, no avalanche of shame, sweet damn all—just relief, even a quiet elation.

"That's what celibacy does for you, Padre," Luanne said.

"What in God's name would you know about celibacy?" he thundered, and then, as if seeing her for the first time, examined her many curves with growing interest. She blushed and he remarked matter-of-factly, "I quit this mornin'."

"You what?" Ringo said.

"I've been tryin' to tell yez all night, but as usual, no one would listen."

"Jesus Christ," Montana swore.

"No, just plain old George Harrison, I'm afraid."

"Are you all right, mate?"

"Yeah, never better. Reckon it's just like you said: can't hide behind a collar all me life."

"Ah, Christ!" Montana took another swig. "The whole bloody thing is just water under the bridge now."

"No, that's where you're wrong," George said. "I missed out on something, and I still have to find out what it was."

Julian watched and listened through the cracked kitchen door. The soft night rain dripped down his face. He made no attempt to wipe it off, and it covered him in a fine, webbed dampness. He'd waited for some words of wisdom, but in matters that concerned his father, wisdom, as always, was at a premium. He could feel little other than an aching emptiness. He'd thrown away the one concrete thing that had made any sense to him, and replaced it with what?

He knew he should get down to Central Office before 'Arry reported him. But he was unable to move—as if he must wait for some inevitable dénouement to be acted out. All he could hear seeping from the kitchen were rehashed memories of everything that had made his life a misery. Nothing would change for these people: They'd continue to plod along, chained to a past they were unable to let go of. The die had been cast, and no matter how much they questioned it, or even fought against it, none of them had the strength to move on and come baldly face-to-face with the present.

Down at Central Office, there was still a chance. He could blame his actions on the heat of the moment or lack of discipline in the ranks. He was one of the Chosen. They'd believe him. He was the future, not the past personified by 'Arry's drunken boot boys. He stood out, he was going places, he could adapt and fit in handily with the new order. 'Arry and his mates were no less locked in the past than the whiners within.

And yet, he knew he, too, was a captive. He'd compromised himself with Luanne and didn't have the heart to use her as a hostage; then, when it came right down to it, he'd defended his father and turned his back on his own people—and for what? Even though he'd had no hand in it, the past had him in thrall. And so he listened while the seconds ticked away and 'Arry, no doubt, spun his self-serving side of the story.

Then the drizzle intensified into a short, violent shower, and he had to move, one way or the other. He slid open the door, slipped into the room, and could no longer keep his cool: He aimed his words like darts at George. "It was all a daydream, Padre. Just four spoiled little boys who didn't want to grow up."

He expected his mother's beam of patronizing affection; it was second nature whenever he caught her off guard. But he was hardly prepared for the vigor with which she replied.

"No, it was more than that. I believed in it too."

"Yeah, and look what happened to you."

"I don't care about that! There were other times—when anything was possible."

He sneered at her but, for once, without conviction. He knew she loved him unconditionally; he could walk all over her, and she'd still find a way to forgive him. Couldn't she see he didn't want her to get hurt again? And what was she doing here anyway? Always getting in the way of him straightening things out.

But she barely noticed him. He was stunned by her intensity when she grabbed Maureen by the elbow. "Remember, luv, all the plans we used to make! What we were going to do in America, the clothes we were going to wear, all the famous people we'd meet."

"Oh God, Cyn! Everything would have been so different, wouldn't it?"

"It was all over that damned single!" George strode around the room, tightly wound as a twelve-gauge E string. "If only Parlophone had let us be what we were."

"Yeah," Ringo said. "Eppy should have stood his ground with 'Please Please Me.'"

"Why did we ever trust that Childwall queer anyway?"

Lennon's slur was too much for Montana. Eppy didn't deserve this kind of treatment. Besides, none of the others had to watch his daily disintegration, far from home. None of them had stood by him through thick and thin with their careers at stake. And none of them had buried him on a furnace of a day in Vegas, when he had to pay a couple of casino bums to make up a ragged quorum at his lonely, disgraced funeral. "We trusted him because he did right by us," he snarled. "So shut the fuck up! I've had it up to here with you and your warped memory."

"I remember everything," Lennon said.

"Yeah! The way you want to. We could have done 'Please Please Me' as a follow-up."

"They would have backed down if you hadn't sold out."

"Bullshit! We had a shot and you guys wouldn't take it!"

"I would have taken it," said Ringo. "I didn't care if we did 'Moon bloody River.'"

"So why didn't you stay, then?" Paul was right in his face.

"I had to stand by me mates."

"I was your mate too. I thought yez had just gone to the pub. The next thing I hear, you're back in Liverpool."

Ringo shook his head, confused as ever by this self-same issue.

But George held the fort. "You should have come back up for us. We could have started all over again and done it right."

"And go back to playing six hours a night in sweaty little clubs to a crowd of scrubbers and teddy boys?" Paul said. "No way! There was a whole world waitin' out there, and the record company was right. 'Till There Was You' was a million seller. And I remember your very words, John"—he parodied Lennon in rough, guttural strains—"'the punters won't buy this heap of shit!' Well, you were wrong! So why don't you just admit it?"

"Okay! Okay! I admit it, I was wrong. But it's still no less a piece of shit! 'Please Please Me' was different. It would have put us in a different league. Listen to it! It still stands up."

He threw open a dresser door and hauled out a battered Grundig tape recorder and a dusty collection of old reel-to-reels, the tape streaming from their boxes. He flung the whole lot down on the kitchen table and furiously scattered them.

"Can never find nothing in this bloody house!" he howled in frustration, and scowled at Cynthia. Then he pounced on a box bearing the official Parlophone trademark. He tore the lid off, locked the spool in place, ran the tape through the heads, and looped it around the empty right-hand reel. He looked up at them, his face quivering with a strange enigmatic arrogance; then he hit the play switch and turned his back.

There was a creaky silence, then a hiss of white noise. The track had never been edited, so the first sound was Ringo's authoritative four-beat count. And then they were off, the guitars and reverberated harmonica meshing seamlessly on the intro, until Lennon's voice sliced through the speakers. Young, arrogant, and amazingly sexy, it tore around the room, sweeping dust off the walls and their collective memories.

No one moved until the end of the second verse, when George, anticipating his guitar break, hammered his fingers on imaginary frets. Ringo caught his eye, winked, and rode time on his cymbal. Maureen beamed at him—all his years and failings dropping away—once again the flashy young charmer she'd have died for. She linked his arm and reached for his hand; he pulled her tight, kissed her hair, then swung her onto the floor, jiving to the eight-note. Eyes now only for each other, they were alone together, lost behind a sprinkling of stardust, catapulted head over heels back into the first dizzying days of their sassy passion.

Montana watched the images of what might have been crowding in and splintering around him into clusters of what-ifs and maybes; he barely noticed that Luanne was trying to shield him—from what, she didn't know—but she could sense the danger lurking behind the magic of this music. Still, as she saw him being stripped of all his masks and pretences, she knew that even though she would never totally understand him, she loved the solitary person in front of her and always would.

Cynthia stared at Lennon's back, and when the bridge spoke about complainin' and rainin' in his heart, she remembered exactly how and when she lost him. It didn't matter that she didn't know any better—that they should never have married in the first place—the words of the song still burned like glowing anthracite. Surely there was something she could have done? But she was what she was, and there was no way she could have changed herself, even for him.

No matter! Just as long as she had Julian. But he seemed pale and displaced, awash in memories of a father who played that tape endlessly on little-boy nights when just the two of them sat in that kitchen—one slouched over the table strangled by the past, the other frightened out of his wits by the depth of his father's black despair.

It wasn't until the end of the bridge that China realized she'd been holding her breath since Ringo's count. And when she heard the lines about pleasin' and reason, it struck her that there wasn't a glimmer of logic in the way she felt for this man. She should turn on her heel and walk out now, while she still had the chance. There had to be someone out there who could make her feel herself—even half the way he did—someone young and vital who wasn't forever shackled to the past, someone with whom she could have a family, someone who could dream dreams that she alone would star in. How could she even imagine that there would be anything but a bitter end to this madness? Instead she stayed, her feet anchored in concrete, and studied the linoleum on his kitchen floor.

When he heard the lyrical balls-up in the third verse, George smiled; he shimmied over and clipped Montana on the ear. Dragged back to reality, the bass player protested his innocence and pointed an accusing finger at Lennon's back. But George didn't care—they'd never fix it now, and maybe it was better as it was, a monument to a more innocent time, when a thing was right even though it might have a whole lot wrong within it. He'd never be totally fixed either, he'd always be teetering on the edge—half in, half out; but it no longer mattered, he'd found a way to live with the past— he could go on. He would go on. The memories might still be overwhelming, but now he could wade into them without fear of drowning and be himself again—George Harrison, guitar player extraordinary. He took Montana in his arms, hugged his oldest friend mightily, kissed him on the cheek, and forgave him everything.

On the last notes, Ringo beat out a final roll and swung Maureen back into his arms. No one moved lest they break the spell. Then the tape spun off, and nothing remained but the hum of the old Grundig.

Lennon bent down, hit the stop switch, and even the hum

disappeared. "Go on, McCartney," he whispered. "Tell me that's not a hit."

"It's good, John. It's probably the best thing I've ever done."

"That's not enough."

"What more do you want?"

"I want the truth! Just the bloody truth! That's all I've ever wanted!"

"I don't have that to give, mate . . . it was a different time, and America wasn't ready."

"Oh, fuck America! They would have bought it by the bucketful. They invented rock & roll—Chuck Berry, Gene Vincent, Eddy Cochran. . . ."

"Little Richard, Bill Haley, Buddy Holly! I know the names as well as you. But where are those guys now? They're either basket cases or they're pushin' up daisies! I didn't want to end up like that. I wanted to sing and entertain and take a little bit of the misery out of people's lives. I wanted to be me. Just me!"

Lennon let him run on until he staggered to a halt, breathless and trembling, his last words a lonely echo. Then, gentle as the rustle of silk, he said: "Yeah, but who are you, Paulie?"

"I'm me, goddammit, I'm me!"

"No, you're not! You could have been the greatest. But look at you!" And he searched for the young McCartney trapped inside Montana's finery. "When all is said and done, you're nothin' more than a second-rate Humperdinck."

"Hey, you say what you like about me, man, but at least I was in the arena. I didn't sit up here on me arse, livin' some kind of fantasy."

"It's not a fantasy! George saw it too. He saw the crowds out there screamin'. We've all seen bits of it. Cyn's seen some of it. Ringo has. Even Maureen . . ."

"It's history. Why can't you get that into your thick skull?

What's done is done. And now we've got a chance to go on and do something for real, something we can all be proud of." Montana took a slug from his flask. He wiped his lips and waited for the liquor to light him up. "And you've still got a chance to pull your family together."

He instantly regretted it. How could he say such a stupid thing? He could feel Cynthia's outrage behind him, Julian clenching his fists, his own wives and children traipsing noisily across his conscience.

"My family may be arse over elbow," Lennon said quietly, his face pale, a tiny blue vein throbbing on his forehead. "I've no one to blame for that except meself. But they've got one consolation—I never sold out. You blew your chance—and you blew mine too."

The bourbon flamed through Montana's veins all the way down his shoulders to the tips of his toes, and both remorse and conscience took to their heels before it. Now he wanted to grab Lennon, kick the shit out of him, and shake him back into some semblance of reality. "No! You did it. You blew the whole thing, and all because someone stood up to you for a change. You were just too proud—you had to be right."

"I was right! I am right! And you know it. We could have turned the world upside fucking down!"

They were so close, they could feel each other's breath. It was like the old fights back in Hamburg—hepped to the eyebrows on speed and booze—neither of them willing to give in.

"So why didn't you?" Montana asked quietly.

"Because . . ." Lennon was sure he knew, but the words just wouldn't come. And then it hit him in all its numbing finality. ". . . I couldn't do it without you, Paul. I couldn't do it without you, mate."

They stood there, looking at each other—locked together.

Lennon was laid bare. Paul had never seen him like this before. The desolation in his face was unsettling, and he made no attempt to hide it. No jokes, put-downs, or change-the-topic tricks now. It was the open face of the little boy, abandoned by both parents, before he'd learned how to mask the pain and keep the world at bay with sarcasm and wit. And Paul knew that his own wounded image was staring back at him. Sure, he'd accomplished a lot, climbed a whole range of Himalayas. But in the end, what did it all amount to? Just another hill of middle-aged beans. And now they were back, right where they'd started, two battered magnets facing each other, still ineffably attracted despite the ruptured years.

He wanted to reach out and touch the other half of himself, tell him it was okay, but what was the point? Words would only make things worse, and the boy would scurry back inside the conditioned adult, throw up his barriers once again. No, it was better to drink in the moment, let it last as long as was possible before the world got in the way again.

China bit her lip. She knew that Lennon needed to drag these words of admission out into the light of day. But once uttered, what would remain of the man himself? Would he still be her John—sure of himself and brimming over with bitter, vivid life—or some pale, limpid imitation, shuffling from pub to pub, shorn of all his illusions?

As if to hammer home her worst fears, Cynthia brushed past her, took John in her arms, and rocked him like a baby. At first he stiffened, surprised by the novelty of her once-familiar body. Then he held on for dear life.

China's heart stopped as he whispered, "I've missed you." Cynthia didn't reply, just caressed the back of his head and shushed him into silence.

China was already on her way out of the room when

Cynthia murmured, "This is for old time's sake." As she turned to close the door, she saw Cynthia take John's face in her hands and kiss him. In the hallway, through her tears, she fumbled for the front door lock; and while running down the garden path, she barely noticed an angry man leaning on the horn of his white car.

"Damn him and his Volvo!" Cynthia broke away from John's grasp and hurried to the kitchen sink. She freshened up her lipstick and said, "C'mon, Julian, before he has a heart attack."

"I hope he dies roarin'." Julian didn't stir from his slouch by the kitchen door.

Cynthia appealed wordlessly to Lennon.

"Let the lad stay," he said, almost a whisper.

"No, John, he's going back to university to make a future for himself. Don't let him end up like this."

Lennon looked around at the mess and confusion. He didn't even try to see it through her eyes. He could still feel the fire. What did she feel? Sweet damn all. She never understood what was going on, just got swept up in the energy, and when the heat got too much for her, she ran back to Cheshire and conformity. And now she didn't even know what made her own son tick. Because in his own crooked way, the lad was right—for all his dumb dreams of a new order. But in twenty-five years, would he still be right? Would his fire still be burning?

Maybe she had a point. If he went back to school, he'd get a chance to think things through—make a rational choice for himself. If stayed here, there'd be no thinking, just being—day in, day out—with life kicking him and his principles up the arse, testing him every single minute. Did he have that kind of fire? Was he up to that kind of test?

When Lennon appeared to waver, Julian snapped out of his slouch. "You can't be serious?"

Lennon shrugged. He knew what he had to do. But first he had to find his mask of nonchalance. He plastered it on, just in time.

"So, she was right. You never really did want me, did you, Dad?"

"No."

"I don't believe you."

"Your problem."

Lennon turned his back. His fingers were sticky and trembling when he fumbled for a beer. Julian never noticed. He stalked out the door.

Cynthia hurried her good-byes and kisses but hesitated with her hand on the doorknob. "Good-bye, John."

She didn't expect or receive a reply. The Volvo's horn blared again. "Oh shut up, I'm coming," she shouted, and closed the door behind her.

At the garden gate, she almost stumbled over China, head down, long hair hiding her face. The rivalry still prickled, but she'd won, hadn't she? Got what she'd come for—her son, back safe and sound, a new beginning ahead of him.

She raised the young woman and pushed the wet hair out of her eyes. "Listen, luv, my time is done. He's your cross to bear now—if you still want him."

Then she closed the gate behind her and called out, "Julian."

Chapter Twenty-four

INSIDE THE KITCHEN, Paul asked, "What time's the set tomorrow night?"

"You still want to do it?" Ringo said.

"Yes, goddammit, I do! What about you?"

"I've never been readier, mate!" George was emphatic.

"So what's stopping us? We can blow the shit out of everyone—just the four of us."

"Bloody well right!" Ringo banged his fist on the table, the bottles and cans jumping in agreement.

"Yeah! A couple of rehearsals and nothin' will stop us." George punched his own fist in the air.

"Ooh, it'll be fab!" Maureen said, linking arms with Ringo. "I'm goin' to wear me mini all the way up to me arse and them shiny black boots I found up in the attic." She threw her arms around her husband and dragged George into their circle. They swayed merrily around the room.

"What about Queen Di, Paul?" Luanne asked.

"To hell with her and with you too, if that's all you care about!"

"All I care about is you, honey." She took his hand. "As long as you're happy."

"I've never felt better. Thanks, babe." He kissed her and she held on to him. "Are you in?" He glanced over her shoulder at Herbie.

As if emerging from deep freeze, the manager kicked out the jams and shook himself from head to toe. "Eh, yeah, sure thing! Make it a gig for peace or reconciliation or whatever. Just for friends and celebrities—keep the media out, then float 'em a few passes—be the hottest ticket in town. Hey, where's the nearest phone?"

Paul nodded. Things were starting to fall into place, and about time too. "We can start with 'Long Tall Sally,' just like down the Cavern."

"I've been thinkin' about a new middle-eight that'll blow the roof off that one." George's eyes were glowing like flamethrowers. "No point in gettin' stuck in the past."

"That's the spirit! What'll we do second, John? How about 'Dizzy Miss Lizzy'? Shit! We can start with 'Twist and Shout' if you like." Paul was electric. He grabbed Lennon by the shoulder. "C'mon, mate, I know what you're feelin'. I know all the problems, but we can do it. I know we can!"

The words repeated on a slow delay. Lennon reached out, tried to grab them and solder them back into some kind of reality. But he was too late. They splintered off and faded down the back alleys of some endless reverb chamber.

Paul could feel him slipping away. "I can't do it all on me own, John, you have to help me."

Lennon could sense the young McCartney enveloping him with all the old raw innocence and optimism. He had only to turn around, say the word, and Paul would come home to Liverpool, or move the whole lot of them lock, stock, and barrel out to the States. But what then? Paul Montana would be eaten alive Merseyside; and what would John Lennon do in Las Vegas: spend his days working the slots and his nights playing second fiddle—no matter how golden an instrument?

It couldn't be that way. You couldn't step back into a dream and jump-start it right where you'd awoken. No, he'd bollocksed up his life here in Liverpool, and only on home ground could he set it right. For better or worse, they'd both made their choices a long time ago, and now they had to work out the consequences—alone.

Lennon turned around and gently removed Paul's hand.

And then the same truth hit Montana square between the eyes. This was 1962 all over again. There was no room for compromise in Lennon's world. Neither of them was right or wrong. They just had different ways of seeing things. He nodded his acceptance at Lennon. Lennon didn't turn away until he was sure his friend understood.

Montana fumbled for his hip flask, but instead of taking a drink, he tightened the cap. "I must have been out of my skull," he whispered.

"No, Paul, you weren't. He wasn't, was he, Richie?" Maureen pleaded.

"What was I thinkin' of?"

"We'd definitely pack the place. No two ways about that, mate," Ringo urged.

"I gotta go." Montana picked through a pile of damp overcoats, searching for his jacket. As if psychically summoned, Herbie appeared at his shoulder.

"What are you starin' at?" Montana snapped out of his daze, and then in rapid fire: "Get your ass out to the stretch and make sure Whalen's sober. He's gotta drive to London. And I don't want to hear shit about no left or right side. C'mon, get a move on. I got a nut of fifty grand a month to cover. Get your things," he said to Luanne.

"But I thought you wanted to stay, Paulie?"

"It's late, babe, we got a full schedule tomorrow."

"But what about . . . your friends?" She looked around the room kindly, even regretfully.

He didn't seem to hear her. "Let's go, Ringo, I'll give you and Maureen a ride home." He motioned to the door.

The drummer began to move, then stopped dead and looked at his wife. She took his arm and slipped it over her shoulders. "No thanks, Paul," she said. "We'll stay and help John clean up."

"You're serious, mate, no gig?" Ringo gave it one last shot.

"Not right now, man, I'll give you my number. We'll work something out."

"Just like that?" said George.

"I'll make it up to you, guys, don't worry. We'll do a benefit or somethin'."

"A benefit? . . . ." George's voice trailed off.

"Somethin', I don't know . . . we'll talk in the next week or two."

He watched Luanne stroll into the toilet. He tried to glaze George over with a smile, but it was no use. "I'm sorry . . . I gave it my best."

George finally relented. He held out his arms, and Montana stumbled into them. "I know you did, mate. As me novice master used to say, you can't make a silk purse out of a sow's ear."

"Give that novice master me number, will you? I could use him in Vegas," Montana said, then he looked in Lennon's direction. "You'll look after him, right?"

"Yeah, it'll be fine." George nodded, then turned to Ringo. "Well, now that I won't be Vivaing Las Vegas . . . stay with you tonight, Rings?"

"With us?"

"Well, I'm not goin' back to that funny farm in Cheshire, that's for sure certain."

"Yeah, sure thing. There's always a kip for you at our place, right, Maur?"

"Of course there is, Father . . . I mean, George." She blushed. "I'll make up the couch for you. You'll be nice and comfy."

Montana fidgeted as he awaited the inevitable flushing of the toilet. Finally, he banged on the door. "Are you goin' to stay in there the whole friggin' night?"

"Maybe you hadn't noticed, but there are no restrooms in a limo," a tinny voice replied from within.

He tried avoiding Lennon, but it was no use—no matter where he looked, he was always drawn back. He couldn't leave with the wound still open. He strode over, hand outstretched. But George was wiser and quicker off the mark, blocking his path and signaling for him to go, just leave it be.

Then the toilet flushed and the spell was broken; Montana put on his shades and swayed unsteadily—grateful for the darkness. George draped a kindly arm over him and escorted him down the hall. Once, he tried to glance backward, but George held on tightly until they were out into the wet night. Luanne followed, lipstick in hand, eyebrows arched to her Redeemer in heaven.

"Thanks for the tights." She hugged Maureen. "You and me are gonna do the Strip some night. Okay?" As she closed the door behind her, she blew the most discreet of kisses to Ringo and called out, "Salt and vinegar, right?"

For once, Maureen didn't comment. She was already on her way to the window, where she pulled back the curtain and looked out. Ringo yawned—regret tinted by relief—a great gig down the drain, but a loose cannon safely out of sight and sound. He scrounged around the table and miraculously discovered a last unopened beer. Things were already looking up. When the cap flew off the bottle on to the linoleum, he waited for his wife's reprimand, but it never came. The limo's engine purred into action, and they both cast anxious glances at Lennon's back. He seemed frozen—not a muscle moving.

The car lurched into gear and took off with a roar and a shudder from the clutch. There was a squeal of brakes on the corner and a long acceleration, finally dimming into silence. No one moved until George opened the door and said, "Look what the cat dragged in."

At first, no one appeared, but then China shuffled in.

"Will you look at the state of you, girl!" Maureen scolded her. "You're positively dripping wet. Dry that hair of yours this instant or you'll get your death of cold."

Lennon didn't turn around, but he did straighten up a centimeter or so. Ringo winked at George and motioned to the door. He took Maureen by the arm and shushed her protestations.

"Good night, mate, I'll be 'round in the mornin'," George said as casually as possible. "We can run through some chords."

When Maureen wasn't looking, Ringo stuffed the few remaining bedraggled shrimp in his pocket. "You should come with us. Them bastards know where you live now."

Still, Lennon refused to turn around. Maureen flung her dish cloth down on the table. "Oh, won't you talk some sense into him, girl. What are you goin' to do if they come back?"

But China wouldn't acknowledge her—just kept staring at Lennon's back.

"Well, I've done me best." Maureen put on her coat. George opened the door, but Ringo shoved them both ahead. He scratched his head and burped long and mightily.

Then he patted his gut and called back. "Tomorrow night, mate, Horse and Jockey. Be on time, will you? You know what Gerry's like."

Then the door closed and it was just the two of them. She heard Ringo kick the gate, then help Maureen up on the dustbin and over the wall into George's waiting arms. A snatch or two of their fading conversation and then silence.

She moved up close and touched his arm. When he didn't tense, she slipped her hand under his elbow. Though he didn't take it, he did squeeze back. Acknowledging the intimacy, she leaned into his back and buried her face in the soft, damp leather.

They both froze as the door inched open, and the light was turned off. Even this quiet moment forbidden them. They turned around wearily to face the Fronters. Lennon pushed her behind him and squinted into the shadows. Black upon black, a figure was pointing something at them. It moved stealthily to the kitchen sink, arm still outstretched, trigger cocked.

The figure switched on the shaving light and turned to face them.

Father and son stared at each other. Then, with a glance, Julian drew their attention to the twenty-pound note in his hand. It seemed to glow in the dim light, a barrier between them. When he let it flutter to the ground, Lennon briefly nodded.

Julian began to shove the furniture up against door and windows. His father watched for a moment, then took off his leather jacket and lent a hand.